Bloodland

Alan Glynn is a graduate of Trinity College Dublin, where he studied English Literature, and has worked in magazine publishing in New York and as an EFL teacher in Italy. His second novel, *Winterland*, was published to huge acclaim in 2009, while his first novel *The Dark Fields* was released as the film *Limitless* – starring Bradley Cooper and Robert De Niro – in spring 2011.

Praise for *Bloodland*:

'There are, as the publishers claim, echoes of John le Carré, *24* and James Ellroy here, but Glynn's talent is all his own, and his ability to ratchet up the tension is eye-popping.' Laura Wilson, *Guardian*

'An intelligent, well-written and compelling thriller . . . while *Bloodland* makes some serious points, it never forgets that a good thriller is there to entertain the reader as well as to make her think – and this is a very entertaining book.' *Irish Times*

'Glynn's writing is engaging and urgent. Each line counts as he expertly develops his characters and plot without sacrificing his wonderful skill for evocative prose. *Bloodland* will enrage that sleeping anarchist within. More of the same, please, Mister Glynn.' *CrimeSceneNI*

'Rattles along at a fair old lick ... the revelations of corruption come thick and fast, keeping you turning the pages.' *Sunday Times Ireland*

'The tone is fast and lively, but not frenetic . . . Among the very talented crop of Irish crime writers on the scene today, Glynn has the most global outlook ... [*Winterland* and *Bloodland* are] very vivid stories of today's low and high crimes, and very much tied to a base in contemporary Ireland.' *InternationalNoir*

'Glynn is garnering a reputation for unpredictable thrillers, and *Bloodland* is no exception ... *Bloodland* could stand up to Hollywood treatment ... A tightly plotted thriller ... an absorbing read.' *Manchester Evening News*

'Whips along at a fair pace.' *Metro*

Also by Alan Glynn

THE DARK FIELDS/LIMITLESS
WINTERLAND

Bloodland

ALAN GLYNN

faber and faber

First published in 2011
by Faber and Faber Limited
Bloomsbury House
74–77 Great Russell Street
London WC1B 3DA
This paperback edition published 2012

A CIP record for this book
is available from the British Library

ISBN 978-0-571-27544-1

2 4 6 8 10 9 7 5 3 1

Again, and always, for Eithne, Rory and Cian

One

The way his heart is beating is unreal, the rate, the intensity – it's like a jackhammer drilling into rock. He puts a hand up to his chest, and waits, gauges. This has to be close to some upper limit of what his or anyone else's heart is capable of enduring, because it's only an organ after all, a pump, a piece of meat, dark, red, wet – and incessant, naturally . . . but not imperishable, not indestructible.

You can push it, but only so far.

Weird thing is, however, he's not actually doing *anything right now – he's not on a treadmill, or on top of some girl, he's not running from anyone or engaged in direct combat. What he's doing is sitting in the passenger seat of an SUV next to the most chilled-out motherfucker he's ever met in his entire life. They're both former servicemen, he and this other guy, and are virtual clones to look at – the buzz cuts, the pumped-up muscles, the armoured vests, the mirrored shades – but Ray Kroner is prepared to lay even money that whereas* he *is ramped up to the max, his dial straining at eleven, Tom Szymanski here is barely a notch or two above clinically dead.*

OK, Ray has got 600 milligrams of Provigil in his system, but that's not what this is. Big in the military, and even bigger now in the PMCs, Provigil will keep you awake for days on end, but it's not speed, it's not even coffee, it's just like an off switch right next to the sleep option in your brain – press it and one thing you won't have to worry about anymore is getting tired.

Ray looks out at the passing terrain.

This two-mile dirt track they're on runs from the compound to the landing strip. The SUV he and Szymanski are in is the last in a convoy of three, with the 'package' just up ahead, and it's a safe route, they do it all the time, no need for armoured personnel carriers or anything.

So that's not what this is about either.

Could it be the heat then? Because man, it's hot here, and not dry hot like Iraq, or even Phoenix, it's humid, sweltering, you can't breathe – four in the morning and you're like a beached fucking whale. It's unbearable. Pretty much like everything else in this shithole of a country.

Except of course that he can bear it, because he's trained to, and he's experienced – and if hot weather really was a problem for him, he wouldn't be here in the first place, would he?

So what is his problem?

Why is his heart racing like this?

Is it the choices he's made? Quitting work last spring? Walking out on Janice? Selling the car, the computer, even Pop's old vinyls? Scraping enough money together to pay for the six-week training course? And all so he could do this again, hold a Bushmaster M4 in his hands? In his arms? Cradle it? Stroke it? The hard chrome, the matt black finish, the coated steel and aluminium?

Nah.

Those choices were inevitable, pre-ordained. The six months he spent at home after his tour in Iraq were a disaster and when the momentum started building in his head after he read that magazine article about Gideon Global he just knew where it was *leading and he went with it, didn't resist, let it envelop him. Janice was pretty much an alien by this stage anyway, with all that delusional new-age self-help shit she'd been gorging on while he was away, not that he's blaming her or anything, he just couldn't listen to it, the gossamer-light optimism, the breezy promises . . . not after what he'd seen.*

And wanted to see again.

He closes his eyes.

Wants to see again.

But strangely enough still hasn't.

Because what's ironic is that this country is ten times more of a catastrophe than Iraq ever was, or ever will be, with millions dead, literally, and the kind of barbarism going on every day that even a sick fuck like him would be hard-pressed to imagine.

On top of which, as a private contractor, he's getting paid ten times more for being here.

It's weird.

He opens his eyes again, and looks around.

In Baghdad he often went on convoy runs like this one, from the Green Zone to the airport, but along what was essentially a six-mile shooting gallery of snipers and car-bombers, a flat, sunbaked road with endless blackened auto husks and rotting corpses strewn on either side of it.

Here on this route it's just, well . . . countryside, scrubland, lush green hills, faraway mountain peaks, and one roadside village – up ahead a bit now – which is little more than a cluster of wooden huts with aluminium roofs and a single-storey concrete structure, dusty and shell-like, that has a faded Coca-Cola sign hanging off the front of it.

A village.

With never too much going on.

Which is the exact opposite of what it was like in Baghdad, where something was happening all the time – a guy pretending to repair his stalled car over here, a vehicle suddenly cutting across the median over there, and people just standing around, random pedestrians, old men, raggedy kids, spooky-looking women in black chadors, everyone gazing up at you with suspicion or even hatred in their eyes . . .

It meant you were permanently on edge, coiled tight, ready to respond at any second.

Which is something about here, actually, that he misses.

But then, curiously, in that very moment – and unlike his heartbeat – the convoy starts to slow down.

'What the fuck,' Szymanski says under his breath.

They're approaching the edge of the village, where something seems to be happening.

They both crane forward, and sideways a bit, to try and get a better view.

Then the radio crackles into life.

'Deep Six, stand by, some kind of bullshit here.'

Szymanski is Deep Six. His radio call sign. The guy up ahead, in the lead vehicle – Peter Lutz, their unit commander – is Tube.

Ray is Ashes. As in rising from. And Phoenix. His home-town.

After another few seconds, the convoy – flush now with a cluster of huts on the right and the concrete structure on the left – comes to a complete halt.

'Man,' Szymanski says, with a weary sigh, and leans forward over the steering wheel.

Ray stares out of the window.

The village, he thinks – half in wonder, half in disgust – the village. What is a fucking village anyway? Do they even have them anymore, outside of fairy tales, and Europe, and Vietnam, and godforsaken shitholes like this one?

The village.

Against all protocol, he suddenly turns, opens the door of the SUV and gets out.

'The fuck, man,' *Szymanski says.*

The door remains open.

'Ashes, what are you doing?' *an alarmed Tube adds, over the radio.*

Ignoring them both, and with a firm grip on his M4, Ray steps away from the convoy to get a proper view of what is going on.

'Get back in, man. Jesus.'

In the second car, the package – some grey-suited fuck from New York or Washington – has his window down and is looking over at the wooden huts, clearly nervous.

Up ahead, Ray sees what is wrong – there's a pile of vegetables or some shit spilled in the middle of the road, and two women are frantically loading whatever it is back into a large wicker basket.

Behind them, playing, are three small children.

Ray glances across at the wooden huts and thinks he detects something . . . inside one of them, movement . . . someone . . . moving. Then he turns in the other direction and looks towards the concrete structure, only a sliver of which he can actually see, due to the position of the two SUVs. But framed there in the space between them is a tall man leaning against the wall, staring right back at him.

The man's face is long and drawn, his expression intense, his eyes bloodshot.

He seems restive, restless . . . shifty.

Ray hears the crackle of another radio communication from inside the car, but he can't make out what is being said.

He looks around again, rapidly – at the huts, between the SUVs, up ahead – the only difference this time being that the two women have stopped doing what they were doing.

Perfectly still now, crouched on the ground, they too are staring directly at him.

And that's when it dawns on Ray what's going on, what this is – it's not fear, not anxiety, not regret, it's anticipation . . . a sickly, pounding realisation of what might happen here, of what he might do, of what he might be capable of doing, and while there's no way he could have known in advance they were going to stop in this village, not consciously anyway, it's as if his body knew, as if every nerve ending in his system knew, recognised the signals, picked up on them, so that now, as he raises his weapon a little higher, he feels the rhythm of his heartbeat falling into sync with the rhythm of this unfolding situation . . .

He directs the muzzle of the gun at the huts, then at the women and children.

'Kroner, Jesus, are you fucking crazy?'

Ray glances back at the car, Deep Six more animated than he has ever seen him.

In the middle car, the package is still staring out of the window, a look of horror forming on his face. It's as though the anticipation has spread, as though it's a virus, or a stain, alive somehow, crimson and thirsty.

Ray swallows.

He's thirsty himself, the feeling in his veins now inexorable, like a dark, slowly uncoiling sexual desire that senses imminent release.

He puts his finger on the trigger.

A few feet away, the door of the lead car opens slightly, just a crack.

'RAY.'

This is shouted.

Ray exerts a tiny amount of pressure on the trigger.

'Tube,' he shouts back. 'DON'T.'

The car door clicks shut again.

Ray refocuses, taking everything in.

But there's no longer any movement he can detect from inside the huts. And the man at the concrete wall is inert now, frozen – like a splash of detail from some busy urban mural.

The women ahead are frozen too, and still staring at him – though the children in the background seem oblivious, unaware . . .

Hopping, dancing.

Licks of flames.

In the oppressive heat, Ray shivers.

He really doesn't have any idea what he is doing, or why, but one thing he does know – there is nothing on earth, nothing on the vast continent of Africa, nothing in the even greater interior vastness of Congo itself, that can stop him now from doing it.

Phone rings.

Jimmy puts his coffee down and reaches across the desk to answer it.

He glances at the display, vaguely recognises the number, can't quite place it.

'Yeah?'

'Well, well, young Mr Gilroy. Phil Sweeney.'

Jimmy's pulse quickens. Of course. The voice is unmistakable. He straightens up. '*Phil?* God, it's been a while. How are you doing?'

'Not bad. Keeping busy. You?'

'Pretty good, yeah.'

And after *this*, Jimmy thinking, maybe a little better.

'So that was a shame there, all those cutbacks. Hard going, I imagine.'

'Yeah.' Jimmy nods. 'It's not exactly front page news anymore, though.'

'No, no, of course not. But come here. Listen.' Formalities out of the way, it seems. Very Phil. 'Is it true what I hear?'

'Er . . . I don't know, Phil. What do you hear?'

'That you're writing an article or something . . . about Susie Monaghan?'

Jimmy looks at the block of text on the screen of his iMac.

'Yeah,' he says, after a pause. 'But it's not an article. It's a book.' Cagey now. 'A biography.'

'Jesus, Jimmy.'

'*What?*'

'I'm no editor, but . . . Susie Monaghan? Give me a break. Tell me it's not the prospect of the last chapter they're drooling over.'

Jimmy is taken aback at this – celebrity drool, as he remembers it, always having been something of a Phil Sweeney speciality. Though he's right in one respect. The paragraphs Jimmy currently has on the screen are from the last chapter, the longest and most detailed in the book and the one he's tackling first.

'Yeah,' he says. 'But that's not all they're interested in. There's plenty of other stuff. The boyfriends, the drugs, the tantrums.'

'Which no one outside of the *Daily Star* demographic would give a shit about if it wasn't for how she died.'

Jimmy shrugs. 'Not necessarily. It's an intriguing story, her death, the timing of it, what it exemplified.' He pauses. 'What it . . . meant.' He shifts in his chair, picks up a pen, fiddles with it. There was a time when a call from Phil Sweeney was a good thing. It meant a lead, a tip-off, information.

This he's not so sure about.

Jimmy's old man and Phil Sweeney had been in business together in the late nineties. They were good friends. Then the old man died and Sweeney started taking an interest in Jimmy's career. He kept an eye out for him, introduced him to people.

Fed him stories.

'Oh come *on*, Jimmy.'

But those days, it would appear, are over.

'I'm sorry, Phil, I'm not with you. What *is* this?'

There is a long sigh from the other end of the line.

Jimmy glances over at the door. He can hear voices. The students from across the hall. Are they arguing again? Fighting? He's not sure, but it might come in handy as an excuse to get off the phone, if he needs one, if this conversation gets any weirder.

'Look,' he says, no longer attempting to hide his frustration. 'I'm doing a bio of Susie Monaghan, OK? Sneer if you want to, but *I'm* taking it seriously.' He hesitates, then adds, 'Because you know what, Phil? It's *work*, something I haven't had a lot of recently.'

He tightens his grip on the phone.

'Yeah, Jimmy, I know, I know, but –'

'Well, I don't think you do actually –'

'I *do*, I get it, you need the assignment, and that's fine, it's just –'

'Oh, what? I'm supposed to run all my proposals by you now, is that it?'

'No, Jimmy, please, it's just . . . all this focus on the crash –'

'It's where the story *is*, Phil, where the different elements converge. And yeah, to justify the advance, I've promised to pull out all the stops, sure, but . . .' He pauses. 'I mean, what the hell do you care?'

Sweeney doesn't answer.

'No, tell me,' Jimmy goes on. 'What's it to you? Really, I don't understand.'

Sweeney draws a breath. 'OK, look,' he says, 'just slow down for a second, yeah? This advance you mentioned. How much is it? I'm sure we could come to some –'

Jimmy hangs up, *stands* up – backs away, stares at the phone appalled, as if it had unexpectedly come to slithering, slimy life in his hand.

When it starts ringing again, he doesn't move. He lets it ring out, waits a bit and then checks to see if there's a message.

There is.

'Jimmy, Jesus, for fuck's sake, I was only *saying*. Look, we can go over this again, but just be careful who you talk to. This isn't about Susie Monaghan. And call me, yeah?' He pauses. 'Take care of yourself.'

Jimmy exhales, deflates.

He flips the phone closed and puts it on the desk. He sits down again.

Be careful who you talk to.

This from Phil fucking Sweeney? PR guru, media advisor, strategist, fixer, bagman, God knows what else? Someone for whom talking to people was – and presumably still is – nothing less than the primary operating system of the universe? Be careful who he *talks* to? Jesus Christ. What about Maria Monaghan, Susie's older sister? A woman he's been pestering for the last two weeks. He's meeting her this evening.

Does *that* count?

Jimmy gets up and wanders across the room. He stops at the window and gazes out.

This is all too weird. Not to mention awkward. Because he really does need the assignment. It's his first decent opportunity in nearly two years.

The bay is cloudy, overcast. The tide is coming in.

Jimmy releases a weary sigh.

Two years ago he was still at the paper and doing really well, especially with that ministerial expenses story. He'd made connections and built up sources – assisted in no small way, it has to be said, by Phil Sweeney. Then these lay-offs were announced. Eighty-five jobs across the board, last in, first out. Among the thirty or so editorial staff affected Jimmy was in the middle somewhere and didn't stand a chance. He eventually found a part-time job covering the Mulcahy Tribunal for *City* magazine, but after six months of that not only did the tribunal come to an end *City* magazine itself did as well, and the work more or less dried up. He did a few bits and pieces over the next year and a half for local papers and trade publications, as well as some online stuff, but nothing that paid much or was regular enough to count as a real job.

Then, about a month ago, this came up.

It was through an old contact at *City* who was running the Irish office of a London publisher and looking for someone, preferably a journalist, to slap together a book on Susie Monaghan in time for the Christmas market. Jimmy didn't have to think about it for very long. The advance was modest, but it was still a lot more than anything he'd earned recently.

He turns away from the window.

But what is this bullshit now with Phil Sweeney? Did he even understand it correctly? Was Sweeney asking him *not* to do the book? To drop it? It seems incredible, but that's what it sounded like.

Jimmy glances over at his desk.

The advance. How much is it? I'm sure we could come to some –

Oh God.

– to some what? Some arrangement?

On one level, Jimmy shouldn't even be questioning this.

Because it's not as if he doesn't owe Phil Sweeney, and owe him big. He does. Of course he does. But dropping a story? That's different. Being paid to drop a story? That's fucking outrageous.

And why?

He doesn't understand. Is Phil representing someone? An interested party? A client? What's going on?

Jimmy walks over to the desk.

All of the materials laid out here – transcripts of interviews, old *Hello*s and *VIP*s, Google-generated printouts, endless photos – relate directly to Susie.

He selects one of the photos and looks at it.

Susie in a nightclub, champagne flute held up, shoulder strap askew.

She looks tired – wrecked, in fact – like she's been trying too hard and it's not working anymore.

But Jesus, that face . . . those eyes.

It didn't matter how tawdry the setting, how tacky or low-rent the gig, Susie's eyes always had this extraordinary effect of making everything around her seem urgent and weighted and mysterious.

As he replaces the photo, Jimmy wonders what the sister will be like. He's spoken to her on the phone a few times and they've exchanged maybe a dozen e-mails – his focus always on getting her to say yes.

To talk to him.

The primary operating system of the universe.

Jimmy sits down and faces the computer. He looks at the words on the screen. Drums his fingers on the desk. Wonders how he got from investigating a ministerial expenses scandal, and doing it in a busy newsroom, to writing about a dead actress, and in a one-bedroom apartment he can barely afford the monthly repayments on.

But then something more pressing occurs to him.

How did Phil know what he was working on in the first place? Who did he hear it from? In what circumstances would Phil Sweeney be talking to someone – or would someone be talking to Phil Sweeney – where the subject might possibly come up?

Jimmy doesn't like this one bit.

Nor is it the kind of thing he responds well to, being put under pressure, nudged in a certain direction, told what to do or what not to do. And OK, an unauthorised showbiz biography isn't exactly Watergate, or uncovering My Lai, but still, he should be free to write whatever he wants to.

That's how it's supposed to work, isn't it?

He stares for another while at the block of text on the screen.

But he's no longer in the mood.

He checks his coffee. It has gone cold.

He looks back at the screen.

Shit.

He reaches over to the keyboard, saves the document and puts the computer to sleep.

*

'I watch a *lot* of TV.'

He just blurts it out.

It's not how he'd answer the same question if it came from a journalist, but God, could he not dredge up something a *little* more interesting for Dave Conway? Travel maybe? Or a bit of consultancy? The Clinton Foundation? Bilderberg?

Standing at the window, phone cradled on his shoulder, Larry Bolger gazes out over the rooftops of Donnybrook.

Usually when a journalist asks him how he's spending his time these days he'll say he's serving on various boards, which is true, and then add that he's started writing his memoirs, which isn't. But at least he gives the impression of being busy. And that's important.

Or is it?

Maybe not.

Serving as a corporate director, in any case, doesn't take up that much time, and not writing your memoirs doesn't take up any time at all . . . so, yeah, big deal, he *does* have a lot of time on his hands. But is it anyone's business how he chooses to spend it? No, and if that means he watches six episodes of *CSI* in a row, or a whole season of *Scrubs*, or the Hermann Goering Week on the History Channel *in its entirety*, well then, so be it.

Because there's no manual for this, no seven-step recovery programme, no Dr Phil or Deepak-whatshisname bestseller. If you're an ex-head of state, and you don't have anything lined up on the jobs front, then that's pretty much it, you're on your own.

'What,' Conway asks, 'like *Primetime*, *Newsnight*?'

'Yeah, that kind of thing. Current affairs.'

'Keeping ahead of the curve?'

'Yeah.'

Bolger throws his eyes up. He didn't phone Dave Conway for this, for a chat.

'So listen,' he says, 'this week some time, are you free?'

'Er, I'm –'

'I won't keep you long.'

'OK, Larry. Sure.'

They make an arrangement for the following morning. Here in the hotel.

After he hangs up Bolger trades the phone for the remote. He stands in the middle of the room and points it at the 42-inch plasma screen on the wall.

When he read that thing in the paper last week, he wasn't sure what to make of it – though it certainly put the shits up him. What use talking to Dave Conway will be he doesn't know either, probably none, but he needs to talk to someone. He needs reassurance. Besides, he hasn't had much contact with any of the old crowd since leaving office over a year ago and he's been feeling isolated.

He fiddles with the remote.

It's amazing, he thinks, how quickly you get cut out of the loop.

He even swallowed his pride and tried phoning James Vaughan a couple of times, but the old fucker won't return his calls. They haven't spoken for about six months, not since that debacle over the IMF job Bolger had been up for and really wanted. Vaughan had championed his candidacy in Washington, or so it had seemed at the time, but then without any ex-planation he'd blocked it.

It was awful. Bolger had had everything mapped out, his tra-jectory over the next ten years – a solid stint at the IMF to hoover up connections and kudos, then a move to some post at the UN, in Trade and Development or one of the agen-cies or maybe even, if the timing was right, Secretary General.

Why not? But *if* not, Trade, Human Rights, Aid, whatever. It was his dream, his 4 a.m. fantasy, and when Vaughan chose for whatever reason to snuff it out, Bolger was devastated. Because it wasn't just that job, the first phase of the trajectory, it was the whole fucking trajectory. The thing is, you don't survive getting passed over like that, it's too public, too humiliating, so you may as well stuff your CV in a drawer and dig out your golf clubs.

That is, if you play golf.

The former Taoiseach, in any case, reckons that James Vaughan owes him at least a phone call.

But apparently not.

Bolger often thinks of that lunch in the Wilson Hotel, what was it, four, five years ago now?

How times change.

He goes into 'My Recordings' on the digital box, which is still clogged up with movies and documentaries he hasn't got around to watching yet. He flicks down through everything on it now, but nothing catches his eye. He turns over to Sky News and watches that for a bit.

They appear to be having an off day.

The news is scrappy, unfocused, nothing with any real heat in it. They need a good natural disaster, or a high-profile sex scandal, or a child abduction.

Get their juices flowing.

Bastards.

He turns the TV off and throws the remote onto the sofa.

He looks around the room. Bolger likes living in a hotel, it's convenient and private. You don't have pain-in-the-arse neighbours to deal with. He and Mary have had an apartment here since they sold the house in Deansgrange, and with the girls in college now it suits them just fine.

He looks at his watch, and then over at the drinks cabinet.

Mary is out.

Bridge night. He could have gone with her, but he can't stand the fucking chatter. All these people in their late fifties and early sixties sitting round playing cards. It's too much like some sort of a retirement community for his taste. His excuse is that he's absorbed in writing his memoirs and has little or no time for socialising, something he even has Mary believing – and to look at his desk in the study, with all the papers laid out on it, and the permanently open laptop, you'd be forgiven for thinking it was true. Which of course it should be. Because working on his memoirs would be good for him. It'd keep his mind occupied, keep him out of trouble.

But he has no idea how to write a book – how he should structure it or where he should even begin. He's actually sorry now he signed the contract.

He looks over at the drinks cabinet again.

Ever since last week – Monday, Tuesday, whatever day it was – Bolger has been acutely aware of this piece of furniture in the corner of the room. Prior to that, it was just an object, albeit a beautiful one, with its art deco walnut veneer and sliding glass doors. It never bothered him in any way. He liked it. When required, he even served people drinks from it. But then he saw that report in the paper and something happened. It was almost as if the damn thing came to life, as if the bottles inside it, and the various clear and amber liquids inside them, lit up and started pulsating.

Gin, vodka, whiskey, brandy.

Fire water . . . water of life . . .

Burning bright.

He has no intention of doing anything about this, of course. He won't act on it. Not after all these years. But it isn't easy.

He stares at the door leading to his study, and hesitates.

Then he goes over to the sofa again, sits down and picks up the remote control.

*

Dave Conway has a headache.

He's had it for a couple of days now and it's driving him up the wall.

He's taken Solpadeine and Nurofen and been to the doctor. But apparently there's nothing wrong with him.

It's just tension – he's exhausted and needs a rest.

And to be told this he has to pay sixty-five euro?

It's ridiculous.

He pulls into the gravel driveway of his house and parks in his usual spot, next to the stables. The spot beside it is empty.

Which means Ruth isn't home yet.

As he gets out of the car, Conway feels a dart of pain behind his eyes – the sudden convergence, he imagines, of half a dozen little pulses of anxiety: there's the ongoing disaster that is Tara Meadows, the fact that his liabilities now exceed his assets, and the possibility that one of the banks he's in hock to may seek to have a liquidator appointed in a bid to seize control of his company.

Conway approaches the house.

There's also this gorgeous French au pair inside he has to

look at now and talk to without weeping, without feeling drab and ashen and like some agèd minion of Death . . .

How many is that?

There's his children, seven, five and two, disturbed, speculative visions of whose unknowable futures haunt his every waking hour, to say nothing of the sleeping ones.

He puts his key in the front door.

And then there's just . . . *dread*. A general sense of it. Vague, insidious, nameless.

He opens the door.

Always there, always on.

As he steps into the hall, Molly is emerging at high speed from the playroom.

He refocuses.

She's clutching the Sheriff Woody doll.

'It's *mine* –'

'I had it *first* –'

He watches as Molly heads in the direction of the kitchen and disappears.

A distraught Danny, outmanoeuvred once again by his kid sister, can be seen through the open door of the playroom, burying his face in the beanbag. Standing behind him, the baby – they still think of Jack as the baby – looks on, serene as usual, taking notes.

Corinne appears at the door, in hot pursuit of the dragon lady. For once, she looks flustered.

'Oh Dave, sorry, I –'

Stepping forward, he holds up a hand to stop her.

'It's OK, don't worry, she's fine.'

'I think there must be a full moon or something. They're acting like crazy today.'

'Didn't you know? There's always a full moon in this house.'

Dumb joke, but Corinne smiles.

Dave's insides do a little flip.

They're standing next to each other, almost framed in the doorway, and it's a little overwhelming – Corinne's scent, her perfect skin, her searching eyes that –

Oh *enough*, Conway thinks, and steps into the playroom.

He winks at Jack, and hunkers down in front of the beanbag. Danny turns around, tears welling in his eyes, and says, 'Where's Mommy?'

'She'll be home soon,' Conway says.

'I had it *first*.'

'I know, I know. We'll get it back in a minute. Come here.'

He reaches across, retrieves Danny from the beanbag, hitches him over his shoulder and stands up.

This manoeuvre used to be so easy, so natural, but now that Danny is bigger and heavier it requires a lot more effort. He squeezes his son's still-small frame in his arms, and then breathes him in, like a vampire, waiting for that familiar emotional rush.

'I've just changed Jack,' Corinne is saying. 'It was quite loose. What's that word you use . . . *splatty*?'

'Yes,' he says. 'Splatty. A splatty poo. Very nice.'

Or not.

Or surreal. Or whatever.

Before Conway can say anything else, his phone rings. He lowers Danny to the floor and gets the phone out of his jacket pocket. He nods at Corinne. She bends down to distract Danny.

'Come on,' she says. 'Time for dinner.'

As Conway moves away, he raises the phone to his ear.

'Yeah?'

'Dave? Phil Sweeney.'

'Phil. How are you?'

'Good. Listen, have you got a minute?'

'Yeah.' Conway heads for the door. 'What's up?'

'Just something that's come to my attention. Thought you should know about it.'

'OK.'

As Conway listens, he walks across the hall and into the front reception room.

Phil Sweeney is an occasional PR consultant. He does strategic communications, perception management, media analysis. He identifies and tracks, Echelon-style, issues that might have a bearing on his clients' companies.

Or lives.

Like this one.

'And the weird thing is,' he's saying, 'I actually know the guy. His old man and I worked together, back in the early days of Marino.'

'Right.' Conway is confused, unsure if he's getting this. 'Susie Monaghan, you said?'

'Yeah.'

'Jesus.'

Susie Monaghan.

Drumcoolie Castle.

Conway lets out a deep, plaintive sigh here, as always happens

23

whenever this comes up, each of the sighs like an instalment, a staged payment against the principal, itself a lump sum of a sigh so great that to release the whole thing in one go would be enough, he imagines, to kill him.

'So what is this guy,' he says, 'a journalist?'

'Yeah. Young, very smart. But he needs the work. That's part of the problem. He got laid off back when all this meltdown shit started. So I suppose he sees it as an opportunity.'

'Right.'

'But look, don't worry. I'll talk him out of it.'

'OK,' Conway says, nodding. 'Or maybe, I don't know . . .' He pauses. 'Maybe we could find something else for him to do.' A signature Dave Conway technique. Misdirection. He's been in business for over fifteen years and it always seems to work. If there's a problem with staff, some kind of dispute or disagreement, redirect their attention. Get them thinking about something else.

He walks over to the bay window.

'Yeah,' Sweeney says, 'I did offer to buy out his advance, but –'

'*No*. Jesus.' With his free hand Conway massages his left temple. 'That's not going to work.' He looks out over the front lawn. 'Not if he's young. Not if he thinks he's Bob fucking Woodward.'

'Yeah, you're probably right. But he does owe me. So we'll get around it one way or another. I just wanted to let you know.'

'Thanks.'

'I'll keep you posted.'

'Yeah.'

After he hangs up, Conway stands for a while staring out of the window.

Susie Monaghan.

OK. Fine.

But doesn't he have other, more pressing shit to be concerned about?

Yes.

Like Conway Holdings going down the tubes, for instance.

Unquestionably.

So why then does he have a knot in his stomach? Why is the pounding inside his skull so much more intense now than it was five minutes ago?

*

Jimmy Gilroy is sitting at the quiet end of the bar. Arranged in front of him on the dark wood surface is an untouched pint of Guinness, some loose change, his keys, his phone and that morning's paper.

It's like a still life, familiar and comforting.

Take away the phone, replace it with twenty Major and a box of matches and this could be any time over the last fifty years. In fact, Jimmy could easily be his old man sitting here – or even *his* old man.

He takes a sip from his pint.

Though you'd definitely need the cigarettes and matches. And he'd need to be wearing a suit.

And they wouldn't be Major, they'd be Benson & Hedges. Senior Service in his grandfather's case, as he remembers – and not matches, a gold Ronson lighter.

Shut up.

And the paper. The paper would be crumpled, having been read from cover to cover.

Sports pages, obituaries, letters to the editor, classifieds.

Leaning back on his stool, head tilted to one side, Jimmy looks at the scene again. But the argument for continuity seems even thinner this time, a little less authentic. And it's not just the lack of smokes, or the mobile phone, or that USB memory stick attached to his key ring.

It's the unread paper.

He bought it on the way here, in the SPAR on the corner, but the truth is he'd already read most of it online earlier in the day.

Jimmy takes another sip from his pint.

He worries for the health of the printed newspaper.

Unfortunately, his own direct experience of the business was cut short by an industry-wide epidemic of falling ad revenues. But even in the few years prior to that things had started feeling pretty thinned-out. Some of the senior reporters and specialist correspondents still had good sources and were out there on a regular basis gathering actual news, but as a recent hire Jimmy spent most of his days in front of a terminal recycling wire copy and PR material, a lot of it already second-hand and very little of it fact-checked. If it hadn't been for Phil Sweeney, Jimmy mightn't ever have had the chance to work on anything more exciting.

The barman passes, rubbing his cloth along the wooden surface of the bar as he goes.

Jimmy reaches for his glass again.

In those final months, Sweeney steered him in the direction of quite a few stories he was able to get his teeth into, and although most of his time was still spent chained to a desk, he put in the extra hours at his own expense and managed to score a couple of direct hits. He'd been building up considerable momentum – and was even due for a review – when the axe fell.

Which is why after six months at *City* and a further eighteen of intermittent and even lower-grade 'churnalism', Jimmy leapt at this chance of doing the Susie Monaghan book.

It may sound like a rationalisation, but he welcomed the change. OK, no more job security, but also no more multiple daily deadlines, no more shameless lifting of news-in-brief items from other sources, and no more frantic, soul-sapping last-minute reliance on Google and Wikipedia.

And while the Susie story might not exactly be news anymore, it still resonates.

Jimmy downs a good third of his pint in one go. He puts the glass back on the bar and stares at it.

Susie Monaghan was a tabloid celebrity, a bottom-feeding soap-star socialite from a few years ago who the entire country seemed fixated on for a while. Every aspect of her life was covered and analysed in excruciating detail, the outfits, the tans, the openings, the reality-show appearances, even the comings and goings of the character she played on that primetime soap.

But then her story took on a whole new dimension when she and five others died in a helicopter crash somewhere along the north Donegal coast. The outpouring of national grief that followed was phenomenal and curiosity about her lingered in the ether for months.

So while the book may be an attempt by Jimmy's publisher to cash in on an early wave of nostalgia, Jimmy himself sees it as more than that – because as far as *he's* concerned, whatever nostalgia there might be is not just for the dead girl, it's for the dead boom as well, for the vanished good times she'd been the potent, scented, stockinged, lubricious poster-girl for . . .

In any case, the point is: it's an angle. He has ideas. He's excited. He's getting paid.

And, in ten minutes' time, he's meeting the dead girl's sister.

A first-hand source.

But then it hits him again, comes in another wave. Phil Sweeney wants to pay him to drop the story?

It's insane.

Tell me it's not the prospect of the last chapter they're drooling over.

For fuck's sake.

The last chapter of the book, covering the twenty-four hours leading up to the crash, was always going to be the most interesting one – Susie still in crisis over the whole *Celebrity Death Row* controversy, Susie turning up uninvited at Drumcoolie Castle, Susie sending that weird series of texts, Susie's last-minute decision to go along for the helicopter ride.

Jimmy shifts on the stool.

Susie's unerring, compulsively watchable, creepily addictive little *Totentanz* . . .

He stares at a row of bottles behind the bar.

It's so obvious now that Phil Sweeney is covering for someone, a friend or a client, some balding, paunchy fuck who was maybe having an affair with Susie at the time and doesn't want the whole thing dredged up again now, doesn't want his name associated with her, doesn't want his reputation or his marriage put in jeopardy.

Jimmy lifts his glass.

But could it really be as banal as that, and as predictable? Unprepossessing rich bloke, gorgeous girl on a fast-ticking career clock? Then this grubby, undignified attempt a few years later to pretend it never happened?

He downs most of what's left in the glass.

He thinks of all that research material laid out on his desk. He's gone through it a hundred times, but maybe he needs to go through it again, with a fresh eye, a colder eye – in case he missed something: a detail in a photo maybe, a telling glance, a bit of furtive hand-holding.

Evidence.

Not that it'll make any difference, because even if something does turn up, what's he supposed to do? *Not* write the book just to save the blushes of some solicitor or banker friend of Phil Sweeney's?

Jimmy drains his glass and puts it back on the bar.

This is only speculation, of course. But it means he's going to have to phone Sweeney back. Find out what the story is.

Out of respect, if for no other reason.

And the sooner he does so the better.

He looks at his watch.

But not before this meeting with Maria Monaghan.

Jimmy gets off the stool and gathers up his stuff from the bar – keys, phone and change. They go in various pockets. The newspaper he takes in his hand. He looks at it for a moment, then leaves it on the stool.

He nods at the barman on his way out.

*

Conway moves away from the window, head still pounding. He walks over to the doorway, hears voices and follows them. In the kitchen Danny is drawing quietly at the table and Jack is playing on the floor. Corinne is cooking something in a wok. Molly is beside her, looking up, her nose wrinkled in distaste.

'I don't *like* that.'

'But sweetheart, you don't even know what it is.'

'I don't *like* it.'

Conway stands for a while by the fridge, observing the scene. He is about to make a comment when he hears a key in the front door.

Everyone turns around.

'*MOMMY.*'

A few moments later, Ruth walks into the kitchen. Within seconds she is being harangued, pulled at, climbed on.

'MOMMY, MOMMY, LOOK AT THIS! MOMMY!'

'I'm looking,' Ruth says. 'I'm *looking.*'

'She took my Woody,' Danny says, 'and hid him in the washing machine.'

'I didn't hide him there,' Molly says, stopping short of adding *your Honour*, 'I *put* him there.'

Conway starts massaging his temples.

Ruth catches his eye.

'You OK?'

He nods *yes*, but it's not very convincing.

'*MOMMY.*'

Raising her arms over Danny in exasperation, Ruth says, 'Please, chicken, quiet for a second, Mommy needs to talk to Daddy.'

Corinne intervenes. 'OK, guys, dinner is ready. Time to wash hands.'

She herds them off.

In the sudden calm that follows, Ruth looks at Conway. 'So, did you go to the doctor?'

He nods another unconvincing *yes*.

'And?'

'Nothing. He said it was tension.'

'I could have told you that. I *did* tell you that.' She takes a grape from a bowl on the counter. 'You worry too much.'

He doesn't say anything. It's not an argument he can win without getting into areas he doesn't want to get into.

He watches as she breaks another grape off and pops it in her mouth.

Ruth is a redhead, with green eyes and pale, freckled skin. After three kids, she's heavier than she used to be – but then again, and without her perfectly reasonable excuse, so is he. She's still good-looking though, gorgeous in fact, curvier than before and therefore, as far as Conway is concerned, sexier . . . a perception these days, it must be said, that is filtered through the alienating prism of extreme and permanent exhaustion.

'Did you get to talk to Larry Bolger?'

'Yeah, this afternoon. Finally.'

They'd been playing phone tag for a couple of days.

'What did he want?'

'I'm not sure really. I'm meeting him tomorrow.'

'He didn't say?'

'No.'

'Strange.' She reaches across the counter for a bottle of Evian. 'I wonder what he's up to these days. He probably just wants to talk. Rake over old times. Revisit old grievances.' She opens the bottle of water and takes a sip from it. 'Summon up old ghosts.'

Conway stares at her.

Shit.

Of course.

That's precisely what the old bastard wants to do. He must have heard the same thing Phil Sweeney heard.

Susie Monaghan.

Old ghosts . . .

Ruth returns his stare. 'What?'

'Nothing.' Conway shakes his head. 'I've just . . . remembered something.'

Realised something.

The headache. He's had it since the other night, since around the time he first heard Bolger had phoned looking for him. Which means it really is tension – but not because of the banks, or Tara Meadows, or his kids, or some stupid crush he might have on the au pair.

It's because of . . .

'Honey,' Ruth says. 'What's wrong?'

. . . a very different convergence . . .

'You've gone pale.'

. . . of very different pulses . . .

He shakes his head again.

. . . of anxiety.

'No,' he says, 'I'm . . . I'm fine.'

Conway mightn't have seen the dots straightaway, mightn't have wanted to see them.

Ruth leans forward. 'You sure?'

But he sees them now, sees where they connect.

'Yeah,' he says, and reaches up to open a cupboard. 'I just . . . I need to take something for this damn headache.'

*

Jimmy spots her straightaway, and it's the weirdest thing: she's unmistakably Susie Monaghan's sister – same posture, same shape, same bone structure even . . . but she . . .

What is it?

She didn't get that extra little shuffle of the genetic deck that Susie obviously got. There's nothing wrong with her. You just wouldn't put her on the cover of a glossy magazine.

Is that unfair?

Jimmy doesn't mean it to be.

No one would put *him* on the cover of a magazine, glossy or otherwise.

He moves away from the revolving doors and starts crossing the lobby. Maria is on the far side of it, standing by a large potted palm tree. She's wearing a conservative business suit – navy jacket, skirt, flat shoes – conservative but also very stylish and expensive-looking. Her hair is dark and short. She's glancing around, and doesn't seem very comfortable.

Jimmy approaches her with his hand outstretched.

'Maria? Jimmy Gilroy.'

She turns and looks at him. She shakes his hand. 'Maria Monaghan.'

The next few minutes are awkward. They find a table in the lounge and as they are getting settled a bar girl appears.

Jimmy orders a coffee, Maria a glass of white wine.

The bar girl moves away.

'So,' Jimmy says. And waits.

Sitting on the edge of her chair, eyes down, Maria smoothes out a wrinkle in her navy skirt. 'OK,' she says eventually, eyes still down. 'Let me make one thing clear. I've agreed to meet you, but I haven't agreed to anything else. I haven't agreed to co-operate, whatever that might involve, or to go on the record. I'm just meeting you because you've been so bloody persistent.'

'Yes. Sorry about that.'

She looks at him. 'Sure you are.'

He holds up his hands. 'How else would you have agreed to meet me?'

'I wouldn't.'

'See? But that doesn't have to mean I'm hustling you, does it? The thing is, if I do this book I want to do it right. I want to be fair.'

She leans forward slightly. 'That's easy to say, but what does it mean?'

'It means I want to tell your sister's story as truthfully as I possibly can.'

'Right,' she says, and nods. 'So where the hell were *you* three years ago?'

Jimmy hesitates. He doesn't have an answer. He sits back in his chair.

The media had a field day when it came to poor Susie. They were having one already before the accident, but afterwards it was extreme. In the previous few months, they'd crawled over every aspect of her life, like maggots, and now they had her actual corpse, twisted and torn, to gorge on.

They.

Jimmy sits up. 'We didn't exactly cover ourselves in glory, did we?'

Maria snorts, but doesn't say anything.

'For what it's worth,' Jimmy goes on, 'I was little more than a trainee at the time. I didn't even –'

'For what it's *worth*, Jimmy,' Maria interrupts, 'little Susie Monaghan loved every minute of it. Right up to, and possibly including, the very end.'

Jimmy nods.

What did she just say?

The bar girl arrives and as she's transferring the coffee things and glass of wine from her tray to the table, Jimmy studies Maria closely. He remembers reading that she was two years older than Susie, which would make her twenty-eight now, or twenty-nine.

His age, give or take.

Though she seems older in a way, more serious.

Maria picks up her glass of wine and takes a sip from it. Jimmy pours milk into his coffee.

What was that, *up to and including*? He wants to ask her to explain this, but he needs to pace himself. He doesn't want to scare her off. What he says instead is, 'What do you do, Maria?'

'I'm an administrator. At the Fairleigh Clinic. Not very glamorous, I suppose, but at least I'm still alive.'

Jimmy nods again. Doesn't seem like she's going to *let* him pace himself. He leans forward in his chair.

'I'm sensing a little resentment here, Maria.'

'Oh you are, are you?'

She looks as if she's about to tear strips off him, but suddenly her eyes well up. She puts her glass down and stifles a sob. After a moment she produces a tissue from her pocket. She dabs her eyes with it and then blows her nose.

'Sorry.'

Jimmy shrugs. 'For what?'

Maria holds up the tissue. 'This,' she says, and shrugs too. 'I don't know. But you're right about one thing. I do feel resentment. A lot of resentment.' She tucks the tissue into her sleeve. 'When I was younger I resented Susie. I resented her looks and her success. Then I resented the way she squandered her success and didn't seem to care, didn't even seem to notice. I resented the media, and the cops, and her friends, anyone we had to deal with after the crash. I resented the fact that Mum and Dad had to suffer so much, and not just the grief, but the indignity, the intrusion. Now they're both dead and for some reason I resent them, too. Don't ask me why. And of course I resent *you*. But you're easy. You want to revive the whole thing, drag me into it, get me talking. So what do you expect? In fact, if you're not careful I might pile all my resentments into one big basket and slap *your* name on it.'

Looking at her now, listening to this, Jimmy already sees a different Maria from the one he spotted out in the lobby only a few minutes earlier, a different Maria from the one he pictured in his head through all those phone calls and e-mails. For one thing – and he can't believe he's only seeing this now – she's actually *very* attractive. Not in the way Susie was, but in her own way. She's tough, and she's vulnerable, and there's a light in her eyes, a spark of something, of spirit, of real intelligence.

'I get that,' he says. 'I do. It makes sense. But you have to understand . . . a lot of people are interested in your sister, still interested. She struck a chord.'

36

'Oh bullshit. She was a celebrity, and one of the best kind, too, the kind who dies.'

Jimmy raises an eyebrow at this.

'Don't get me wrong,' Maria goes on. 'I loved my sister. I just wish things had been different.'

'In what way?'

'Between *us*. For *her*. In every way.'

'Right.'

Jimmy has a sense that this isn't going to be easy. As usual with a human-interest story you talk to someone, look them in the eye, and what happens? Things get knotty, ambivalence creeps in, black merges with white and you end up with an amorphous headachy grey.

'Susie loved being famous,' Maria says, reaching for her wine again. 'She really wanted it, always did, but it gnawed at her soul that that was *all* what she wanted . . . because she knew on some level . . . she knew it was *nothing*.' Maria takes a sip from her glass. 'And that made her do reckless things, made her *be* reckless.'

Jimmy hesitates, then says, 'That's a whole narrative right there, Maria. It's a perspective no one's heard before. People will be interested in that.'

Maria looks alarmed. 'Yeah, but they won't be hearing it from *me*. I'm just shooting my mouth off. Being a little reckless myself.' She takes another sip of wine. Then she furrows her brow. 'Is this some technique you're using here? Getting me to talk?' She pauses. 'You have a sympathetic face. Maybe that's it.' She pauses again. 'But I suppose the real question is do you know you have a sympathetic face and use that fact, or is it just –'

She stops, looks away, shakes her head.

'Jesus, listen to me. This is why I didn't want to meet you, you know. I'm a talker. I *talk*. And what happened to my sister is something I haven't talked about in a very long time, to anyone. And the thing is I want to. So you're probably the last person I should be sitting in front of.'

She leans forward and puts her glass back onto the table.

Jimmy looks at his untouched coffee, which is probably lukewarm by now.

He should have ordered a drink.

'Maria,' he says, 'all I can do is try to reassure you. I don't work for a tabloid. I'm not out to trap you. This is a *book*, commissioned by a publisher. And yeah, there's a sales and marketing aspect to it, of course there is, but I want to do a good job, and your insights can only help to round it out, give it substance.'

Maria looks at him, holds his gaze for what feels like a long time. She seems to be calculating something. Then she says, 'You know what I'm afraid of? I'm afraid something will come out.'

Jimmy swallows. 'Like what?'

'I don't know, but . . . the crash? There was never really any explanation for it, was there? There was no faulty or missing *bit* they could find, nothing mechanical, the weather wasn't particularly bad. It was just a crash, a disaster. What was the verdict at the inquest? Accidental death? Then, case closed. Just like that.'

'Yes.'

'Well, I'll be honest with you, Jimmy, I knew Susie better than anyone, and she was wild, she liked to make scenes and kick up a fuss for no apparent reason. So my darkest fear, what

I'm afraid might come out, is that in some way . . .' She stops for a moment and takes a deep breath. 'Look, it was a helicopter, right, a small, confined space, six people, she was probably coked out of it, even at that time of the day, plus she'd been sending those weird texts, and clearly wasn't in a stable frame of mind, so . . . who knows?' Maria's eyes well up again. 'Maybe she made some kind of a scene, maybe she got hysterical about something, went crazy. Maybe the accident was *her* fault.' Maria pulls the tissue out of her sleeve again. 'There, I said it.'

Jimmy's heart is racing. 'This is just . . . speculation, right?'

'Yes. Of course. But I can see it. I can visualise it. It'd be so typical, so . . . *Susie.*' .

'Jesus.'

'This idea has haunted me for three years, Jimmy. I still have nightmares about it.' She pauses, wipes a tear from her cheek. 'Though you could never write that I said that. I'd sue you if you did –'

'I wouldn't.'

She looks him in the eye again.

'But then with that . . . that *image* in my head, how could I possibly co-operate on a book with you, how could –'

'Maria –'

Jimmy doesn't know what to say, blindsided himself by what she has conjured up.

'Look,' Maria goes on, 'I know I'm probably not being very rational here, but –'

'No, no, you are. Jesus. You're fine. You're allowed.'

She nods, then blows her nose again. As she does so, Jimmy looks down at the floor, gazes at a pattern in the carpet.

Some sort of commotion in the cockpit? Instigated by Susie?

It's a tantalising idea. But even if that's what happened, who could prove it now?

Who would want to?

He would. That's for sure. And Maria, if it ever came to it – the thing is – probably wouldn't.

See?

This is how it goes. You get talking to someone, you interact, and it all starts to fall apart.

Then something occurs to him.

'Those texts,' he says. 'Did Susie send one to *you*?'

'Yes.'

'From the actual helicopter?'

She shakes her head.

'It was before. From the hotel. From her room.'

Jimmy waits. He wants to ask her what was in the text, but he's assuming that if she's prepared to tell him she will. When she doesn't, he says, 'In all the documentation there is reference to four texts she sent that morning. Yours would make it five.'

Maria shrugs. 'It was just a text. It was no smoking gun, believe me. Susie was a text head. She would have loved Twitter.'

'She sounded kind of hysterical in the one she sent to her agent.'

'Yeah.' Maria pauses, and almost smiles. 'Look at you. You're all intrigued now, aren't you? I'm sorry. This is precisely the opposite of what I wanted to happen.'

'Intrigued by this or not, Maria, I still want to write the book. There's enough there as it is. But it'd be great if you went on the record.'

She studies him for a moment.

'You know,' she says, 'you do have a sympathetic face. But I actually don't think you're trying to hustle me.'

Jimmy remains silent.

She picks up her glass of wine again and takes a sip from it. 'Nothing in life is easy, is it?' she says.

Jimmy smiles. 'No. So does that mean you'll talk to me?'

*

Flanked by two senior civil servants, he emerges from Government Buildings and steps out onto the landscaped courtyard, where a car is waiting. But something isn't right . . . it's one of the civil servants . . . he turns to look . . .

The man is bleeding from his eyes . . .

Bolger grunts, shifts in the armchair.

'What?'

The door clicks shut. He opens his eyes. The TV is still on, Frasier Crane, looking harried.

What time is it?

He turns. 'Mary?'

'Hi, were you asleep?'

She approaches, stands over him.

'Christ,' he says. 'What time is it?'

'Not late. Just after ten, I think.'

'Why are you home so early?'

He has the feeling of being caught out. She wouldn't normally be home before eleven, and by that time he'd have ensconced himself in the study with a cup of hot chocolate.

To make it seem like he'd been slaving away all evening.

'I had a bit of a headache,' she says. 'I wasn't in the mood.'

He feels guilty, slumped here in the armchair, watching television.

'Will you have a cup of tea?' she then asks, turning and unbuttoning her coat.

'Yes, thanks.'

He rubs his eyes. How long was he asleep?

A civil servant bleeding from . . .

What is wrong with him? He stands up and walks around the room, trying to get his circulation going. Mary is in the kitchen now. He can see her through the door filling the kettle.

'Did you get any work done?' she asks over her shoulder.

'A little, yeah.'

He throws his eyes up.

Chapter a hundred.

He has barely started is the truth. He doesn't know *where* to start.

Chapter one. I grew up in the shadow of my older brother, and despite how things may have come to seem in later years – I never really got out from under it . . .

Yeah. Fuck off.

'How are the crowd anyway?' he says, deflecting a follow-up question.

'They're grand. Everyone asking for you.'

Mary comes out of the kitchen, smiling, grabs her coat from the back of the chair where she left it and heads into the bedroom.

Bolger stands in front of the fireplace, looking down at the carpet, listening as the dull hum of the kettle in the next room ascends to a muffled roar.

He is sick with anxiety, and that's about the size of it.

Meeting Dave Conway tomorrow is supposed to make him feel like he's taking some kind of action. But he won't be really. All he'll be doing is asking Dave if he saw that thing in the paper last week.

Saying, *I* saw it. Did *you* see it? *I* saw it.

And I haven't been right since.

Reading the *Irish Independent* that morning, alone in the apartment, Bolger came as close as he has in nearly ten years to falling off the wagon.

He glances over once again at the corner of the room, at the drinks cabinet.

Takes a deep breath, holds it in.

Couple out walking their dog. In Wicklow. Remains of a body in a ditch – just bones really, and a set of clothes. Reckoned to have been there for at least two years. Unidentified, but no shortage of speculation.

He breathes out slowly.

Mary emerges from the bedroom in her at-homes and goes back into the kitchen.

Bolger stands there, not moving.

Couple out walking their dog.

In Wicklow.

Is this it? Is this beginning?

*

It's nearly eleven thirty.

Too late to phone now, but then again maybe the perfect time to phone. Catch him off guard.

Jimmy is walking along by St Stephen's Green.

He left Maria at the top of Grafton Street and while they didn't make a specific arrangement to meet again, the understanding is that they'll be in touch – once Maria has had a little time to think, and maybe consult a lawyer. Once *he's* had time – not that this came up in conversation – to clear the decks with Phil Sweeney.

He gets his phone out and looks at it.

There's no point in putting this off. Besides, things have changed. He's on his own now, no longer a valuable asset working at a national newspaper . . .

He finds the number.

What has he got to lose?

He brings the phone up to his ear, and waits.

He glances over at the Shelbourne Hotel.

'*Jimmy?*'

'Phil. Hi. I hope I'm not calling too late.'

'No, no, you're grand. Thanks for getting back to me. I appreciate it. I wouldn't want there to be a misunderstanding.'

'Oh?' Jimmy says, deciding to get straight into it. 'Really? What'll we call it then, an *absence* of understanding? Because you know what? I'm at a loss here. You call me up –'

'I was just trying to help –'

'How? By insulting me? And where did you hear about what I'm working on anyway?'

There's probably no straight answer Sweeney can give to this, at least not one Jimmy will find acceptable.

'The flow of information,' he says. 'I pay attention to it.'

'Oh *please*.'

'Look, I often hear things I don't necessarily ask about,

44

things I maybe shouldn't even be privy to. Whatever. It is what it is.' He pauses. 'So, did you have a think about what I said?'

'Yeah, I did, and the thing is –'

'No, Jimmy, there's no thing. Just take it on board, OK? Please.'

Jimmy stops in his tracks. A group of American tourists walk past him, one of them talking loudly, a big guy with a beard saying something about 'this giant Ponzi scheme'.

At the taxi rank to his left a young couple appear to be having an argument.

'I *told* you, he's from *work*.'

Beyond them are lights, colours, a kaleidoscope, traffic stopping and starting.

Jimmy turns, takes a few steps towards the railings of the Green.

'For Christ's sake, Phil,' he says in a loud whisper, 'you can't just dangle something like this in my face, and not expect me to bite. I'm supposed to be a fucking journalist.'

Sweeney exhales loudly.

'It's not like that,' he says. 'There's no story here. It's not –'

'Susie Monaghan? No story? Her name on a magazine cover, let alone her *picture*, and you still get a huge spike in circulation, even after all this time, so don't tell me –'

'It's not about her. Believe me.'

Jimmy reaches out and takes a hold of one of the railings.

'Then what *is* it about?'

Sweeney clicks his tongue. 'I know this is tricky for you,' he says, 'professionally, being told, being *asked*, to stay away from something, a story, it goes against the grain, I get that, but . . . the thing is, I'm good friends with Freddie Walker. Yeah?' He

45

pauses. 'Ted Walker's brother? And . . . they're still suffering. Every time the story comes up, every time Susie Monaghan's name gets mentioned, it brings the whole thing back, the tragedy, everything, and the prospect of a book, with all the publicity, the photos, dredging through the details again, and having it all be about *her*, with only a cursory mention of Ted and the others who died, it's . . . well, frankly it'd be fucking torture for them.' He pauses again. 'So I'm asking you, Jimmy. As a favour. Give it a miss.' He clears his throat. 'And I certainly didn't mean to insult you.'

Jimmy squeezes the railings until his knuckles are white.

Mother*fucker*.

He didn't see this coming.

Black, white, headachy grey.

'Freddie Walker?' he says.

This is a question, sort of, but they both know what the answer is. It's a no-brainer. It's *Yeah, sonny Jim, back in your box now and shut the fuck up*.

Jimmy releases his grip on the railing. Behind him is kinesis, light and noise, the streets. Ahead, through the bars, is stillness, a dark blanket of shadows, the Green at night.

'Yeah,' Sweeney says, 'Freddie Walker, he's a client, lovely guy, you'd really like him, and of course –'

'No,' Jimmy says. 'Stop it, right? I'm not listening to any more of this.' He turns around and walks towards the head of the taxi rank. 'Good night, Phil. I'm sorry, I can't help you out.'

He snaps the phone shut and puts it away.

Steps around the arguing couple.

'Hey –'

And opens the back door of the waiting taxi –

'That's our –'

– anticipating a musty whiff, the residue of long hours, long *years*, of sweat, smoke and overheated opinion.

'Take that one,' Jimmy says, pointing at the next car along, and gets in the back of the Nissan.

Maria will talk to him, he's pretty sure of that, and it'll add a whole new dimension to the story.

'Sandymount,' he says to the driver, 'Strand Road.'

So Phil Sweeney can just . . .

'That's not a bad one.'

'No,' Jimmy says, as they cruise past the spot where he left Maria a few minutes earlier, 'no, not a bad one at all.'

*

On his way down in the elevator of the BRX Building in Manhattan, Clark Rundle is about to flick through the latest issue of *Vanity Fair* to look for the article when he gets a call from Don Ribcoff.

'Yeah, Don,' he says, putting the magazine under his arm, 'what's up?'

'Clark, I need five minutes. Are you around?'

Rundle looks at his watch. 'It's nearly seven o'clock, Don. I'm leaving the building. It's been a long day.' He's also had this copy of *Vanity Fair* in his possession since lunchtime, and has managed to hold off opening it until now. He resents the intrusion.

'Can't it wait?'

'Not really, Clark, no. Where are you headed? Let me meet you there.'

'I'm going to the Orpheus Room. I'm meeting Jimmy

Vaughan for a drink.' He hesitates, then says, 'Look, why don't you join us?'

'Twenty minutes?'

'Fine.'

Rundle closes the phone. The elevator door hums open and he steps out into the lobby area.

Seems he's not the only one leaving the building.

As he walks through the crowds, Rundle keeps the *Vanity Fair* under his arm, with the cover concealed. It's absurd, but he feels a little self-conscious. He's been interviewed before, many times, but usually under controlled conditions and not until multiple confidentiality clauses have been agreed to and signed.

None of which applied with *Vanity Fair*, of course.

Rundle didn't mind, though. He was doing it for J.J., for this campaign he might be running. Plus, he finds there's a certain cachet to being profiled in *VF* that even *he* isn't immune to.

He'll read the article in the car.

Out on Fifth it is warm. The air is still heavy and the evening sun is struggling to break through the haze.

He crosses the sidewalk. His driver holds open the door of the waiting limo and he gets in. As far as Rundle is concerned, the interior of a car like this, with its tinted windows and chilled hum, is a refuge, one of the modern world's few remaining private spaces. Advances in telecommunications haven't helped much in this regard, but he still tries his best. Phone-time is kept to a minimum, and e-mails are ignored.

Settling in now, he places the magazine in his lap and looks at the cover. It shows an actress he doesn't recognise. She is pale and blonde, with icy blue eyes. She's got blood-red lipstick on and is wearing a mantilla.

Pastiche forties.

A Veronica Lake wannabe. A Veronica Lake-alike. She's pretty cute, though.

Her name, apparently, is Brandi Klugmann and she's in some new blockbuster franchise.

He scans the rest of the cover for article titles. He finds what he's looking for at the bottom.

The Rundle Supremacy. How brothers Senator John Rundle and BRX chairman Clark Rundle are taking on the world . . . and winning.

He reads this over a couple of times and nods, as though in agreement with someone sitting in front of him. He then lifts the magazine and gives a preliminary riffle through its glossy, scented pages, catching a rush of images, ads mostly, promissory shards of the erotic and the streamlined.

Perfume, watches, banks, celebs, real estate porn.

He looks up and out of the window for a moment. Traffic is light and flowing easily. They'll be at the Orpheus Room sooner than he expected.

He goes back to the magazine and quickly locates the article.

It opens with a two-page spread of photos, some colour, some black and white – he and J.J. at various stages in their lives, together and apart . . . grainy images, weird clothes and, of course, *hair*, from the seventies, suits thereafter, and less hair . . . J.J. with Karl Rove, J.J. on *Meet the Press* . . . Clark looking inscrutable at some charity ball, Clark in the cabin of his G-V.

He scans the text.

It actually *is* something of a puff piece – the Rundle brothers,

49

John, 50, and Clark, 48, sons of the legendary Henry C. Rundle, each on a trajectory to stellar success, one in politics, setting his sights on the White House, and the other in business, steering long-held family concern, mining and engineering giant BRX, to global domination. The 'narrative' in the article is how close the brothers are, no sibling rivalry, just mutual support, the kind of bond you'd expect from identical twins sort of thing, with anecdotes emanating from the usual sources, how J.J. ceded control of his part of the company to Clark against all legal advice, and how Clark chose to withdraw his name for consideration as commerce secretary under Bush so as not to steal J.J.'s thunder.

He closes the magazine and puts it on the seat beside him.

It's strange reading about yourself. The material usually feels diluted and one-dimensional. By the same token there's nothing in the article here he needs to call his lawyers about. It's accurate enough, he supposes, and will achieve what it was intended to achieve – at least as far as J.J.'s press office is concerned – and that is to help pave the way for this possible nomination.

Rundle wonders if J.J. has seen it yet. He's on a foreign trip at the moment – doing Clark a favour, as it happens – so it's unlikely.

But then again the article is probably available online.

In which case, knowing J.J., he'll definitely have seen it.

And will be in touch about it the first chance he gets.

The limo pulls up outside the Orpheus Room on Fifty-fourth Street. Rundle waits for the driver to open the door and then gets out. As he straightens his jacket he glances at the passing traffic down a bit on Park and something occurs to him. It's easy to forget this, but it's true what was in the article. There *is* no rivalry between them, none, and they genuinely do root for each other. In taking BRX Mining & Engineering to new levels of success, Clark has remained largely anonymous, and that's been fine. J.J. was always the attention-seeker anyway, the approval junkie. But if that's what his brother wants, a shot at the presidency – which until now, being honest about it, Clark hasn't really taken that seriously – then why not? And why shouldn't Clark do everything in his considerable power to help make it happen?

Add 'kingmaker' to his list of achievements.

Stick it one more time to the old man.

Fuck, yeah.

He heads in under the sidewalk canopy.

Realigning his headspace.

Inside, Jimmy Vaughan is sitting at his regular table, nursing what looks like a fruit juice.

Rundle approaches the table with his hand outstretched. 'Jimmy, how are you?'

Vaughan looks up. He shakes Rundle's hand and indicates for him to sit down. 'How *am* I? I'm eighty-two years old, Clark, what do you want me to tell you?'

Rundle laughs at this and sits down. 'Well, if I could look half as good as you do, Jimmy, and I mean *now*, let alone when I'm eighty-two, I'd be a happy man.'

This is bullshit, of course, palaver, but on one level he actually means it. Vaughan is extraordinary for his age, his steely blue eyes displaying an undimmed and ferocious intelligence. As chairman of private equity firm the Oberon Capital Group – as well as sitting member of the Council on Foreign Relations and the Trilateral Commission – Vaughan is something of an *éminence grise* around these parts.

A waiter appears at Rundle's side. 'Your usual, sir?'

Rundle nods.

A gimlet. For his sins.

He looks at Vaughan. 'How's Meredith?'

Vaughan waves a hand over the table. 'She's . . . *well*.'

Meredith is Vaughan's umpteenth wife. They got married about four years ago, and she's at least forty-five years his junior. Which maybe explains a lot.

She's even younger than Rundle's own wife.

'And Eve?'

'She's good. She's in England at the moment, Oxford. Checking up on Daisy.'

Vaughan smiles.

Wives, daughters, whatever.

'Listen,' he says, leaning forward, getting down to business, 'this thing with the Chinese?'

Rundle nods.

'It isn't going to go away, Clark. I mean, let's say our friend the colonel turns down their offer, yeah? Let's say we pull that off. It just means they'll come back with a bigger offer. That's the kicker in all of this, it isn't *about* money.' Vaughan makes a puffing sound and throws his hands up. 'It's like we have to learn a whole new language.'

Rundle is all too aware of this, but hearing Vaughan articulate it, hearing him sound even vaguely defeatist – *that's* a little unnerving.

'Yeah,' he says, 'or maybe we have to *re*learn a language we once knew, but have forgotten.'

Vaughan looks at him for a moment. Then he reaches over and pats him on the arm. 'Oh lord, Clark,' he says. 'That's a bit subtle, even for me.' He laughs. 'Or . . . or what's that other word . . . inscrutable?'

'Well, I wouldn't –'

'Gentlemen.'

They both look up.

It's Don Ribcoff. He has arrived at the table in what seems like a frantic rush. He sits down, nods at Vaughan, but then faces Rundle.

'Forgive me, Clark,' he says, 'I wouldn't normally barge in on you like this, but I thought it'd be better not to talk over the phone.'

Rundle nods, wondering what this is about – the urgency, the not talking on the phone. Especially the not talking on the phone. But also thinking who'd be a better judge of something like that than the CEO of Gideon Global?

He turns to Vaughan. 'I didn't mention it to you Jimmy, but I spoke to Don earlier and asked him to join us.'

'Of course, of course,' Vaughan says, and makes an inclusive gesture with his hand. 'Don, what are you drinking?'

Ribcoff bites his lip. 'Er, water, please.'

Vaughan raises a finger and a waiter seems to materialise out of thin air. Instructions are given, two chilled 330 ml bottles of Veen, one velvet, one effervescent. Almost immediately a second waiter appears with the gimlet and as the drink is being transferred from the tray to the table Rundle takes a moment to study Don Ribcoff.

He seems uncharacteristically ruffled. Still only in his mid-thirties, Ribcoff is a hugely capable young man, good-looking, fit, and incredibly focused when it comes to his business. He also provides an invaluable service to people like Rundle, Vaughan and many others. The privatisation of the security and intelligence industries has been nothing short of revolutionary and the Don Ribcoffs of this world, who have spearheaded that revolution, are men to be cherished and nurtured.

Which is why it's disturbing to see him like this.

As soon as the waiter withdraws, Rundle reaches for his gimlet.

Gin and lime juice.

Who could ask for anything more?

He takes a sip.

And then it strikes him that the reason Ribcoff is agitated is because he wants to talk to *him*.

He refocuses.

Vaughan and Ribcoff are looking in his direction.

'What?'

Ribcoff clears his throat, shifts his weight in the chair and then says, 'Look, er, this trip the Senator is on? It's run into a little trouble. I'm afraid we might have to think things over.'

Rundle immediately says, 'What things?'

And then adds, after a beat, *'What trouble?'*

2

As they cross the lobby, various people greet Larry Bolger by name. He's been living in the hotel for over a year now, in one of the penthouse suites, but his presence down here, or in the bar, will still cause a stir.

How's it going, Larry? they'll say. *Would you not fancy your old job back? The country needs you.*

Stuff like that.

He only wishes Irish people weren't so bloody informal. Bill still gets called Mister President wherever he goes, Bolger has seen it. Not that he wants *that* particularly, a title or anything, grovelling. Just a little respect.

Mister Bolger mightn't be a bad place to start.

'How are Mary and the girls?' Dave Conway asks, keeping up the small talk until they get settled at a table.

'They're grand, thanks, yeah. Lisa's just got her MBA.'

'Another Bolger out of the traps, eh?'

'I'm telling you, I don't know where she got it from, her mother maybe, but she's got it.'

They take a table at the back. It's early and the dining room next door is crowded, breakfast in full swing, but there's almost no one in here, in the Avondale Lounge. It's eerily quiet, with at least half of the room – the half they've chosen to sit in – still in semi-darkness.

'So,' Bolger says, and shifts his weight in the chair. 'How are things with *you*?'

Why is he so nervous?

'Yeah, not too bad, Larry, I suppose. We've managed to avoid the worst of it. So far, anyway.'

Dave Conway is one of the canniest businessmen Bolger has ever met and for a while there he was a trusted member of the inner circle, of the kitchen cabinet. It was Dave, in fact, who persuaded Bolger to go to Drumcoolie Castle in the first place.

To that corporate ethics conference.

Bolger hadn't wanted to go.

Of course. Story of his bloody life.

A waiter approaches the table, an older guy with a dickie-bow and a silver tray under one arm. Bolger squints at him for a second and scrolls through his mental database.

'Sean,' he then says, 'how are you? A pot of coffee will do us fine here, thanks.'

The waiter nods in acknowledgement and retreats.

Bolger turns back.

'So,' Conway says, 'how are the memoirs coming along?'

'Oh God.' Bolger groans. 'Not very well, I'm afraid. What's that old song? "I Can't Get Started"?'

'Really? I thought –'

'Writing's not my strong suit, Dave. I don't know why I ever agreed to do the damn thing. I sit there for hours and nothing happens. It's a total waste of time.'

'Do you have a deadline?'

'Yeah, but that's become a bit of a moveable feast. It was supposed to be due two months ago.' He shrugs. 'Now . . . I don't know.'

Conway nods, but doesn't say anything.

Bolger thinks Dave looks a little peaky this morning, tired, not his usual self. Bolger has noticed this quite a bit recently. People he runs into from the old days aren't as healthy-looking as they used to be.

'Anyway,' he says, after a long pause, 'here we are.'

'Yes,' Conway responds, 'here we are.'

Bolger hates this. He's always been known for his direct, no-bullshit approach – it worked with the unions, with the employers, and even occasionally, on the international stage, with fellow heads of government – so what's up with him now, why is he being so coy? It's not as though Dave is any kind of a threat to him. If anything, it's the other way around.

Two young men in suits come into the lounge and take a table near the entrance. One of them is talking on his phone, the other one is texting.

Bolger clears his throat.

'OK,' he says, straightening up in his chair. 'Reason I asked you in here? That thing in the paper? About a week ago? Did you see it? In Wicklow? The fella they found in the woods?'

Conway furrows his brow. 'No. I didn't. I was away for most of last week.' He pauses, then his eyes widen. 'The *woods*?'

'Yeah,' Bolger says. He looks around the room, over at the two suits, back at Dave. 'In Wicklow. A *body*.'

Conway stares at him, going pale.

Or was he pale already?

'Shit,' he says. 'Has there been anything about it since?'

'Not as far as I've seen, no. But still. I mean.'

'Right.' Conway nods, considering this.

Bolger glances around again, biting his lip.

Couple out walking their dog.

Jesus.

He looks back at Dave. 'But if there *is* any more about it . . .'

'What?'

'I don't know. We'd have to . . . *do* something, wouldn't we?'

Conway looks puzzled. 'I'm sorry, *do* something? Like what?'

'Ah, come on, Dave, you know what I mean. For fuck's sake.'

Bolger hears the incipient panic in his own voice and it irritates him. Before coming down here this morning, he'd decided he was going to remain calm, not lose his cool, tease this out . . . maybe draw on some of the old magic . . .

'We'd have to have a word with someone,' he says.

Conway leans forward at this. 'A word? With *who*?' He holds his hands up. 'Jesus, Larry, would you cop on to yourself. I know you ran the country for, what was it, three years or something, but you're not running it now.'

Bolger flinches. 'I *realise* that.'

'Because I mean . . . that's not how things work anymore.'

'OK, OK,' Bolger whispers loudly. 'Whatever. I get it.'

He sits back in his chair, and glances around, doing his best to absorb this.

He's not an idiot.

He just thought . . .

In any case, what he's *now* thinking is . . . three years? It wasn't very long, was it? Not the five or even ten years Paddy Norton had dangled before him that night in his office. He led a heave and then, eventually, after a disastrous election campaign, got heaved himself. Ignominious, inglorious, call it what you will – but holy God, those three years in the middle there were brilliant, golden . . . nothing like them before or since.

Certainly not since.

And he doesn't want them being tampered with now, or re-interpreted, or rewritten in any way, or decon-*fucking*-structed because of some stupid, bloody *thing* he had shag-all to do with in the first place. But that's exactly what he's afraid is going to happen.

It's what has been eating him alive, from the inside out, for the last week and a half.

'So,' he says eventually, a slight tremor in his voice. 'Where does that leave us?'

Conway shrugs. 'I don't know. You said it yourself, there hasn't been any further mention of it in the papers. Maybe there's no cause for concern.'

'Yes, but it's bound to resurface at some point, isn't it? At an inquest or whatever. Details. Probing. Jesus Christ.'

Bolger can't stand himself right now. If Dave is being aloof and somewhat enigmatic here, *he's* being whiny and insecure.

But he can't help it.

'Listen,' Conway is saying, leaning forward again, 'do you want to know why we've got nothing to worry about? And this is totally apart from the fact that there's probably, I don't know, *dozens* of bodies buried up in the Wicklow hills.' He pauses. 'It's because none of *us* had anything to do with it. With what happened. It's that simple. So there's no traceability. There can't be.' He pauses again. 'Are you with me?'

Bolger nods along. 'Yeah, I know, I get it,' he says, 'no traceability, and I like that, I do, but we're not fucking rogue pig farmers here, Dave, are we? I mean *are* we? There's always traceability, there's always *someone* . . . some . . .'

He trails off, his fist clenched.

'Jesus Christ,' Conway says, looking around as well now, 'take it easy.' He draws back a little and screws his eyes up, as though to focus better. 'Are you OK, Larry?'

'Yeah, I'm fine, I'm fine.'

But he isn't, and it's in that very moment, as the waiter approaches – silver tray held aloft, aroma of coffee wafting through the air – that Bolger realises something. As soon as he can get rid of Dave Conway here he's going to head straight back upstairs to the apartment. He's going to shut the door behind him. He's going to walk over to the drinks cabinet in the corner. He's going to take out a bottle of whiskey. He's going to pour himself a large measure. He's going to fucking *drink* it.

*

The voices come, a dizzying swirl of them, hectoring and ceaseless . . . it's the incomprehensible babble, he *suspects*, of Irishmen and Chinamen building the transcontinental Union Pacific Railroad . . .

He suspects?

Rundle opens his eyes.

Yes, he –

The voices –

But where he is? For a moment he's not sure.

Then . . . Manhattan. Of course. The Celestial.

He struggles up and looks at the clock on the bedside table.

4:18.

Shit.

He throws back the covers and climbs out of bed. He goes to the door and stands for a moment in the dense nighttime stillness.

With Daisy gone to college it didn't take long for the place to start feeling lonely, but now with Eve gone, too – even if only for a couple of weeks – it's positively desolate.

He should have called Nora, told her to come over, to drop whatever she was doing, whoever she was with.

That he was in a platinum-rates frame of mind.

She would have understood. Nora always understands.

He walks along the corridor and goes into the living room.

He didn't get in until after midnight – stuck there at the Orpheus with Jimmy Vaughan and Don Ribcoff, trying to piece together what had happened, trying to come up with a strategy for dealing with it.

Frantic about consequences, about fallout.

Rundle especially frantic about J.J.

He wanders over to the window and stands there, gazing out – the city below, coruscating busily. *It* may never sleep, but he wishes to fuck he could, even occasionally – wishes he could get a decent night's shut-eye, and one without these stupid, scrappy dreams he keeps having. The Union Pacific Railroad? Irishmen and Chinamen?

For *Christ's* sake.

He turns around and checks the time on one of the room's displays.

4:39.

What'd that be in Paris? A quarter to eleven almost, morning-time in full swing, coffee and croissants.

Cigarettes.

Where'd he leave his phone?

He's not going to wait any longer.

Because he should have heard from J.J. by now, even a quick reply to that text he sent last night.

He finds his cell phone next to his keys on a counter in the kitchen and tries J.J.'s number. It rings. There's no answer. It goes into message.

Then he tries a number he has for Herb Felder, J.J.'s director of communications. It rings twice.

'Yep?'

'Herb. Clark Rundle.'

'Oh. Mr Rundle. Hi.'

'How is he?'

'Er, he's fine, he's fine. A little shaken. He's going to need some surgery on his hand, but all things considered he's fine. He's actually sleeping right now.'

Rundle nods. There's nothing new in this, nothing different from what Don Ribcoff was able to tell him last night, but still, he's relieved to have it confirmed first-hand.

'You're in the American Hospital?'

'Yeah.'

OK.

So, next stage.

'Tell me, Herb, have you thought about how to handle this?'

'Er . . . I've *thought* about it, sure, Mr Rundle, but I'm at something of a disadvantage here.' He pauses. 'In that I'm not exactly in possession of all the facts. The Senator goes AWOL for a couple of days and then turns up with a serious injury? No real explanation? I've been dealt better hands in my time.'

Rundle clicks his tongue.

'Right.' He turns around and leans back against the marble counter. 'What have the doctors said? Is he going to need a plaster cast? A brace of some kind? How's it going to look?'

Herb Felder sighs, probably frustrated at not having his concerns addressed. When he replies his tone is more clipped than before. 'He'll have a brace. There won't be any way of hiding it.'

Now Rundle sighs.

'OK,' he says. 'Here's what we do. I'm going to talk to Don Ribcoff. He's got people on the ground over there –'

'But I thought Gideon –'

'PR people, it's an affiliate company. They do strategic communications. The Jordan Group.'

'Oh.'

Oh? Rundle makes a face. What the fuck? The guy's feelings are hurt? 'Look,' he says, 'it's better if they take care of this. Better if *you* stay out of it, in fact.'

'Why?'

'In case it comes back and bites you in the ass, that's why. The Jordan people will feed something into the news cycle and you just run with it. The less you know about how it got there the better.'

'Mr Rundle, with respect, I *know* how this works.'

Rundle rolls his eyes. 'Well then, I shouldn't have to tell you how important maintaining distance and deniability is, should I?'

He pictures Herb Felder rolling *his* eyes.

'No, Mr Rundle, I suppose not.'

Herb's a smart guy and will probably go all the way with J.J., but he's a wonk, his strong suit is policy, explaining it, packaging it.

This is a little different.

Some of the other aides around J.J. – the campaign veterans, the oppo men – would be more up to speed, more *au fait* with the techniques here, with the philosophy, but Herb's the one he got through to.

'So when the Senator wakes up, Herb, tell him we spoke, yeah?'

'Yeah.'

'And tell him to call me.'

63

Rundle closes the phone and puts it back on the counter. He looks around.

What does he do now?

He can either put on some coffee and work for a bit – send a few e-mails, read the online editions of the morning papers – *or* he can go back to bed and just lie there tormenting himself with different shit until it's time to get up.

He looks at the display on the cooker.

5:01.

He knows what the old man would do. Or, at any rate, would have done. Taken advantage of the situation. Maximised it.

Rundle reaches up to an overhead shelf and takes down the coffee grinder.

Though no doubt old Henry C. would have been up at five in any case, so it's a moot point.

He puts beans in the grinder and switches it on.

But to be fair – he thinks, holding the grinder down – fair to *himself* . . . hasn't he always maximised his opportunities? Hasn't he transformed BRX Mining & Engineering out of all recognition, way beyond anything the old man, if he were alive today, would even comprehend?

Yeah, yeah.

He releases the grinder. Its whirr slows gradually, then stops.

So does that mean he can go back to bed?

He actually considers it for a moment.

But what would be the point? It'd only lead to more dreams. More Irishmen and Chinamen.

Forget it.

He looks around for the coffee filters.

*

From the moment he wakes up Jimmy Gilroy is aware that things are different, that there's been a fundamental shift – tectonic plates, paradigm, take your pick. Yesterday he was working his way in isolation through a mountain of research material. This morning – bloodied, in full view – he's caught in the barbed wire of human contact.

He gets up and goes over to the bathroom. He didn't sleep well and he's tired. He looks in the mirror, holds his own gaze for a moment, sees the old man, then looks away. Everyone says it, and it's true . . . after a certain age you're never alone in front of a mirror.

Sitting on the toilet, he wonders what Phil Sweeney is up to. Is he really representing the family of one of the other victims? It's not implausible and is certainly the sort of thing he might do for a client – though it could just as easily be a strategic move, a ruse.

But if so, what's behind it?

He gets in the shower.

Then there's Maria. If she decides to talk to him, to trust him, what will she say? And how much of what she does say will she allow him to put in the book?

After his shower Jimmy gets dressed, puts on coffee, checks his e-mails.

Distracted throughout.

Sweeney pulling him one way, Maria the other.

Then he logs on to the Bank of Ireland website and checks his current account. He knows what he's going to find here, but seeing it on the screen, the column of figures, is always a shock

– and that's just what he needs. Because whatever arguments there might be for not doing the book, there's no arguing with *this* – no arguing with the fact that he has spent half of the advance and would have to return all of it if he abandoned the project.

And then have none of it.

He looks away from the screen, over at the window.

But Phil Sweeney buying out the advance is unthinkable, too. He'd rather pack it in, and starve. It's a matter of . . . principle maybe, of self-respect – but also, to be honest, of what the old man might think

If he were still here.

Jimmy leans back in the chair.

Phil Sweeney and Dec Gilroy were partners for a time, co-founders of Marino Communications, and good friends, but as basic types they were very different. The old man was a political junkie. He grew up on the Arms Trial and Watergate, on GUBU and Iran-Contra. He was interested in what made public figures tick, psychologically, which meant that the move from clinical work into PR and media training shouldn't have been that much of a stretch for him. You would think. But it turned out that he was markedly better at analysis than he was at manipulation, and it wasn't long before the new job started wearing him down.

Phil Sweeney, on the other hand, was a natural and in many ways a more skilled politician than a lot of the people they were dealing with. He'd studied in the US and worked there for years before coming back to set up Marino. The organisational brains behind the outfit, he was also the one with big plans, and this led to a certain amount of friction. In fact, by the time

Jimmy's old man got sick and had to start withdrawing from the business, the process of expanding it beyond all recognition had already begun.

Which maybe explains why Dec Gilroy was so happy when his teenage son first expressed an interest in journalism. He felt that here was a possible route back, a second chance almost. As a result, he pulled down his battered, dog-eared Penguins and Picadors and turned Jimmy on to Mencken, Woodstein, Hunter S. Thompson, Seymour Hersh, Jonathan Schell, others. More than just a crash course in journalism, however, in styles and approaches, this was a declaration of values, a sort of retro-active mission statement.

It's something that Jimmy has never forgotten, and hopes he never will.

He gets up now, walks over to the window and gazes out. The bay is shrouded in mist.

But that's not the only reason he won't be taking Phil Sweeney up on his offer. There's a second dynamic at work here, and it has to do with Maria.

The thing is, now that they've met, and talked, it's not so much that the story has gone from uncomplicated black and white to ambivalent grey, it has gone from dreary monochrome to full-on colour, from one dimension to three, from glossy pixels to flesh and blood. Maria's perspective in the mix, her intimate knowledge of Susie, always had the potential to take the project from a showbiz cut-and-paste job to something a bit more substantial – that's why he wanted to meet her in the first place.

But this is something else.

The fact is he liked her. He enjoyed her company. And now

he's excited at the prospect of seeing her again. The only problem is, last night at the top of Grafton Street they sort of semi-agreed that next time *she* should be the one to make contact.

If, and when – that is – she felt ready.

Jimmy turns around.

But that mightn't be for days, weeks even.

He looks over at the research material laid out on his desk, at the folders, notes, printouts – all of it generated from secondary sources, all of it useful . . . but all of it fairly limited. So his impulse is to pick up the phone right now and call her.

He could rationalise this in six different ways.

But it'd still be ridiculous.

She only agreed to meet him last night because he'd been so persistent. If he pushes it now, she mightn't ever talk to him again.

He leans back against the window and surveys the room. The bookshelves to the left contain those Penguins and Picadors he inherited, along with hundreds more, and hundreds of his own. To the right is his cluttered workspace, desk, computer, printer, and then a music system of stacked stereo separates – another legacy of the old man's and about as anachronistic-looking as a Bakelite telephone. Two leather sofas in the middle, and a coffee table. Kitchen at the back. Kitchen*ette*. Adjoining bedroom and tiny bathroom.

Fourth floor. Small seafront apartment building.

Thirty-two years to go on the mortgage.

For that money he could have got a slightly bigger place somewhere else, but as far as Jimmy was concerned the living space wasn't what mattered. His apartment could just as easily have been a tent, or a nice arrangement of cardboard boxes.

68

What mattered was the view, the ability at any time of the day or night to look out of his window and behold – to open his window and *breathe in* – the sea.

To be beside the.

Jimmy then finds himself wondering where Maria lives, and if she is involved with anyone. Or married even. He didn't notice if she was wearing a ring.

He slides down and sits on the windowsill.

At which point his phone rings.

He hesitates for a second, then gets up and goes over to the desk. He can see who it is before his hand has even reached the phone.

'Hello?'

'Jimmy, hi, it's Maria.'

'Hi. How are *you*?'

'I'm fine. But listen.' He's listening. 'You've started me thinking about this, and now I can't stop. But I need to do more than think about it, I need to *talk* about it.'

'OK.'

'So can we meet again?' She pauses. 'Today?'

'Yeah.'

Yeah.

'How about for lunch?'

'Sure.' Leaning his free hand on the desk, he turns and slowly lowers himself into the chair. 'Where did you have in mind?'

*

He acts like it's the most natural thing in the world. He takes the bottle of Jameson's from the cabinet and places it on the

69

fold-out shelf. He takes a glass – Waterford cut crystal, one of a set, a gift from Paddy Norton – and drops four ice cubes into it. Then, as he opens the bottle, whiskey fumes hit his nostrils – molecules of it rising to his brain, like tracker scouts, seeking out receptive lobes and cortices. He tilts the bottle and pours, watching mesmerised as the golden liquid cascades over the ice cubes, one of which cracks loudly and splits. When the glass is nearly full he puts the bottle down and screws the cap back on, an act which feels measured, grown-up.

He looks over his shoulder.

He's alone here, but you never know. Mary's in town and the girls are off doing whatever they're doing. They don't even live here anymore, but they both have keys.

He doesn't want to be disturbed.

He takes the glass in his hand, ice cubes clinking.

Tinkling.

Oh Jesus, like *music*.

But has he overdone it? It's a greedy-looking affair, practically full to the brim. He'd never *serve* a drink like this. On top of which it's not even lunchtime. It's not even mid-morning. But does that matter? The time of day it is? If it was half past seven in the evening and he was in a tuxedo holding a Manhattan in his hand he'd still be a fucking alcoholic.

Still be a degenerate lowlife.

Still be –

Oh just shut up and drink the bloody thing.

He raises the glass to his lips and slurps.

Slurps whiskey.

The taste of it, the feel of it going down.

Oh.

My.

God.

He holds the glass in front of him, stares at it in disbelief. Raises it to his lips again. Takes a couple of genteel sips. Just for confirmation.

Then another slurp.

Puts the glass down. Turns around.

Stands, waits.

Already he can feel it, that burning sensation in his stomach, that hesitant acceleration in his brain chemistry, like a fluorescent tube-light clicking and stuttering into life. Already he can feel those familiar cravings, sudden and impatient . . .

For a cigarette, for company . . . for another sip . . .

He turns around and takes one.

Then goes over and switches on the radio. He picks up the remote and switches on the TV as well, tunes it to Sky. He presses the mute button and drops the remote onto the sofa.

He goes back to the corner and retrieves his drink.

He stands there, taking sips, looking into the glass, swirling its contents around.

The last time he did this was nearly ten years ago. He was a cabinet minister trying to stay on top of a very difficult portfolio. But he was gambling at the same time – and obsessively, any chance he could get, the races, card games, whether this or that bill would pass and by how many votes, whatever. Plus, to crown it all, he was having an affair with his bookie's wife, Avril Byrne. It was the only time he ever cheated on Mary, but it was enough to last him a lifetime. Big and messy, it was all hotel corridors, hidden credit card bills, misplaced packets of condoms, blinding headaches, rows, shouting, lies, more lies and fucking *endless* rivers of booze. He doesn't know how he survived it. A few of the lads – including Paddy Norton – took him aside one day and told him he was becoming a liability. They said that if he wanted his shot at the leadership – which had always been on the cards, sort of – then he'd have to get his shit together in pretty quick order.

And weirdly enough that's just what he did. He stopped. From one day to the next.

The gambling was little more than a question of impulse control, which he'd let slip, so apart from a huge pile of unpaid debts there was no problem there. Avril was easy, too – he never liked her that much anyway, and besides, she seemed more relieved than he was.

No, it was the other part that was really hard, the not drinking part. That part took forever. The shakes, the sweats, the vivid dreams, my sweet Jesus. But it worked out in the end. He lost weight, got in shape, had the laser surgery on his eyes, smartened up.

Moved up.

Ironically, a few years later, it was the affair and the gambling that nearly scuppered his leadership chances. Some prick at party HQ loyal to the Taoiseach resurrected the whole thing and leaked it to the press in some sort of preemptive strike. But he weathered that one as well and took power soon afterwards.

In fact, the closest he came to taking a drink during all of that time was when Mark Griffin showed up, and when Paddy Norton –

Bolger clicks his tongue.

Fuck it.

He's not going *there*.

He takes another sip, and then two more.

The weather girl is on Sky – though not the one he fancies. There's some choral thing on the radio.

He looks into his glass.

He's fallen off the wagon now. It's official. He can release a statement to the media. Ex-Taoiseach succumbs to demons, has a little drinkie, feels he deserves it . . .

But then, in the next moment –

Couple out walking their dog.

To which he says, fuck it, he's not going *there* either.

He turns around and replenishes his drink.

But what does he do now? Trapped in the apartment like this, a caged beast, the clock ticking until Mary gets back.

He looks at his watch.

There's plenty of time, though – hours in fact. He'll be able to sleep it off, drink some coffee, say he's feeling under the weather, say he even detects a cold coming on . . .

He grunts. Sniffs.

Jesus, what is he, *twelve*?

He takes another long slurp from the glass and wipes his mouth with the sleeve of his jacket.

Then he walks across the room, glass in hand, not sure where he's going exactly. He almost loses his footing at one point, but somehow ends up in the study.

Standing over his desk.

He picks up a wad of pages, photocopies from a folder, and looks at them for a while.

What? Is he kidding? In these memoirs the publishers aren't going to want him re-hashing some select committee report on quarterly budget estimates – if that's what this is, he can't quite

73

focus on it properly – they're going to want juicy anecdotes, an interesting angle on events, they're going to want a book people can *read*.

He sits down and puts his drink on the desk.

What he should do is lay everything out straight, shoot from the hip, no pussyfooting around or lilding the gilly. Gilding the lily. He should write a warts-and-all account of what it's like to hold down the top job – the in-fighting, the petty rivalries, the smoke-filled back rooms, all of that stuff, of which there was plenty, though without the smoke of course, because no one does *that* anymore.

He sees the whole thing in a flash – the hardcover edition, press quotes on the back.

Shocking. Brilliant. Urgent.

He takes a sip from his drink.

With blistering honesty and a prose style that wouldn't be out of place on a Man Booker shortlist, Larry Bolger's essay on the nature of power will be required reading for generations to come.

He hits a key on his laptop and the screen lights up. He opens Word.

He takes another sip from his drink, hesitates. Stares at the blank screen.

But there's something he needs to do first.

He gets up and strides out of the room.

Where's his phone?

He finds it on the table in the kitchen. Scrolls down through the list of names.

V for Vaughan.

It's only when it's ringing that he realises what time it is. That they're five hours behind in New York. And probably all still asleep.

It goes into message. 'You have reached . . .'

He waits for the beep.

'Mr Vaughan? It's Larry Bolger.' He pauses. 'How are you?' His voice sounds strange, heavy, a bit slurred. It sounds drunk. *He* sounds drunk. He *is* drunk. 'I called you a few months ago, left a message on your machine, but you never got back to me. Why didn't you get back to me?' Now he sounds like a fucking teenager. It's how he feels, though – angry, frustrated, *thwarted*. 'I don't see . . . I don't see why you couldn't have got back to me. A simple phone call. Is it . . . is it because you're so fucking high and mighty? Is that it? You're so important?' He pauses, possibly for a long time, before eventually saying, '*Prick*.'

Then he holds the phone out in front of him and looks at it, a little confused, as though someone has just called *him* a prick.

He puts the phone back to his ear and listens for a second. Nothing. He holds it out again and presses End Call.

Puts it on the table. Furrows his brow.

Huh.

He goes back into the living room.

What was he doing?

Oh yeah. A drink. He looks over at the cabinet in the corner. He was going to have another drink.

*

As he comes off the roundabout and approaches the entrance to Tara Meadows, Dave Conway can't believe what he's seeing. It's only been three weeks since he last came out here and

75

already it's as if a ravenous Mother Nature has reclaimed substantial sections of the development for her own.

He goes through the gates and drives on for a hundred yards or so before pulling up at the kerb. He takes a small torch from the glove compartment, puts it in his pocket and gets out.

He looks around.

The perimeter fences are entwined with prickly bushes and briars. Nettles are everywhere and weeds – thick, green, poisonous ones – are growing, it seems, at an alarming rate, rushing up in busy clusters overnight.

The rows of detached houses on the right and left – the only residential units to be completed so far – seem forlorn, as though abandoned after some environmental catastrophe. Windows have been smashed and walls have been daubed with slogans and graffiti. The other houses – the ones on the far side of the so-called town square – have been abandoned, too, but not by their occupiers. These have been abandoned midway through construction by the very people who were building them – the contractors, the bricklayers, the electricians. From what Conway can make out, most of these houses are roofless and surrounded by half-erected scaffolding. Diggers and cement mixers lie awkwardly on the roads in front of them, entrenched in gullies of dried mud, like dinosaur skeletons.

Conway walks along the left-hand pathway of what was to be called Tara Boulevard. At the end of it lies the town square. They hadn't decided on an official name for this and had been toying with the idea of simply calling it the Piazza. Or the Plaza. Conway still thinks of it – from the early design and development days – as the Concourse, which is how the architect always referred to it.

It's an impressive space – airy and adaptable, at least in theory. Surrounding it are the completed 'civic buildings', what were to be the heart of this new urban development – a town hall, a hotel, two apartment blocks and a shopping mall. It's short on the 'civic' perhaps, but all of that stuff was grandiose brochure-speak in any case. The truth is that Tara Meadows was never intended to be much more than an upscale commuter-belt housing development (with an expected first phase of buyers feeding in from the nearby Paloma Electronics and Eiben-Chemcorp industrial plants).

He walks across the eerily deserted Concourse. It's midday and this place should be buzzing. There should be cafés open, restaurants, a hairdresser's, a SPAR, a multiplex.

There should be *people*.

Busily crisscrossing the square.

With money in their pockets.

Driving our economy forward.

Yeah, right.

Conway approaches the entrance to the as yet unnamed two-hundred-and-fifty-room hotel.

As yet unfurnished, unfitted, unwired.

He wanders across the lobby area, glancing in at the vast darkened ballroom over to the right.

As he enters the stairwell he takes the torch out of his pocket and uses it to light his way.

He goes up six flights of stairs and comes out onto a long dim corridor. There are no carpets or skirting boards. Cables hang from the ceilings. The air is simultaneously dank and dusty. A few doors are open and these let in enough light from the outside for him to put the torch away.

He walks along the corridor, slowly, and stops at the first open door he comes to. He looks inside.

It's just an empty hotel room. Concrete floor. Plastered walls. Bare, fitted windows. Sliding glass door leading to a balcony. Nothing else.

He nudges the door fully open and goes inside. He crosses the room, opens the sliding door and steps out onto the balcony. He looks directly down onto the deserted Concourse, and then beyond it to the entire development.

Tara Meadows has imprinted itself on the landscape, no question about it. From this perspective the whole thing is stunning – so much more than just another soulless grid of housing units.

Which is why he comes up here every now and again. To see the big picture – quite literally. It gives him a degree of satisfaction, of reassurance.

He leans forward now, hands on the balcony rail.

But there's nothing of that sort on offer today. How could there be? Conway Holdings borrowed a total of two hundred and twenty million euro for this project, with the promise of a further eighty million to keep the wheels turning. One of the banks he borrowed from, however, North Atlantic Commercial, is looking for its money back, and none of the other banks are lending anymore. The problem is, without the further eighty million there's no way he can keep the wheels turning, and without the wheels turning there's no way he can hope to pay back any of the original money.

Naturally, he's trying to scare up alternative financing – he's in negotiations at the moment with a team from Black Vine Partners, a private equity fund – but unless he's prepared to go as far as collateralising the internal organs of his three children there may be no practical way out of this.

All of which should be enough – you would *imagine* – for any man to have to worry about.

But right now this isn't even the issue for Dave. This is just background noise, like a headache you can't shift when you've got something more important to think about – such as, for instance, that little chat he had earlier on with Larry Bolger. He'd been convinced that Larry had somehow heard the same thing he'd heard, about the Susie Monaghan book, and was rattled about that, needlessly as it would have turned out.

But that wasn't it at all.

The fella they found in the woods.

What was it Ruth had said last night, about summoning up old ghosts?

But the weird thing is it's not the body in the woods he's worried about. Not *only*. There are degrees of separation there. It's Bolger he's worried about. The man was unhinged this morning. Maybe it's that he's bored or frustrated, or that retirement doesn't suit him and he has too much time on his hands, but it almost seemed as if in some perverse way he was looking for trouble.

What the man needs is a job. To chair some committee or head up a review group or something.

Keep him busy, keep him distracted.

Because the last thing Conway himself needs, as he bargains for his financial survival with these Black Vine people, is to be linked, however tenuously, to the three-year-old disappearance of a security guard . . . who then turns up in a shallow grave in the Wicklow hills.

Unable to dwell on this, even for a second, Conway turns and goes back inside. He rushes across the room and out into the corridor. He switches his torch on again and makes his way back to the stairwell. On the way down, he focuses on taking the steps two at a time.

As he's approaching the second floor, he hears a weird sound and stops. He remains still for a moment. There is silence. Then he hears the sound again.

It's a dog barking.

He hears it a third time.

It's close by.

He steps out into the second-floor corridor. It's much darker down here, and the air is heavier, dustier. He stops and listens carefully.

The dog barks again, a yappy sound – it's probably some sort of terrier.

Conway looks at an open door a little further along the corridor and thinks he detects movement inside. He quickly realises that it's something flickering – a form of light, a flame perhaps, a candle.

Slowly, he moves towards it.

His heart jumps when the dog barks again.

He peers in through the door. The windows have been blacked out with plastic sacks. Protruding from a bottle on the floor is a red candle. In the middle of the room there is an empty shopping trolley and tied to the trolley with a dirty piece of rope is the dog, a scruffy little terrier.

The place reeks of piss.

The dog barks again.

Conway shines his torch over the room. In one corner he sees what at first appears to be a bundle of old clothes and news-papers. After a second he realises that the bundle is moving, that there's someone lying there. A pair of eyes stare up at him, squinting, a hand raised to block out the light from the torch.

'Ah fuck, *pal.*' It's a man. 'What's going on? What do you want?'

For a fleeting moment it is on the tip of Dave's tongue to re-spond, 'What do *I* want? What do you mean? This is *my* hotel.'

Pal.

But he knows how absurd that would sound.

He goes on pointing the torch, and staring.

The man goes on squinting and holding up his hand but he doesn't say anything else – all resistance spent, seemingly, in those first few words.

The dog, who has been quiet for a bit, starts yapping again. It tugs at the rope and causes the shopping trolley to move.

Conway is startled by this. He retreats, walks quickly back to the stairwell and down to the ground floor. He rushes across the lobby and out onto the Concourse, all the time wondering how many of the other rooms are . . . *occupied*? Is that the cor-rect word? And how many of the houses? There's no security here, there's no surveillance. The money ran out, work stopped and the place was just abandoned.

With a sick feeling in his stomach Conway makes his way back along Tara Boulevard and gets into his car.

Holy fuck.

What is happening?

These bastards at Black Vine had better come through with the funding, otherwise this place will be devoured.

His life will be devoured.

81

And not just by overgrowth and weeds and graffiti and tramps and squatters.

He starts the car.

It will be devoured by lawyers and creditors and injunctions and journalists.

Appalling vista number two.

He does a three-point turn and heads for the exit.

But going back to the first appalling vista, the more immediate one, what does he do about Larry Bolger? There's no way he can possibly allow this sad sack of a man – who also lives in a hotel, as it happens – to jeopardise everything Conway Holdings has built up.

He stops at the exit.

And then it hits him.

That other little pulse of anxiety, the one from yesterday afternoon . . .

Misdirection.

Displacement.

He pulls out his mobile, finds the number and dials.

As he waits, he glances to the right and up at the peeling billboard for Tara Meadows. It shows an artist's impression of the development – spectral, stick-insect people with shopping bags crisscross the Piazza. The strap reads: 'First line of defence, last word in sophistication.'

'Dave?'

He refocuses.

'Phil.'

'Two days in a row? This must be a record.'

'Yeah. How are you?' He leans forward, over the steering

wheel. 'But listen, Phil, that thing we were talking about yesterday? I've just had an idea.'

*

It is reported in an afternoon edition of *France-Soir* that a middle-aged man, believed to be an American tourist, has been seriously injured at the scene of a motorcycle accident in central Paris. The incident took place at about 6 a.m., not far from the man's hotel.

The story gets picked up straightaway and within an hour three different American news websites are speculating that the 'tourist' in question might be none other than US Senator John Rundle, who is currently in Paris as part of a trade delegation. The story is then confirmed a couple of hours later on another website. Sitting in his office now, Clark Rundle is going through this report line by line.

The Senator was apparently out jogging alone in the early hours when he witnessed a motorcyclist careering out of a laneway and colliding with a bollard. He ran to help, but in attempting to get the man out from underneath his bike, the senator slipped in some oil, lost his grip and fell. Part of the motorcycle, a 1500cc Kawasaki, then collapsed on the senator's hand, crushing two fingers and breaking several bones. He remains in the American Hospital in Paris and a spokesperson says that although surgery will definitely be required the fifty-year-old pol is nevertheless in good spirits.

The motorcyclist himself received only minor injuries and has praised the senator for his quick reflexes and extraordinary courage.

83

Hhmmmm.

Clark Rundle turns away from his computer terminal.

Slightly overcooked, he would have thought.

It'll do the job, though.

He hasn't heard from J.J. in person yet but understands that because he's still on strong pain-relief medication he might need a little more time to clear his head.

Rundle *will* have to talk with him, however, and soon. Because J.J. is the only one who can fill him in on what the colonel is thinking – and not just in relation to the Chinese, but now in relation to this Buenke incident, as well.

Details of which conversation Rundle himself will then have to pass on to Jimmy Vaughan.

It's a delicate set of circumstances, a delicate balance. You've got a PR nightmare on two fronts, each one potentially feeding into the other, which means if either one of them blows up they both do, and if *that* happens the whole fucking shebang blows up.

He rubs his stomach.

But even if they're successful in extracting J.J. from the equation and in smoothing over Buenke, there's still no guaranteeing the whole shebang won't blow up anyway. No guaranteeing the colonel won't side with the Chinese and take their infrastructure deal. No guaranteeing he won't unravel years of hard work on BRX's part and sign away the rights to . . . whatever it is . . .

They worked it out last night.

Utterly unthinkable.

But what do they *do*?

Rundle rubs his stomach again. He presses it at different points. There's something going on in there, ulcers or . . .

Or *what*? Go on, say it.

Stomach cancer.

It's what killed his mother. Came out of the blue, then *bam*, six weeks and she was gone.

He takes a deep breath.

But that was after six *decades* of corrosive boredom, of Pall Malls and dissatisfaction, of private education and public marriage, of being an heiress, a corporate wife, a matriarch.

A socialite and a churchgoer.

Rundle stands up.

This isn't boredom, though. This is coiling, knotty anxiety. It's fear. Fear of losing control, of not measuring up, of not having measured up in the past. It's any number of unresolved issues.

He glances around the office, wondering which is more corrosive, boredom or fear, and if it has to be a competition.

Newly redesigned, the office is all ultra-thin tempered glass and different coloured metals.

All transparency and jagged edges.

It gets on his nerves.

What he needs is an hour or two with Nora. He'll call her later. He might even call her this afternoon. Arrange to meet her at the Wilson.

He swallows, rubs his stomach one more time.

Maybe it's indigestion. Unresolved *dinner*.

They were all pretty tense in there last night, in the Orpheus Room – talking over each other, mapping out different scenarios, calculating the potential loss in offtake, working their

BlackBerrys like a trio of hopped-up beboppers. And Orpheus food is good, but it's not that good. It wouldn't ever be his first choice, and certainly not for dinner.

Rundle stands up suddenly, grabs the *Times* from his desk and rushes across the office to the door in the corner that leads to his private washroom.

*

Jimmy watches as Maria stirs three sugars into her double espresso, an energy fix he imagines she'll need to make up for the energy she's just expended in talking to him about her sister.

He takes his own espresso without sugar. Not that he even needs the caffeine. Listening to Maria for the last hour or so has energised him in a way he hasn't experienced for ages, and had almost forgotten could happen.

They met here at Rastelli's just after one o'clock, found a table and got straight into it. Maria said she'd been thinking about their conversation non-stop since last night and couldn't see that she had a choice. Once Jimmy had put the idea out there – released the genie from the bottle, so to speak – there was no going back. They *had* to do this.

And *for* Susie.

Not that Maria imagined the book would turn out to be some kind of cheesy tribute or anything, a hagiography – more an honest account of how Susie had lived her life, but with no backing away from the ugly stuff either, the behaviour, the compulsions, the stuff that had made her sister who she was. Maria said she hated the word 'closure', didn't even know what it meant, but felt that after three years here might be a chance to grab a little of it, see what everyone was talking about.

Jimmy nodded along to most of this, taken aback at the shift in mood and tone. Last night Maria had been subdued, circumspect, now she was . . . what? Ebullient? Irrationally exuberant? Off her meds? *On* her meds? He didn't know. Maybe she was crazy. Though she didn't seem to be. If he didn't know any better – and actually he didn't – he might have thought she was drunk.

But then again, at the same time, she seemed quite . . . centred.

Self-possessed.

Maybe she was just sold on the idea all of a sudden.

Maybe he'd done a better job last night than he was giving himself credit for.

Plus . . . it was as if she . . .

As if –

But he didn't really have time to think here, or editorialise. She was talking too fast, covering too much ground, giving him in broad strokes what they would have to go back over later on, but in excruciating, forensic slo-mo – Susie the wild schoolgirl, for instance, in her white blouse and plaid skirt (replete with tell-tale residues, cigarette smoke, vodka, Red Bull, bubblegum, cum), Susie on the modelling circuit, alternating between blind ambition and almost existential despair, Susie's first line of coke, first magazine cover, first potential husband, then *that* audition for *Phoenix Road* and how her personal input into the character of Sharon O'Dwyer transformed a bit part into a pivotal one, a whiny young drug-dealer's girlfriend into a semi-tragic gangland widow . . . a pretty face on TV into nothing less than a national sweetheart, all of which was followed by an increasingly desperate need to *escape* the role and take her career to what everyone around her, agents, publicists, showbiz columnists, insisted on calling, maddeningly, 'the next level'. Which would be what? A presenting gig on TV? A part in a *movie*? She didn't know, but on the road to this chimerical future there always seemed to be one more opening to go to, one more reality show to take part in – the last of these being the ill-fated *Celebrity Death Row*, in which Susie and seven others were to court the public vote in order to be spared a mock execution in the series finale. But accusations of bad taste and a frenzied debate over declining standards led to the show being cancelled after only two episodes, and hot on the heels of *that* came a messy break-up with corporate executive, Gary Lynch, number five in Susie's usual-suspects line-up of potential husbands. The last few weeks of Susie's life, therefore – and this seemed to be emerging as Maria's central thesis – were extremely difficult ones. OK, she was out of control, taking too many drugs, smoking too many cigarettes, operating on little more than seething resentment and the energy rush that comes from a suppressed appetite – but she was also suffering at a much deeper level . . . she was miserably, *profoundly* unhappy and didn't have the first clue what to do about it . . .

Watching Maria as she tells him all of this, Jimmy is struck by how animated she is, but also by how beautiful – and not in that overly obvious, cosmetics-model way that Susie had, it's something more natural than that, and more vivid. In fact, it's as if Maria has come alive, as if all along, despite appearances, each sister had been playing the other one's role, and now in the quickening light of an outsider's attention these roles were reversing, reverting.

Susie no longer alive.

Maria no longer dead.

As he drains his espresso, Jimmy is acutely aware of how twisted and fucked-up it is of him to be thinking like this, how unprofessional – but that's what can happen when you leave the second-hand stuff on your desk and engage directly with a source, the game sometimes changes.

You lose your bearings.

Maria drains her espresso now, too. Looking around her in silence, she seems a little dazed from all the talking.

Jimmy studies her face – the devouring eyes, the pale skin, the freckles around her nose.

Then she starts up again. 'So. Told you I was a talker. It feels good, though, and I suppose it means I trust you, Jimmy. Or that I've decided to trust you. Or something.'

He smiles. 'That's great, Maria, because as far as I'm concerned the more you talk the better it'll be. But more talk will also mean more work.' He gives a little back-and-forth flick to his hand. 'More meetings like this one. Because up to now I've been focusing on the last chapter.' He pauses. 'The idea was to kind of . . . to try and get that out of the way first, and then –'

'I understand,' Maria says. 'But don't . . .' She hesitates. 'Look, in a weird way the crash *should* be the focus of the story. It's what it builds up to. And it's almost like the perfect metaphor. I mean, we'll never know exactly what happened, but everything in Susie's life seemed to be . . . inclining towards that moment.'

Jimmy swallows, then nods in agreement.

He wants to remind her that the metaphor mightn't quite

work for the other victims, but he holds back. It's a tricky enough point – and maybe on one level Phil Sweeney is right – but they'll find a way around it.

He'll find a way around it. It's his job.

Maria picks up her phone and looks at it. 'I have to get back to work.'

'Sure.'

Outside on Dawson Street they chat for a bit and seem reluctant to separate. At least that's how it feels to Jimmy. After they do say their goodbyes, and Jimmy is heading along Duke Street – in something, it has to be said, of a dreamy haze – his phone rings.

He pulls it out and looks at the display.

Shit.

He hesitates, but then answers it. 'Hi, Phil.'

'Jimmy, how are you doing? Look, I've been feeling bad since yesterday. I didn't mean to put you on the spot like that, I really didn't, it was a terrible thing to do, and I'm sorry.' Jimmy slows down, doesn't say anything, waits. 'So I thought of you today when something else came up, a job you might be interested in.'

'I'm already working on a job, Phil.'

'There are jobs, Jimmy, and there are jobs. This is a fucking *job.*'

'But –'

'Just listen to me for a minute, will you? The Susie Monaghan book, dress it up whatever way you like, it's only fluff, it'll cause a blip in the Christmas market if you're lucky and then that's it, no one'll ever hear of it again. But what I've got –'

'Jesus, Phil –'

'No wait, and don't hang up on me, Jimmy, please. What *I've* got – and this only came up today, I swear to you – is a sub-stantial piece of work. It's something your old man would have *loved*.'

Jimmy stops.

'It's political. A political memoir. You'd get to shape something that'll be read and mulled over and put in reference libraries.' He lets that hang for a second, then goes on. 'Larry Bolger, yeah? He's supposed to be putting his memoirs togeth-er, but the man can't write to save his life, he needs help, someone who can organise his notes, interview him, someone who can turn a decent phrase . . . a fucking *writer*.'

Jimmy stands there, outside the Bailey, with the phone up to his ear.

He doesn't speak.

Sweeney goes on. 'You get access to his private papers, details of his meetings with Bush, Putin, the *Pope*, everyone, plus all the domestic stuff, the heaves and backroom intrigues, all that shit you love.' Another pause. 'Plus. *Plus*. It hasn't been worked out yet, hasn't been finalised, but what might actually turn out to be the most substantial part in all of this is the fee. Larry's got a big contract, so you'd do pretty well out of it. Might even get to pay off that mortgage of yours . . .'

He leaves it there.

Jimmy's insides turn. He stares down at the pavement. People pass in both directions, but no one gives him a second glance. Nothing odd in that, not anymore – man standing alone in the street, hand up at the side of his head, staring into space.

'Jimmy? You interested? There's a clock running on this. He's already missed one deadline.'

Still nothing.

'Jimmy? *Jimmy*? You there?'

After a long pause, Jimmy exhales loudly.

'Yeah, Phil,' he says, 'take it easy.' He closes his eyes. 'I'm here.'

3

Bolger's mouth feels like the bottom of a birdcage. He's slumped in the armchair and suspects he has been asleep, though he can't be sure. There weren't any dreams, which for him would be weird, because his brain usually manages to concoct *some* twisted combination of . . . of . . .

Of what? He can't even think of an example. His brain won't oblige.

He looks around.

Oh *fuck*.

What time is it?

The plan was to clean up and *then* go for a nap. There are at least two empty glasses he can see from here, one on the dining table and the other on the arm of the sofa. The drinks cabinet looks like a bomb site. He can also smell cigarette smoke. There was an old packet of Silk Cut he found in a bag in the wardrobe. It must have been there for, what, six, seven years?

He takes a deep breath.

What time is it?

Mary will be home soon.

Then he hears a sound from the kitchen, a clattering of implements, and realises that Mary is already home, and that he *was* asleep. He looks over at the door.

'Mary,' he says, in a loud voice, louder than he intended, 'what time is it?'

There is silence.

After a moment she appears in the doorway. Bolger can't be sure from this distance, but her eyes look a bit red.

Oh Jesus.

It's then, too, that he remembers leaving a message on James Vaughan's answering machine or voicemail or whatever the fuck it was.

He groans. Feels a hot flush of shame and humiliation. Why did he do this? What on earth drove him to it, what could possib—

Oh yeah.

Of course.

He remembers now.

Couple out walking their dog. Body in the woods. Paranoia, anxiety . . . traceability, rogue pig farmers . . .

Pig farmers?

What is he, *still* drunk?

Mary steps forward from the doorway. 'Larry, I don't . . . I –'

'*WHAT FUCKING TIME IS IT, WOMAN?*' he roars.

In that same moment he sees what time it is on the display of the digital decoder box. Then, as he watches Mary cower in shock and retreat into the kitchen, he remembers something else: what a mean fucking drunk he was.

Is.

The thought lingers for a moment, becomes unstuck and dissolves. Some time passes, a minute, maybe two. During this brief period his mind remains blank. Then he struggles up out of the armchair, feeling twenty years older than he did when he got out of bed that morning. His head is splitting. The room shifts slightly, its relationship to gravity and fixed points seeming like a loose enough arrangement.

He walks over to the dining table and leans on it with both hands. Next to the empty glass there is a saucer. In it is a dirty pile of cigarette ash and four stubbed-out butts.

He groans again and puts a hand up to his head, as if that will ease the pounding.

It doesn't.

He looks in the direction of the kitchen.

How is he going to finesse this with Mary?

When he packed in the drink all those years ago certain promises were made, behaviours renounced, habits eschewed.

Not that she knew the half of it.

But it was a serious pledge nonetheless, and he meant it. So what he has done now by taking a drink is not only an act of stupidity – which it patently is, look at the *state* of him – it is an act of betrayal as well.

And shouting at her just now? What was that an act of?

He shakes his head. He could rationalise it on the grounds that he was groggy, and had just woken up, that it didn't have anything to do with the booze.

But –

When's the last time he raised his voice at her?

Exactly.

He lifts his hands from the table and as he straightens up what feels like a current of electricity shoots through his skull. It's five o'clock in the afternoon and he's *this* hungover?

Classy.

He did have his reasons, but the curious thing is these don't seem quite so urgent anymore, or relevant. Also, the anxiety and paranoia have receded. Somewhat. Because Dave Conway was probably right, the truth is they *weren't* actually involved. So why get all worked up about it?

What hasn't receded, though, is this seemingly permanent fog of insecurity he's been living with, insecurity about his legacy, about his future – and, OK, getting drunk and leaving inappropriate messages on people's machines may not be the optimum solution here, but what is?

What it's always been, *work*.

It's just that as an unemployable ex-premier the only job opportunity he has right now is this stupid book he's supposed to be writing.

And isn't.

Which sparks something . . . a vague . . .

Does he remember sitting down at his desk earlier on? All fired up and ready to get started? Possibly. Yes. But didn't he then go off straightaway to do something else?

His usual m.o.

He walks over and looks through the door of the study, for confirmation – and indeed there it is, his cluttered desk, untouched, exactly as it has been for days, weeks.

He could sit down now and get started. If he didn't feel nauseous, that is. If he didn't have to devote whatever shred of energy he might be able to muster over the next few minutes to mollifying, or attempting to mollify, his wife. If he knew how to string two coherent sentences together.

He turns around and heads over to the kitchen. No point in delaying the inevitable.

He stands in the doorway. Mary has her back to him. She's at the counter and appears to be busy, chopping or peeling something. After a moment, she turns around. The look she gives him is withering.

'How *dare* –'

And then the phone rings. It's beside her on the counter.

'*Jesus.*'

She picks it up. Incapable of not.

'Hello?'

This is a reprieve for Bolger, but not one that lasts.

'Yes.' Tight-lipped. 'Hello, Dave.'

When she looks away for a split second, Bolger rolls his eyes. This micro movement sends a shockwave of nausea through his system. He puts one hand on his stomach and holds the other one out in front of him, flaps it frantically, indicating to Mary that he's not here.

'Yes, Dave, he's here. Sure. I'll put him on.'

She approaches quickly, holding the phone up. It looks like she's about to strike him with it. He recoils, but still ends up taking it in his hand, Mary gliding past him out of the room, mouthing something he doesn't catch.

*

Clark Rundle gazes down at Madison Avenue from the window of his tenth-floor suite in the Wilson Hotel. It is just after two in the afternoon. That's eight in the evening in Paris, which means it'll be nine by the time Nora is leaving, so if he hasn't heard from J.J. by then he'll have to call someone at the hospital and demand that they put him on.

Below, traffic flows silently along Madison, only the occasional honking of a horn or wail of a siren making it through the thick glass of the hotel windows. It is a beautiful spring day in Manhattan, cold, crisp and sunny, but inside here it is warm and the atmosphere, along with every nerve ending in Rundle's body, tingles with expectancy.

There is a gentle rap at the door.

He turns and crosses the room, which is a refuge of elegance, with its embroidered drapes and silk wall coverings, its mahogany furnishings and marble floors.

He opens the door and in she glides.

Nora is twenty-four years old and very beautiful – extraordinarily so, in fact – with exotic colouring, perfect bone structure and eyes so dark and mysterious they could bring down an empire. She is from Haiti, so her name probably isn't actually Nora, but Rundle has never got around to asking her about this, or about a whole lot else for that matter. When he's with her he tends to talk about himself. He was going to say that it's cheaper than therapy, but actually it isn't. Nora is very expensive. He's had an account with Regal Select for over five years now but has spent more in the last eighteen months since Nora showed up than in all of the time prior to that put together. He doesn't feel guilty about this, nor is he stupid enough to have fallen in love with her, but he does regard their time together as essential, each appointment as a sort of pit stop, something entirely related to the rhythms and requirements of his working life.

It's not just that he's paying for her to leave, as the conventional wisdom runs. It's a bit more complex than that. He's paying for what sociologists have recently taken to calling 'relief from the burden of reciprocity'.

In other words, he already has a wife.

Nora removes her coat. She places it on the back of a chair. She then does a half turn and glances at Rundle, coquettishly, her lips glistening, her tongue just visible.

Hard-on in place, check.

She can do this *every* time. Just walk into the room. What wife can do that?

More than once J.J. has begged Clark to hook him up with Regal, but of course that's never going to happen.

J.J. doesn't get to do this.

Especially since he's on the brink of submitting to the most rigorous vetting process known to man. Even before the media get involved, he'll have to offer himself up on a platter to the party handlers: his education and employment histories, every tax return he's ever filed, every investment made, every gift received . . . his *medical* records, and all of them, copies of lab results, bloods, electrocardiograms, even down to such stuff as the size of his prostate and how much Pepto-Bismol he uses.

So no room for peccadilloes.

'How are you, Nora?'

'I'm good.'

She walks over to the window, though it's more like sashays. He follows. Puts his hands on her shoulders, applies pressure, breathes in her scent – nose in her hair, hard-on nuzzling against her ass.

Rhythm starting.

She's wearing that silky dress he likes, it's a –

Look, forget it.

They have their habits, like any couple, stuff they do and say – but only in some alternative universe could the details of this be any of your fucking business. Set up a sting operation and nab J.J., fine, you'd get to justify that on the grounds of public interest, so-called. But not here, not in this case.

Say hello to the *private* sector.

So, between one thing and another, a little time passes.

Nora then takes off to the bathroom for a shower and Rundle lies back recalling what it was like in his younger days, at this juncture, to smoke a cigarette.

Just after half past his cell phone rings.

This could be anyone, but he has a feeling about it. He sits up and reaches over to the bedside table for his phone.

He's right.

'J.J.? Shit, how are you?'

'I'm fine, fucking *traum*atised, but fine. And it's not like there isn't plenty going on over here to distract me, or going on over *there*, I should say with all this stuff being generated.'

'I'm sorry?' Rundle slides off the bed. 'Stuff? What stuff?' He goes over to the window.

'You haven't been following it? Seriously?'

'No. What?'

'You're the one who kicked this whole thing off, man. Stroke of genius.'

'Kicked *what* off?'

'It's all over the internet. *I'm* all over the internet. Senator saves motorcyclist. Senator in Parisian rescue drama. I've been getting calls all day, interview requests. I'm telling you, Clark, you couldn't pay for this kind of exposure.'

Rundle thinks back. He was busy for most of the morning, paperwork, meetings, this and that. He skipped lunch and came directly here. He doesn't have time for Twitter or any of that shit, so it's not like he's been monitoring developments.

'Jesus . . .'

'Yeah, it's amazing. Political coverage, but with a dollop of feelgood on top? I mean come *on*.'

'OK, I suppose . . .'

'You *suppose*? Clark, I'm sitting here in my hospital bed doing a Google news search and it's like, *Washington Post* two hours ago, *San Francisco Chronicle* nineteen minutes ago, it's just story after story. I mean, look at this, *People* magazine four minutes ago. I was calling you *up* four minutes ago. This is phenomenal.'

Rundle isn't sure. It's not what he expected, certainly not what he intended. 'OK, J.J.,' he says, 'but play it down, let *them* do the work. I mean, this is tricky territory. The bigger the story gets, the more likely they are to go looking for this motorcyclist.'

'Who cares? I'm getting a bump out of it, a chance to build up my profile. This afternoon? Fucking Wolf Blitzer's people called. I'm telling you, there's some serious traction to be had here.'

Rundle throws his eyes up.

'Wolf Blitzer? Jesus Christ, J.J., let me remind you of something, OK? An important detail. There *is* no motorcyclist. It didn't *happen*. So this is a dangerous little game we're playing.'

'You wouldn't say that if you saw my hand, Clark.'

'Well, *sure*, but –'

'Because believe me, this injury is *very* real.'

'I know –'

'I mean, the whole thing was insane, man. I'll never forget it, I –'

'OK,' Rundle says. 'Sure.' He glances over his shoulder at the bathroom door. Is the shower still running? 'We still need to be careful, though.'

'We're *being* careful. God. And what about that guy from the Jordan Group? We spoke about an hour ago. He seemed pretty smart. On top of things. They'll handle it.'

'Yeah, but what I'm saying is, they might have overreached themselves a bit, that's all. These things can take on a life of their own.'

A long pause follows. Rundle can hear . . .

Is J.J. grinding his teeth?

It sounds like it. Maybe it's the medication he's on, or some kind of adrenaline rush. Maybe it's the onset of PTSD. According to what Don Ribcoff was able to find out the incident *was* fairly horrendous, but J.J.'s involvement was minimal, his injury minor, and they managed to get him out of there pretty damn fast. The important thing is it happened after he saw Colonel Kimbela.

'Anyway, look,' Rundle goes on, clearing his throat, 'I'm sure it was awful, but we need to talk.'

'About what?'

'About what did happen. Beforehand, I mean. The colonel. About what he had to say.'

'Right.'

Rundle waits. He glances over at the bathroom door again – anticipates it opening, anticipates Nora emerging . . . her dark glistening skin as it contrasts with the white cotton of her towelling robe, the belt loosely knotted, pullable . . .

'The thing is, Clark, I . . .'

Start of round two.

'Yeah?'

Value for his four grand.

'I'm a little confused. I –'

Rundle turns back to the window, his eyes widening all of a sudden. He presses the phone to his ear, listens hard. Is J.J. . . . is he *crying*?

'*J.J.?*'

'I'm sorry, Clark, I –'

'*What?*'

'Look, you've no idea what it was like, the noise, looking down the barrel of that gun, blood everywhere, those *kids* . . .'

'*J.J.*'

'And what happened beforehand? Meeting with Kimbela? Talking to him? That's all a blur now. I'm just not sure I can recall any of it.'

*

Jimmy spends the rest of the afternoon and that evening in front of his iMac trawling the web for articles about Larry Bolger. He has a knot in his stomach the whole time. The evening is punctuated by three further calls from Phil Sweeney. The first, at around seven o'clock, is to go over a few ground rules – terms of reference, what's off limits, what isn't, contractual details, conditions. This is stuff they clear up easily enough. The second, an hour later, is to announce that

Bolger has agreed to the arrangement, in principle at least, but would like a face to face with Jimmy before making his final decision – a meeting he thinks should take place quite soon, within the next week or so. The third call, after ten, is to say that Bolger has been in touch again and would actually like to get moving straightaway, so is Jimmy available to meet the following morning?

At Bolger's hotel, say, ten o'clock?

For what will be, in effect, a job interview.

With the phone cradled on his shoulder, Jimmy stares at an article on the screen about the 'palace coup' that originally led to Bolger taking over as Taoiseach. It's a fascinating analysis of the intrigues, the backstabbings and the fallout, but at the same time, as with so much of this kind of stuff, it is tantalisingly in-complete and raises more questions than it answers.

Yes, he says.

Knot still in his stomach.

One of the conditions – and Jimmy's not sure if this comes directly from Bolger himself or just from Phil Sweeney – is that the job is to be exclusive. He must suspend or abandon any work he currently has in hand and must turn down any new offers of work.

For the duration of the project.

Which could take anything up to six months or a year. And occupy his every waking hour. But also help pay off his mortgage. *And* enhance his reputation. Phil Sweeney has said he wouldn't be ghosting the book, he'd be getting a co-credit. Which, in turn, could lead to any amount of other interesting work.

Jimmy scrolls down through a few more search results.

Squirming in his chair as he does so.

Because while this whole thing is clearly a no-brainer, there's also something deeply insidious about it, about the way it's making him re-evaluate the Susie Monaghan story . . . which all of a sudden has begun to seem inconsequential and tawdry. Why should he spend his time and energy writing about some coke-addled soap star, the argument appears to run, when he could be writing about national politics, and at the highest level?

Quite.

But how is he supposed to explain that to Maria?

In his head, he tries to – spins it one way, then another, con-textualises it, rationalises it, brings in the old man . . .

Ends up feeling sick.

At eleven o'clock he turns off the computer. He tries to watch some television, but can't concentrate. He goes to bed and tries to sleep, but can't do that either. There is a loud bass sound thumping through the walls from across the corridor. It's those students in the apartment directly opposite his. Now and again, he can hear their raised voices as well. What are they arguing about? Climate change? Afghanistan? Quentin Tarantino vs. Shakespeare? Which of them left an open tin of beans on a shelf in the kitchen for five days? They're two guys, maybe three, it varies, modern languages, engineering, he's not sure. He hung out with them once and after two hits on a joint felt so stoned he forgot his own name.

The bass thump goes on and on, works its way into his dreams. When he next looks at the bedside clock, it is 4.35, the thump still there, but muffled now, more like a heartbeat.

He looks over at the window.

It's dark, too early to get up, but he knows that further sleep is out of the question. His *thoughts* are up. And it's the same queasy merry-go-round – excitement about meeting Larry Bolger, shame at having to blow off Maria, excitement about meeting –

He climbs out of bed.

What better way to start a new assignment anyway than in a full-on state of jangly-nerved sleep-deprived anxiety?

Over the next few hours, Jimmy sits at his desk, drinking coffee and trawling through more of the same kind of stuff he was trawling through yesterday. He takes copious notes. He may not be entirely comfortable about the arrangement but he still wants to be prepared. Nor does he have any illusions about Larry Bolger and the kind of book *he'll* probably want to write. As a senior politician, Bolger's impulse will be to whitewash everything, to be self-serving and epically disingenuous. But the process itself will be fascinating – watching the big beast up close, getting to see how his mind works.

There was a time when Jimmy and his old man shared a fascination for another and considerably bigger beast, Richard Nixon – a man about whom they conversed and theorised endlessly. A key event in this shared mythology was the occasion in 1972 when Hunter S. Thompson rode with Nixon in the back of a presidential limousine between campaign stops. All they talked about, apparently, was football, but Thompson still managed to transmute the base metal of this banal conversation into psychological gold.

As a result, in some obscure corner of his mind – and the feeling has been building slowly, quietly, since yesterday – Jimmy sees the Bolger assignment as *his* chance for a backseat ride in that same limo. He knows this is a bit fanciful, but he also knows that it's how the old man, if he were alive today, would see it too.

At eight o'clock, Jimmy has a shower and gets dressed. He puts on a jacket and tie. He eats a bowl of cereal and drinks more coffee. He checks his e-mails and does a quick round of a few newspaper websites. He puts his notebook into his jacket pocket. He heads out a few minutes after nine.

The hotel is up in Ballsbridge, so he can walk there in about twenty or thirty minutes. Jimmy has a motorbike, an old Honda, but he only uses it occasionally. He prefers to walk whenever he can.

It's a beautiful morning, sunny and fresh, though it's supposed to rain later.

Walking along Strand Road, towards Sydney Parade Avenue, Jimmy slows down and stops. His plan was to phone Maria later on and tell her what he was doing, but now he doesn't think he should wait. Now he thinks he should tell her what he's going to do, not what he has done.

Be straight with her.

Whatever about hedging his bets with his editor, doesn't he owe Maria that much?

As he crosses the road and walks towards a seafront bench, he takes out his phone and looks for her number.

He sits down. The tide is in and is lapping gently up onto the strand.

A middle-aged lady walking her dog strides past.

He presses Dial.

It rings. She'll be at work. Maybe this is unfair, maybe he should –

'Jimmy?'

'Hi, Maria.'

The knot tightens in his stomach.

'What's wrong?'

How does she know something is wrong?

'Nothing is wrong . . . well, I mean, in the sense that –' He pauses for a moment and regroups. The whole point of this was not to dissemble. To be straight. He breathes in, looks across the bay at Howth. He starts explaining.

It doesn't take him long.

Then silence.

Oh fuck.

'I'm sorry, Maria.'

He can hear her breathing.

'Don't be. I'm the one who's sorry. I'm the one who opened up and talked. I'm the one who trusted a *journalist*.' Her voice rising. 'I believed you, Jimmy, I really did, but . . . Larry Bolger's memoirs? You've got to be –'

'Look, I –'

'No, Jimmy, don't, please.'

He doesn't.

After a long pause, she says, 'My sister, right? She was a fuck-up, a disaster-zone, and maybe she was responsible for what happened, I don't know, but I was prepared to face up to the fact, and to live with it. Because I thought you were interested in getting at the truth. That's what you told me.' She pauses. 'But Larry Bolger?' She laughs at this, her tone cold, almost harsh. 'Jimmy, do you really think that someone like Larry Bolger is going to tell *you* the truth?'

'Maria –'

She hangs up.

Jimmy swallows. He lowers his hand slowly and stares at the phone. After a few seconds he flips it closed and puts it away.

He stands up.

He could have made a stronger argument. He could have pointed out that the truth of what had happened on that day would always elude them. That all they could ever do was speculate.

Whereas with Bolger . . .

But to what end?

No amount of logic can reverse what he has just done.

He pictures Maria sitting opposite him, talking like an express train.

Those eyes, the freckles around her nose.

After a moment, he refocuses. He has no choice. He stares out to sea, follows the line on the horizon. Then he turns away. He looks at his watch and starts walking. He has thirty minutes to get to the hotel.

He doesn't want to be late.

*

Bolger paces back and forth across the living room. He's got a large mug of black coffee in his hand and takes occasional sips from it. He's wearing a suit and tie. The place has been aired, a combination of open windows and multiple assaults from a pine-fresh aerosol spray. The stench of cigarette smoke lingered for most of the previous evening, heavy and acrid – not unlike the atmosphere between himself and Mary.

But that's all been taken care of now.

He came clean with her as they were going to bed, or at any rate made it appear that he was coming clean. First, he apologised – cried and begged her to forgive him. Then he explained. The two things you're never supposed to do. Who was it said that? Wellington? Disraeli? Anyway, he's pretty sure it doesn't apply to wives. What he told her wasn't untrue, but it was still something of a convenient retrofit. He told her he was in utter despair over this book he's writing and that that's why he'd fallen off the wagon. He also told her that Dave Conway's phone call had been fortuitous. That Dave might just have come up with the perfect solution.

A bit too neat, perhaps, but it did the job. Besides, where else could Mary go with this? He'd only had a lousy few drinks, after all. It's not like he was off with someone's wife, or having his way with one of the hotel maids. Apropos of *which*, however – he did see a tiny flicker of panic in Mary's eyes when he told her what Dave Conway had in mind, i.e. that a young journalist would come here to the hotel and help him out. He'd said 'journalist', not specifying male or female, and he let her stew in that for a while, let her picture some gorgeous young bird with a degree in politics and history from Trinity, someone she'd be forced to leave him alone with for hours on end each day, as they debated, and exchanged views, he inevitably becoming aroused in the presence of such an attractive, brainy young woman, and she, with equal inevitability, falling under the spell of the older man's undoubted charms.

But at that point he had her where he wanted her, so he casually dropped in a gender-specific pronoun. 'He'll be here at around ten in the morning.'

He.

Checkmate.

Mary was all for it after that, of course – suddenly conciliatory and accommodating. She had stuff to do in town and would get out of his way. Then *she* apologised. To *him*. For overreacting. He waved this off.

The soul of magnanimity.

Bolger doesn't feel quite so smug now, though. He didn't sleep well last night, tossing and turning until the early hours, his mind teeming with partial reconstructions of the previous afternoon. When he got up he felt irritable and had to restrain himself from snapping at Mary. Now he's afraid he might snap at this young journalist. Even though he's quite ambivalent about the whole thing anyway.

Feels Dave Conway maybe railroaded him into it.

The journalist's name is Jimmy Gilroy, Dec Gilroy's son, as it turns out. Of Marino Communications. Dave Conway says he's perfect for the job – smart and fairly experienced, but not to the extent that he has an ego to fuel, or an agenda to push. The balance is just right and Bolger should have no problems getting him to do what he wants.

Still.

Can you trust these bastards? Because what he's also reticent about is exposing his inner demons – not to mention his indolence, and indiscipline – to a complete stranger . . .

For all his notoriety, Bolger considers himself a very private person, even a shy one, and there's nothing about this situation that he finds reassuring.

He looks into his coffee.

And then glances at the time on one of the displays.

9:47.

He looks over at the drinks cabinet.

What do the Italians call it? *Caffè corretto*. A corrected coffee.

Leave it to the wops.

A coffee with manners on it.

How civilised can you get?

After a moment's hesitation he goes over to the cabinet. He opens it and takes out the bottle of Jameson's. He unscrews the cap and pours a drop into his mug of coffee. Then a second drop, a slightly extended one, a glug really.

He tastes it. It's nice. Though the coffee *has* gone a bit cold.

He knocks the whole thing back in one go.

Start again.

He pours another substantial measure of whiskey into the mug, puts the bottle away and closes the cabinet. He goes into the kitchen and turns on the kettle. There's some coffee left in the cafetiere. He pours this into the mug. When the water in the kettle boils, he adds some of that into the mix.

He takes a sip.

Hhmm.

It is just as he's coming away from his second visit to the drinks cabinet a few minutes later that the phone rings.

It's reception.

'Mr Bolger, there's a Mr Gilroy here to see you.'

'Right,' Bolger says, passing the mug under his nose, as though it were a fine claret. 'Send him up.'

*

The first thing that strikes Jimmy is how small Bolger is. He's smaller than he looks on TV. He's also a little heavier, but that could well be a more recent development.

Bolger extends a hand and they shake. Then he waves Jimmy in. 'Take a seat. Make yourself comfortable. Would you like something, tea, coffee?'

Jimmy enters a large, expensively furnished living room, lots of chintz, lace and mahogany. A deep-pile carpet. Some antiquey-looking stuff. No books. Above the fireplace there is a huge wall-mounted plasma TV screen.

'I'm fine, thanks,' he says, 'I've already had enough coffee this morning to do me for a week.'

He sits at one end of a long sofa.

Bolger retrieves a mug from the dining table and carefully lowers himself onto a sofa directly opposite the one Jimmy is sitting in.

He crosses his legs and takes a sip from the mug.

'So,' he says. 'Jimmy Gilroy. I knew your father.'

'Yeah?'

'Well, I *met* him a few times. I did one of those media courses. At Marino Communications. He was pretty good, I have to say.'

Jimmy nods. Most of the guys of Bolger's vintage would have passed through Marino at one point or another and had at least some dealings with the old man – though they'd all have known Phil Sweeney much better.

Walking up here from Sandymount, Jimmy thought about turning back more than once. If he'd been struck earlier by how tawdry the Susie Monaghan story was, out on Ailesbury Road he couldn't shake the idea that *this* story was potentially even worse, a spider's web of cheap connections and called-in favours, of nods and winks, of underhand deals and impenetrable lies.

With various forms of collateral damage being par for the course.

The hurt he himself has ended up inflicting on Maria, for instance, is something that won't easily be eradicated, and he's seeing now that it won't easily be contained either.

Because he's looking at Bolger in the light of it.

And hates him already.

Nor will it be long before he starts hating himself too, spinning his own little web of compromises – can't turn back, must play along, need the money.

'He was very thorough,' Bolger is saying. 'Very intense. He had quite a clinical approach, as I remember.'

'Well, he came from a clinical background,' Jimmy says, knowing that that isn't exactly what Bolger meant. 'He trained as a psychiatrist.'

Can we please not talk about my old man?

Bolger laughs. 'A psychiatrist? I'll tell you what, we could have done with a few more of those back in my day.' He laughs again. 'Could do with a few now, am I right?'

Jimmy smiles in response. But is he . . . is he imagining it, or is there something slightly loose, almost intemperate, in the way Bolger is speaking, as if –

No –

Bolger takes another sip from his mug.

No, Jimmy thinks, it couldn't be.

But as they continue chatting nothing happens to dispel this impression.

For a while Bolger discusses his ideas about how to shape the book – he has some grandiose notion of dividing it into three volumes – but as he's doing this *Jimmy gets it.*

The smell of alcohol.

Whiskey fumes.

They aren't exactly wafting across the room, but he's in no doubt about what his nose is telling him. And it just corroborates what he's seeing and hearing anyway.

If the whole thing wasn't so alarming, so weird, it'd be hilarious.

Larry Bolger is pissed.

Well, maybe not pissed, but he's tight. He's sipping whiskey from a *mug*.

Jimmy shifts his position on the sofa.

What the hell is he supposed to do now? He can't work with someone who's drunk at ten o'clock in the morning, can he?

'So, I don't know,' Bolger is saying, beginning to slur his words a little, 'anything less than seven or eight hundred pages and it's just not at the races as far as I'm concerned. Gravitas wise. You need bulk, a good *heft* to it. What do you think?'

'Yeah, I agree.' Jimmy swallows. 'Hit nine and I think you might be pushing it. Definitely not a thousand. But yeah, seven or eight sounds good.'

Get me the fuck out *of here.*

Bolger drains the mug, leans his head right back. Then he places the mug on the arm of the sofa.

'So,' he says, after a long pause. 'Jimmy Gilroy. Tell me who Jimmy Gilroy is.' He flicks his hand back and forth between them. 'Tell me why this is going to work.'

What Jimmy needs to do here is stay calm. He needs to extricate himself from the situation as quickly and efficiently as possible. Then he can go and talk to Phil Sweeney, clear things up. Not that that will leave Jimmy in any great position of strength. The Susie Monaghan book he can return to – he hasn't talked to the editor who commissioned it yet – but as far as Maria is concerned . . .

'Ever since the economy tanked,' he says, feeling deflated all of a sudden, 'I've been working freelance. Picking up bits and pieces here and there.' At this stage no point in holding back. 'It hasn't been great.'

'What have you worked on recently? Anything I might have seen?'

'I doubt it. Unless you read trade magazines, stuff aimed at the pharmaceutical and automotive industries.' He shrugs. 'Though for the past few weeks I've been doing a bit of . . .' He pauses. 'Research.'

Bolger stares at him, waiting for more. 'Well? Research into *what*? Jesus, it's like trying to get blood from a stone here. You'd want to up your game a bit, son. If you want to work with me.'

Jimmy feels horribly self-conscious. It's as if he has been cornered at a family gathering by a drunk uncle he hasn't seen in years.

'Er, I was commissioned to write a book. A biography. Of Susie Monaghan.' He hesitates, then adds, 'the actress.'

Bolger nods. 'Oh, I'm aware of who Susie Monaghan is all right. Of who she *was*. Well aware.'

There's something in the way he says this.

Jimmy leans forward. 'Did you know her?'

Bolger shakes his head. 'Not exactly, no. She was a gorgeous-looking bird, though, wasn't she?'

Jimmy stares at him. *A gorgeous-looking bird?* How is he supposed to respond to that? *Yeah, she was a ride.* Will that do? He nods. 'Actually, I find her very interesting,' he says. 'Her story, that whole crash-and-burn dynamic. She was a real product of the times.'

Bolger looks at him for a second and then bursts out laughing.

Jimmy is taken aback. He bristles. '*What?*'

'No, no, I'm sorry,' Bolger says, still laughing. 'Don't get me wrong, but I can see what you're doing, I can see the temptation to mythologise her, to make her into some kind of an emblem. Death and the maiden sort of thing. To conflate the economy with . . .' He stops and gives a firm shake to his head. 'Because . . .' Suddenly he's not laughing any more. It's as though a dark cloud has passed over him. 'Because you see that isn't what *happened.* I was there. Not at the crash site, of course. I was at the conference. I was at Drumcoolie Castle.' He puffs his cheeks up and exhales loudly. 'There's an untold story *there*, my friend. Holy God.'

Jimmy doesn't move a muscle. He waits. Bolger seems to be lost in thought now, staring into space. Every couple of seconds he gives another little shake to his head.

Jimmy isn't sure what he should say here, but he desperately wants to say something, anything.

Just as he thinks the moment might have passed, Bolger continues. 'And do you know what the ironic thing is?' He picks the mug up from the arm of the sofa. Jimmy shakes his head, though Bolger isn't even looking at him, not directly. 'It was supposed to be a conference on corporate fucking *ethics.* Can you believe that?' He tilts the mug towards him and peers into it. What does he see in there? A tiny dribble? A golden droplet of deliverance? Is it worth the effort? He goes for it, knocking his head all the way back again. The sigh that follows tells its own story. 'Anyway,' he says, 'I went down on the Saturday, just to put in an appearance. Have dinner with the big guns. Ha. The Clark Rundles and the Don fucking Ribcoffs. The *boys*.'

Jimmy knows all about this conference from his research. It was held one July weekend over three years ago at Drumcoolie Castle in Co. Tipperary and was attended by executives from companies such as Hewlett-Packard, Shell, Nike, Dell, Paloma, Chipco, Sony and BRX. Executives from several Irish companies were also in attendance. One of these was Gary Lynch, a re-cent ex-*fiancé* of Susie Monaghan's.

The break-up, apparently, hadn't been Susie's idea, and she'd tagged along to see if there might be any chance of negotiating – or indeed, of engineering – a reconciliation.

Bolger makes another puffing sound. 'Wish to fuck I'd never gone.'

'Why?' Jimmy hears himself ask.

'Because then I wouldn't have . . .' He leans forward on the sofa. 'I wouldn't have been present when certain conversations took place, when certain things were said.' He looks Jimmy in the eye now. 'I wouldn't know what I know.'

'Certain things,' Jimmy says slowly, tentatively, not wanting to break the spell, 'about Susie Monaghan?'

Bolger's eyes widen and a pained expression comes over his face. 'Susie Monaghan? *No.* Jesus Christ, have you not been listening to me? This has nothing to do with Susie Monaghan.' He flops back onto the sofa and stretches his arm out over the side of it, the mug dangling from his hand. 'Did you never hear the expression "collateral damage"? That's what *she* was. A nice piece of misdirection is all.'

Jimmy is speechless. He scrambles in his head for the next question to ask, the right question. 'So who *does* it have to do with?'

Bolger makes a loud guttural sound, somewhere between a harrumph and a belch.

'Well, not Susie,' he says finally. 'That's for sure. Not poor little Susie.' He drops the mug. It falls silently onto the shag carpet. 'Suzi Quatro . . . Sweet Sue.' He's gazing off into space again. 'A boy named . . .'

'*Mr Bolger*,' Jimmy says. '*Who?*'

Bolger looks back, stares at him for a second. 'Think about it. She wasn't the only one.'

'The only one what?'

'The only one who died in the fucking *crash*, you gobshite.'

Two

Ashes was always wound pretty tight but this is something else. This is insane . . .

Tom Szymanski shifts over to the passenger seat and puts his hand on the open door, ready to jump out if necessary.

'Deep Six,' Tube is whispering over the radio, 'defcon fucking one here, man, what is going on?'

'I don't know . . . I . . .'

That's all he can come up with, at least for now, though one or two theories are definitely forming in his brain.

He leans out a bit and when he sees where Ashes is aiming his weapon, he whispers loudly, 'Kroner, Jesus, are you fucking crazy?'

Ashes glances back at him, this strange look in his eyes, no shit, but after a second he turns away and looks at the middle car, in at the package, then up ahead again.

Szymanski retreats into the SUV.

It's not that Ashes has been acting weird lately, it occurs to him, he's been acting weird since the day they first met, which was what, three, four months ago now? Though in this context 'weird' is certainly a relative term. Szymanski has seen all kinds of weird himself, been all kinds of weird, but he has also been equipped to deal with it, blessed or cursed with the kind of intelligence that can process shit, transform it, sit on it till the time is right, keeping any unpleasant consequences at bay or at least to a minimum. He knows he has this exterior, too, that he comes over all chilled-out, like nothing fazes him, but that's a shell he's developed down through the years and of course every shell has an interior, his being stuffed full of crazy just like anyone else's.

And for crazy, for weird, read PTSD.

The acronym of choice among the private military companies.

The PMCs.

Because on the menu of symptoms you can just take your pick: depression, guilt, nightmares, alienation, isolation, psychic numbing, denial, fear of intimacy, dependence, abuse, startle reflex, panic attacks, compulsive behaviours, high-risk behaviours – we're getting there, we're getting there – suicidal ideation, homicidal *ideation* . . .

'RAY.'

Oh God.

'Tube . . . DON'T.'

So he's not saying Ashes doesn't fit in with the unit, or is a loner, or a loser or anything, which would actually be fine in the 3rd Infantry Division or the 82nd Airborne or whatever – you're in with who you're in with there, it's not like you have a choice in the matter, the sad sacks line out with the best and the brightest, no questions asked – but in the PMCs it's a bit different, they like you to fit in, they like you to get along, because having some freak of nature in the unit everyone can pick on is all very well, but it's not exactly cost-effective, and Gideon Global is supposed to be a business operation, tight, well-oiled, not some toxic dumping ground for the twisted and the dispossessed.

Which he's not saying Ashes is, but –

What the fuck is the guy up to? He needs to blow off a little steam or something? Scare the shit out of everyone?

Really?

The first shots are unlike any Szymanski has ever heard, and he's heard thousands of the motherfuckers. These have a quality to them, an unreality, it's like even they *don't believe they've been discharged.*

But the second burst is business as usual, as is the third.

At which point, no more than about three seconds into this, with Tube's radio voice crackling 'STOP HIM, STOP HIM' in the background, Szymanski piles out of the passenger side of the SUV, hits the ground and rolls forward into the back of Ray Kroner's legs, bringing the dumbass cracker down in an awkward pile on top of him.

And right in front of the passenger door of the middle car.

The handle of which Ashes uses for leverage to get himself up again.

But also, in the process, manages to pull toward him.

So that from below, through the open door, Szymanski gets to see the terrified package flailing inside, one hand gripping the headrest in front of him, the other hand holding onto the door jamb.

Ashes facing him now, the muzzle of his M4 pointing in.

And as Szymanski scrambles to get up, his arm hurting like shit, he catches a flash of someone through the lowered window of the car door . . . Tube . . . rushing forward . . . kicking the door shut again, raising his hand with a Sig Sauer pistol in it and putting a bullet point blank into the side of Ray Kroner's head.

There is silence, but only for a second. What follows it isn't the delayed wailing of women and children, as Szymanski might have expected, it's the agonised screaming of their executive package here who's just had his hand badly crushed in the car door . . .

When Tube slammed it shut with his boot.

But hey, fuck him.

Szymanski staggers backwards a few feet – away from Ray Kroner's crumpled body, and his twisted face, away from what at first you might be forgiven for thinking was the 'primary scene'.

But then he gets it, gets why there's no screaming other than that of the suit in the car, why there's no wailing of women and children.

They're all fucking dead.

Up ahead, and everywhere around him, he sees it.

Three short bursts of fire.

Over to the left, splayed against the wall of the concrete struc-ture, his skull fucking daubed against it, is the tall skinny man with the bloodshot eyes. Over to the right, the wooden huts look all riddled to shit. And there, directly in front of the convoy, in a heap, along with their baskets of spilled produce, rivulets of blood trickling out in different directions, are the two women and the three small children.

4

'So,' Dave Conway says, 'what do you think of our chances?'

As he considers how to respond to this, Martin Boyle swivels his chair from side to side. He's in his early-sixties, grey and paunchy, a solicitor for forty years, third generation, the law ingrained in his face, in his posture, in his syntax.

'That depends.' He clears his throat. 'Notwithstanding all the work we'll have completed here by, with any luck, Sunday night, your best chance with these people will actually be down to something else entirely, something quite intangible.'

Conway has just learnt there's to be a make-or-break meeting with the Black Vine people on Monday. A team at McGowan Boyle is trying to come up with a convincing business model – which is what Boyle insists on calling it, having issued a blanket ban on the term 'survival plan'.

Conway looks at him. 'What's that?'

'*You*. The Conway Holdings *brand*.' Boyle leans forward and plants his elbows on the desk. 'Black Vine aren't stupid, they see what's going on. You've overextended, the market's dead, it's a simple equation and if they were a bank they wouldn't give you a second look, but they're not a bank, they're an equity fund, they play a smarter game than that, they look five, ten, fifteen years into the future. They look for value in the *long* term. And I'm convinced that when they sit down with you that's what they're going to see.'

'Hhmm.' As Conway gives this some thought, he glances around the office, at the messy piles, on every surface, of folders, lever-arch files and back numbers of law journals. The window behind Boyle's desk is slightly opaque, long made grimy by the Dublin rain.

'Look, Dave, I know you might be a bit disheartened at the moment, but believe me, Conway Holdings has a serious track record. This is the first real speed bump you've ever hit, and everyone else is hitting it at the same time. With a little luck, you'll recover. Most of them won't.'

Maybe Boyle has a point.

For thirty years, under Dave's late father, Conway & Co. was a solid, profitable operation that had started out in cement and building supplies and then diversified into mining and property development, with interests in the UK, Eastern Europe and Africa. When Conway took over he expanded the development portfolio, but he was always fairly cautious. A turning point in the company's history came when he sold First Continental Resources, a virtually abandoned copper mine in the Democratic Republic of Congo, to the multinational engineering giant, BRX.

For a huge profit.

That freed things up and the newly named Conway Holdings just mushroomed. If Conway was ever guilty of being reckless, it was only at the end of the boom.

In its last five minutes.

And only with Tara Meadows.

He pumped everything he had into it, and when he needed more, he started borrowing.

Like everyone else.

Like every other pig at the fucking trough.

'The thing is,' Boyle goes on, waving his hand in the air, indicating the surrounding offices, 'this business plan we're drawing up here, the new accountants' reports, the fresh valuations, it's all smoke and mirrors, it's for show. *You're* what counts. Dave Conway, the serious businessman, the dealmaker. Not some flash git who lost his head in the boom. I've met these Black Vine guys and I know how they think. They'll look at the record. They'll want to talk about stuff like that First Continental Resources deal – which, by the way, I don't mind telling you, they are *very* curious about.' He sits back in his chair. 'Go in there and talk about *that*, tell them *that* story, and you'll have them eating out of the palm of your hand.'

Conway flashes Boyle a look. What does *he* know about the First Continental deal?

McGowan Boyle only came on board afterwards – new solicitors, new accountants, new arrangements. A lot of things changed for Conway around that time.

New house, new lifestyle.

'OK,' he says, 'but it's still a crapshoot, right?'

'There's always an element of the crapshoot to these things. But go in there and explain to them how you got a multinational corporation to bend over like that, how you got them to shell out a hundred million dollars for an abandoned copper mine in some godforsaken shithole, and I think the odds just might tilt in your favour.'

As Conway opens his mouth to speak, to object – because this is a direction he really doesn't want to go in – his phone starts vibrating in his pocket.

He sighs and pulls it out in order to switch it off completely.

But then he sees who it is.

Lifting the phone to his ear, he looks over at Boyle, holds up an index finger. 'I'm sorry, Martin. I have to take this.'

Boyle nods.

'Larry?' he then says into the phone, rising from his chair. 'What . . . what's the matter? Take it easy.'

*

It's ironic.

Having read only yesterday in *Vanity Fair* how well he's supposed to get on with his brother, Clark Rundle is now seething with anger and resentment towards him. He understands that J.J. had a rough time of it out there – he had his hand crushed in the door of an SUV and witnessed some scary stuff, OK – but how can the guy not be able to recall a simple conversation he had thirty minutes prior to that? It seems ridiculous.

Rundle is sitting at his desk, waiting for Don Ribcoff to arrive with the latest update.

Don has already tried to put it down to post-traumatic stress disorder, but Rundle isn't buying. It's too easy. J.J. is due back this morning and he'd better have his head sorted out by then or Rundle doesn't know what he's going to do. J.J. doesn't appear to have any problem dealing with all the publicity they've inadvertently managed to whip up with this Paris thing – which is why he's flying home so soon, and against, apparently, all medical advice – but one slip-up before the cameras, one hint that the senator's 'heroics' might not be entirely on the level, and the man will be roasted alive in the full glare of the world's media.

And that, of course, unlikely though it may be, would have unintended consequences – easily the least of which, as far as Rundle is concerned, would be the ignominious end of J.J.'s bid for a presidential nomination. More seriously, it would undermine Rundle's own credibility as an unofficial power broker.

In the colonel's eyes. In James Vaughan's eyes.

Not that Rundle gives a shit what the colonel thinks. He doesn't. Kimbela's a deranged megalomaniac who just happens to be sitting on some very valuable mineral deposits.

Rundle leans back in his chair.

What James Vaughan thinks, though, is a different matter altogether. That runs a little deeper. Rundle has known Jimmy Vaughan since he was a small boy – back when Vaughan and the old man were knee-deep in Middle Eastern construction projects, building pipelines and refinery facilities, as well as networking and schmoozing.

The company and the Company.

As it were.

Rundle remembers a trip to Saudi in the mid-seventies, when he was a teenager – has this vivid image in his mind of old Henry C. in his short-sleeved shirt and wide tie, with his clipboard and his pocket calculator, Jimmy Vaughan standing next to him in a white linen suit, straw panama hat and dark glasses.

The weird thing is, and maybe it's not weird at all, is that Rundle never put any effort into trying to impress the old man (if anything it was the opposite), but he couldn't help himself when it came to Mr Vaughan. And now, ten years after the old man croaked it – right in front of him, in the study of the house in Connecticut – here he is, middle-aged, in his eight-thousand-dollar suit, still worried about how Vaughan will react to something he has done, or is doing, or is contemplating doing.

It isn't that simple, of course. It isn't just dollar-book Freud. It's actually – when he thinks about it – just *dollars*.

Period.

Fuck the Freud.

As chairman of BRX, Rundle is little more than a bean counter, a storekeeper, like the old man was. And for his part, J.J. is a Beltway pol, a grafter, a ballot-box hustler. But Jimmy Vaughan is different. He's one of those extraordinary guys, and there aren't that many of them, who somehow float between the two, and it's not that he's both – businessman *and* politician – it's actually that he's *neither*. He's something else again, something more evolved than that. For him, it's not about making money and having it, or about having money and spending it.

It's –

He's –

Rundle doesn't know.

It's like he's the very *embodiment* of money. Cash made carnate.

Flesh and the devil. Flesh *of* the devil.

And back then, even when he was sixteen or seventeen, Rundle caught a whiff of this, and it has never left him. It's in his nostrils now, as he sits here, staring down through tempered glass at the gleaming white floor of his office.

When he looks up, he sees his assistant standing in the doorway, ushering Don Ribcoff in.

Ribcoff comes over, takes a seat and the two men exchange pleasantries. Ribcoff settles some papers in his lap. He's here to provide an update on what they have taken to calling 'the Buenke incident'. After another few moments, Rundle gives him the nod to proceed.

'OK,' Ribcoff says, leaning forward and placing a sheet of paper on the desk. 'Nine dead, including the contractor. This is a layout of the village.' He then indicates different points on the sheet of paper with a pen. 'The two women and three children *here*, the man *here*, and the other two, who were elderly women, in the huts *here*. The contractor was Ray Kroner, twenty-eight years old, from Phoenix. Ex-army, two combat tours in Iraq. Armed Forces Expeditionary Medal. Global War on Terrorism Service Medal. No prior behavioural problems. Seems he just went postal.'

'Goddamn.'

'Yeah, look, it's a hazard. These guys are well paid, but the pressure they're under is phenomenal. Having said that, at Gideon we pride ourselves on the quality of our work, and in seven years of ops we've only ever had two incidents that might even vaguely be comparable to this one. Both in Nasiriyah.'

Rundle doesn't believe this for a second, but he's not about to argue.

'What about fallout?'

'So far we're good. No witnesses, which means it's a closed system, more or less.' Rundle leans back a little from the desk. 'And you know, to be honest, Clark, this is nothing. It's a drop in the ocean. Village massacres are a dime a dozen over there.'

'Right.'

'If it weren't for the senator being part of the equation we wouldn't even be talking about this. But to the extent that it happened, and that we might have to address it? In *some* form?

Our cover story would be that the convoy was responding to hostile fire.' He shrugs. 'After all, we have a body on our hands to prove it.'

Rundle nods. 'And the contractor's family?'

'They'll be informed. In due course.'

'Which means?'

'In due course. We have considerable latitude here, Clark. It's not like a regular casualty situation. I mean, when a member of the armed forces dies, next of kin have to be informed within forty-eight hours. Then you're talking Arlington, a twenty-one gun salute, taps, flag draped over the casket, the whole bit. It's a little different for private contractors. There's no fanfare. At *all*. There isn't even an official list anywhere of contractor casualties.'

Rundle sits back in his chair and considers this. After a while, he says, 'OK, no witnesses, but what about the others?'

'The other contractors?' Ribcoff shakes his head vigorously. 'No. They're the ones who took Ray Kroner *out*. Because they deemed the senator to be in danger. These are men of the highest calibre, Clark. Loyalty is their watchword.' He shakes his head again. 'This situation, this *incident*, is in effective lockdown, believe me.'

Rundle nods. The nightmare scenario here would be disclosure, some kind of inquiry, prosecution even. It would be in no one's interests – not BRX's, not Gideon's. And if J.J.'s presence at the scene were to become public knowledge the consequences would be unimaginable.

But Don appears to be on top of things.

'OK,' he says. 'What about Kimbela?'

'That's not so straightforward. He's a hard man to pin down.

He won't use a phone, as you know. He plays video games *online*, but he won't do e-mail.' Ribcoff makes a face. 'Plus, he's always on the move. Our man on the ground over there is doing his best to make direct contact, but it could be a day or two, and you know how cagey he is, even at the best of times.'

'Yeah.'

Rundle gets a sinking feeling in his stomach. Sending J.J. down there on a lightning trip from Paris to suss out the colonel's position vis-à-vis the Chinese seemed like a good idea at the time – sprinkle a little political stardust into the mix, play to the man's vanity – but it doesn't feel like such a smart move now.

Inevitably, Rundle will to have to go and see Vaughan later on, to give *him* an update, but his plan is to have cornered J.J. by then and extracted an account of the meeting.

He and Kimbela sat down together for over an hour.

He has to remember *something*.

Rundle shifts in his chair. 'Don,' he says, 'what time does the flight get in from Paris?'

Ribcoff looks up from his papers and then checks his watch. 'Around midday. Twelve fifteen, I think.'

'Don't let him out of your sight. I want a piece of him before he starts talking to CNN and Fox.'

Ribcoff nods. He shuffles his papers together and stands up. 'I'll keep you posted, Clark.'

Rundle watches as Ribcoff crosses the office and leaves. Then he swivels his chair around and sits for a while staring out of the window.

*

It's late in the afternoon before Jimmy starts to slow down. He remembers at one point that he hasn't eaten anything since breakfast and goes over to the kitchen to make a sandwich. As he is drizzling olive oil over mozzarella, he runs a reconstruction of the morning's events through his head.

This is maybe the hundredth time he has done this.

There are variations, but each time it's essentially the same.

He arrived at the hotel as arranged and met Larry Bolger. They started talking. It quickly became apparent that Bolger was drunk. Bolger then dropped this incredible bombshell.

And after that, it was pretty much downhill.

Jimmy tried to pretend that nothing had happened, but it didn't really work. Bolger knew he'd said something he shouldn't have, and though he seemed to be a little confused about what that was exactly, it didn't take him long to turn the tables and start accusing Jimmy of having tricked him.

Jimmy said he hadn't tricked anyone, that they were just talking.

Bolger grunted and sidled over towards the corner of the room.

Jimmy did his best to get the conversation back on track, thinking that maybe in a while he could broach the subject again, but within minutes Bolger was pointing at the door and shouting at him, 'Get out, you bowsie.'

Jimmy left without protest.

On the way down in the elevator he was too stunned to think of writing anything in his notebook. But then outside, walking along Merrion Road, his heart pounding, something would come to him that he didn't want to forget – a name or a phrase Bolger had used – and he'd stop to jot it down.

When he got back to the apartment he took his notebook out and got straight to work. Names: Clark Rundle, Don Ribcoff. *Who were these people?* Phrases: collateral damage; a nice piece of misdirection; not the only one. *Could these really mean what he thought they meant?*

He's been hard at it ever since, rearranging all the material on his desk, but factoring Susie out this time, trying to reconfigure the narrative, to find a new pattern, an alternative meaning.

Because . . .

He takes his sandwich and a bottle of water back across the room.

Because Bolger implied – fuck it, he more or less *said* – that the helicopter crash three years ago hadn't been an accident. Bolger was drunk, at least as far as Jimmy could tell, and the conversation was off the record, fine, so he can't *prove* Bolger said it.

But –

The thing is, if it somehow turns out to be true, then it won't matter that Bolger said it. It won't matter who said it. Who *said* it won't be the story.

If it's true.

But how does he prove that?

Jimmy eats the sandwich, barely aware of its taste or texture. He chews, swallows, takes occasional sips of water, at the same time casting his eye over various open notebooks, printouts, the computer screen.

His phone.

From which, to his surprise, there hasn't been a peep all afternoon. There *will* be, though. He knows that. Because it's inconceivable that Phil Sweeney hasn't already been alerted and fully briefed. Inconceivable that there won't be significant fall-out from this.

He finishes the sandwich, brings the plate back over to the kitchen and puts on some coffee. As he's waiting for the water to heat up, he stares at the wall.

And if it *is* true, of course, *he'll* have to alert and fully brief Maria.

Which he'd be more than happy to do.

But then he thinks . . . this is insane, *he's* insane. Larry Bolger was drunk and barely coherent. Why would anyone think for a second that a claim like the one he made even *might* be true? *In vino veritas*, sure, but also a lot of the time in vino bullshit. In vino paranoia and delusion. Because if the claim is true, if the crash wasn't an accident, then what was it? Some sort of a conspiracy? Involving who? These names that were mentioned? And why? Something to do with one of the other passengers?

Suddenly, it all seems a bit far-fetched.

As he makes the coffee, Jimmy considers the possibility that what has happened here is pretty simple: *he* has just blown a good job prospect.

Maybe Larry Bolger likes to tie one on in the mornings and tell stories. So fucking what? Winston Churchill used to have champagne for breakfast. And anyway, wouldn't that have made the job – and the book – infinitely more interesting?

Or maybe it's just that Bolger was testing him, seeing how he'd react.

Like an idiot, as it turns out.

He brings his coffee back over to the desk.

On the screen he has pulled up an article from the most recent online edition of *Vanity Fair*. It's about one of the people

Bolger mentioned, Clark Rundle, CEO of something-or-other, and his brother, a US senator.

Jimmy starts reading, but gives up after a few paragraphs.

Some bloke out of *Vanity Fair*?

Fuck off.

He's tired now, and cranky, this sense creeping up on him that he's been mugged somehow – by circumstance, by coincidence, by his own stupidity.

He takes a sip of coffee.

His phone rings.

He shakes his head, and picks it up.

*

By the time he gets to the hotel, Dave Conway is exhausted. He has spent most of the afternoon with Martin Boyle discussing how best to make his pitch to the Black Vine people on Monday and although his concentration mightn't have been great to start with, the call from Larry Bolger threw him off completely. Dave's not even sure he fully understood what Bolger was on about – something to do with the young journalist. But the easiest way to get him off the phone was to promise he'd call around and see him later on. Conway then tried Phil Sweeney, but Phil was in a meeting, so he had to leave a message – a message that he found was becoming, in the course of leaving it, increasingly urgent.

On his way up in the elevator now he takes out his mobile and switches it to vibrate.

When Mary Bolger opens the door of the apartment, Conway immediately sees the distress in her face. She doesn't say anything, just leads him in and points across the room at Bolger, who is slumped in an armchair.

Then she disappears into the kitchen.

No greeting. No peck on the cheek. No offer of tea or a drink. All the usual formalities dispensed with.

Bolger looks over at him and nods, distress equally evident in *his* face.

Conway approaches. He stops at the dining table and pulls out a chair. He turns it around and sits in it. Yesterday, down in the Avondale Lounge, it had seemed as if Bolger was looking for trouble. Today it seems – Conway can't help thinking – as if he might have found it.

There is silence for a while.

Then Conway says, 'Right. What is it, Larry? Come on.'

Bolger groans.

Conway doesn't think he is going to have much patience for this. After all, he's the one who came up with the idea in the first place, kill two birds with one stone sort of thing, and now Bolger is the one, it appears, who has gone and fucked it up.

'*So?*' he says, an edge entering his voice.

Bolger sighs and runs a hand over his stubble. He has always been one of those men who needs to shave in the afternoon. But not today, apparently. 'Listen,' he says, 'I've done something stupid.'

'O-kay,' Conway says, and nods, feeling like a priest in the confessional. Then he sees that not only has Bolger not shaved, his eyes look bleary, and his face is a little puffy.

'Larry,' he says, 'have you been *drinking*?'

'Yes.'

Conway closes his eyes. He didn't know Bolger in his drinking days, but he's heard the stories. And he knows how all of this works. He opens his eyes again.

'Meeting was that bad, yeah?'

Bolger grunts, then says, 'This was before he arrived.'

'What?'

'I was well on when he got here.'

Oh Jesus.

'And this stupid thing you did, I assume it wasn't just *having* the drink . . .'

Bolger shakes his head.

'. . . it was something you said?'

'Yeah.'

Whatever Bolger may have said to this journalist, and even if he didn't say anything at all, the mere fact that he had drink on him, and so early in the day, would be enough of a story in itself – a bullshit *tabloid* story, but a story nonetheless – to do him irreparable damage.

Conway shrugs. 'So, what did you say to him?'

Bolger exhales, though it's more of a shudder. 'I don't fucking know, Dave. I don't remember exactly. We were talking about other stuff he's done and he said he'd been working on a book, a biography –'

Dave's heart sinks.

'– of Susie Monaghan, and –'

'Larry, don't tell me you –'

'I didn't go into any detail, none at all, but I may have . . . I may have intimated that –'

'*What?*'

'– that . . . things weren't what they seemed.'

'Why?'

'*Why?* Because we were talking and because *I was fucking drunk*, that's why.'

'*Jesus*, Larry.'

Bolger leans forward, animated all of a sudden. 'And do you want to know why I was drunk? Do you? Because I'm tired of all this bullshit is why. I'm tired of sitting around in this fucking hotel, I'm tired of watching TV and pretending I'm writing my memoirs, I'm tired of all the remarks and sly comments I have to read every day in the papers, Larry Bolger this, Larry Bolger that, what now for Larry fucking Bolger? I'm tired of being treated as a joke. I'm tired of arrogant pricks like James Vaughan not returning my calls, I'm –'

Conway holds up a hand. '*What?*'

Bolger looks at him. 'James Vaughan? That bastard *owes* me. He did me out of that IMF job and now he won't talk to me, won't return my calls.' He stops here, as something seems to occur to him. 'But he *will* return my calls, and you know why? Because this Jimmy Gilroy prick has nothing, nada, he can't prove a bloody thing. But *I* can. And if Vaughan doesn't start showing a little respect, maybe exert a bit of that legendary influence he's supposed to have, then I might just be forced to –'

'Jesus *Christ*, Larry.' Conway gets up from his chair. 'Are you out of your fucking mind? Do you have any idea what you're *saying*?'

Bolger leans back in the armchair. 'You know what, Dave? A little bit of respect from *you* mightn't go amiss either.'

'What? Is that a threat? Were you smoking crack as well?'

'Watch it.'

Conway throws his arms up. This is unbelievable. The irrationality of it is breathtaking. 'Larry,' he says, a slightly more pleading tone to his voice than he'd like, 'yesterday you were worried about some small item in the paper, worried that someone might start asking questions, and today you're ready to, what, *blackmail* James Vaughan? And if that doesn't work, what? Is there a plan here? Go on fucking *Liveline*? You have to see how insane this is.'

'I don't bel—'

'You have to see that not only would James Vaughan not allow it, *I* wouldn't allow it, I *couldn't*. I'm in enough trouble as it is, you drag me into this shit, and I'd be destroyed.'

Bolger looks at him and shakes his head. 'I don't believe what I'm hearing here. *Allow*? You couldn't *allow* it? You see . . . you see, this is what I'm talking about, and frankly I've had enough. I'm not putting up with any more of it.' He bangs his fist on the side of the armchair. 'I was the fucking Taoiseach for Christ's sake.'

Conway turns around and runs a hand over his hair.

He takes a deep breath.

This is a nightmare.

He wants to just walk out of here, but he can't. He has to talk Bolger down, has to bring him back from the precipice.

Plus, he has to find out what Jimmy Gilroy knows.

'OK,' he says, turning around again, 'OK,' and then adds, in an attempt to defuse the tension, 'Larry, any chance I could get a cup of coffee or something?'

*

Jimmy sees from the caller ID that it's Phil Sweeney. For a second or two he toys with the idea of letting it go into message. But that would just drag things out. He'd have to call him back at *some* point.

He answers it.

'Phil?'

'Jimmy. What's going on?'

'Er . . . what do you mean?'

'I mean what's going on? I heard something happened. I got a message. But I've been in meetings all day.'

'You don't know?'

'No. It's something to do with Larry, isn't it? *Tell* me.'

Jimmy hesitates, but then decides to get straight into it. What's the point in being coy, he thinks, or in dissembling? He'll just tell it straight, describe what happened, because Sweeney is probably going to ridicule him anyway. Then, in hearing himself tell the story, Jimmy realises afresh – with each passing word, with each new detail – just how ridiculous it actually is.

How ridiculous *he* is.

And how he'll fully deserve to be ridiculed.

But –

Curiously.

That isn't what happens.

'Holy *fuck*, Jimmy.'

'What?'

'What do you mean *what*? Jesus. Are *you* drunk now, too?' He pauses. 'Listen to me, Jimmy, this is . . . this is *very* fucking serious.'

Jimmy stares at the *Vanity Fair* page on the computer screen. Why is it so serious? Is it the fact that Larry Bolger was drunk at ten o'clock in the morning? Is *that* what Sweeney is afraid will get out?

It'd make sense.

Because it can hardly be the other thing.

'Jimmy?'

'Yeah.'

'Do you *hear* me? I said this is very serious. You cannot repeat a word of what Bolger said, not to anyone.'

'But –'

'If this gets out it will be a complete fucking disaster.'

Jimmy swallows. 'If *what* gets out, Phil, the fact that he was drunk?'

'*No*, shit, that's the least –'

And then he stops, obviously struck by what he is about to say.

But Jimmy is struck by it, too. He looks again at the stuff on his desk. 'The least *what*, Phil?' he says. 'The least of his problems?' There is a long silence, which tells Jimmy more than any possible answer to the question. 'Phil,' he says eventually, 'you can't be serious. I was ready to dismiss this. I thought if there was a story here it might be, I don't know, his struggle with the booze or something, his struggle with *reality*, which certainly wouldn't be anything *I'd* want to write about.' He pauses. 'But *this* –'

'*Write?* You won't fucking write anything, Jimmy. I set you up with this and if it didn't work out, fine, you walk away from it, we'll find you something else, but –'

'No thanks, Phil, and I'll write whatever the hell I want to write.'

'That was a confidential conversation, Jimmy, you can't go around quoting –'

'I have no intention of quoting him, or even of referring to him. All I'm going to do is look into this. I'm a journalist, Phil. What do you expect me to do?'

No answer. Another pause. Sweeney regrouping. Then, 'Look, Jimmy, you're not going to find anything, you're –'

'How do you know?'

'Because . . . oh *fuck*.'

Jimmy feels strangely calm through all of this, relieved almost, as though he has been liberated. It's a feeling that has crept up on him, and as he listens to the normally confidant and sure-footed Phil Sweeney floundering at the other end of the line, he grows in confidence himself.

'Maybe I won't find anything, Phil. But this is way too serious an allegation to ignore.' Glancing at the screen again, and then at one of his notebooks, he decides to take a chance. 'With too many serious names in the mix. Clark Rundle.' He pauses. 'Don Ribcoff.'

As the silence that follows this expands to fill the room, Jimmy's eyes widen. Eventually, he says, 'Phil?'

After another moment he hears a slow, laboured intake of breath. 'Jimmy, listen to me. Leave this alone, will you? I'm serious. You've *no* idea what you're getting into here.'

Jimmy agrees but he isn't about to say so.

'I'll see you around, Phil,' he says and hangs up.

*

On three separate occasions, as he sits in Bolger's apartment, Dave Conway feels his phone vibrate in his pocket.

Afterwards, walking along the corridor towards the elevator, he takes the phone out and checks it – three missed calls, all from Phil Sweeney.

He stops at the elevator and presses the 'down' button.

His hand is shaking.

The elevator door opens and he steps inside.

What can Phil Sweeney tell him at this stage that he doesn't already know? The damage is done.

He calls him anyway.

'Phil.'

'Dave, my God, where have you been? This is a nightmare. Larry and the kid? We shouldn't have put the two of them to-gether, *big* fucking mistake.'

See?

'Yeah.' Conway presses the button for the ground floor. 'But how much does this . . . what's his name again? The kid?'

'Jimmy Gilroy.'

'Right. How much does he know?'

'Not much, as far as I can tell. But of course now he's like a dog after a bone. Plus, he's got names. Whether these came from Larry or not I don't know. It wasn't clear.'

'Names, what do you mean, names?'

As the elevator car descends, floor by floor, Conway feels his insides descending even faster.

'He mentioned Rundle. And Don Ribcoff.'

'*What?*'

'I think he was bluffing, but it means he's not working in a vacuum.'

'Well, can you take care of him?'

The elevator door opens onto the hotel lobby.

'That depends, Dave. What do you mean exactly?'

Conway doesn't know. He needs time to think.

He steps out of the elevator.

He needs time to remember. Because how much, actually, does Phil Sweeney himself know? Not everything, that's for sure. He'd know that certain things happened – but not, in every case, how or why they happened. He'd know names and dates – but not, in every case, their full significance.

There's a balance to be struck here and Conway needs to be careful. In any case, Phil Sweeney probably isn't who he should be talking to about this.

Not anymore. Not going forward.

'Talk him out of it', he says. 'That's what I meant.'

'Well, I'll see what I can do, Dave. I suppose there's still a couple of buttons I can press.' He pauses. 'Did you talk to Larry?'

'Yeah, he's . . .' Conway swallows, still in shock. 'I don't know, he's out of control.' He stands next to a marble pillar in the lobby. 'Right now, he's the very fucking definition of a loose cannon.'

'So what are you going to do?'

'I'm not sure, Phil. But I'll tell you one thing. I'm up to my neck in this rescue package at the moment and I'm not going to let anything jeopardise it.'

What's he saying here?

'Right.'

He's saying that if this shit gets dredged up again, if questions are asked, if names are mentioned and dots are joined – then that's it. He may as well pack it in. But that also, basically, he's not going to *allow* that to happen.

So who *does* he talk to?

'Look, Phil,' he says, resolve hardening. 'You deal with this Gilroy fella, OK? Call him off, do whatever you have to do, because I don't ever want to hear his name again. As for Larry, I really don't know. I'm going to have to think about it.'

But the fact is he's already thought about it.

Already thought it *through*.

And it didn't take him long.

The important decisions usually don't.

After he's done with Phil Sweeney, he keeps the phone in his hand. He crosses the lobby and goes outside. There's an early evening chill in the air. He stands under the portico.

He gazes out over the hotel's manicured front lawn.

He looks back at the phone and scrolls through his list of contacts. He finds what he's looking for. It's a long time since he's used this number.

He calls it. He waits. It rings.

'Good morning, Gideon Global. How may I help you?'

'Yes, can you put me through to Don Ribcoff, please.'

5

Jimmy has been handed something on a plate here, it's just that he doesn't know what it is exactly. If Phil Sweeney had opted for Bolger being drunk as the major cause of concern, Jimmy would have had no inclination to take the matter any further. But Sweeney was rattled on the phone and made it obvious that the real problem was *what* Bolger said, not the state he was in when he said it – a position that only moments earlier Jimmy himself, and all on his own, had somehow managed to reason his way out of.

Now he's right back into it.

But with no sense of direction, no compass.

A clue to the answer may lie somewhere among all this stuff on his desk. Or it may not. But so far that's all he's got.

He sorts through the papers again and reorganises them.

The event at Drumcoolie Castle was the Fifth International Conference on Corporate and Business Ethics, previous ones having been held in places such as Seattle and Johannesburg. It was a three-day event – a wall-to-wall roster of papers, panels, lunches, receptions and dinners, and with an extremely impressive list of attendees. But reading through the programme and subsequent newspaper reports, Jimmy gets no real sense of what the event was like, no sense that it was anything other than as intensely boring as it seems now on paper.

He goes through the list of attendees again.

Apart from a few obvious and well-known ones, the only name that sticks out on the list is one of the two that Bolger mentioned – Clark Rundle. The other name he mentioned, Don Ribcoff, doesn't appear on the list – or, indeed, in any of the other materials Jimmy has assembled about the conference. But that doesn't have to be significant. Nothing he has found out about Rundle means anything to him either.

Clark Rundle is the Chairman and CEO of BRX, which is a privately owned engineering and mining conglomerate with operations in over seventy countries around the world. Founded in the late nineteenth century by his great-grandfather, Benjamin Rundle, the company quickly went from producing machine parts to building railroads, highways, pipelines and hydro-electric dams. Over the decades there seems to have been a revolving door of sorts between the boards of BRX and various administrations in Washington, but that, Jimmy assumes, is standard operating procedure at this level.

None of which, in the context of what Jimmy is concerned about here, means or proves anything.

Same with the second guy. A quick internet search reveals Don Ribcoff to be the CEO of Gideon Global, a private security company with operations in dozens of countries worldwide – including Iraq and Afghanistan. Lately, according to one report that Jimmy finds, Gideon have been withdrawing from direct military engagement and increasing their presence in the areas of corporate competitive intelligence and domestic surveillance.

But again, so what? This is shit he has found on Wikipedia. It brings him no nearer to formulating even the bones of a theory about what might have happened. He could gather similar information on the dozens of other executives at the conference, but what good would it do? While there must be some reason Bolger singled out these two names, Jimmy doesn't believe he's going to find it on the internet.

He gets up and goes over to the window.

As he gazes out across the bay, which is disappearing behind a shroud of evening mist, Jimmy re-runs the conversation with Bolger in his head.

'Think about it. She wasn't the only one.'

'The only one what?'

'The only one who died in the fucking crash, you gobshite.'

And suddenly it seems so obvious.

He goes back to his desk, shuffles through some papers and finds what he's looking for.

The passenger list.

It was a privately leased helicopter, piloted by Liam Egan, with five passengers on board. Apart from Susie Monaghan, there was Ted Walker, Gianni Bonacci, Ben Schnitz and Niall Feeley. He has extensive notes on each of these men, and he glances through them now. But nothing new jumps out at him.

It's stuff he's been over a hundred times before.

Ted Walker was a top executive at Eiben-Chemcorp, thirty-eight years old and big into extreme sports. The trip was believed to have been organised by him in order to showcase to fellow danger junkie Ben Schnitz some ideal paragliding spots along the north Donegal coastline. Schnitz was a senior vice president at Paloma Electronics.

Also assumed to have been an extreme sports enthusiast, Gianni Bonacci was director of a UN Corporate Affairs Commission, and Niall Feeley, an executive at Hibinvest, was known to have been a close friend of both Ted Walker's and Gary Lynch's – Gary Lynch having been the guy Susie Monaghan had just broken up with.

The theory at the time was that Susie went along with Feeley in a desperate attempt to make Lynch jealous.

Fine.

But according to Bolger, Susie was collateral damage. So does this eliminate Niall Feeley too? Was he collateral damage as well? Is Ted Walker's brother being a friend of Phil Sweeney's significant? And what about the other two?

Jimmy looks over the papers again. He doesn't know what to think. Nothing presents itself as significant, and everything does. Which isn't much of a help.

He needs to widen his frame of reference. He needs to get out there and talk to someone.

But where does he start?

It takes him a few minutes of rummaging around – through notebooks, the phone directory, online – to come up with a couple of numbers.

Ted Walker's brother, Freddie. This is a brash move and it will probably piss Phil Sweeney off no end, but he feels it's legitimate.

He dials the number. It rings and then goes into message. He hangs up.

The second number he has unearthed is for Gary Lynch.

It's the same story.

But this time he leaves a message.

Please give me a call.

*

Rundle sits at his usual table at the Orpheus Room, nursing a gimlet, waiting for J.J. to arrive. Don Ribcoff did his best this afternoon, but apparently the senator couldn't be dissuaded from engaging with the media pack at JFK or from then doing a couple of hastily arranged appearances on cable news shows. Rundle caught one of these back at the office and although the whole time he was watching it his heart was in his mouth nothing disastrous happened. Apart from the brace on his hand and wrist, J.J. looked good. He was calm, composed, and constantly made the point that he didn't want all of this hoopla to be a distraction from the more serious issues he and his fellow delegates had been so focused on in Paris. It was a performance, of course, but Rundle was relieved to see that J.J. seemed to be in full control of his faculties.

He's due any minute now, so hopefully they can clear things up and move on. Because Rundle has invested a huge amount in this already – time, energy, money.

He set up the Buenke operation at James Vaughan's behest, and has kept it ticking over for him, but the bottom line is if he blows the current negotiations Vaughan won't forgive him – he'll cut him loose and leave him in the wilderness, as he has done with so many others in the past.

Rundle reaches for his gimlet.

He's in too deep now to let this slip away.

He looks over at the entrance. There is a flurry of activity. This will be the senatorial entourage – handlers, advisors, security. He spots Herb Felder and one or two other people he knows. After a moment the seas part and J.J. appears. He strolls over, nodding and smiling at various people on the way. He arrives and sits down, but with his back to the room.

Rundle's eye is immediately drawn to the brace, an elaborate and uncomfortable-looking affair of wire and gauze, but it's the expression on J.J.'s face that he finds particularly disturbing. Away from the cameras now, and sitting with a family member, pressure off, he seems pale, reduced somehow, as if he needs to be taken in hand.

'How are you, J.J.?'

'I'm all right, Clark. I'm tired. It's been a crazy few days.' A waiter approaches but J.J. waves him away. 'This has been good for me, but I can't let it drift. I can't let it dissipate. I've got to take it to the next level, you know, keep the traction but change the conversation.'

Rundle stares at him. 'Change the conversation?'

'Yeah, away from Paris, get into some policy thing, an issue. Move it forward.'

Rundle nods. 'Look, J.J., I sent you down there for a reason. It was important. And this –' he points at the brace, then indicates behind him, at Herb Felder and the others '– it's all very well, and I hope it works out for you, I do, but right this minute I couldn't give a fuck about any of it.' He leans forward, hands out, pleading. 'I need to know what Kimbela said to you.'

J.J. sighs and slumps back in his chair.

'I know, Clark, I know. I've been trying.'

'You've been *trying*? I need comprehensive notes on what you guys talked about. I need minutes. Come on, J.J., you've sat on a thousand committees, you know the drill.'

'This wasn't like any committee, Clark. This was the weirdest fucking experience of my life.' He leans forward as well. 'And I'm not just talking about the shooting, which was bad enough, believe me, because I can still see . . . I can still see the pools of blood, and those little vacant, limp faces, *shit* –'

'OK, OK.' Rundle glances around. 'Take it easy.'

'But it was already weird before that, at the compound, from the very moment I arrived there. It's bizarre, he has this half-built . . . villa, with a portico and fake-looking Louis Quinze shit inside it, and then nearby there's this row of concrete shacks, like interrogation rooms or something, whatever, I don't know. And that's where we went, straight from the house into one of these, Kimbela leading the way, his permanent entourage right behind him, these heavily armed, heavily drugged *children* . . . and meanwhile all *I've* got on either side of me is a couple of pumped-up Gideon guys –'

'J.J. –'

'One of whom, by the way, turns out to be *a complete fucking psycho*.'

'J.J. –'

'I'm just telling you what happened, Clark, OK?' He shakes his head. 'So we're in this shack, right, sitting at a metal table, bare light bulb hanging from the ceiling, it's dank and smelly, and I'm waiting for . . . I don't know *what* I'm waiting for . . . a pair of pliers to be produced, a blowtorch, a chainsaw, but then in comes this little girl, eight or nine years old, real cute from a distance, but scrawny up close, and with these sunken eye sockets, like a fucking zombie or something, and she's carrying a tray of . . . *tea things*, which she then puts on the table and proceeds to serve us *tea* from, this ornate pot, these old china cups, it was the creepiest thing I've ever seen. Meanwhile Kimbela is sitting opposite me, talking his fat sweaty face off, arms flailing, every part of him in constant motion, and the thing is Clark, I'm so freaked out by this stage, I'm so fucking terrified, that I'm just not taking anything in, I'm not hearing a word he's saying.'

Rundle can feel himself deflating.

'Did you even –'

He stops and looks his brother in the eye. What was he thinking of, sending him down there? J.J. has never done anything real in his life. It's all been campaigns and poll numbers, finance bills and select committees, he's never served in the armed forces, hasn't travelled that much outside of trade delegations, and he has certainly never met anyone remotely like Arnold Kimbela before.

Rundle thinks back to when he first met the colonel himself. It was about three years ago, and in Paris of all places. A darkened apartment in the Bastille district, Rundle sitting opposite the enigmatic, chunky thirty-nine-year-old, armed guards lurking in the shadows. It was a master class, as he recalls it, in various dark arts, in contract negotiation, in price structuring, in sheer *ballsiness*. And he expected J.J. to be able to do something similar? And not even in the familiar surroundings of a western city, but actually down in the insane heat and chaos of Congo itself.

He must have been out of his mind.

'Look, J.J.,' he says, one last shot. 'Did you hear any mention of renegotiating the terms? Anything about redrafting –'

'Clark, listen to me, it's a miracle I didn't shit in my pants, OK? And if I'd known what was round the corner, on the ride back to the airstrip, I . . . Jesus, even thinking about it now.'

'Relax, J.J., would you? You did what you could, and I'm grateful.'

'I'm sorry, Clark.'

Rundle shrugs. He leans back in his chair.

Damn.

*

It comes to him as he's having a dump in the *en suite* bathroom. Humiliation. If you're looking for a unified field theory of all things Larry Bolger, then that's it, humiliation. It's the linking thread, the connective tissue, it's the recurring theme throughout his life and career. When he was a young man, for instance, his father treated him like a fool, kept comparing him unfavourably to his older brother, Frank. Then there was Paddy Norton, who bossed him around – effectively bullied him – and for the best part of twenty-five years. There was his disastrous visit to Tokyo. His interview with *Hot Press*. That series of snubs by the German Chancellor when he was EU Council president. And also, let's not forget, the ignominy of being forced out of office by the same Gang of Three who got him into office in the first place.

Bolger can't dwell on that one for too long.

But now he has, what? James Vaughan giving him the run-around and the likes of Dave Conway telling him what he is or isn't *allowed* to do.

Not to mention that little prick of a journalist.

A sudden rap on the door interrupts his train of thought.

Coming here and . . .

'Are we all right in there?'

. . . having the nerve to . . .

Bolger closes his eyes.

'Yes, Mary,' he says, '*we* are all right.'

Jesus.

Silence follows, then footsteps moving quietly away.

Bolger clenches his fists now, and winces. Something is happening.

Finally.

In agony, he fixes his gaze on the gleaming white tiles of the bathroom floor, his fists still clenched. He's going to have to do something about this, go to the doctor with it, get it seen to.

Which of course will mean only one thing. More fucking humiliation.

After a while, his mind in a fog, the pain subsides.

He finishes up, and a few minutes later he's back out in the living room, pacing up and down. Mary is running a bath and he's decided to wait until she's in it before he –

Before he –

Places the call.

Through the open door of the bathroom, the roar of the water comes to a sudden halt.

He glances over at the drinks cabinet, but doesn't feel a thing. In fact, the thought now of a drink makes him a little nauseous.

He's still hungover and suspects he will remain so well into tomorrow.

He hears Mary getting into the bath, the gentle slosh of the water, the displacement – your man, what's his name, Archimedes.

He gets his mobile phone from the table and sits down in the armchair, facing the TV. He puts on *Sky News* with the sound off. He finds the number and hits Call.

It'll be the same as before, he bets, straight into message. He's not even sure what this number is, if it's an office or home number, a service, or what.

'You have reached . . .'

Bolger rolls his eyes, waits.

'Yes, Mr Vaughan, it's Larry Bolger again. Listen, I've been thinking and I've come to a decision. You promised me that

IMF thing, and fine, maybe it didn't work out for some reason, whatever, but it seems to me that your obligation in the matter remains . . . unfulfilled.' He stares at the TV as he speaks, at the Sky newscaster, his heart pounding. 'Well, time is running out, let's put it that way. Or let's put it another way. I want a *job*. Do you understand me? A real position, something commensurate with my experience. Like we talked about. Because here's the deal. Drumcoolie Castle, yeah? Are you with me?' He clears his throat. 'I was at that table along with the rest of them, don't forget that. I heard everything. Yeah? And I followed it all afterwards, too.' He lets that hang in the air for a second. 'Now, the thing is . . . there's a nuclear option here, which I won't hesitate to use, believe me. And I think you know what I mean.' He clears his throat again. 'So I expect to hear back from you this time.'

He pauses, and hangs up.

His heart is still pounding.

He almost laughs.

*

At around eleven thirty Jimmy gets a callback from Gary Lynch.

'I got your message,' the voice says. 'So. Who are you? What do you want?'

Jimmy explains. He's a journalist. He has some questions about Susie Monaghan. Any chance they could meet?

'Susie? Holy fuck.' Lynch sounds drunk. There's noise in the background, voices, music. He's in a pub somewhere or a club.

156

'Yeah,' he then says. 'Why not. I'm in Alba, in town. I'll be here for another hour or two.'

He hangs up.

Jimmy looks at his phone.

That's it?

Does he go and meet him? It's late, but if Lynch is drunk, then yes – going on today's form. Now is probably the perfect time to go and meet him.

He gets ready in a hurry and heads out. He flags down a taxi on Strand Road and makes it into town in about twenty minutes.

Alba is a club just off George's Street, over a trendy bistro called Montmartre.

As he is going up the stairs to the club Jimmy realises that he doesn't know what Gary Lynch looks like. He's probably seen photographs of him, but none that he remembers, none that stuck. He walks into the main room, which is bright and airy, with a long bar running along the back. The place is crowded but not hectically so, not as crowded on a Thursday night as it would have been a couple of years ago.

There is music. It is loud, pounding.

He is greeted by a hostess.

'Hi,' he shouts. 'Gary Lynch?'

The hostess smiles and points over to a side room.

'Can I take your jacket?'

Jimmy shakes his head. 'No, you're grand,' he says, and smiles back. He makes his way through the crowd. As he approaches the side room, he sees that it's a small lounge area with leather sofas and armchairs. Two couples, facing each other across a low table, occupy one part of the room. They're drinking pints and talking loudly. To the right, sitting alone in a deep arm-chair, and looking slightly forlorn, is a guy in a suit. He's about forty. He's slim, has thinning dark hair and a goatee. In his right hand he's holding a glass of what looks like whiskey or brandy.

Jimmy leans forward. 'Gary?'

The man looks up. He seems puzzled. After a moment, he says, 'Holy shit, that was fast. You're the journalist?'

Jimmy nods and sits down in the armchair next to the one Gary Lynch is sitting in.

He holds out a hand, 'Jimmy Gilroy.'

They shake.

'So,' Gary Lynch says, 'Susie Monaghan? That was another lifetime.' He grunts. 'Man, another *planet*.'

Jimmy leans forward to hear properly.

'In what sense?' he says.

'Well.' Lynch takes a sip from his glass and then explains that, what was it, three, four years ago, he was a corporate execut-ive on a salary of two hundred and fifty K per annum, with the same again in bonuses and perks. That he was footloose and fancy free, always had the latest Beemer, city breaks every fuck-ing weekend. But that *two* years ago he lost his job, company upped sticks and relocated to Poland, go figure. And that since *then* he's done a stint as a taxi-driver, he's worked at a call centre and he's now the manager of a shoe shop around the corner on George's Street. 'Keeping the head above water, you know?'

'Yeah,' Jimmy says, debating whether or not he should pitch in with a reference to his own circumstances.

'I'm only glad I never got married,' Lynch goes on. 'Though I came close with Susie. Guys I know from the old days? Stuck now with kids, debts, mortgages they can't afford. It's a nightmare.'

Looking around, Jimmy wonders where some of these guys are tonight – at home, probably, watching *CSI* or an old Leinster schools cup final on Setanta.

'Talk to me,' Jimmy says, 'about that weekend, the conference. Drumcoolie Castle.'

Lynch looks at him and laughs nervously. 'Jesus, cut to the chase, why don't you? What kind of journalist are you anyway? Is this an article or –'

'I'm writing a biography of Susie,' Jimmy says firmly. This may no longer be true, but it sounds good, and it works.

'Oh, well then,' Lynch says, nodding his head sagely, 'a biography. Cool. Am I going to be in it?'

'That depends. I reckon so. You were engaged to Susie, weren't you?'

'Yeah. For a while.' He takes another sip from his glass. 'But I couldn't keep up with her, to be honest. And I was small potatoes anyway, where Susie was concerned. I may have effectively been on half a million per annum, but back then that was nothing. I didn't own anything, I didn't *run* anything. What Susie needed was someone with assets, property, money in the bank. Staying power. There were guys before me like that, but I guess they didn't work out either. And probably for the same reason. Couldn't keep up with her.'

'Meaning?'

'Oh.' He groans. 'Do I have to spell it out? She was a fucking pig when it came to the coke.' He clicks his tongue and shakes his head. 'What she was, basically, was a coke whore, no other

159

word for it. That's what was going on that weekend. It was all about the charlie.'

Jimmy's heart sinks. Does he want to hear this?

'What do you mean?'

'Look, I'm not a hundred per cent certain, but I had this feeling at the time that she was involved in setting up some sort of a . . . deal, and a pretty big one. I bumped into her late on the Saturday night and she more or less told me that straight out. But when I pressed her for details, she went all coy.'

'A coke deal?'

'I assumed so, yeah.'

A bar girl appears at this point and Lynch holds up his glass. Jimmy nods at her and says, 'Yeah, whatever that is, and I'll have the same.'

The bar girl smiles and makes a face that says, gents, er, I'm not a mind reader.

'Oh, sorry,' Lynch says, 'a triple Hennessy.'

Jimmy swallows and nods.

The bar girl retreats.

'So,' Jimmy says, after a suitable pause, 'why did she go for the helicopter ride? The story doing the rounds was that she was trying to make *you* jealous. Heading off with Niall Feeley.'

'Hah. I heard that one, too, and you know what? Niall Feeley was a close friend of mine, but he was big into the show tunes as well as the paragliding, so that doesn't wash. There was something else going on.'

He stops there, looks into his glass and swirls what's left in it around.

Jimmy waits.

Lynch then knocks the brandy back in one go. He holds the

glass aloft, allowing the burning sensation to work its little bit of magic.

Jimmy fights the impulse to reach over and shake him. After a moment, he says, quietly, 'So, what do you think was going on?'

'I don't know. For the life of me.' He pauses. 'Jimmy, isn't it?'

Jimmy nods.

'Look, Jimmy, Susie was great, she was funny, she was different – she was the light of *my* fucking life for a while, I can tell you that – but by the end there, by that weekend, she was in serious trouble, she was strung out, and I just didn't want to get involved. I didn't want to know. So what I'm telling you is, there was something going on, sure . . . but what that was exactly? I haven't a bloody clue.'

Jimmy is about to respond to this when the bar girl re-appears. She lays the two drinks down and hands Jimmy the bill.

Thirty-eight euro. For *fuck's* sake.

He takes out his wallet, hands over a fifty and waits for the change. He doesn't look at the bar girl. When she's gone, he lifts his glass and takes a sip from it.

Lynch does the same.

Then Jimmy says, 'What about Ted Walker?'

'No, Ted organised the whole thing, him and Niall. They were showing off, trying to impress Ben Schnitz. It was all a bit . . . it was a *scene*. If you catch my drift.'

Jimmy nods along. Then something occurs to him.

'What about the other guy? The Italian? Gianni something. Bon . . . Bonacci?'

Lynch raises his eyebrows and stares into space for a while, thinking. 'Yeah,' he says eventually. 'Right, the Italian guy. I forgot about him.'

'Was he . . .?'

'No, he was . . . come to think of it, he was with Susie, but not . . . he wasn't *with* her, I mean, as such, no one thought that, because he was a weedy little guy, short, with glasses. But you know that was typical Susie as well, she was always picking up strays and oddballs. She was a tease. She'd play with them for a while and then send them packing, usually with an irreversible hard-on and a broken heart for their troubles.'

'So he wasn't *with* her, strictly speaking, and he wasn't *with* the paragliding contingent?'

Lynch considers this. 'No.'

'Then what do you –'

'I don't know. He wasn't even an executive. He was some kind of a UN inspector or something.'

'Right.'

Lynch puts his glass down and stands up. 'I'm going to the jacks,' he mutters.

Jimmy watches him as he wanders off. None of this is clear. But at the same time, in a way, it's crystal clear.

Because it's the same thing he's heard over and over again. Directly or indirectly.

This isn't about Susie Monaghan.

Which means it's about someone else.

And it seems obvious to Jimmy now – without any evidence at all – that that someone else is Gianni Bonacci.

*

162

Clark Rundle stands under the sidewalk canopy and watches the evening traffic drift by on Park. This is another of those times when he wishes he still smoked. The doorman is only a few feet behind him and probably has a pack of butts in his coat pocket, or inside somewhere, behind his little desk or in his cubbyhole. But what's Rundle going to do here? Turn and ask the guy, maybe make a face, all pally and conspiratorial, wait for the pack to be produced . . . then someone comes along and he gets caught bumming a cigarette off of Jimmy Vaughan's doorman?

Nice.

Besides, it's more than a smoke he needs.

More than an afternoon with Nora. More than a week in the Bahamas.

He rubs his hands together in the cold.

It's . . .

A moment later, Don Ribcoff's limo pulls up at the kerb. The doorman appears from behind Rundle, has it covered. Ribcoff emerges from the back of the car looking solemn, anxious even.

'Clark.'

'Don.'

They spoke briefly on the phone a little earlier. Ribcoff explained about the call he got from Dave Conway in Dublin and Rundle explained about his sit-down with J.J.

A follow-up with the old man seemed inevitable.

But when Rundle got on to him Vaughan said he was busy, said he had some people around and could maybe squeeze out ten minutes if they showed up before seven thirty. Rundle felt like saying he was busy too, but that seeing as how they were looking at a potential catastrophe here – a total and utter melt-down, in fact – he for one didn't have a problem *cancelling his fucking dinner plans*.

What he said was, OK, whatever, they'd see him at his place at seven twenty.

Rundle and Ribcoff go through the lobby now and take the private elevator up to Vaughan's apartment. The interior of the elevator cab is something to behold, with its wood panelling, its brass insets, its chandelier and mirrors, its little red velvet bench. Rundle compares it to the stainless steel panels and tubular handrails of his own elevator cab in the Celestial. If that one is maybe a bit too spare and minimalist, a bit too late modern, Vaughan's one is an outrageous throwback to the Gilded Age.

Ribcoff looks around and makes a low whistling sound.

'You think this is bad,' Rundle says, 'wait till you see the actual apartment.'

They are greeted in the entry foyer by one of Vaughan's staff and then ushered into the library. In this high-ceilinged, mahogany-panelled room the two men wait – and for the best part of their allotted ten minutes. When Vaughan eventually appears, wearing a tuxedo and smoking a cigar, he seems a little preoccupied. He makes no attempt at small talk, nor does he ask them to sit down or offer them anything to drink.

'So?'

Rundle begins. He explains that J.J. bottled it and came back from Congo with nothing. The Buenke incident has been contained, he says, but they currently have no idea what Kimbela's position is vis-à-vis them, vis-à-vis the Chinese, nothing. On top of *which*, he goes on, there appears to be some sort of a situation brewing over in Dublin.

Vaughan furrows his brow.

Ribcoff takes a step forward. 'I got a call this afternoon,' he says. 'From Dave Conway. Remember him?'

Vaughan nods.

'Well, he told me that Larry Bolger has been hitting the bottle, running his mouth off. Seems he spoke to some journalist.'

Vaughan's reaction to this is somewhat muted.

After a long silence, Rundle says, 'You're not surprised by that, Jimmy?'

'No, I'm not.' The old man gives him a cryptic look and then takes a puff from his cigar. 'The truth is, Larry Bolger has been running his mouth off to *me*. Leaving voice messages. It's actually getting out of hand. It's as close now to blackmail as makes no difference.'

Rundle's heart sinks. 'Jesus H. Christ.'

Ribcoff exhales audibly, but doesn't say anything.

Vaughan paces back and forth across the room, taking occasional puffs from his cigar.

Rundle takes a step backwards and leans on the end of the red leather couch behind him. What he actually does need, thinking about it, is a week in the Bahamas *with* Nora.

And a carton of Lucky Strikes.

Which'd just be for openers.

'Don,' Vaughan says eventually. 'We've got to do something about this.'

Ribcoff nods in acknowledgement.

Vaughan points his cigar at him. 'Come to my office first

thing in the morning. We can talk about it then.' He pauses. 'And Clark?'

'Yeah?'

'Seems to me that you need to take a trip.'

Rundle's stomach does a little somersault.

'Excuse me?'

'You need to take a *trip*,' Vaughan repeats. 'To the Congo. Democratic Republic *of*. See our friend. Get some answers.' He studies the glowing ash at the tip of his cigar. 'Because it's clear that your idiot of a brother wasn't up to the job.' He lets that hang in the air for a moment. 'Though presumably *you* will be.' He looks up, meets Rundle's hard stare. 'Won't you?'

6

'*Pronto.*'

Holding up the notebook, Jimmy Gilroy braces himself.

'Er . . . *posso parlare con la Signora Bonacci, per favore?*'

'*Non e a casa addesso.*'

What?

'Er –'

'*Chi parla?*'

Shit.

Panic.

That didn't take long.

'Er, *non parlo italiano.*'

There is a pause.

'English?'

'Yes. English. I *speak* English. I'm Irish. *Sono irlandese.*'

'Oh.' Another pause. '*Irlandese.*'

Jimmy isn't sure but even after these few brief seconds . . . does he detect a change of tone?

'Yes, er . . . *si.*' What does he think he's doing? He got one of the students across the hall to come over and write a few phrases down in this notebook. But the hope was that Signora Bonacci might have a bit of English herself and that they could muddle through.

'What I can . . . what . . . what is it you want?'

The voice is young, female. Signor*ina* Bonacci?

'My name is Jimmy Gilroy,' he says, swivelling in his chair. 'I am a journalist.' The next bit he already feels guilty about, because – he doesn't know – is it even true? 'I am investigating the air crash three years ago in which Gianni Bonacci was killed.'

'*O dio mio.*'

Jimmy winces. 'I'm sorry.'

There is a long silence, and then, 'I am Francesca Bonacci. Gianni's daughter.'

'Hello.' Jimmy winces again. How young is she? A teenager? A kid? It's hard to tell. Bonacci was forty-five when he died. 'May I ask how old you are, Francesca?'

'Seventeen.'

He needs to be careful here.

'Look, I'm sorry to disturb you in this way, but . . . I would like to speak with your mother sometime, if that is possible. Does she speak English?'

'No. She does not speak *any* English.'

This sounds slightly defensive, even a bit confrontational.

Has he offended her? 'Could I ask *you* some questions?' he then says, with nowhere else to go. 'Or ask her some questions through you?'

'What kind of questions? What is it you are investigating, mister, er . . .?'

'Gilroy. But please, call me Jimmy.' He pauses. 'I'm not sure what I'm investigating, Francesca, and that's the truth. I realise this must be very painful for you, and I apologise for the intrusion, but I just need to gather some information first before I can –'

'Gather?'

'What? Er . . . collect. Get.' He looks around. Where was he? 'Before I can . . .' He trails off, unsure how to proceed.

'Accuse.'

'Pardon?'

'Accuse. Before you can accuse somebody. Is that what you mean?'

Jimmy looks again at the notebook in his hand, stares at the spidery scrawl, as though it were some type of code, something he could use to turn this situation around. But the fact is, there's nothing left here to decipher – these are just simple phrases and he has already used them up.

He tosses the notebook onto the desk.

'I don't know,' he says, almost to himself, 'maybe. But accuse who, and of what?'

Francesca Bonacci scoffs at this. 'Now you are looking for answers? *Now*? What about three years ago, eh?'

That's exactly what Maria Monaghan said to him.

'What do you mean?'

'When *we* wanted answers to those questions, my mother,

my uncles, the lawyers, no one would talk to us, in Ireland, no one would give us any information. We found what was the phrase, someone told me, a *brick wall*.'

She's angry. It also strikes Jimmy how remarkably self-possessed she seems to be for seventeen. But at the same time, what is she saying?

'I don't understand, Francesca. Questions? Answers? If what happened was an accident –'

'Oh, *per piacere*,' – from the tone he takes this to mean *oh, please* – 'you really believe that?'

'Well, it's what I'm trying to find out.'

There is silence for a moment. Then she says, 'What is your e-mail address?'

His impulse is to ask why, but he just gives it to her. This could well be a step in the right direction.

'You will need a translator,' she says.

He's not sure what this means. Something she is going to send him?

'OK. No problem.'

'I must go now,' she says.

He doesn't argue. 'Thank you, Francesca.'

The line goes dead.

Jimmy closes the phone and puts it down. He sits back and stares at the computer screen.

He's exhausted.

It took him over an hour and several phone calls to locate that number. This was followed by an awkward twenty minutes with the student from across the hall, who was clearly hungover and kept insisting it'd be easier if he made the call himself. But Jimmy couldn't take the chance.

Then . . . *questions, answers, a brick wall . . . you really believe that?* Bonacci's widow and daughter making the same claim that Larry Bolger made?

A few minutes later things get even knottier when he hears the ping of an incoming e-mail. It's from Francesca. There is no message, just a single hyperlink. He clicks on it and his browser opens up onto the homepage of what looks like an Italian news website.

At first it makes no sense to him. It's in Italian. He doesn't understand any of it. He considers bothering the student across the hall again when suddenly something comes into focus for him. He recognises a few names clustered together – Enrico Mattei, Giuseppe Pinelli, Aldo Moro, Marco Biagi, Carlo Giuliani. As far as he remembers, from things he's read and seen over the years, these men were all high-profile victims of political assassination.

In some form or other. At least in *theory*.

At which point he realises this must be a website devoted to, or specialising in, Italian conspiracy theories. Aldo Moro, for example, was the ex-prime minister who was kidnapped and killed in 1978, allegedly by the Red Brigades. Enrico Mattei was a politician who challenged the oligopoly of the international oil markets and died in a mysterious plane crash in the early 1960s.

Jimmy flicks around the site for a while, scans various chunks of text at random. Eventually, in a sidebar, he comes across Gianni Bonacci's name. He is unable to decipher the text that surrounds it, but the very presence of Bonacci's name *here*, on a website of this nature, surely indicates that –

What?

When Jimmy Googled Bonacci's name before, he filtered out any stuff that wasn't in English. The stuff he did look at was UN-related and fairly uninteresting. He Googles the name again now and sees that there are references to him on dozens of Italian sites, many of which – at a glance – also contain references to Mattei, Moro and others. In addition to this, he repeatedly comes across words such as *omicidio, assassinio, vittima, cospirazione.*

From what Jimmy can make out, Bonacci would be fairly low down on any league table of political assassinations, but the mere fact that his death is perceived by some people in this way at all comes as quite a shock.

And there must be a reason for it.

He swivels his chair around, looks across the room at his bookshelves.

Mustn't there?

Or is even posing this question a first and dangerous step into the delusional, self-perpetuating fog that is the mindset of the conspiracy theorist?

He swivels back around.

It doesn't matter, though. It's fine. Someone else's perception of the truth – however outlandish or irrational – is a valid starting point for any investigation.

He sets up a reply to Francesca's e-mail. He thinks about what to say. He starts typing. But when he is half a sentence in, his buzzer sounds.

Damn.

He gets up and goes over to the intercom, presses the button. 'Yeah. Who is it?'

'Hi, Jimmy. It's Phil Sweeney.'

Jimmy closes his eyes for a second. He turns away from the intercom. He groans.

Why didn't he just leave it?

*

Rundle gets up at six and puts on some coffee. He takes a shower and then spends at least twenty minutes in the walk-in closet choosing which of his fifty or sixty suits to wear. There is no real reason for him to do this. He doesn't have any particular thing on today. But he finds it relaxes him, the ritual of it, moving down the line, checking out the different fabrics, feeling the subtle variations in texture . . . vicuna, merino, cashmere, silk.

It's distracting. It keeps his mind occupied.

Though admitting this fact sort of defeats the purpose.

So he eventually just picks one out at random – a charcoal grey William Fioravanti.

He goes back to the kitchen and pours himself a cup of coffee.

The thing is, he doesn't mind travelling to the Congo – in a way he's looking forward to it, taking the reins, settling this thing once and for all – but what he does resent is being *told* to go. It's the attitude he has a problem with, the tone. Rundle is well used to Vaughan's quasi-imperial style – he grew up with it, and most of the time he even enjoys it – but last night was simply too much. The contempt Vaughan displayed for Rundle, and right there in front of Don Ribcoff, was . . .

Well, it was unacceptable.

And it wasn't only the offhand manner, or the business of the ten-minute 'audience'. No, Vaughan had said earlier he was having some people around, but it soon became clear that these weren't just any people. Crossing the foyer on his way out, Rundle caught a glimpse through the door of the main reception room, which was ajar, and he's pretty sure he recognised Dick Cheney standing there talking to the CEO of Chipco and the Chairman of the Joint Chiefs. Nice little get-together. And what, all of them casually over for canapés and a glass of white wine? A quick tour of the walk-in humidor?

Rundle could care less about Vaughan's social life, but he *has* taken to seeing himself – at some level – in the role of Vaughan's protégé. He also knows that Vaughan has come to depend on *him* for certain things – that the Buenke project, for example, always significant, has assumed an even-greater urgency of late. So why, Rundle wonders, would Vaughan exclude him from such a high-level gathering of luminaries and policy-makers? Why would he have him scuttled in and out of the apartment as though he were no more than an errand boy?

Rundle doesn't wish to be unkind, but he half suspects that James Vaughan may be succumbing to a mild form of dementia, a strain of clinical paranoia perhaps, and one that is specifically associated with old age. Vaughan settles in his mind that he can no longer fulfil his ambitions unaided, that he is now dependent on this younger man – and he kicks out in rebellion, as though to ward off death, to deny its proximity.

One day he lionises the younger man, the next day he humiliates him.

Rundle considers himself a student of human nature and can understand the dynamic at play here – not that he enjoys being on the receiving end of it. Nail this Congo thing, however, and maybe the game changes. Maybe he'll have Vaughan exactly where he wants him.

Until then he can put up with the mood swings and the abuse.

Rundle finishes his coffee and gets moving.

Outside, his car is waiting.

On the way to the office, Thirty-fourth Street flitting past, he makes some notes. If this really is to be a game changer, he'll need to be heading down there with some serious leverage under his arm. J.J. wasn't authorised to make any offers; he was just supposed to listen. But the time for that has passed.

He pencils in a few calls for the morning.

Then, of course, he'll have to discuss travel and security arrangements with Don Ribcoff.

*

Phil Sweeney arrives at the open door and gives it a little tap.

Jimmy is at his computer, pretending to be absorbed in something. He waits a couple of seconds before looking up from the screen. 'Phil, how's it going?'

'Not bad, Jimmy, not bad.'

'Come in, sit down.'

Phil Sweeney has aged quite a bit since Jimmy last saw him. As usual, he's wearing a very expensive suit, and he's got the shoes, the watch, the cologne. But he's also lost weight, and it doesn't look like the kind you lose because you're eating better and taking care of yourself. He is tall and imposing, no change there, but definitely more stooped than Jimmy remembers.

'So,' Sweeney says, not sitting down. 'You know why I'm here.'

Jimmy stands up. 'You want some coffee?'

'Yeah, that's why I'm here, Jimmy, I want some *coffee*.'

Jimmy sighs, sits back down. 'Tell you the truth, Phil, I *don't* know why you're here. Unless you've got something new you want to talk about.'

'Don't get smart, Jimmy. This is serious shit and *you're* in over your head.'

'If it's as serious as you say, Phil, then I think everyone's in over their head.'

That sounds clever, but Jimmy isn't really sure what it means.

'Listen to me,' Sweeney says, palms forward, switching gears. 'Let's back up here for a minute, yeah? Larry Bolger is not a well man. It's pretty obvious he's got a drink problem. There's depression there, too. Adjustment issues. All *I* was trying to do was help him out.'

Jimmy says nothing, nods along.

'So when he starts mouthing on about this or that, the past, making bizarre statements, like he did today, I think we can safely assume it's the bottle talking, yeah? And to be honest with you, I didn't realise he was that far gone.'

Looking at Sweeney, Jimmy feels a little strange. When he was younger, and the old man was still alive, Jimmy was in awe of Phil Sweeney, afraid of him even. When the old man was dying, and for a while afterwards, Sweeney was a big man in his life, a commanding presence. He exuded confidence and authority. You listened to him. You didn't cross him.

Now Sweeney is stooped, tired-looking, maybe a little sick himself.

Now someone is about to cross him.

'Phil,' Jimmy says quietly, 'we've been over it. On the phone. This isn't about Larry Bolger. I'm not interested in Larry Bolger. I just want to look into what he said, check it out, see if there's anything to it.'

Sweeney hesitates, then explodes. 'Oh, for fuck's sake, Jimmy, do you not *get* it? How many different ways do I have to *say* it? Back off. Leave it alone.' He leans forward. '*This isn't for you.*'

Jimmy stares at him in disbelief. 'Don't you see that telling me that only makes it worse?'

'I'm warning you, Jimmy. For the last time. Jesus Christ.' Sweeney is shouting now, pointing his finger. 'And don't forget something, you *owe* me.'

Jimmy stands up. 'I do, yeah, but not this, Phil, I don't owe you *this*. You helped me along, fine, and I'm grateful –'

'Damn sure I helped you along, Jimmy. But I also played you like a fucking fiddle. Every story I fed you had an agenda, *my* agenda.' Sweeney makes a sound here, a laugh, but it's hard, mirthless. 'And you were *so* easy. You were *so* eager to get ahead.'

Jimmy swallows. He'll need a little time to process that one. 'Yeah,' he says, 'for all the good it did me.'

'Oh, and what, that's *my* fault? Take some responsibility for yourself, would you?' Sweeney glances around the room. 'I mean, look at where you live. It's a shithole. What do you think your old man would make of this?'

Jimmy stiffens. He doesn't answer.

'What do you think he'd make of you, now, today?' Sweeney shakes his head. 'Dec Gilroy. I'm telling you, *there* was a man who knew how to play the game, knew when to speak up and when to shut up.'

Jimmy takes a step forward. 'Shut up about *what*, though? Something like *this*? I don't think so, Phil. In fact, it was playing the game, playing your game, that made him sick in the first place, shutting up about stuff . . . but it was the small stuff, the tawdry stuff, the personal stuff, not anything like this.' He pauses. 'And tell me Phil, do you actually know what *this* is, what we're talking about here?'

Phil Sweeney stares back at him. He doesn't answer.

'A helicopter crash, six people dead, *but not an accident*? That's the allegation that came out of Larry Bolger's mouth. And that's what you want *me* to shut up about? That's what you think Dec Gilroy would shut up about?'

'Yeah, but come on, it's ridiculous –'

'Is it? I don't know, Phil. I've already peeled away a layer or two and I'm not so sure.' He pauses. 'And how can *you* be so sure?'

'Because –'

'Who are you representing anyway? Not Larry Bolger surely, not directly. And I doubt that it's Ted Walker's family, so –'

'*Shut up.*'

Jimmy is taken aback at this, but to his surprise he does shut up.

He turns around and goes back to the desk. He sits down.

There is silence for a while. Phil Sweeney remains standing in the middle of the room, swaying gently, almost imperceptibly, like a tall building.

Jimmy closes his eyes. An image comes to him, of the old man lying in his bed, gaunt, reduced, getting weaker by the day, diminishing, but never diminished . . .

Eventually, in a quiet voice, Phil Sweeney says, 'What layers, Jimmy? Peeled away what layers? What have you . . .'

Jimmy opens his eyes, looks up, meets his gaze. 'Just stuff, Phil. Leads.' He lays a hand on some papers on the desk.

Phil Sweeney stares at him for a moment, then exhales loudly. He turns and heads for the door, slamming it shut as he leaves.

Jimmy moves his hand from the papers on the desk to the keyboard. He straightens up. He clicks a few keys and within seconds is on the Ryanair website checking out prices and times for a flight to Verona.

*

All through the function – the annual Leinster Vintners Society lunch – Larry Bolger feels horribly queasy. He'd forgotten that he promised to attend this and when Mary reminded him of it earlier he immediately started looking for a reason to cancel. But she was having none of it. He attends very few events these days, only the occasional dinner or speaking engagement, and Mary's feeling is that he needs to get out more – especially after what happened yesterday, and *especially* if he wants to get back in the game, as he keeps saying.

But Bolger doesn't understand why kick-starting this get-out-more policy has to coincide with his first hangover in a decade. Or is it his second already? A thick, extended hangover it is anyway, one laced with shame, anxiety, dread, and one that, just possibly, it's beginning to feel, might never end. He doesn't have to speak today, which is a gargantuan mercy, but he does have to smile and chat and act like he's on the brink of staging a military coup in order to get this benighted country *back on its feet*.

He has to shake a lot of hands, and the comments come thick and fast.

You can't beat Bolger.

Go on, you good thing.

But he gets through it, even managing to crack the odd joke himself.

The queasiness never lifts, though – and whenever the details of this bloody mess he's created for himself pop into his head, which is about once every ten minutes, it actually intensifies. Talking to the young journalist was bad enough, but leaving that message for James Vaughan was insane. It remains to be seen what the consequences of any of this will be, but it's hard to imagine that they won't be extreme.

On the return journey, alone in the back of the state car – which is provided to him for life by the Irish taxpayer – Bolger reacquaints himself with that purest form of melancholy, the brittle, unforgiving, all-pervading kind that comes with an acute hangover. As he gazes out at the passing city, his city, he sees no route forward anymore, no plausible future for himself, nothing new beyond what he's got, which is retirement and anonymity, and a curdling sense of his own worth.

Because his last act as a political animal may well prove to be that pathetic phone call to James Vaughan. Silence and exile maybe, but certainly not cunning.

I want a job . . . or else . . .

Vaughan isn't going to take a threat like that seriously. He isn't even going to dignify it with a response. But it also means that Bolger has effectively disqualified himself from consideration for any future employment opportunities – proper ones, at any rate. International ones. The only kind he's interested in.

At the hotel, things are quiet and he manages to get across the lobby and into an elevator without having to engage with any staff members or random, excitable guests. On the way up it occurs to him that his hangover might actually be far enough along now for him to be in danger of . . . a little bit of . . .

Temptation.

A little bit of recidivism.

Very sweet, and very welcome.

Because frankly, what difference would it make?

Walking along the corridor, he feels his body chemistry stirring.

It would make a difference to Mary, he supposes, but maybe Mary is just going to have to get used to it.

Anyway, she's out at the moment.

He gets to the door of the apartment and as he's opening it he hears the phone ringing.

Shit.

He gets inside and grabs the cordless unit from the table.

'Hello?'

'Mr Bolger?'

'Speaking.'

He doesn't recognise the voice. Not many people have this number.

'Good afternoon, Mr Bolger, my name is Bernard Lund from Adelphi Solutions in London.'

An accent. Australian, or maybe South African.

'Who? Adel—'

'Adelphi Solutions. We are an affiliate of the Jordan Group.'

The name's vaguely familiar. He glances over at the drinks cabinet. 'OK, Mr Lund.'

'I am calling on behalf of a private client –'

Bolger's eyes widen. 'Sorry, what . . . *private*?'

'Yes.'

There is brief silence.

'And?'

'Well, we were wondering if you would you be available to present for an interview on Monday of next week? In London?'

'An interview?'

'Yes, Mr Bolger. I am not at liberty to be more specific over the phone, as I'm sure you will appreciate, but our client is looking to promote a suitable candidate for a high-level position in a leading international regulatory agency.'

*

Ruth groans. 'Not *again*.'

'I got it,' Conway says, and rolls out of the bed.

He was wide awake in any case.

Stomach jumping, head racing.

He wanders down the corridor and into Jack's room, the small night lamp by the cot illuminating this cyclorama of Pooh and Piglet and Tigger.

Tiny face looking up.

Wide awake, too.

And displaying something like smug satisfaction. No sign of the distress he was clearly faking half a minute earlier.

Conway reaches down and pulls him up, rests his head on his shoulder.

Molly and Danny were always good sleepers. From day one, Jack was a nightmare.

Conway brings him downstairs. He heads towards the kitchen, but stops at the door, hesitates. It's not a bottle Jack wants, it's company, body heat, someone else's pulse and rhythm.

He turns back. They go into the big reception room at the front.

Over to the window.

Conway looks out at the darkness, which is tinged now with the merest hint of blue. The tall trees beyond the lawn are swaying in the wind.

He can hear Jack breathing, a tiny whistle, back to sleep already.

So.

Where was he? Larry Bolger. Don Ribcoff. Susie Monaghan.

Fuck.

Couple out walking their dog.

Fuck.

Black Vine people on Monday, and a big part of what they want to talk about, apparently, is the First Continental deal.

Fuck, fuck, fuck.

It's all going round in circles.

And he can't make it stop.

He turns, wanders over to the sofa.

The jumping in his stomach won't stop either. Which means *he's* not going to get any sleep. A drink would smother it, but only for a while. Then he'd have to have another. And another.

It wouldn't work.

Besides, it's too late. Too close to morning.

In a way, he'd prefer to have a headache, because with a headache, you can't think straight. It drowns everything out, blurs everything. With this, it's different. What you're thinking *is* what you're feeling – in an objective correlative sort of way, each stabbing sensation a specific reminder of some awful fact or memory.

He sits down in the semi-darkness, settles Jack in his arms.

Swallows.

Earlier Ruth asked, in passing, why it was so long since they'd been to Guilbaud's.

Conway laughed at her.

Doesn't she get it?

The house here? The stables? *This* little bastard? His inheritance? Any sense of entitlement he might be expected to feel growing up? Let *alone* one more dinner at Guilbaud's for Mum and Dad?

It's all gone. It's over.

Effectively.

Not that he said that to her, or anything like it, but maybe he should have. From the perspective of 4 a.m. it seems self-evident, undeniable.

It's not *her* perspective, though. It's his, and is based on stuff only he knows. It's also a perspective he resolves not to carry with him through the weekend, resolves not to impose on Ruth, on the kids. This is partly because he's aware he'd more than likely crack under the pressure. Which wouldn't be pleasant, or edifying, for anyone.

And partly because he *has* to believe there's still a chance.

*

Jimmy spends Saturday morning trawling websites for references to Gianni Bonacci and builds up quite a collection of articles and quotes, none of which he understands a word of. In the afternoon he goes and knocks on the door of the students' apartment across the hall. The engineering one answers, looking tired and not a little bleary.

'How's it going?' Rubbing his eyes. 'Jimmy, isn't it?'

'Yeah. Not bad, thanks. Er, I can't remember your –'

'Matt.'

'Right. Is Finbarr around?'

The modern languages one.

'Yeah, come on in.'

The place is in semi-darkness, windows closed, curtains drawn. The air is dense, toxic.

'Sit down,' Matt says, turning. 'And, er, 'scuse the . . .' He waves a hand around to indicate the entire apartment. 'I'll get Finbarr.'

Jimmy doesn't sit. He looks down at a low table in front of the sofa – coffee mugs, sticky spoons, ashtrays, controllers, remotes, crushed cans, crisp packets, socks.

Last time he was in here was months ago, and it was late at night, and he was drunk.

He's not drunk now and would very much like to leave.

'*Ciao, bello.*'

He turns around to see Finbarr emerging from a bedroom. Sweats and a T-shirt, glasses, stubble, thick curly black hair.

Jimmy was going to ask Finbarr to translate a few things for him but now he decides against it.

Let Francesca do all the explaining.

'Hi, Finbarr.'

'What can I do you for at this ungodly hour?' There's a beat. 'What time is it anyway?'

'It's three o'clock,' Jimmy says. Another beat. 'In the afternoon.'

A loud groan.

'Miss something?'

Finbarr looks at him. 'No, just . . . where does all the *time* go, you know?'

'Tell me about it. Listen, I'm going to Italy on Monday morning and I was wondering if you'd keep an eye on the place for me.'

'Sure.'

'Thanks. Let me give you my mobile number.'

He takes a page from his notebook and writes it down.

Finbarr looks at it. 'Where are you headed? What part?'

'Verona. Flying to Treviso.'

'Cool.'

'Ever been there?'

'Once. Day trip from Venice.' He scratches his belly. 'It's gorgeous.'

'Glad to hear it.'

They move towards the door.

'So,' Finbarr stifling a yawn, 'what's the scoop?'

Jimmy steps out into the corridor, turns around, looks at Finbarr. 'The scoop? I'm not sure, to tell you the truth.' He clicks his tongue. 'Remains to be seen.'

*

At Mass on Sunday morning, during the homily – that Zen

space between the Gospel and the Eucharist – Bolger goes over the situation one more time in his head. He thinks he's got it figured out. James Vaughan has capitulated, but very much on his own terms. Which is typical of the man. He's not folding outright, he's playing a little hardball first, saying fine, you want a job that bad, *here's* a job.

Now, it may not be what Bolger had in mind, he may even have to jump through a few hoops to get it, but – and this would seem to be Vaughan's point – given Bolger's behaviour of late, his recalcitrance, to put it mildly, isn't running an international regulatory agency about as much as he can reasonably expect?

No real argument from Bolger there, and he can decipher the code, as well – do *this* right for a couple of years, behave, and who knows? Besides, it's often performance at these quiet, under-the-radar jobs that really counts when it comes to choosing candidates for the bigger, more high-profile jobs later on.

Not to get ahead of himself or anything.

He glances around, at the congregation, up at the priest.

It still surprises Bolger that his own little bit of hardball actually paid off. It wasn't so much a high-risk strategy, being honest about it, as sheer recklessness on his part. Still, Vaughan seems to have responded to it, and who knows, maybe even on some level respects him for it.

He's trying to be low-key with Mary about the whole thing, to play it cool, but it's not easy. After Mass, they're having lunch in town with Lisa, and he won't be able to resist telling *her*.

Of course, Bolger has no details yet, no idea of what the job will entail. Or of where they'll be based.

Brussels, maybe, or Strasbourg.

Or London – given that that's where the interview is taking place. In fact, he wouldn't mind London at all, and is looking forward to his trip there tomorrow.

The priest wraps up his homily, turns from the lectern and walks back to the altar.

Bolger shuffles forward and kneels.

He isn't superstitious, but he's almost reluctant to admit it – this is the most excited, the most energised, he has felt in a long time.

*

Conway has been doing well all weekend, compartmentalising like fuck, spending some time with his family, and some with his legal team, but never enough with either, or with anyone else, to lose perspective. Until late on Sunday evening, that is, when the doorbell rings and he opens it to find Phil Sweeney standing there, looking – is Conway imagining it? – slightly the worse for wear.

'Phil. This is a surprise.'

More than. It's not like he's ever told Phil Sweeney to drop by the house if he happened to be passing. Their relationship is a business one, conducted mainly over the phone or by e-mail. Down through the years, there have been sensitive issues, of course, and conversations that have occasionally crossed a shadowy line between the professional and the personal, but they've maintained their distance.

That's not what this is.

'Can I come in? Have a question I need to ask.'

Conway stands back, gets the tell-tale whiff from Sweeney's breath as he passes.

They go into the main reception room. Conway automatically heads for where the booze is kept.

'Drink?'

'Yeah, whiskey.' Some throat clearing. 'Please.'

As Conway fixes the drinks, thinking maybe this isn't such a good idea, Sweeney – standing right behind him – starts talking.

'I can't do anything about Jimmy Gilroy, Dave, I tried, he's got his teeth into this thing, and . . . you said so yourself, he's young, he thinks he's Bob fucking Woodward, thinks he's – I don't know – *on* to something. But the thing is, and here's my question, how *could* he be? *On* to something, I mean?' Conway listening, not moving, bottle suspended over a glass. 'I flagged this Susie Monaghan thing for you because my understanding is that you don't want anything out there drawing attention to the First Continental deal. Which means the conference. Which means *that* weekend. And which also means, for whatever reason – I never asked, but you were very clear about it at the time – *her.*'

Conway pours a measure into the glass, turns around and hands it to Sweeney.

He doesn't say anything.

'I assumed you'd had a thing with her, didn't want connections being made.'

What *is* this?

'And?'

'Now Larry Bolger is . . .'

'*Larry?* Jesus, Phil, have you gone soft in the head? The man is demented. He's delusional.'

'Isn't that supposed to be *my* line, Dave?'

'Yeah, well, why aren't you sticking to it?'

'Because . . . I don't know . . .'

'*What?*'

'I don't know what's real here and what isn't, what's spin and what's truth.'

'I thought that was the whole point, Phil. Of Marino Communications. Of *you*. Of why we all pay you so much.'

'For the little stuff, maybe, expense sheets and zipper trouble, for papering over the cracks, but this . . .' He shrugs, shakes his head, searching for the words.

'*This*, Phil?'

'Something about *this* stinks to high heaven.'

Conway's had enough, and snaps. He swipes the glass out of Sweeney's hand. 'Get out of my house, Phil. And you know what? I don't think I'll need your services anymore. Consider yourself fired.' He puts the glass down. 'Go on, get out.'

Sweeney stares at him. 'So Jimmy's on the right track, is that what you're telling me?'

'I'm not *telling* you anything, Phil. You can choose to believe whatever shit you like. That's what you do best, isn't it?'

Sweeney flinches. 'Fuck you, Dave.' He turns and walks out of the room.

A few seconds later, Conway hears the hall door slamming shut. He reaches around for the drink he took from Sweeney. He knocks it back in one go. He pours another one and knocks that back. Then he notices the one he poured for himself and knocks that back, too.

7

Jimmy doesn't e-mail Francesca Bonacci again until he arrives in Treviso on Monday morning. This is deliberate. He wants to exert a little pressure – both on her and on himself. He tells her he's getting a train to Verona and will be there by early afternoon. Can they meet? Can he call by? Talk to her mother?

He sends this while he's still in the airport terminal.

Then, in the taxi and on the train, he keeps checking for a reply, until he remembers that she's seventeen and is probably still at school.

He has the phone number, but decides to wait a while before using it, at least until he's settled somewhere, in a hotel or a *pensione*.

At this point he allows himself to take it easy for a bit. He sits back, looks out of the window and registers, almost for the first time, that he's in Italy.

The views flitting past are a curious mix – lush countryside and dense pockets of industrial activity, rolling green hills and boxy grey factory units. As the train snakes into the city, this gives way to another curious mix – dusty, high-rise apartment blocks and elegant two-storey villas with pink slate roofing and green shutters.

He gets a taxi from the station into the city centre. It takes no more than five minutes. He could have easily walked it, but he didn't know. This is because he omitted to do any travel research before leaving Dublin, a situation he now rectifies by stopping at a newsstand and buying a guidebook.

It's a beautiful day, sunny and warm, and as he sits on a bench in Piazza Bra, beneath the cedar trees, looking through the gushing fountain to the Arena, Jimmy wonders what he's doing here. He has a very limited budget and his grand plan doesn't seem to extend a whole lot beyond doorstepping Gianni Bonacci's widow.

But what choice does he have? What other course of action was open to him? None that he can think of. Because talking on the phone and exchanging e-mails wasn't ever going to be enough. To get at the truth, you need eye contact, body language. Especially with a story like this. In any case, he'll give it a couple of days, and see. Maybe something will come of it. Maybe nothing will.

Isn't that how it works?

He flicks through the guidebook and marks down three possible places to stay.

He walks along Via Mazzini, a narrow pedestrianised street of luxury boutiques and jewellery shops. This leads onto another piazza, one dominated by an enormous medieval tower.

He keeps wandering, and consulting the map in his guidebook, until he eventually finds the first of the three hotels. It's fine – cheap and clean – and when he's checked in he falls on the bed and dozes for a while. Then he takes a shower.

At about five o'clock, an e-mail arrives from Francesca.

She seems slightly alarmed that he's here and says she'll have to talk with her mother first, before anything can happen.

Jimmy replies, giving her his mobile number. Then he flops onto the bed again, and waits. He turns on the TV and flicks around for a while, but there's no CNN or Sky, just what seem like local channels, with endless ads, cartoons and chat shows. None of which he can follow. After about twenty minutes, his mobile rings.

He reaches over and grabs it. 'Hello?'

'Mr Gilroy?'

'Yes. Hi. Francesca.'

'Hi. Mr Gilroy. How are you?'

'I'm fine, thanks.' He shunts over and sits up on the edge of the bed. 'But please, call me Jimmy.'

'OK. Jimmy.'

'And how are *you*?'

'I am well. Thank you. Jimmy.'

'Good, good.' *This* is awkward. He stands up. 'So?'

'Er, *allora*, I spoke with my mother, and –'

'Yes?'

Jimmy braces himself.

'She would like to invite you to dinner. At our house. For this evening. If you are free.'

*

Sitting in the back of a black taxi, as it inches its way along Whitehall towards Trafalgar Square, Bolger sends Mary a quick text. He tells her he's arrived and is on his way to the hotel. Over the weekend, they'd talked about her coming with him, for moral support, but they eventually decided against it. Bolger's exclusive focus, they agreed, should be on the interview. All going to plan, however, there's no reason they couldn't both come over in the near future, and do some shopping, or maybe even, if appropriate, a spot of house hunting.

The traffic in London this morning is heavy and the weather is unseasonably warm. Bolger feels a headache coming on.

When he gets to the hotel in Bloomsbury he takes a quick shower and then goes over some notes he made. The interview is at three o'clock. It's in another hotel, somewhere in Knightsbridge.

Though really, *interview*.

It's not quite how he sees it, not quite the word he'd use.

A process maybe, a getting-to-know-you type of thing.

Terms and conditions.

He's never actually sat for a job interview before. Unless you count getting elected. Multiple times. The closest he's probably ever come was that lunch in the Wilson, which –

Oh.

He sees it now. Another hotel. A certain symmetry.

The hand of Vaughan.

Well, whatever. He'll do what he has to do. The jobs pool for ex-prime ministers isn't that big. There also tends to be a window for these things and he hasn't exactly been making the best use of his time. The manner in which he was forced to relinquish office didn't help either, of course. And he'll admit it now, he left in a huff. He withdrew from public life altogether, wouldn't give interviews, didn't take a staff with him. It wasn't a good strategy. It wasn't a strategy at all. The two things he did do were lobby for that IMF job and sign the contract to write his memoirs – but look how he got on with both of *those*.

So in a sense this is a reprieve – a second chance, maybe even a last chance – and he's determined not to squander it. He's still quite nervous, though. And with good reason. He might have dodged one bullet, from Vaughan, but there are others out there – that thing in the paper last week, the couple out walking their dog, and then the young journalist he shot his mouth off to. That was an extraordinary lapse of judgement. OK, he'd been drinking, but when was that ever a valid excuse? Anyway, he's heard nothing about it since, and can only suppose that Dave Conway has taken the matter in hand.

Bolger has a light lunch in the hotel restaurant. Then he freshens up – shaves, changes – and gets ready to go.

As the porter is hailing him a cab, a text message arrives from Mary, wishing him luck. In the cab he sends her one back, saying that he doesn't need luck, he has *her*. Bolger doesn't often get sentimental, but he's not a fool either, he appreciates what he's got in Mary, the love, the attentiveness, the unquestioning support. Without it, he wouldn't be able to function. Without it, his career would have gone belly-up years ago.

The hotel in Knightsbridge is called the Marlow and is a boutique establishment owned – Bolger is assuming – by the Oberon Capital Group. It's a medium-sized modern building sandwiched in between two ugly redbrick residential piles typical of this part of London.

He enters the lobby, which is spacious and very chic, a swirl of design elements he couldn't possibly absorb at a single glance. He approaches the desk and is greeted by the receptionist, an attractive young woman in a discreet uniform. She is blonde and has bright blue eyes.

And blood-red lipstick.

'Good afternoon, sir. Welcome to the Marlow.'

And a slightly haughty English accent of the kind that Bolger, as an Irishman of a certain age, still finds it impossible, somewhere deep inside himself, not to be intimidated by.

'Good afternoon.' He clears his throat. 'Er . . . for Mr Lund. I'm Mr Bolger.'

'Oh yes, Mr Bolger, of course. Would you care to take a seat?' She indicates an area next to a decorative reflection pond in the centre of the lobby. 'Mr Lund will be with you shortly.'

'Thank you.'

He turns away from the desk and glances around. Then he walks over towards the reflection pond.

When he was Taoiseach, Bolger would never have found himself alone at a location like this. There would always have been staff, civil servants, advisors, not to mention a security detail.

You wouldn't get a former British PM wandering around alone. It's a difference in scale, he supposes, between the two countries. Or a question of resources. Until recently, the Irish state provided round-the-clock security outside the homes of its former leaders. Then, for whatever reason, they decided to pull the plug.

He's lucky he still has the state car.

'Excuse me.'

Bolger turns around. Standing there with his hand extended is a pale young man in his late twenties.

'Mr Bolger? I am Bernard Lund.'

'Mr Lund.'

They shake. Lund is certainly young but he seems terribly serious. He's wearing a grey suit and a blue tie. He's got rimless glasses on and is practically bald. He's also wearing a tiny wireless ear-piece.

'Would you come this way, please?'

Bolger follows. They head towards the elevators.

They wait in silence. An elevator door opens, some people come out, Bolger and Lund step in.

Lund presses eight.

'So, Mr Lund,' Bolger says, 'what is the procedure here this afternoon?'

Lund turns slightly. 'A senior representative from Adelphi Solutions will see you in our executive suite. Any questions you have, you may address to him.'

Very clipped. Definitely South African.

The elevator hums open and they step out into a long, empty corridor. Lund leads the way.

They stop at a room near the end of the corridor. Lund swipes a card and they go in.

Unlike that time at the Wilson, the room is empty, not a senator or a Nobel laureate in sight. Bolger looks around. They are in a contemporary living area, with a modern brushed-steel fireplace in front of which there is a glass coffee table and some black leather armchairs.

Lund indicates for Bolger to sit down.

'Our representative will be with you shortly.'

Bolger sighs at hearing this, and sits down.

Shortly? Who *are* these people? He looks at his watch and wonders what the chances are of getting a cup of tea.

He turns to see Bernard Lund over by the door, mobile at his ear.

Bolger takes out his own mobile and switches it to silent.

When he looks back, Lund has gone.

Bolger sits there for a while, in the stillness and the silence.

Five minutes pass, ten minutes. He eventually stands up, walks around, stretches his legs.

Every now and again he glances over at the door.

Thinking, this is ridiculous.

When it reaches the thirty-minute mark, he decides he's had enough. He won't be taken for a fool.

Because what *is* this? Some kind of a joke on Vaughan's part?

He heads for the door.

*

Jimmy has no difficulty finding the address. It's in Via Grimaldi, a dark, narrow street behind Piazza Erbe. A lot of the city centre is pedestrianised, but not this street. The footpath is barely wide enough to accommodate a single pedestrian and as you walk along there's a constant stream of cars rushing past. It's not a stretch you'd want to find yourself on after a few drinks.

The entrance to the apartment building where the Bonaccis live is a high, arched wooden doorway. He presses their buzzer and is let in. The contrast between the street outside and the courtyard in here is quite striking. There are colonnades, hanging flower baskets and, in the centre, what looks like an old stone well.

There is a stairway to the left and Jimmy goes up two flights. Here, at an open door, he is greeted by a slim, studious-looking teenage girl in jeans and a black T-shirt.

'Francesca?'

'Hello.' She nods, extends her hand. 'Jimmy.'

They shake, and she leads him into a small entrance hall.

'May I present my mother,' Francesca says, as an elegant woman in her mid-forties appears from behind her.

Jimmy steps forward and shakes hands with Signora Bonacci. He can see the resemblance straightaway, same eyes, cheekbones, mouth. She is casually dressed as well, though more expensively than her daughter, and with more jewellery. Her smile is open and friendly, but there is something guarded about her – naturally enough, Jimmy supposes, letting a stranger into her house, and a journalist at that.

'It's very kind of you to see me,' he says. 'Signora Bonacci.'

Francesca laughs – at his pronunciation, he assumes. 'You can call her Pina,' she says. 'Everybody does.'

Jimmy looks at her. 'Pina?'

'It's short for Giuseppina.'

'And of course,' her mother adds, 'it's easier to pronounce.'

'Ah, you do speak English.'

'A little. Francesca is better at it.' She smiles again. 'I understand . . . most . . . of things.'

'OK, that's good, because I would like to explain myself.'

'Yes, but . . . please,' Pina Bonacci says, indicating for him to follow her.

They move to the main living area, which is bright and spacious, with marble floors and high ceilings. There are some modern touches – a plasma TV, metal-grey bookshelves and track lighting – but the room has a conservative, old-fashioned feel to it.

They sit in chintzy sofas around a low antique table. In the middle of the table there is a glass bowl filled with fruit.

'Once again,' Jimmy says, 'thank you for seeing me.' In as straight a way as possible, he then explains who he is and what he is doing. He makes no great claims for himself and is clear about his reasons for coming. He really has nothing to offer them, he says, except for a series of questions. And he makes no promises either, except to say that he will go wherever their answers take him.

Pina Bonacci nods along to most of this, and Jimmy is fairly certain that she understands him. Francesca remains still, with her head down.

When he finishes speaking, she looks up. 'So. These questions. What are they?'

Jimmy shifts his position slightly on the sofa. He's not sure what to make of her tone. 'Well, first of all, Francesca, I know very little about your father. Can you tell me what he was like?'

There is silence for a moment. Then the mother and daughter turn to each other, and smile.

Jimmy is relieved at this.

'Gianni was a good man,' Pina says, looking at him. 'A good husband and father.' She turns back to Francesca. 'Husband, *giusto*?'

Francesca nods, and then laughs. '*Mamma, dai.*'

Jimmy stares at them both. They're a good double act. This could have been quite difficult, but so far they seem on a fairly even keel. If anything, Francesca is the more unpredictable of the two, the harder one to read.

'My father was very serious,' she says, and smiles again. 'Like me.'

She certainly looks serious, with her glasses and hair pulled back into a ponytail. Jimmy imagines that the ordeal she went through three years ago must have accelerated the growing up process quite a bit.

At the same time, it appears, she can be quite playful.

'Serious in what way?' he says. 'Your father, I mean.'

Over the next thirty minutes or so, taking it in turns, both in English and Italian – sometimes translated for him, sometimes not – Francesca and Pina talk breathlessly about their Gianni. Jimmy gets the impression that this is something they've maybe wanted and needed to do for some considerable time, but just haven't had the right audience, the right opportunity – which he's now providing, and they're seizing on with barely contained glee. He wonders what it is, the mechanism here – is it the fact that he's a foreigner and this somehow gives them a licence to talk freely, as though it doesn't really count? Or is it him, what Maria Monaghan called his sympathetic face? Possibly a bit of both, not that it matters.

The point is, they're *talking*.

Though so far it's all been about Gianni Bonacci's life, nothing about his death. They tell him he was passionate about movies and jazz, that he inherited hundreds of albums from his own father, Blue Note LPs with all the original cover art, that there's an annual jazz festival here at the Teatro Romano and Gianni never missed a gig; that he was a great cook, did the best porcini risotto you've ever tasted; and wine – *o dio mio* – how Gianni loved his wine; but that he was also sporty, and went cycling and skiing.

At one point, Francesca gets up and retrieves some photos from a drawer to show Jimmy: Gianni with her, with Pina, with both of them, Gianni on the slopes of Madonna di Campiglio, Gianni in an office, at a restaurant, outside the UN Headquarters in New York, Gianni in a jeep somewhere, by a river, up a mountain.

'He travelled a lot, for his work,' Francesca says, as she hands him another picture.

Jimmy remembers Gary Lynch's description of Bonacci . . . what was it, short and weedy? From here, that seems a little unfair. He's not tall, and his thick black-rimmed glasses make him look a bit nerdy, but the image Jimmy is getting of the man from his wife and daughter is an altogether more rounded one than that.

It occurs to Jimmy then that any mention of Susie Monaghan will have to be handled very delicately.

'Tell me about his work,' he says.

'Well, my father was an employee of l'ONU, the UN. He worked for the Directorate of Ethics in Geneva, but had an office in Milan. He went to many conferences and visited . . . sites, industrial plants, all over the world. He was responsible for formulating policy and procedures on corporate ethics. Accountability, implementation, that sort of thing.' She pauses. 'He was a lawyer, of Criminal Justice, but also had degrees in Organisational Psychology and Labour Relations.'

Jimmy gets the impression that this isn't the first time she's reeled off these facts.

'He was very well respected.'

'I'm sure he was. Of course. I have no doubt.'

'But,' Pina Bonacci leans forward. 'He had, er . . .' She turns and whispers something to Francesca, who whispers something back. Then she faces Jimmy again. 'He had enemies. He *made* enemies. Because of his work.'

Jimmy nods. 'Can you elaborate on that?'

Pina remains hunched forward, searching for the words. She seems pained.

Definite mood shift.

'He had no real power, but . . .' Clicking her fingers, she turns to Francesca and releases a torrent of Italian. Francesca listens, then takes a deep breath and looks at Jimmy. 'The Directorate of Ethics couldn't enforce change or impose new practices on corporations, but their reports could create pressures, public relations pressures. In certain cases, these could be – *were*, in fact – extremely damaging.'

'I see.'

'Contracts were cancelled. Losses were incurred.'

Jimmy looks at her. Something is either very close here, or it isn't. The answer Francesca gives to his next question is either going to be very specific or maddeningly vague.

He suspects he knows which.

'Francesca,' he says, leaning forward, 'can you trace a direct line between the two, between something your father ever wrote or said and one of these examples of, let's call it . . . corporate discontent?'

She shrugs. 'Did you not look at that link I sent you?'

'Yeah, I did, of course.' He pauses, sighs. 'Well, sort of. It was in *Italian*, Francesca.'

'OK.' She holds up a hand. 'One second.' She and Pina then exchange another few rapid, labyrinthine sentences. When they've finished, Pina stands up. 'Jimmy, I hope you like, er . . .' She looks at Francesca. '*Frutti di mare?*'

'Seafood.'

She looks back at Jimmy. 'I hope you like seafood.'

He nods. 'Yes, absolutely.'

'Good. Now, please excuse me.' She turns and heads over towards what Jimmy sees through an open door is the kitchen.

Then Francesca stands up as well. 'Wait here a moment,' she says. 'I will get my laptop.'

*

Sitting across from Dave Conway are three pink-faced little pricks in expensive suits and sober ties. Spread out before them on the glass table are BlackBerrys and bottles of water, though no laptops – that's because there won't be any third degree here today, no advanced interrogation techniques. It's all meant to be informal and getting-to-know-you. Black Vine Partners is a Philadelphia-based private equity fund and these boys – which is what they are – have flown in to 'scope out' Conway Holdings.

It's just that Dave Conway is in no mood this afternoon to be scoped out.

Hollowed out is more how he feels.

That whiskey he drank last night after Phil Sweeney left – the three original shots followed by another four or five – certainly took their toll. When he got up this morning he felt like shit and the feeling hasn't really lifted.

All day, too, he's been trying to calculate the cost of pissing Phil Sweeney off. Traditionally, Sweeney has been the great buffer zone between bad things happening, and how, when or even if those bad things show up in the news cycle – so he's not someone you want to have outside of your tent, unzipping his fly.

But then again, in his hungover state, Conway can no longer even be sure there *is* a tent.

Across the table, Black Vine's Director of Investor Relations, the pink-faced little prick in the middle, is delivering a tedious monologue on the European debt crisis.

Conway is only half listening. His sense of things falling apart is too acute now for any of this to matter. Even if he manages to get the investment money from these guys, which is doubtful, it won't stem the tide. Susie Monaghan is out there, Larry Bolger is out there, this Jimmy Gilroy is out there . . . not to mention all the lies and misinformation, all the suspicion and paranoia.

He closes his eyes.

Everyone running for cover. It's been building for days. And what was *his* solution? In the circumstances? It was only a two-minute phone call, but the more he replays it in his head, the less it makes sense to him.

'Mr Conway?'

Because what did he imagine it was going to achieve? In fact, what on earth was he *thinking*?

'Mr Conway?'

And what on earth – for that matter – was he thinking three years ago when he last spoke to Don Ribcoff?

'*Mr Conway?*'

'Yeah.' He opens his eyes. 'What?'

The Director of Investor Relations is smiling at him, but it's a smile of bewilderment. 'We were wondering,' he says, reaching for his bottle of water, 'if you could tell us something about the sale of First Continental Resources to BRX?'

Conway looks at him, and then at the others. These guys are at it now, too? Martin Boyle had warned him that they'd want to talk about this, but suddenly their interest seems a little pointed. What do they want to know? And why?

He shrugs. 'It was . . . a straightforward deal. Nothing special.'

'Oh come now, Mr Conway, a hundred million dollars for a disused copper mine?' He half turns, for support, to the guy on his left. 'There must be an interesting story behind *that*.'

Oh come now? This irritates the shit out of Conway and he can feel any sense of perspective he's supposed to have slipping away. He's just glad that Martin Boyle isn't in the room. 'Well, if there is,' he says, '*you're* not going to hear it.'

'Excuse me?'

Where would he begin in any case? It's not something that easily lends itself to being told as an anecdote – which was true from the start, even long before that interfering little bastard Gianni Bonacci entered the equation.

'It's not something I wish to discuss.'

'It's not –' The Director of Investor Relations leans forward, barely able to conceal his disbelief. 'Can you explain that? I don't understand.'

Conway leans forward to meet him. 'There's nothing to understand. I don't want to talk about it.'

'Oh.'

The three little pricks turn to each other, muttering and pulling confused faces.

'But Mr Conway,' the one on the right then says, 'this is your party piece. Nothing else you've got distinguishes you in *any* way. If we don't hear this' – he clicks his tongue – 'we're not hearing anything.'

Conway nods his head in silence for a while. 'Right,' he says eventually, 'I guess this meeting is over then.'

*

As Bolger opens the door of the hotel room and steps out into the corridor, he feels a certain measure of relief. This is uncharted territory here and it'd be very easy to make a mistake, to rush into something he'd later regret. On reflection, what he should have done was play a longer game, more hardball, make it so that *he* was calling the shots. He should have asked for details, the terms and conditions, got *them* to sweat for a bit.

Another couple of days at least.

In any case, this messing around, the waiting – it has helped him to make up his mind.

And it's fine.

Though as he walks along the corridor, his irritation increases.

Shortly.

What was he, waiting at the dentist's? After all, he's a former prime minister, a retired national leader. Isn't that deserving of a little respect? Not that he means this in an arrogant way, or that he's brimming over with self-belief or anything. In fact, he has as much of a store of self-loathing and Catholic guilt as the next man – the next Irishman, at any rate – but these Adelphi people wouldn't know that. They wouldn't be aware of his personal failings, or of the torment he's been suffering recently.

So there's no reason he can't just look them in the eye and tell them where to get off.

He arrives at the elevator and is about to press the button when he hears someone calling his name.

He turns around.

It's Bernard Lund, walking towards him.

'Wait, please.'

Where did he come from?

'What is it?' Bolger says, and looks at his watch. 'I'm leaving.'

'Please, Mr Bolger. You must accept my apologies.'

'I don't think so. I've been sitting in that bloody room for half an hour.'

'Yes, yes, I'm sorry, but –' He turns away, holding one hand up and pressing the other to his ear, the one with the wireless device in it. 'I'm just . . . yes.' He turns back. 'Our representative is arriving now.'

Bolger sighs. 'This is unacceptable, you know.'

'Yes, and I apologise, but there has been some delay with traffic. An accident, I believe.' He nods his head at the elevator. 'They're coming now.'

Bolger turns and sees the pulsating green light.

A moment later the elevator door hums open.

Two men in suits emerge, one tall and thin with grey hair, the other one short, stocky and with a buzz cut. The first weird thing that Bolger notices is that neither of them looks directly at him. The tall, grey-haired one makes eye contact with Lund and seems to be trying to communicate something to him. The stocky one just keeps his head down. He also remains at the elevator, holding the door open with his arm.

That's the second weird thing that Bolger notices.

But for sheer, unalloyed weirdness it is nothing compared to what happens over the next few seconds.

Bernard Lund glances over his shoulder at the still-empty corridor and turns back. Then, as Bolger is about to say something, to ask him what the hell is going on, Lund makes a sudden forward movement, pushes up against him, arms outstretched as though about to lock him in sort of a bear hug. Pushing against him in the same way, but from behind, is the tall, grey-haired man, who proceeds to restrain Bolger by putting an arm around his neck.

What the –

Bolger struggles, splutters, unable to speak. He is helpless, sandwiched between these two bodies. But then, for a fleeting moment – force and resistance in perfect balance – everything is still. He can hear them breathing. He can smell their cologne. He just can't move.

Or understand.

Or think.

He feels a sudden extra stab of pressure in his lower back and a second later is released, the two men stepping away, peering around them, breathing heavily.

Bolger looks down at the carpet, shakes his head, says nothing. He doesn't know what it is, but something makes him realise there's nothing *to* say.

There'll be no talking here.

Or eye contact.

Besides, he's feeling dizzy now, and doesn't want to talk.

He looks up, and around.

Lund and the tall, grey-haired man are already halfway along the corridor. The short stocky man with the buzz cut is still at the elevator. He holds out his free hand to Bolger and beckons him over.

Bolger feels dopey all of a sudden, and sluggish, a bit stupid even. He complies, steps over. The man with the buzz cut takes him by the elbow and guides him into the elevator car. The man then reaches in, presses a button and withdraws.

Bolger turns and stands gazing out. The now empty hotel corridor stretches off, it seems, to infinity, and as the elevator door closes, cutting off his view, he starts to feel a tremendous weight bearing in on his chest.

*

It turns out that the most recent stuff on the website Francesca shows Jimmy is at least two years old, and that any references he came across over the weekend on other websites were merely rehashed versions of what's on this one. With a bit of gentle prodding, he also finds out from Francesca that today is the first time in over a year, possibly longer, that she and Pina have talked to anyone about the circumstances surrounding Gianni's death – which maybe explains why they're so eager to talk about it now. After the crash, there was a flurry of activity, people online and in the mainstream media speculating, theorising, asking questions, but a combination of the brick wall in Dublin and a battening down of the corporate hatches generally meant that no answers were ever forthcoming. Then the questions started to peter out. They finally stopped altogether and this long period of silence followed.

The stuff that is on the website relates mainly to a report Gianni wrote about three pharmaceutical companies – only one of which, as far as Jimmy can remember, was represented at the conference in Drumcoolie Castle. And the one that *was* there – from what he understands after a cursory glance at the report – would have been the least culpable in terms of any criticisms Gianni had made, and therefore the least likely to have wanted or needed to silence him.

When Jimmy points this out, Francesca makes the entirely reasonable point that neither of the other two companies, if they'd been intent on assassinating Gianni, would have necessarily had to have an official presence at the conference.

Indeed.

Except that it's not a reasonable point at all. It's more of a tipping point in fact, one between evidence-based supposition and classic paranoid theorising. Because there simply isn't enough evidence here. Nor is Jimmy convinced of the basic premise anyway, that corporations go around assassinating people who criticise them. 'And since the report was already out,' he says, hammering the point home, 'wouldn't it have been too late anyway, a case of closing the stable door . . .' Francesca looks at him, brow furrowed. '. . . after the horse has bolted.'

He then starts to explain the phrase, but she quickly nods, yes, yes, yes, and after a moment says what he takes to be its equivalent in Italian.

But now, having traded idioms, they fall into an awkward silence. Because with remarkable ease, he has undermined the basis of their suspicions and also more or less debunked what he himself came here hoping to find out in the first place.

The awkwardness continues as they move over to the table and start dinner.

When Francesca fills her mother in on what she and Jimmy have been saying, Pina shrugs and seems unfazed.

Francesca argues with her, making gestures, rolling her eyes. Pina responds in kind. It gets heated.

Jimmy puts his head down, and concentrates on the plate of pasta in front of him, spaghetti with mussels and clams. If he was looking for a distraction, he has certainly found one, because this is delicious. He wants to compliment Pina on it but the moment doesn't seem right.

After a while, Francesca turns to him. She sighs dramatically. 'Look, Pina is not so much concerned about a . . . what is that expression, a smoking gun?'

Jimmy nods.

'Because she knows Gianni, *knew* Gianni, and is in no doubt that he was in danger in Ireland. His death only confirmed this.'

'How does she know –' Jimmy stops and turns to Pina. 'How do you know that he was in danger?'

'Because he told me.'

He looks at her, fork suspended over his plate. 'Told you how?'

'On the phone. We spoke. Every day.'

Jimmy waits. 'And?'

Pina hesitates. She and Francesca exchange a look. Then Francesca turns to Jimmy. 'The day before the crash Gianni said that he had discovered something. He was excited about it, but also angry. He said that just knowing what he knew put him in a very dangerous position.'

She takes a deep breath, and exhales slowly.

Again, Jimmy waits for more. 'So? What was it?'

'We don't know. He didn't say. He didn't want to be specific over the phone.'

Jimmy puts his fork down. 'There's no mention of this anywhere, Francesca, at least not that I've seen. Not on that website, or in any of the reports.'

'Yes, I know.' She shrugs. 'We *did* tell the police, here and in Ireland, again and again, but they ignored it, they said it wasn't relevant. Gianni died in a crash, an accident, along with five others. And what *we* were saying, what *we* were implying, according to them, was ridiculous. They didn't investigate anything.'

There is silence for a while. Then Pina says something to Francesca. She speaks quietly, and takes her time about it. After another silence Francesca turns to Jimmy. 'My mother says she's not a conspiracy theorist, she's not obsessed with this, she's not crazy. She just believes what her husband told her . . . and from everything she has seen and heard over the years, she also believes that none of this is implausible.'

Jimmy nods along, feeling a sudden weight of responsibility. 'Of course. Of course.'

'But I'm different,' Francesca continues. 'I *am* a little crazy, as you can see. I want to know the truth.'

'That's not crazy,' Jimmy says, and pauses. 'I want to know the truth, as well.'

But do they have anything? Not really. Pina's conviction, based on . . . what? Love, trust, experience? And the claims of a drunken fool based on he doesn't know what. Guilt? Maybe, but that's not enough.

A smoking gun is precisely what they do need.

So far Jimmy has been very circumspect here about anything he might know – he hasn't mentioned Larry Bolger, for instance, and isn't going to – but he decides now to throw out at least some of what he's got.

He turns to Pina. 'Did Gianni mention any names when he spoke to you? People he was meeting. Clark Rundle, for instance?'

Pina considers this, but shakes her head.

'Don Ribcoff?'

'No.'

Francesca cuts in, 'Who are these people?'

'Just other delegates, at the conference, people he –'

'Wait,' Pina says. 'Maybe. Say those names again.'

He repeats them.

'I don't know,' she says. 'On a business card, perhaps. Clark Rundle. It's a strange name. Funny.' She turns to Francesca again and talks in Italian. When Francesca is ready she turns back to Jimmy.

'Gianni's briefcase, and some clothes. That's all we have left of my father, from Ireland. In the briefcase he had some documents, and business cards. He always had so many.' She nods back at Pina. 'Maybe she saw that name on one of those.' She pauses. 'But who is this person?'

Jimmy ignores the question. 'Do you still have the briefcase?'

'Of course.'

He leans forward. 'Can I see it?'

Francesca and Pina look at each other.

The briefcase is quite small, a black leather doctor's bag. Pina handles it with great care. She carries it across the room and places it on the free end of the table and opens it. From the main compartment she takes out a sheaf of documents. At a glance, Jimmy sees that they are on UN-headed paper and are in Italian. From a smaller front compartment, she takes out a handful of business cards and puts them down in front of him.

He picks them up and starts flicking through them.

'The police looked at this stuff,' Francesca says, 'but it was . . . two minutes. They didn't care. They didn't see any point.'

'What about his cell phone?' Jimmy asks, flicking through more cards. 'His laptop?'

'No. They were . . . the police said they must have been destroyed in the crash.'

Jimmy stops, holds up a card. 'Clark Rundle.'

He studies it. Chairman and CEO of BRX Mining & Engineering Corporation.

He flips it over.

There is something handwritten on the back of it.

Jimmy tries to make out what it says, but can't. The handwriting is illegible. Francesca takes the card from him and looks at it. She shakes her head.

'Can you make it out?'

'Yes,' she says, staring at the card. 'I think it's a name.' She pauses. 'Dave . . . Conway?'

*

As the elevator descends, Larry Bolger presses his hands very hard against his chest to try and relieve the pain.

It doesn't work.

He's in shock.

Fuck.

Did . . . ?

Where *is* he again? London. *Why London?* Oh yeah, that inter . . . international regulatory . . . something . . .

But –

In his stomach now too, there's an intense . . . sensation. He looks up . . . the numbers . . .

Falling, sinking . . . into . . .

2008.

The top job, at last, seal of office, seal of approval, two fingers to all his critics down through the years, nothing like it.

Falling, sinking.

1999.

First time in cabinet, though not ready for it, not ready at all, no, drowning in a sea of whiskey and self-pity, and what's-her-name, Avril Byrne.

Falling.

1983.

How many was it . . . over six thousand first-preference votes, elected on the first count, hoisted up in the air, to deafening cheers . . . but he was only three months back from Boston at that point, still in a tailspin over Frank, and still clutching at the straws of what he'd been forced to leave behind, that other life, with all its golden possibilities, unfulfilled now, and unfulfillable . . . dimming, dimmed, his lost trajectory . . .

Falling . . .

1968.

Brother Cornelius, looming in a dank, musty corridor, chalk dust on his soutane and a leather strap hiding in his pocket, waiting to be whipped out, like a dark, brooding, permanent erection . . .

Sinking . . .

1964.

At a match in Croke Park with Frank and the old man, but feeling left out, excluded, unable to join in any of the conversation, and not tall enough either to see a fucking thing, first time he properly remembers *that* sensation, though not the last . . .

His stomach, plummeting . . .

But then it stops.

And the door slides open. He staggers forward, out into the lobby, hands still pressing at his chest, holy Jesus, the *pain* . . . and the people, pointing, standing aside and murmuring . . . their plummy voices, I say, look, *look* . . .

1957.

Dadda, mamma . . . brudder . . .

Falling.

1954.

D.O.B.

*

When Dave Conway pulls into the driveway and sees that Ruth's car is there he leans forward and rests his head on the steering wheel.

Damn.

He managed to avoid Martin Boyle after the meeting by going down the stairs and slipping out a side exit of the building, but given the choice now – an hour or two with his lawyer or the next ten minutes with his wife – he'd happily head back into the arms of his lawyer.

Ruth knew the meeting with the Black Vine people was important, but she didn't know it was critical. Now Conway is going to have to explain to her both that it was critical *and* that he blew it.

And that consequently . . .

He doesn't know.

He straightens up. He gets out of the car.

Ruth isn't stupid, she's just never paid that much attention to her husband's financial affairs. When they met, he was already running several successful businesses and she never felt the need to interrogate him about it. So she'll understand.

But the thing is, she won't forgive him.

Ruth always took it on trust that Conway knew what he was doing. The big deal he negotiated a few years back with BRX confirmed this for her. Not only that, but it also set the bar for her expectations, and set it pretty high. Because as far as Ruth was concerned – *is* concerned – there's no debate about the direction this thing is going in. It's only a matter of time, she believes, recession notwithstanding, before Conway pulls off another spectacular and they move up to the next level.

However, with this Black Vine catastrophe – self-inflicted or not, it doesn't really matter – they've pretty much lost everything.

How does he break *that* to her?

And how does he break it to her that it might even be a lot worse? That the BRX deal itself is in danger of coming apart, of unspooling, and all the way back to that long, wet, complicated summer of three years ago . . .

As he approaches the front door, rummaging for his key, he wonders how he's going to be able to face this now, with the kids pulling at him and screaming for attention.

What he'd like to do is turn around and get back in the car, but where would he go? He has to face Ruth sooner or later.

He puts his key in the door.

Where does he even begin? Does he explain to her that while *he* might be responsible for the financial mess they're in, his old friend and political patron, Larry Bolger, is now a direct threat to their security, to everything they hold dear? That if the man can't keep his mouth shut, Conway and others might actually end up going to *prison*?

When he gets inside the door he hears sounds coming from the playroom to the right. They're watching something on TV. He doesn't go in. He walks straight on towards the kitchen at the back.

Ruth is sitting at the counter, alone, gazing up at the small wall-mounted TV over the fridge.

'Hi,' he says.

She turns to look at him. He is alarmed at the expression on her face. Does she know already? Has Martin Boyle phoned?

'What's wrong?' No response. '*Ruth?*'

She shakes her head slightly. 'Haven't you heard?'

'What?' Panic now. 'No. Heard *what*?'

She points up at the TV screen. It's tuned to Sky News. At first he doesn't understand, it's just a newscaster, saying something about a Lib Dem by-election candidate . . .

But then he sees it.

The crawl.

Running across the bottom of the screen.

BREAKING NEWS: FORMER IRISH PRIME MINISTER LARRY BOLGER DIES SUDDENLY IN LONDON . . . BREAKING NEWS: FORMER IRISH PRIME MINISTER LARRY BOLGER DIES SUDDENLY . . .

*

The elevator door opens onto the underground car park of the

BRX Building and Clark Rundle steps out. His car is waiting, but directly behind it is another car, door open, engine running. Don Ribcoff gets out and walks over.

'Sorry, Clark, this won't take a minute.'

Ribcoff had phoned just as Rundle was leaving for an appointment and he wanted to see him in person. Since Ribcoff doesn't place much trust in electronic forms of communication, most of his business is conducted in this way.

Rundle is slightly agitated. He's en route to the Wilson Hotel, to see Nora. 'What is it?' he says.

'That potential situation we had overseas, with the politician? I've just heard it's been put to bed.' Even with all his security measures in place, Ribcoff still occasionally has a habit of delivering updates in language like this, coded, bleached of specifics.

Rundle finds it strange.

He makes a face. 'That was fast.'

'Well, the old man was pretty adamant.' Ribcoff shrugs. 'It *was* rushed, that's for sure, and they nearly botched it, but it's fine.'

'What about the . . .' Rundle is about to say 'journalist', but stops himself. Might be a bit specific for Ribcoff's taste. 'What about the young guy, the, er . . .' He's not good at this. 'The young guy that the older guy, the politician, talked to?'

'You mean the journalist?'

Jesus.

Rundle nods. 'Yeah.'

'We're going to keep an eye on him, you know, do a sneak and peek, monitor his activities, and . . .' He glances around.

Rundle waits. 'And?'

Ribcoff looks back. 'Take action, if necessary.' He pauses. 'You know, some form of containment.'

'OK.'

Maybe Rundle understands it after all, this need for lingo, for euphemism.

'In the meantime,' Ribcoff says, 'I have some travel details for you.' He reaches into his jacket pocket and takes out a slim envelope. He hands it to Rundle. 'Tomorrow, for Thursday. Is that good?'

'Yes.'

He'll have to clear his diary and let Eve know he won't be here when she gets back from England. He'll also have to arrange to have vaccinations done. Though Ribcoff probably has that set up already.

'You'll be going via Paris to Rwanda, and then over the border to the airstrip at Buenke.'

Rundle nods. This will be a Gideon Global operation all the way. They provide transport in and out of the country, as well as escort security at the site.

He's essentially putting himself in Ribcoff's hands.

'And Kimbela?'

'We've just had word from our guy that he's agreed to a meeting. He's not happy about what happened last week, but we're negotiating a reparation package.'

'And I take it you've already done some form of psych screening of your remaining personnel over there.'

Ribcoff doesn't like this. 'Look,' he says, 'it was a blip, unfortunate yes, but . . . a blip. These things happen. Even Kimbela understands that.'

'Oh, he does? And I'm supposed to take comfort from the fact?'

'Clark, come on –'

'I'm kidding, Don. Jesus, lighten up.'

Actually, he's not kidding, and on the way to his suite at the Wilson he realises just how much he's not kidding. In normal circumstances, by the time he's riding the elevator up to the tenth floor there'd be a certain amount of anticipatory lead in the equation – to adopt Ribcoff's linguistic technique – but not today.

Not even when Nora comes through the door.

He's got a knot in his stomach now, and he reckons he'd better get used to it.

It won't be going away any time soon.

*

Jimmy isn't sure what he's got here, what he's coming away with, and as he walks back to his hotel, through the dark, quiet streets of the city, a fog of ambivalence, as familiar as it is unwelcome, settles over him. He really liked Francesca and Pina – liked their different styles and coping mechanisms, liked the way they were confrontational with each other and supportive at the same time. But that hardly gives him the right to come along and intrude into their lives, does it? He did the same with Maria Monaghan and look how that worked out. It's one thing to interview a pharmaceutical executive for a trade publication and ask about patents or production schedules; it's another thing entirely to sit across from grieving family members who want to understand how and why their loved one died, and know that your questions – your mere presence, in fact – is giving them hope, hope that *you* know in all likelihood to be false.

He didn't make any promises, though. He didn't lie to them.

At least.

Is that enough?

He passes a small bar, an enoteca, one of the few places still open, and is tempted to go in, but he's more anxious to get back to the hotel. He could have used Francesca's laptop to chase up this lead, but he wasn't keen on the idea of having her there the whole time, peering over his shoulder. He's also naturally quite cautious and didn't want to leave a trail of his internet searches on her computer.

Back in his room, he jots down a few quick notes from the evening. Then he opens his laptop and goes online.

Dave Conway.

When Francesca said the name, Jimmy recognised it straightaway. Dave Conway. Conway Holdings. One of the property guys. Hotels, apartment blocks, housing estates. But he had absolutely no idea what connection Dave Conway might have to Clark Rundle or to Gianni Bonacci.

He types in the name.

The thing is, Jimmy calls this a lead, automatically thinks of it that way, but maybe it's nothing.

Maybe it's a different Dave Conway.

He does a search anyway and surfs around for a while – business websites, directories, news archives – not expecting to find anything. To his surprise, however, he quickly comes across a clear, unequivocal connection. Three years ago, it seems, around the time of the conference, Clark Rundle's company,

BRX, bought a Conway Holdings subsidiary, First Continental Resources.

No more than that, no detail, just a reference.

Jimmy is fully aware that this doesn't have to mean anything, that it's a random, neutral fact he has found on the internet.

But –

It certainly joins up a lot of dots.

Larry Bolger, Clark Rundle, Dave Conway, Gianni Bonacci, Susie Monaghan.

What all of this means, in turn, he doesn't really know. But his sense, increasingly, is that it must mean something – that there's simply too much here for it *not* to mean something.

In which case, it occurs to him, shouldn't he be concerned? A little nervous even?

Why?

Because –

Jimmy gets up off the bed and goes over to the window. There isn't much of a view, just red slate roofs in the moonlight. It's quiet, too, with occasional sounds drifting up from a nearby restaurant, cutlery and plates, laughter.

Because if it does mean something, think what that something must be.

Before now all of this had been academic, more or less, supposition, speculation – and at a considerable remove from any reality Jimmy is familiar with. But there's something about being in Italy that changes that, recalibrates it, brings it closer to home. Maybe it's the air or the architecture, he doesn't know, but he has an acute sense right now of time and history, of ceaseless activity and intrigue, of ripeness and rot, of this calcified political culture where literally anything is possible –

where the assassination of a middle-ranking official, for example, would be as routine and banal as the cancellation of an IT support contract.

Jimmy turns around and faces the room.

So what's he saying? All of a sudden this is plausible? It's *thinkable*? But wouldn't that have to apply – logically, sooner or later – to most things? Including, he'd have to suppose, various forms of damage limitation? Damage caused, say, by someone who couldn't keep his mouth shut? And then, in turn, by whoever that someone might have been talking to?

Jimmy is tired and losing perspective. He feels like having that drink now and wonders if it's not too late to head back out.

He goes and sits on the edge of the bed.

Maybe he could find that bar again, the one he passed earlier.

He reaches over for the laptop, pulls it towards him. Before he logs off, he clicks onto the *Irish Times* website.

Force of habit.

It's the first item he sees.

Larry Bolger dead.

One phrase. Three words. No room for ambiguity.

He stares at the headline in shock. Then he clicks onto the main story. It says Bolger died of a heart attack. In the lobby of a London hotel.

Jesus Christ.

But what was he doing in London in the first place? Who was he with? Who was he seeing?

It takes Jimmy a while to understand something here. As he's staring at the screen, scanning the article, it creeps up on him. He realises he's taking it for granted that this isn't what it seems. Based on what? Absolutely nothing. But he's convinced he's right.

He's convinced, too, that it won't – can't – end there.

At which point his phone rings. Without taking his eyes from the screen, he reaches over and picks it up.

'Yeah?'

'Hi, Jimmy, how's it going? It's Finbarr.'

Jimmy stops, looks up, confused. 'Who?'

'Finbarr. From across the hall.'

'Oh. Yeah. Hi. I . . . I was just reading about Larry Bolger.'

'Right. I *know*. Weird, isn't it? But come here, listen.'

'Yeah?'

Something about his tone.

Jimmy braces himself.

'Sorry to lay this on you when you're away and all, but there was a break-in this evening, in the building. Your place got done over. I'm afraid, it's pretty bad.'

Three

Tube steadies himself with a couple of deep, measured breaths, replaces the revolver in his holster and steps away. Behind him now, the package is screaming, but what can he do? Venus and Scratch from the lead car were right behind him so they'll be on it.

Kicking the door closed was dumb, and unnecessary, he could have just gone around it, or through the open window – but he had to feel like he was in a scene from a fucking movie, didn't he? It's the perennial temptation, the age-old problem – which comes first, the war or the stories? Put a gun in your hand and who are you?

He turns around.

Sweet Lord.

Venus looks at him.

Tube nods at the lead car.

'Sir,' he then says to the package, loudly, clearly, and with enough firmness to command the poor bastard's attention, 'these men will escort you to the airstrip. There you will receive immediate medical attention.' He pauses. 'Do you understand?'

The package nods. He's pale, terrified, in agony.

Venus and Scratch take him away, quickly, out of the car and around the body. They shield him as best they can from what's up ahead as well, and bundle him into the other car.

Tube just stands there. In theory, they could be vulnerable to attack here, some kind of retaliation, return fire, but it's highly un-

likely. Gideon controls this whole area, the airstrip, the mine, its immediate environs. Once you get near the compound, OK, things are a little different – the painted kids with bloodshot eyes take over . . . but they're all still on the same side.

Except . . .

He looks around.

Except – you'd think *– when something like this happens.*

The lead car starts up, veers right, moves along the edge of the road for a bit and then speeds off.

Spokane, the driver of the middle car, opens his door and gets out, radio in hand.

He looks over at Tube. 'Support on the way, sir.'

Tube nods.

Support. Clean up. Bags. At least one bag, anyway.

He shakes his head.

What a mess.

A few feet away is Deep Six. He's just standing there, too, looking around.

Guess they're both a little shell-shocked.

The silence now is the strangest thing.

Fuck.

No one moaning, no one crying, nothing.

Crazy, efficient motherfucker.

If anyone had asked him, Tube would have opted for Deep Six here, not Ashes, on the basis that it's always the quiet ones you have to look out for – and Ashes was anything but quiet, fool couldn't keep still for a second, slave to his ADHD or whatever he had, though he never seemed that *disturbed, just a little weird, stupid actually. And that's another thing, it usually isn't the stupid ones who end up doing this kind of thing – for whatever rea-*

son it's the smart ones, like Deep Six . . . who at any rate seems smart, but maybe he isn't, maybe he's as dumb as he lets on. And who knows, go figure, maybe Ray Kroner was smart after all. Doesn't matter now, though, he's gone to the bosom of the Lord and he sure as shit ain't coming back.

Tube looks down at the body.

He didn't like having to do it, not least because it was his first time at such close range, but it was a split second thing anyway, he acted on reflex, and if he hadn't, if Ashes had shot the package – it's just occurring to him now – the fallout would've been . . .

Unimaginable.

There'd be no containing it. Which begs the question – what the hell is Senator John Rundle doing down here anyway? Whatever the strategy is supposed to be, it's a damn risky one. A Beltway insider like Rundle? Coming to the Congo? For a sit-down with Arnold Kimbela?

He guesses the stakes must be pretty high.

Not that it's Tube's job, or his place, to be speculating on such shit, but you can't help it.

He looks over at Deep Six again.

'Hell of a thing,' he says. And that's when he notices the look on Tom Szymanski's face. It's a scowl, brooding, almost baleful. 'What?'

Szymanski shrugs, seemingly unable to speak.

Tube steps over to him. 'I didn't have a choice. That was a US senator, for Christ's sake.' He's whispering this. 'Ashes was going to shoot him.'

Szymanski looks up. 'A senator?'

'Yeah, John Rundle. Big family.' He raises an arm and sweeps it around. 'His brother actually owns all of this, the mine, the airstrip. You know, BRX.' He pauses. 'They write the cheques. So I'm sorry, but Ashes picked the wrong fucking day to go crazy.'

Szymanski considers this, seems to anyway.

'Yeah,' he says eventually, under his breath. 'The wrong fucking day.' It's barely audible.

He walks away.

Tube watches him.

He stops in front of Ray Kroner's body for a second and then walks on.

Venus and Scratch watch in silence as he passes them.

Tube can hear something in the distance now, from behind. It's on the road. A deep rumbling sound.

Support.

One of the armoured humvees.

Tom Szymanski stops when he comes to the scene up ahead.

Tube studies him – his posture, body language. What's he thinking? What's going on inside his head as he looks down at this pile – this fucked-up arrangement – of corpses . . .

Twisted, bullet-riddled, blood-soaked.

Faces frozen in shock.

This calculus of horror.

Two women, one slumped over an empty wicker basket, the other lying sideways in a pile of, what are they, yams . . . and behind them, splayed out on the dirt road, three tiny, limp frames . . .

Is Deep Six straining to take this in, to comprehend it? Is it getting to him? Is he losing his perspective, losing his mind?

Tube exhales, turns around, looks in the opposite direction.

The armoured vehicle is approaching. It gets closer, louder. It pulls up next to the first SUV. Doors and hatches open, support *personnel appear. They spread out, assess the damage, start the clean-up.*

Though Tube is still in charge.

In fact, since the entire Buenke operation is under his command, he'll be the one responsible for shaping and disseminating the official narrative of what happened here.

Which isn't going to be easy.

Because Gideon Global don't do explanations, or apologies.

Tube nods at Venus again and walks over to where he and Scratch are standing. As he does so, he makes a mental note.

Tom Szymanski takes extended leave.

Unpaid.

Effective immediately.

8

On the flight to Paris, Rundle goes over his notes again and then catches up on some of the J.J. stuff from the weekend. He watches various clips – mainly from the Sunday morning talk shows, *This Week* and *Face the Nation* – and has to admit that J.J. did pretty well. He'd said last week that he wanted to hang onto the media traction while changing the conversation, and he appears to have done just that – little or no mention of the 'accident', instead a vigorous assault on the Finance Reform bill. Of course, the high-visibility brace on his hand leaves no one in any doubt about the narrative subtext that's being peddled here.

But nicely done. All round. No question about it.

Nor has it taken long for the speculation to ramp up about J.J. possibly running for the White House in two years' time. No one has officially put their hat in the ring yet – it's too early for that – but the more times you get asked the question, the less plausible, conveniently enough, your coy and disingenuous denials become.

Rundle can even see it himself now.

What's more, he can see the benefits.

It's become clear to him recently that his position vis-à-vis James Vaughan and the Oberon Capital Group may not be as solid as he'd been assuming. Rundle has played his part, there's no doubt about that, he's kept the supply chain ticking over, and at considerable cost, both financial and otherwise – but there's also no doubt that in relation to certain follow-on matters he has been kept in the dark.

There's a bigger picture here – it's obvious, Rundle can feel it in his bones – but for whatever reason, or reasons, Jimmy Vaughan has consistently made a point of excluding him from it. With J.J. in the White House, however, things would be different. They'd have to be.

It would be a lock.

The Rundle Supremacy.

OK, there's a long way to go before that happens, but in the short term if BRX can sew up the Africa situation, Oberon might be more favourably disposed towards the senator making a bid for the White House.

Maybe pitch in a little.

Quid pro quo sort of thing. Two-way street.

Not that there'd be anything formalised about it, much less illegal or nefarious – nothing, say, for *The Nation* or *Democracy Now* to be getting worked up about.

Because how do these people think shit gets done?

It's just business.

Rundle closes his laptop, leans back and sighs.

He's getting to Paris on his own steam, in the G650, and after that Gideon will be taking over – there'll be a flight in a military plane to Kigali followed by a quick hop over to Bukavu in eastern Congo. Then he'll be taken in a light aircraft to the mine at Buenke. At least the reverse trip, with the scale of comfort ascending, will be a little easier.

And in between he sits down with the colonel.

It'll be a quick turnaround, couple of hours maybe, some

hard talking, lots of back and forth, issues, conditions, whatever.

But a resolution has to be arrived at.

That's the bottom line.

Rundle looks out the window, at the clouds below, billowing furiously.

He has spent his life arriving at solutions – structuring complex deals, negotiating buyouts . . . manipulating, cajoling, sweet-talking, playing hardball where necessary – but it has always been in streamlined air-conditioned spaces, in hotel rooms, office suites and conference centres.

This is going to be very different.

A jungle clearing, kids with Kalashnikovs, a damp hut, a metal table, a bare light bulb. That's how J.J. described it. Equally, depending on his mood, the colonel could choose to hold the meeting in his new palace – so-called, and still half-built by all reports, with its unsuitable antique furniture, staircases leading nowhere and empty Olympic-sized swimming pool.

The point is, it'll be different.

And Rundle has this notion –

He can't help it.

He has this notion that by travelling to Africa in person, by engaging directly with a local warlord, by not flinching, he will come away stronger, empowered somehow, equipped not just with a re-negotiated mining contract but with a psychological edge as well, an air of dark authority. It's as if he expects to be infected, bitten, tainted in some way.

His soul.

Rundle looks away, suddenly uncomfortable with this, a

little embarrassed even. He swivels his seat around to face the empty cabin.

He is aware of all the history here, of the tropes and metaphors routinely used, the clichés even. He's aware of the complex web of interdependencies going back over decades, the involvement of various agencies, corporate, military, intel.

He's aware, too, of the enduring friendship between Jimmy Vaughan and Mobutu Sese Seko.

But –

Rundle swivels back to face the window again.

That would have been confined to Paris, or London, or Washington, wouldn't it? At no point, as far as he knows, did Vaughan himself ever actually *go* to Congo.

He's going, though, and it feels appropriate.

Rundle leans back in his seat and closes his eyes.

He's only sorry now that he didn't arrange to have Nora come along as well.

*

Conway sits at the kitchen counter, distracted, agitated, gazing at Corinne as she cajoles Jack into eating some cereal. What if he were married to *her*, he thinks, and Jack was their first, and they lived in an apartment in Paris, and he ran a successful software or consultancy business? And Corinne adored him, deferred to him, wanted him.

What if . . .

'Well?'

Conway looks up. Ruth is standing there, with her coat on. She nods at the radio.

'Any mention of when the funeral is?'

He straightens up. 'Thursday morning.'

She passes Jack on her way to the fridge and strokes his head.

'Is it going to be a state funeral?'

'Mamma.' Delayed reaction.

'Yeah.'

She opens the fridge and takes out a carton of cranberry juice. 'I still can't believe it.'

'No, me neither.' It's not the only thing he can't believe. His brief phone call to Don Ribcoff and then . . . problem solved?

Again?

Or maybe Larry Bolger simply obliged, succumbed to the enormous pressure he was under, the guilt, the fear, the apprehension.

Ticker couldn't take it any more.

Either way, problem solved.

That problem solved.

Who does Conway phone up now, though, about his other problems? His financial woes, his impending professional meltdown, his own guilt and fear and apprehension?

'Oh,' Ruth says, 'I meant to ask you. How did the meeting go?'

They'd been so caught up last night in the news about Bolger's death that they hadn't talked about anything else.

He pauses. He's about to tell her the truth. But not with Corinne there, not with the baby, not in the *kitchen*.

'It went OK, I think. We'll see.'

Ruth pours some juice into a glass and puts the carton back in the fridge.

'Right,' she says, and knocks the juice back. 'I'm off.'

'Mamma.'

A few minutes later, Conway heads out himself.

Driving into town feels normal enough, like any other morning, but only so long as he keeps the radio off and ignores the constant pinging of his phone. As soon as he arrives at his building, however, the feeling evaporates. Because what awaits him here, up on the sixth floor, especially after yesterday's debacle with the Black Vine people, will bear no resemblance to a normal day at the office. Instead, there'll be frantic messages from Martin Boyle, from the banks, maybe even from business correspondents, people at RTE and Newstalk and the papers. Among the staff, there'll be an air of panic, of incredulity, of how can this be happening.

He'll be expected to say something.

He'll be expected to turn this around.

*

When Jimmy walks into his apartment on Tuesday afternoon he is almost sick. Finbarr warned him that the place had been turned over, but he isn't prepared for the visceral shock of it – the sense of what it'd be like, he imagines, to look in the mirror one morning and see your face unexpectedly disfigured.

He puts his bag down.

Everything has been disturbed, moved, knocked over. The bookshelves have been cleared, with all the books now in messy heaps on the floor.

But he's prepared to bet there isn't a single one missing.

Because burglars don't take books, certainly not old paperbacks. They clear bookshelves because they're *looking* for something.

He goes over to his desk and switches on the computer. It's one of the few objects in the room still in its proper place.

Which will maybe tell its own story.

And, straightaway, does.

Wiped.

Fuck.

It's not the loss of data he's concerned about – he has that on his laptop, on a flash drive, stored online – it's the message this conveys. It's how it makes him think again about what happened in London.

Fuck.

He looks around.

Apparently, two other apartments in the building were broken into as well, but he can only conclude that these were for show.

It's with a certain degree of ambivalence, not to say unease, that he decides to start tidying up. The alternative would be to go and stay with a friend, but this is where he lives. It's his apartment. He isn't going anywhere.

He kneels on the floor, picks up a few books.

Starts there.

Thumbs through a couple of them, ends up reading bits, and quickly feeling indignant.

He picks up a Scribner's *Gatsby*.

A Picador *Dispatches*.

Concrete Island.

It takes him a while.

In fact, it's not until the next morning that Jimmy can bring himself to get back to work.

And effectively this means tracking down Dave Conway.

Without much difficulty he finds an address for Conway's office in town and a reference to his home, which is somewhere near Enniskerry. He also finds a couple of phone numbers and an e-mail address. But initial approaches prove fruitless – a cursory message is taken, a call is not returned, an e-mail gets an automatic out-of-office reply. He makes it as far as the reception area of the building where Conway Holdings has its offices and is told that no one is available to see him.

But he picks up on something here. There's a certain frantic air about the place, maybe even a sense of panic – which is not unusual these days, but he wonders if there's more to it than that.

He considers going out to Enniskerry to see if he can locate Conway's house, but decides against it, reckons that it might be a bit tricky. Or even risky.

Or just pointless.

When he gets back to the apartment, he delves further into a couple of online news archives, and keeps reading, searching, probing, as if some revelation might be at hand, some neat and convenient tying together of the various threads.

It's not quite *that*, but a significant fact does emerge from the acres of material he manages to scan – Dave Conway and Larry Bolger were close. During Bolger's time in office reference after reference puts the two men together, at meetings, in corridors, on the phone.

In photographs.

Jimmy looks at a few of these and tries to parse the body language, to extract some meaning from the position of a hand on a shoulder or the direction of a gaze.

It proves difficult, elusive.

Ultimately what he gets from the photographs is pretty obvious. And simple. It's the realisation that as a result of this close association between the two men, Dave Conway will more than likely be attending Larry Bolger's state funeral tomorrow morning in the church at Donnybrook and then later out at St Felim's Cemetery.

*

'I see the way you *look* at her.'

This is whispered. Ruth only whispers when she's about to explode. Or when there's no choice, when she's at something like a funeral, and a state funeral at that.

And at the bloody *graveside*.

'I *don't* look at her,' he says. 'Jesus.'

Conway has been blindsided by this. Of *course* he looks at Corinne. The girl is so beautiful she breaks his fucking heart every time he sees her – but he's not fourteen, he's not an idiot.

He swallows.

'You *do*.'

'I *don't*.'

He swallows again.

OK . . . maybe it's not inconceivable – lately, at any rate – that Ruth has caught him staring at the au pair.

For inappropriately long periods of time.

But whatever she might think it's not actually sexual. He doesn't want to fuck her. He's old enough to be her father.

He just –

He wants to envelop himself in the fragrant *idea* of her, and disappear.

Basically.

Evaporate. Escape.

Which might well be worse. From Ruth's perspective. Mightn't it?

A more serious transgression.

He should shut up.

It's been a long day. Two hours in the church, readings, tributes, poetry, the interminable shuffle back along the aisle to get out, then the car park, the cortège, the lined streets.

And now they're out here at St Felim's, at the graveside.

Waiting.

For the oration. Which is to be delivered by another former Taoiseach, and will no doubt be tedious beyond belief.

'I don't understand. What is *wrong* with you?'

Ruth doesn't look at him when she says this. It's more of a rhetorical question. He's reluctant to fight with her, but it's inevitable, he supposes.

They're a few rows back from the graveside, seated, and it's chilly, uncomfortably so. He doesn't recognise anyone on either side of them. No one seems to be listening anyway, everyone caught up in their own whispered conversations.

He stares at her, waits until she turns.

'What's wrong with me?' he then says, almost giddy with the knowledge that he's about to obliterate any annoying thoughts she might have about him and the au pair. 'I'm as close to being bankrupt as makes no difference. That's what.'

She stares at him, eyes widening.

His stomach turns.

He can see her trying to take this in.

But he won't have to say anything more, that much is clear. She gets it. Every time he tried to imagine the scene it took him ages, working through it, just to *explain*.

Not necessary, it seems.

Ruth can put the pieces together. And can probably extrapolate from it, too, see the ramifications.

All the way to the poor house.

'You *fool*,' she hisses.

God, Conway thinks, if only that's all I was.

'And what about the kids? *Jesus*.'

At least he doesn't have to go into any of the other stuff with her. The Larry Bolger stuff. The Susie Monaghan stuff.

The Don Ribcoff stuff.

'The house is in your name,' he says quietly, aware now of her starting to tremble beside him. 'Remember? So are half of the companies. It'll take ten years to sort it all out.'

Something occurs to him at that point. Phil Sweeney. Where is he? He didn't see him at the church. He should be here somewhere.

Conway looks around, over his shoulder.

He's assuming that despite their little falling-out things are OK there. With Phil. With the young guy, whatshisname, Jimmy Gilroy.

Now that Bolger is –

Well . . .

He's just assuming.

Big crowd here. He turns back, stares straight ahead, at the grave, at the coffin.

But maybe he shouldn't be making assumptions like that.

In the distance, a black state car glides into view.

Maybe he shouldn't be making assumptions like that at all.

*

Jimmy sits huddled behind his Honda on a low wall opposite the entrance to the cemetery. There's a large crowd here and they've all just watched the funeral cortège snake its way along the Cherryvale Road and disappear in through the imposing iron gates of St Felim's.

Earlier on, Jimmy spotted Dave Conway and his wife coming out of the church in Donnybrook and getting into a dark green BMW. There was a large crowd there too and it wasn't easy, but Jimmy knew it was him – recognised him from photographs. He wasn't going to be able to follow them directly, because of how the cortège was organised, but he knew where they were headed and made his own way out. He took an alternative and much quicker route, but when he arrived at the cemetery he found, not surprisingly, that access to it was restricted.

With more crowds gathering, he decided to pick a spot, sit down and just let the afternoon unfold at its own glacial pace.

He glances over at the gates again now.

The thing is, Conway will reappear at some point and Jimmy will follow him.

Until then all he can do is watch and wait. Besides, it's a nice day, cool, intermittently sunny, and there's a gentle breeze.

There are worse things he could be doing.

He feels strange, though. He's not here as a punter, not here to gawk or pay his respects. Nor does he feel, at the same time, like one of the journalists or photographers he keeps spotting about the place, guys he knows from his days at the paper.

In any case, they wouldn't allow that. He's officially out of the system, on the fringes at best.

They're a very protected species.

When one of them wanders past, in fact, Jimmy gets the look, the slight double-take.

Fuck are *you* doing here?

'Hi, Chris.'

'Jimmy.'

'How's it going?'

'Not bad. Nice day for it.'

Chris Sullivan. Political correspondent. Late forties. Inside track on just about everything.

Jimmy looks up at him, squints. 'Shouldn't you be inside?'

'On my way.' Sullivan checks his watch. 'Larry's not going anywhere.' Then, eyebrows furrowed, 'You working?'

It crosses Jimmy's mind to say something here, maybe even to say everything. He has what he has, information-wise, story-wise. What he doesn't have is the back-up and resources of a legitimate news organisation.

If there is such a thing anymore.

'No,' he says. 'I wouldn't call it work.' He holds a hand up to his face to block out the light. 'Though mind you, I was wondering.'

'Yeah?'

'What did you make of it?' He gestures towards the cemetery. 'A heart attack? In *London*?'

Sullivan shrugs. 'If that's how you're going, I don't think you get to choose where it happens.'

'He was relatively young, though. Healthy. Bit strange.'

Sullivan looks at him. 'What?' Long pause. Then, 'Would you *fuck* off. Larry Bolger? What are you saying?'

Jimmy hesitates.

That I talked to him a few days ago? That he implicated some pretty influential people in a horrendous crime, and that now he's dead?

He clears his throat.

'Nothing. I'm not saying anything.'

'Apparently.' Sullivan shakes his head. 'And I'd keep it that way. Take it easy, Jimmy.' He walks a few yards along the path, turns and crosses the road.

Jimmy watches as Sullivan approaches the cemetery gates. A uniformed guard lets him in. He disappears.

It wouldn't have worked out.

Jimmy doesn't have anything concrete, and if he did he'd be more or less giving it away. Guys like Chris Sullivan don't share their by-lines.

Jimmy leans forward and rests his head on the side of the motorbike.

He's a long way off a by-line on this one.

But what choice does he have? He has to keep going.

Has to keep waiting.

And it's at least another ninety minutes before the first few cars start trickling out of the cemetery. During this time the crowd pretty much disperses. Nothing left to gawk at.

Jimmy then gets ready and keeps his eyes peeled for the green BMW.

After a couple of minutes, and about five or six cars, he sees it.

9

A Gideon convoy takes Clark Rundle from the airport, which is just inside the Congolese border, to a lakeshore hotel near the old governor's mansion in Bukavu. The hotel has spectacular views of the lake and seems to be fairly comfortable, with spacious rooms and a functioning AC system, but Rundle is focused on only one thing now – seeing Arnold Kimbela and then getting the hell out of here.

It has been the longest two days of his life.

The flight from Paris to Kigali was bad enough, but then there was a ten-hour overnight delay before he could take the short flight to Bukavu. At all times he has been surrounded – cocooned, indeed – by Gideon personnel, and there has never been the slightest question about his safety, but something about the . . . the atmosphere, clammy and dense, and the people, staring faces seen in the distance, harsh voices carried on the air . . . he doesn't know, there's a general hard-to-define looseness here, a dreamlike, nightmarish feeling that everything is about to fall apart, slide into chaos, and it bothers him, it's like an incipient headache, or a rising wave of nausea.

Alone in his room, he gags and rushes to the toilet, but nothing happens.

He feels insecure, almost like a child, and for one or two seconds actually wants to cry. He imagines Nora sitting on the bed, opening her arms to him, but he flinches from the image, and shakes his head.

Then he goes over to the mini-bar, opens it and extracts two small bottles, a Jack Daniel's and a Teacher's. He unscrews these and knocks them back, one straight after the other.

That settles him.

After a while, he takes a shower, shaves, puts on a fresh suit. He looks at himself in the mirror. He straightens his tie.

At noon, they're taking him back to the airport for the last leg of the journey, the one-hour flight to Buenke. They'll be landing at the airstrip, which is a few miles from Kimbela's compound, and a few more again from the mining area itself. With any luck, he should be back here at the hotel by late evening, ready to start the return trip in the morning.

Rundle paces the room for a while, going over various negotiating positions in his head, stuff he might need to pull out later on. Then, suddenly, he stops. He stands at the window and looks out at Lake Kivu. For the first time since arriving here, he feels able to . . . not *relax* exactly, but . . .

Slow down a little.

Look at something directly in front of him and not be thinking about something else. And what's directly in front of him right now, he has to admit, is pretty stunning.

Not so the streets of Bukavu. As the convoy speeds through them a couple of hours later, along Avenue de la Résidence and Avenue Lumumba, past rundown art deco buildings – dusty and peeling, remnants of what must once have been a gorgeous city, probably as far back as the 1950s – Rundle's anxiety returns. It's the shanty town overlay, the air of menace and despair, the realisation that without this armoured SUV he's in, and the ones up ahead and behind, without his Gideon shell, he wouldn't survive ten minutes here, that left to walk any of these streets on his own, he'd be torn apart, limb from limb, then left to rot and decompose.

For the dogs, for the maggots.

The flight to Buenke is in a light aircraft and does nothing to mitigate his feelings of anxiety. They pass over mountainous terrain, jungle and scrubland and while it's all undeniably beautiful he has this queasy sense that he's falling deeper and deeper into some inescapable abyss. This is Congo's 'wild east' after all, a region of the country in which government forces and rebel militias vie for control of the abundant natural resources so coveted by the rest of the world.

Though, OK, *vie for control* . . .

That makes it sound almost civilised, like a game of chess or something. But it's not. The hard fact is, shifting loyalties here and the fluidity of the security situation in general make eastern Congo one of the most unstable and barbarous regions on the entire planet.

If there *is* a real chess game, where it's played out, he supposes, is behind this great cloak of ungovernability, and the players are people like himself, and James Vaughan, and whoever the party leaders in Beijing have sanctioned to come over here and do business. It's like the Cold War, with its drawn-out proxy conflicts, only this time there's no pretext, no talk of a clash of ideologies, no talk of a domino effect.

This time it's strictly business.

At the Buenke airstrip, Rundle is greeted, much to his relief, by Don Ribcoff, who came on ahead to oversee the security arrangements in person. He looks at home here, all dressed-up and heavily armed.

Rundle isn't complaining.

As the two men walk from the plane to another convoy of SUVs, they discuss arrangements. Kimbela is at his compound for the rest of the day and will receive Rundle at 1600 hours. What happens after that – locations, timeframes, catering – will very much depend on how negotiations proceed. At all points along the way Rundle will be accompanied by a team of eight Gideon contractors, and leading the unit will be Peter Lutz, who – as they arrive at the head car of the convoy – Ribcoff now introduces Rundle to.

'Sir,' Lutz say, extending his hand, 'it's an honour.'

Rundle wants to say *at ease* here, or some such, but he knows this isn't the military, knows the PMCs do things differently – he's just not *au fait* with the protocols.

Not, of course – if this was the military – that he'd be saying *at ease* to anyone.

He's a bit thrown at the moment, that's all. The heat here is unbelievable, like New York in August, only ten times worse.

He looks at Ribcoff with renewed respect. The man is more or less wearing battle fatigues and hasn't broken a sweat.

By the same token, Rundle is in a suit and tie, and while he won't claim not to have broken a sweat, he *is* holding his own.

What he says, turning to Lutz, is, 'That business last week?'

Lutz nods, readies himself. 'Very unfortunate, sir, and we all send our best wishes to the Senator, but as far as procedures here are concerned, I can assure you that a definite line has been drawn in the sand.' He pauses, glances around, and although there is no one within earshot, continues in a lower, more discreet tone. 'As you know, sir, during the course of the incident it became necessary to terminate the contractor concerned. It was unavoidable. The only other contractor closely involved, and in a defensive capacity, let me stress, has already shipped out on extended leave, so I think –'

'Why?'

Lutz hesitates, seems surprised by the question. 'Why has he gone on leave, sir?'

'Yes.'

'He appeared to have been traumatised by the incident. I felt it wiser to remove him, for his own sake, and also for the morale of the unit.'

Rundle considers this. 'Makes sense, I guess.'

Ribcoff then nods at Lutz, who extends an arm, indicating to Rundle the middle car.

'OK,' Rundle says, following him, and adding, a little self-consciously, 'Let's get this show on the road.'

It's a phrase he's heard James Vaughan use many times.

*

Conway pulls out of the cemetery onto the Cherryvale Road. There is a big reception being held in a local hotel and everyone will be there, most of the cabinet, various financiers, business people, a bishop or two, the media, celebrities . . .

But at the earliest opportunity – approaching the first main intersection – Ruth takes a deep breath and says, *'Take me home.'* Her voice is shaky, uncertain. These are the first words she's uttered in over an hour.

Although Conway doesn't want to go to the reception either,

he certainly doesn't want to go home. He doesn't want to go anywhere.

But with Ruth in the car what choice does he have?

He takes a left, leaving the main road behind – and the route to the hotel.

He wants to say something, just to break the silence. There is nothing to say, though. Unless they want to have it out and go all the way.

But not in the car.

Not in the kitchen, not in the bedroom, not in front of the au pair, the kids, the *baby*.

Where then?

'Ruth, I'm sorry,' he says. 'It's a mess. North Atlantic are calling in their debts, and –'

'You're only telling me this *now*?' She punches the dashboard. 'You let me go on thinking everything was OK?'

'I didn't want –'

Ruth screams. 'What? You didn't want me to be worried? Don't give me that crap, Dave, I'm not an *idiot*.'

'Well, if you're so on the ball,' Conway says, squeezing the steering wheel, 'why didn't you see this coming? Because it's been staring us in the face for months. You read the papers. You follow the news. Why should *I* be immune? Why should *I* be any different?'

Ruth screams again, but quickly muffles it. 'Because,' she says, the shake still in her voice, 'I thought you *were* different.'

Conway doesn't know how to respond to this.

He says nothing.

Once more, a thick silence descends.

The traffic is heavy and every light seems to be red.

It's torture.

When they pull into their driveway, Ruth straightens up. She opens her side of the car before Conway has even cut the engine. She then storms across the gravel and in through the front door of the house, slamming it behind her.

Conway follows. He moves slowly, digging out his keys. When he gets inside, Ruth is standing in the hallway with the phone up to her ear.

He drops his keys onto the hall stand.

Ruth lowers the phone and presses a button on it.

'Four messages,' she says. 'One from the *Times*, one from the *Sunday Business Post*, two from Martin Boyle. All urgent.' She looks at him. '*Jesus*. So I'm the last to know, is that it?' She flings the phone down onto the hall stand. There are tears in her eyes. '*Bankrupt?*'

Conway picks up the phone and replaces it in its charger. 'Look, I owe the bank a couple of hundred million, Ruth. There's no way I can pay it back.'

'But...'

He looks at her, says nothing.

'What about...?'

At which point Molly and Danny come rushing down the stairs, 'MOMMY, DADDY...'

Followed by Corinne, who is holding Jack.

The next few minutes are chaotic. Everyone moves to the kitchen at the back of the house. The kids dominate, which is fine, it provides convenient cover – because Conway doesn't want to continue the conversation with Ruth, doesn't want to answer any of her questions, her what-abouts. Besides, he knows them all in advance. What about the kids? What about schools?

What about the house? What about the horses? What about Umbria? What about *me*?

But that's all shit they can sort out, with lawyers and accountants, and a little bit of pulling together. What Conway would like to point out to Ruth, but can't, is that this could all be *so* much worse, that they've been *lucky*, that the man whose funeral they've just come from, if he'd lived, was actually on the point of burying *them*.

There's no shame in financial ruin if everyone else is going through it at the same time, is there? But the scandal of a trial for, at the very least, conspiracy to murder, the ignominy of that would be insurmountable, the disgrace of it ineradicable. Then they really would lose the house, and the kids really would suffer.

She doesn't have a clue.

But he can't tell her now, because the simple fact is he didn't tell her *then*. How could he have? Why would he have? It wasn't supposed to get that complicated and messy. He found himself in the situation and he handled it.

He protected his interests.

And moved on.

Not that he's pretending it was easy, or that it didn't leave a mark, it did . . .

He still dreams about it.

But –

And it's just then, as he senses Ruth approaching – rapidly, from the left – that Conway realises what he's doing. His mind might be elsewhere, but he's staring at Corinne again. He has allowed himself to be distracted, mesmerised even, by the revealing gap that appears every so often between the bottom of her short silk top and the top of her sculpted blue jeans. He catches sight of it as she moves about the kitchen, as she reaches up for something, or leans over, his eye tracking this innocent, elusive slit of smooth, tanned skin.

When Ruth gets to him, it happens very fast. She swings her hand back and slaps him hard on the face.

'You *pig*.'

He lurches sideways, sliding off the stool. He brings a hand up to his stinging cheek.

'*Jesus*.'

'*MOMMY!*'

'*Out*,' Ruth says to him, as they both turn to look at a shocked Molly. 'Now. *Out* of here.' She grabs him by the arm and they move towards the door.

Corinne, clearly shocked too, steps forward to distract Molly.

Out in the hallway, door closed behind them, Ruth raises her hand again, but Conway blocks it, takes a firm hold of her wrist.

'*Christ*.'

'Get out of this house,' she says, resisting, her voice no longer shaky.

'Ruth, I –'

'Don't –'

For a few seconds they stay like that, locked in position, staring at each other, and in steely silence – too many words required, too many knotty, complicated sentences, to even *begin* the process of –

But suddenly, Conway releases her. He turns and walks off, grabbing his keys from the stand as he passes it. Without look-

ing back, he goes out the hall door. He is careful not to slam it
behind him.

*

The ride to the compound is fast and bumpy. On the way,
they pass through a tiny village, which Don Ribcoff points out
as the scene of last week's 'incident'. Rundle tries to picture
it, J.J. close to a heart attack as all hell breaks loose around
him, but the images are insubstantial, fleeting, and in any case
are superseded by others – ones nearer the surface, and drawn
from memory, chiefly Rundle and Kimbela in a Paris apartment three years ago, what Rundle likes to think of as his
Africa summit. There were plenty of guns around the place
that day – none of them Rundle's, as it happens – but at least
outside the apartment it was fucking *Paris*.

This is going to be different. Outside wherever they sit down
today it will be Congo.

Democratic Republic *of*.

No surprise then that Rundle's guts are in a knot.

As he recalls, Arnold Kimbela was scary and charming in
about equal measure. But that was then, when Rundle knew
very little about the man – which was mainly that he was a local
force to be reckoned with, commander of a brigade of the Congolese army that operated outside the control of the Congolese
government, but who also, more importantly, ran the mines,
doled out the contracts, a loose enough arrangement by international standards, even by official Congolese standards, but
round here all that you needed.

In the meantime, no doubt, the scariness-to-charm ratio will have shifted considerably. Gregarious and larger-than-life as he was, and probably still is, the colonel has acquired a reputation for brutality.

Extreme methods.

And so on.

Rundle closes his eyes.

He doesn't have much of a stomach for this sort of stuff, but he takes a pragmatic view. Short of invading the continent, there isn't much anyone can do about how these people choose to run their affairs. However, the international trade in mineral resources is a vital one, and is also, frankly, unstoppable, so the cost – and, by extension, awareness of that cost – is extremely difficult to avoid.

Whatever that might mean.

He opens his eyes again.

He's beginning to sound a bit like a politician.

He looks out of the window. Flat grey scrubland rushes past. One minute this place is astonishingly beautiful, and the next it's drab.

And bleak.

Or is that just how he feels?

'You ready for this?' Don Ribcoff says.

Rundle turns to him. 'Yeah. Piece of cake.' He smiles. 'I mean, it's just business, right?'

'Well, I don't –'

'Look, I know, I know, kids with Kalashnikovs, heart of darkness, all of that shit, but at the end of the day it's a meeting, it's negotiations, it's striking a deal. I'm a businessman, he's a businessman. We disagree, what's he going to do, eat me?'

Ribcoff grunts. 'We're not likely to let that happen, but it doesn't mean he wouldn't try.'

'Oh relax, Don. This'll actually be pretty tedious. These mining contracts aren't a barrel of laughs you know.'

This is bluster on Rundle's part. He's nervous, no getting away from it, but after what happened with J.J., he's not about to put it on display. Besides, Don Ribcoff is the hired help here, he's security, and the details of what goes on, of what this is about, are – and must remain – strictly confidential.

Soon the convoy is slowing down and they're turning left in through some gates to a walled enclosure. They follow a heavily tree-lined driveway for about two hundred yards and come out onto a clearing. Then they stop alongside the main entrance to what Rundle takes to be Kimbela's famously unfinished 'villa'. It's the sort of thing a prosperous tea merchant might have built for himself in one of the new suburbs of mid-Victorian London.

Here, of course, it looks absurd.

On the opposite side of the clearing is the row of concrete shacks J.J. talked about.

Rundle glances around. The place appears to be deserted. But within seconds this changes. Jeeps pull up on either side of the convoy, brakes screeching, soldiers piling off, and suddenly they're surrounded.

Rundle stiffens.

Ribcoff rolls his eyes. 'This is Kimbela's praetorian guard. I can't believe we actually *train* these idiots.'

'Really? And who supplies them with those pressed fatigues and crisp felt berets?'

'Who do you think?'

'Yeah?'

Ribcoff laughs. 'Sure.'

Rundle makes a show of laughing along. Then he reaches for the door and opens it. He steps out of this climate-controlled SUV and into a wall of heat.

Ribcoff does the same, followed by Lutz and his team in the other two vehicles.

Everyone stands around for a moment, soldiers, private contractors, but it's barely enough time for any kind of tension or animosity to build. Not that it should, Rundle thinks, given that they're all basically on the same payroll.

'Clark, my old friend.'

The voice is deep and resonant. Rundle turns around and sees Kimbela emerging from behind one of the jeeps. He too is in pressed fatigues and a crisp beret.

And mirrored sunglasses.

Regulation issue.

Rundle gets the impression that they've all dressed up for this, for the occasion. He doesn't think they did it for J.J. And there don't seem to be any drug-crazed children around either.

Should he be flattered?

'Colonel,' he says and extends a hand.

Kimbela steps forward and they shake. The colonel is forty-two now, but he still looks like a slightly excitable, overweight teenager.

With attitude.

Which is exactly what he would have been twenty-five years ago when his old man was running an extortion and racketeering network for Mobutu.

'It's good to see you, Clark. Tell me, how is your brother?' As he says this, Kimbela makes a move towards the house and indicates for Rundle to follow him. Rundle does so, followed in turn by Lutz and several of the Gideon contractors. 'J.J. is well,' he says. 'He's recovering. It wasn't an easy trip for him.' Then, feeling he should amend this, adds, 'It wasn't an easy *time* . . . for anyone.'

'No, no it wasn't.' Solemn here. 'But anyway, look. I saw him on, what is it called, *Face the Nation*? Online? He was good. Very good. The brace is an interesting touch, I think. No?' He turns, looks at Rundle and bursts out laughing. Then, 'American politics, if I may say so, is quite boring. *Fiscal* reform? Please.' He laughs again, even louder this time.

Rundle tries to join in – he wants to be polite, but at the same time feels it shouldn't be all one way. 'Well,' he says, 'at least we have systems that work, we get things *done*, you know?'

Kimbela either doesn't hear this or chooses to ignore it.

They are standing now in a large reception room. The furniture, as J.J. said, is fake Louis Quinze, upholstered chairs, a couple of chaises longues and a credenza arranged in no particular order.

It's like a forgotten corner of some discount home furnishing outlet in a New Jersey shopping mall.

'So, Clark,' the colonel says, turning to Rundle, 'would you like some tea?'

*

Conway gets in the car, reverses quickly on the gravel and turns. He shoots along the driveway, narrowly avoiding a stalled motorbike at the gates. He turns left and takes off.

He has no idea where he's going, but it doesn't matter. He needs time to think. Now that he's come clean with Ruth, and that the *Times* and *Business Post* are clearly on the case, he can start devising a realistic rescue package for the company. And what he mustn't forget is that it *can* be done. Compared to how things might have turned out, it won't be that hard either. Dealing with the media intrusion is going to be tough, but easily preferable to dealing with the cops. And downsizing Conway Holdings? Creative restructuring? Brutal cutbacks? All a hundred times more preferable – how could they not be? – to prison time.

Somehow he has to bring Ruth on board and get her to see things his way.

After driving aimlessly for a while, Conway decides where he's going. From here he can get to Tara Meadows in fifteen minutes. It's quiet there, and isolated. He won't have to talk to anyone. He'll give Ruth a couple of hours to cool off and then he'll phone her.

By that time he'll have worked it out, everything, even a rescue package for their marriage. First off, Corinne will have to go. Not that any of it is her fault, but she's a distraction. They can get some hatchet-faced old biddy to replace her. As he drives, Conway sees that the real issue on the domestic front is that he has hidden things from Ruth. Not just the true nature of the First Continental deal, and what happened at Drumcoolie Castle, all of that, which is understandable, but lots of other stuff as well, ordinary stuff, banal stuff.

And unnecessarily.

Being secretive has become a habit.

Ruth deserves better.

He must *do* better.

Glancing in his rearview mirror a moment later, as he comes off the roundabout, Conway notices something.

There's a motorbike. It's been there for a while. He wonders if it's the same one that was stalled at the gates of his house.

As he was pulling out.

Seemed to be stalled.

Shit.

It's a journalist, has to be.

Approaching the entrance to Tara Meadows now, Conway is undecided. He turns in anyway. At least it will flush this bastard out. He'll hardly just follow him in.

But he does, brazenly.

Right behind him, no hesitation.

Conway proceeds along Tara Boulevard, towards the Concourse. Then he swerves suddenly, pulls in at the kerb and opens the door. He gets out. He stands there on the road, door still open behind him, and glares at the approaching motorcyclist.

The motorcyclist slows down, and stops. He gets off the bike and immediately starts undoing the clasps on his helmet.

Conway readies himself. He's in no mood for this, but there's no point in being overly aggressive either. It won't be his last encounter with one of these guys. As he watches the helmet coming off, he wonders what the angle is going to be, financial or tabloid – figures and statistics or fat-cat confidential?

The guy is quite young. Conway stares at him for a few seconds, but doesn't recognise him. And he's fairly sure he would. Because he knows most of the hacks in this town. Over the years, he's been inter—

Oh Jesus.

It hits him.

Of course. It's so obvious.

Then Conway's whole world dissolves, everything, his plans, his assumptions . . . even his delusions . . .

But what did he expect? What did he think he was paying for all these years?

No more Phil Sweeney, no more buffer zone.

Simple equation.

The young guy turns and hangs his helmet on one of the handlebars of the motorbike. When he turns back, Conway looks him in the eye and says, 'You're Jimmy Gilroy, aren't you?'

*

Jimmy nods.

'Yes, I am.'

How does Conway know this? Probably Phil Sweeney. Not that it matters.

'What do you want?'

Jimmy's a little nervous here. There's no other way of proceeding, though. 'I'd like to ask you a couple of questions.'

Conway doesn't answer straightaway. But his body language is telling. Initially, it was aggressive – hands on hips, ready for a confrontation – then it changed suddenly. Now *he's* the one who seems nervous.

'Questions about what?'

'Different things. It depends.' Jimmy glances around. This is one of those ghost estates – half-built, then abandoned when the money ran out. Despite the late afternoon sunlight, there's a bleak, almost menacing feel to the place. 'Can we go some-where?'

Conway stares at him. He shakes his head. 'What do you want to ask me?'

Jimmy pauses. He's reluctant to begin, standing out in the open air like this. 'Tara Meadows?' he says, with a sweep of his hand, indicating the entire estate. 'Is it one of yours?'

Conway exhales, clearly fighting the urge to snap at him, or worse. '*That's* one of your questions?'

'No. I suppose not.'

'I didn't think so.' He exhales again. He looks up at the sky. He seems to be considering something.

Jimmy remains very still.

'Fine,' Conway says eventually. 'Let's go somewhere.' He turns around, pushes the door of his car closed and starts walk-ing along the road, heading further into the estate.

Jimmy hesitates. He looks back at his bike. He should lock it.

'Follow me,' Conway says over his shoulder. 'I want to show you something.'

Jimmy follows.

They walk along Tara Boulevard and enter a large, deserted town square. Thinking about it, Jimmy remembers an article he read a couple of years back about this development, what it was supposed to be, the great hopes for it. He can't believe what he's seeing now, though – a bleak, windswept square surrounded by empty apartment blocks and office buildings. On the far side of it he spots a group of youths, some on bikes, circling aimlessly, others sitting on a low wall drinking cans of beer.

'You see this?' Conway says, striding now towards the en-trance to one of the buildings. 'Supposed to be a hotel, the five-star . . . something, we didn't have a name for it yet. But you know who's living here now? Yeah?' He holds open the door for Jimmy, who hesitates but then goes in past him.

'No, who?'

'Homeless people. Drunks. I don't know. Squatters, junkies. Anybody who wants to. Welcome to Tara fucking Meadows.'

Jimmy walks straight in and looks around. It's a hotel lobby all right, or would be if they finished it. He can see where the reception desk should go, and the lounge area. Over to the right, double doors, half open, lead into another room, probably a dining area or a function room.

The whole place is dark and musty.

All of a sudden Jimmy isn't sure how comfortable he feels here. Dave Conway, if he wanted to, could stab him in the heart with a knife, repeatedly, leave him there on the floor to die. And how long would it be before anyone – apart from the local rat population – discovered his body? It could be days, weeks even. The only thing is, Conway doesn't look like the sort of person who carries a knife around with him. Or even a gun. Standing in this bare hotel lobby now, he looks exactly like what he *is*, a businessman.

Besides, why would he want to kill Jimmy in the first place?

He hasn't heard any of his questions yet.

And it's entirely possible that he won't have any answers when he does – that he won't have the slightest idea of what Jimmy is talking about.

'So,' Conway says, 'this is it. This is all there is. All that's left.'

'Yeah?'

'Yeah. It's what I'm reduced to, so believe me, I've got

enough on my plate without' – he stops for a moment – 'without whatever Susie Monaghan crap you're peddling.'

Jimmy takes a notebook from his back pocket and flicks it open. 'I'm not peddling anything, Mr Conway, and as people keep pointing out to *me*, this isn't about Susie Monaghan.'

'What *is* it about then, tell me.'

'Well, I'd like to know why Gianni Bonacci wrote your name on the back of a business card belonging to Clark Rundle.'

Conway leans forward. '*Come again?*'

Jimmy doesn't say anything. He waits.

'A business card? So fucking what? I did *business* with the guy.' Conway shakes his head. He seems flustered. 'Who did you hear this from anyway, Larry Bolger?'

'No,' Jimmy says. 'I heard it from Bonacci's wife. His *widow*.'

'His widow?'

'Yeah, I've just come back from Italy. I went to her apartment and talked to her. She showed me the card.'

Conway shrugs. He doesn't say anything for a moment. Then he says, 'Come *on*. What's this about? I'm tired.'

Jimmy shifts his weight from one foot to the other. He wishes they could sit down somewhere. He wishes he knew what he was doing. He wishes he had a job. 'Right,' he says, glancing at his notebook. 'Here it is. Larry Bolger more or less told me that the helicopter crash that weekend wasn't an accident. He said that Susie was collateral damage and implied that one of the other passengers was at the heart of this. I talked to some people and went through the passenger list and, let's put it this way, Gianni Bonacci's name is the only one that I couldn't eliminate. Then I went and spoke to his wife who told me that the day before the crash Gianni had told *her* his life

266

was in danger, that he had come across something, stumbled on it, something significant. Now.' He takes a deep breath. 'Around this time you sold your company First Continental Resources to BRX, a company owned by Clark Rundle, whose name, along with yours, turns up on a business card in Gianni Bonacci's briefcase.' He pauses. 'So, there it is . . . it's just a lead. That's all. I'm pursuing it. I'm here asking if there's anything you can tell me, if you can explain any of this.'

He flicks the notebook closed, as though he was reading from it and is now finished.

Nerves.

He looks up.

Conway is staring at him. 'This is all unsubstantiated, it's . . . it's circumstantial.'

'Yeah, it's circumstantial, sure, but the circumstances keep piling up. A few days after my conversation with Larry Bolger and what happens? He drops dead. Then my apartment is broken into. Nothing of any value is taken, but the hard drive on my computer is wiped. Meanwhile I have people like Phil Sweeney telling me I'm in over my head, and to find another story. Offering me *money*.'

Conway maintains eye contact, but there's something different about him now, about his facial expression. It's as though a key element that was holding it in place has dropped out. Certainty, conviction.

Self-belief.

'Who are you working for?' he says. 'What paper? When is this story coming out?'

Jimmy hesitates. He's not about to throw away his advantage

here by admitting he's not working for anyone. 'Well, probably not this Sunday, but definitely –'

'According to Phil Sweeney you're unemployed.'

Jimmy looks away, then back, sighs. 'OK, maybe, but when I get this figured out, I won't be, all right?' He pauses. 'I mean, do you not remember that crash? *Six* people dead? This is a big fucking story.'

Conway doesn't say anything.

Jimmy waits a beat. 'So. I take it you're the one Phil Sweeney is trying to protect. Is that right?'

Conway takes a deep breath. He holds it in for a few seconds before releasing it as a slow, shuddering sigh. He stares at Jimmy for another few seconds. 'You're not going to let this go, are you?'

'No.'

Conway sighs again, in the same way. 'Well then,' he says, his voice weary, defeated. 'I suppose the answer to your question is yes.'

Jimmy swallows. 'Sorry?'

'Your question. About Phil Sweeney and who he's trying to protect. The answer to it. It's yes.'

*

It quickly becomes clear to Rundle why sending his brother down here was such a miscalculation. Kimbela didn't take J.J. seriously. He didn't think he was expected to.

For his part, Rundle had thought *he* was being clever.

Because who wouldn't be flattered by the attentions of a US

senator, one who comes thousands of miles to pay you a visit, and at *your* convenience?

Arnold Kimbela, apparently.

It turns out that J.J. is a mere politician, not the sort of person – not round here anyway – who commands much respect. Politicians are a joke. They kiss babies and smile for the cameras. They do what they are told. Clark, on the other hand, is a businessman, and one with an international profile. He is – there's an expression for it – a mover and a shaker. He gets things done.

It's on the tip of Rundle's tongue to say, well, what about Mobutu? But he knows what the answer would most likely be. Mobutu wasn't a *politician*. Are you crazy? He was Mobutu Sese Seko Nkuku wa za Banga, the king, the all-powerful warrior who goes from conquest to conquest, leaving fire in his wake.

OK. Fine.

Rundle is tired.

They've been sitting in this room now for over an hour, sipping tea from china cups and shooting what could only loosely be called the breeze. The heat is so overpowering that Rundle feels he might be close to hallucinating. They've had the tea ceremony with the little zombie girl, who turns out to be family – Kimbela's niece or daughter, or maybe even his *wife*, Rundle isn't quite sure. Possibly all three. They've discussed *Lost*, which Kimbela has watched on box sets. They've argued over the new LudeX 3 games console, its place in the market and whether or not it will achieve full spectrum dominance.

And all the time, in the background, soldiers and contractors stand around, smoking, whispering, some obviously bored, others trying to listen in on the conversation.

But at a certain point, Rundle has had enough.

'So, colonel,' he says, 'we have business to discuss.'

'We do?' Kimbela seems puzzled.

Rundle isn't in the mood for games. 'Our ongoing relationship, the contract situation. BRX is very anxious to continue at Buenke, and to help in any way we can, but we do realise that there's competition.' He glances over his shoulder, sees Ribcoff, then looks back at the Colonel. 'A rival bid. From the Chinese.'

Kimbela still looks puzzled. 'But I thought . . .' He leans forward. 'I thought I'd discussed this with your brother. I instructed him to inform you of my position. Isn't that why he came? To deliver a message?'

Rundle suppresses a groan. 'Yes, but . . .' There's no finessing this. 'Look, I didn't get the message, OK? Between one thing and another, what happened here, his injury, he got confused.'

'Aaaaahh,' Kimbela says, drawing it out. 'And look at me, thinking my old friend Clark has come on a *social* visit. To pay his respects.'

'Oh, but I *have*, too, I –'

Kimbela bursts out laughing, and even slaps his thigh. 'Of course you have, of course you have.' He wipes a tear from his cheek. 'But seeing as how you are here, no? Maybe we can clear the matter up, is that it?' He goes on laughing.

Rundle finds this really annoying, and wonders what Ribcoff is making of it all. 'Well, I *do* need to know what you said to J.J.' He's whispering. 'Because, as you can imagine, a lot is riding on it.'

Kimbela nods, all serious again. He shifts his considerable

weight in the chair, which looks as if it could snap under him at any second. 'Very well,' he says. 'These Chinese? Scary people. They want everything, and they want it *now*. And not just in Congo, in all of Africa.' He sighs, and shakes his head.

Naturally, Rundle is aware of this. Even in the three years since BRX bought the mine at Buenke, the Chinese presence in Africa has increased exponentially. And BRX, with substantial oil and mining interests in Angola, Mozambique and Equatorial Guinea, has seen this growth at first hand.

'They send people over,' Kimbela continues, 'who will live in huts and survive on a bowl of rice a day. *You* people?' He gives another of his short, loud bursts of laughter. '*You* people have to have hot dogs and sodas and Taco Bell and reality TV shows and every kind of shit. So the result is, you are being left behind.' He pauses. 'You have . . .' He clicks his fingers. 'Yes, fallen asleep at the wheel.'

Rundle isn't sure what Kimbela is getting at here. Could it actually be the big kiss-off? No reason why not. Because the fact is, like it or lump it, China is going through an accelerated industrial revolution at the moment and has unlimited cash to feed its voracious appetite for natural resources – the kind of cash that the US these days can only dream of.

Highest bidder wins.

But what made the Buenke deal a little different, Rundle thinks, and where BRX were ahead of the curve, was that no one really knew what they were after. People assumed it was copper, and while Buenke certainly had *some* copper, there were better locations elsewhere – farther south, for example – that the Chinese would have been more likely to favour.

Rundle remembers the negotiations the way you might remember a particularly awful root canal procedure. First you had that stupid conference in Ireland, with Gianni Bonacci poking his nose in and Dave Conway pushing for more money. Then, after *that* whole mess was resolved, you had the meeting in Paris with Kimbela and the elaborate sham of pretending they were signing an actual, legally binding contract.

But it suited both parties at the time, and the arrangement has worked perfectly well ever since. That is, until the goddamn Chinese started poking *their* noses in, looking to hoover up a few more mining concessions.

Putting ideas in people's heads.

The problem is, BRX can't just up sticks and go somewhere else. This is site-specific shit here. 'You know,' he says, fixing his gaze at a point on the floor, 'asleep at the wheel, I'm not sure about that. But maybe . . . maybe we haven't been keeping our eye on the ball.'

'As you like,' Kimbela says. 'Though tell me, who is this *we*? The Americans? The West in general?' He pauses. 'Because now, it seems, it's the turn of the East.'

Rundle looks up. Kimbela is staring at him.

This could be awkward.

Without some sort of local support, BRX would have to leave the region, no question about it. Without the *colonel*, however, you could perhaps negotiate some deal with a rival militia group. But that would be a very long shot indeed, and not the outcome from all of this that Jimmy Vaughan wants to hear about.

Nor is it a card that Rundle can play right now, sitting in front of Kimbela, looking him straight in the eye.

Hey fatso, how'd ya like a bullet in the brain?

Rundle leans forward. He's beyond tired at this point. 'Colonel,' he says, 'stop fucking with me, OK? I need to know.' He holds his hands out in surrender. 'What was the message?'

Kimbela laughs at this. It's clear he's lapping up Rundle's unease, his humiliation. But as before, he stops quite abruptly. 'Very well, my friend. The Chinese, yes? They want to build a network here, a spider's web of railroads and highways going out from Congo through Angola and Zambia and Tanzania to ports on either side of the continent. And you know why?' He makes a snorting sound. 'Of course you do. So they can come here, extract every mineral they can find from under the ground and cut down every tree in every forest and ship it all back to China.' He holds up a finger. 'But in exchange they will give us banks and soccer stadiums. Oh, and hospitals, too, and universities. And a functioning sewage system. And they want to do it all themselves, with imported labour, Chinese engineers, Chinese technicians, all living in temporary compounds, speaking Mandarin and eating chow mein. And no talk of human rights, either. None of that paternalistic bullshit we routinely get from *you* people about political transparency and fighting corruption.' He stops and smiles. 'Sounds good, yeah? Sweet? Tempting?' The smile quickly fades. 'If you're in Kinshasa, maybe. If you're already *in* the fucking government. But not for someone like me. Out here. In the hills.' He thumps his chest. 'In this brave new world, there's no place for someone like *me*.'

This is shouted.

Rundle flinches.

'You Americans?' Kimbela goes on. 'You have no real policy for Africa. The politburo in Beijing, they're thinking one hundred years into the future. But what are *you* doing? Setting up AFRICOM? With its headquarters in Stuttgart? Is that meant to be some kind of a joke? No, you've got nothing to offer us but bureaucracy and aid and inefficiency and . . .' – he drags the words out – '*spectacular ignorance*. But you know what? It's fine. I love it. *Plus ça change*.'

Rundle isn't too sure what point Kimbela is trying to make here. He's beginning to understand how J.J. felt, and it obviously shows in his face.

'Look,' Kimbela says, lowering his voice to a conspiratorial whisper, 'what I'm telling you is, this *thing*, this arrangement we have.' He waves a hand back and forth between them. 'It suits me very well. I don't want it to change.' There is a long pause, during which his smile slowly returns. 'And *that*, my friend, is what I told your brother.'

*

'Yes, but . . .' Jimmy looks around this spectral hotel lobby. There's nowhere to go, nowhere to sit. The place is empty. Are they just going to stand here? He looks back at Conway. 'Protect you from what?'

'My part in what happened. Not that Phil Sweeney actually knows what happened. He doesn't. Which is something, by the way, you should get straight in your head right now.'

Jimmy nods.

Conway then seems to brace himself. He picks a spot on the dusty concrete floor to stare at, and starts talking. 'I'd been trying to sell First Continental for years. It was one of my old man's early companies and originally consisted of five copper mines spread out over various parts of eastern Congo, but with what was going on there, the unrest, the *war*, he lost most of the concessions and when he died there was just one left, near a place called Buenke, but even that hadn't been operational for about five or six years. I tried to sell it, couldn't and then more or less forgot about it.' He looks up at Jimmy for a moment and a flicker of doubt crosses his face. 'You do know what I'm talking about, right? My father? Conway & Co.? I'm assuming you've got background on all of this. You actually *are* a journalist?'

Jimmy nods. 'Yeah, of course I am.'

Conway narrows his eyes. 'Right. Anyway, I get this offer, out of the blue, for First Continental and the mine at Buenke. It's from BRX and is decent enough, I suppose, but I'm thinking, they're a huge company, interests everywhere, always expanding, maybe they'll shell out a little more.' He shrugs, half apologetically. 'Look, I'm a businessman. You don't just accept an initial offer without . . .' He hesitates, then waves the point away. 'So. It turns out that Clark Rundle, the CEO of BRX, is coming to Ireland to attend some conference and he suggests that we meet up to discuss the offer. Now at the time, I'll be honest with you, I thought this was pretty weird. A guy like him? Of his stature? Negotiating the sale of an old copper mine?' He pauses. 'But what was I going to do? *Not* go?' He pauses again. 'It was a weekend thing, at Drumcoolie Castle in Tipperary, corporate ethics in the age of globalisation, some crap like that. Anyway, I meet Rundle on the Friday evening, with a couple of his cronies, and we get on pretty well. At first, he seems like a bit of a stuffed shirt, but then he loosens up. I'm flattered too by all the attention I'm receiving, and then doubly so – more, in fact – when I realise just who one of the guys with him is, an old guy, James Vaughan. Of the Oberon Capital Group. Who I'm now looking at and thinking, what's *he* doing here? He isn't listed as one of the delegates – I checked up on it later. Nevertheless, he seems to be paying very close attention to everything that's happening, and in particular to the conversation Rundle and I are having. Strange thing is, as the evening progresses, and although they don't say anything about it explicitly, I get the impression from both of them that they're excited, giddy almost, at the prospect of acquiring this shitty little copper mine in the middle of nowhere.' He pauses. 'Now why would that be, I find myself asking. There's also something arrogant about them, in their attitude to *me*, like I'm stupid and won't notice what's going on. Needless to say, that rankles.' He stops and takes a deep breath. 'Jesus. I can't believe I'm doing this.'

Jimmy doesn't move a muscle.

'OK.' Conway takes another deep breath. 'You know, when I look back at it now, at that evening – we were in the main lounge, the Angler's it's called – I can see that everything was in place for what happened afterwards. *We* were there. Gianni Bonacci was there. He was a couple of tables over, with some of the Nike people. And Susie Monaghan was there, up at the bar with Niall Feeley. It's like a . . . a tableau.' He pauses to visualise it.

Jimmy tries to visualise it, too. Lounge of a big country hotel? Mahogany-panelled walls? Red leather armchairs? Fine art prints of hunting and angling scenes?

He looks at Conway, who seems lost in reverie. Jimmy has some questions here, needs certain things clarified, but does he ask now, or wait? He waits about two seconds. 'How did you know them all?'

Conway looks at him. 'Dublin. Everyone knows everyone. I knew Niall from years back, and of course I knew Susie. Who didn't?' He sighs. 'And for some reason Bonacci stuck out. He didn't have that *executive* look.' He pauses again, his eyes busy, as though he's trying to work out how much he's said so far and if there's any chance he might be able to just cut loose at this point and stop.

Jimmy jumps in. 'So, what then?'

'Well, later on, I got talking to Niall and Susie at the bar, and somehow Gianni Bonacci ended up joining us. You know how it is, people come, people go, but at the same time I think he was mesmerised by Susie. He kept staring at her from his table and eventually just came over and wormed his way in. He started talking to Niall and within ten minutes had got himself invited to go on this big, all-bloke trip Niall and Ted Walker were organising for Sunday. They'd hired a helicopter and were going to be scouring the Donegal coastline for good spots where they could go paragliding later in the summer. Anyway, after a while I got talking to him myself and before I realised he was a UN inspector I was telling him about the mine at Buenke and how I was in the process of selling it to Clark Rundle. I mean, why not? It wasn't a state secret or anything. I didn't go into any of the details, but he seemed very interested and after another couple of drinks started asking me if I knew what was going on in that part of the DRC and if I'd ever heard of Arnold Kimbela. I said of course I had.' He pauses. 'Even though I hadn't.'

'Who?'

'Arnold Kimbela? Local warlord. I checked up on him later,

too. He was originally the leader of a Mobutuist rebel faction, but then he went on to gain control of this huge mineral-rich territory in the east, which he now runs as a sort of *de facto* state. All mining contracts and land sales there have to go through him. He also has an iron grip on the local population. Torture, rape, mutilation, whatever. At its best it's a form of indentured labour, and at its worst . . . I don't know. When First Continental was running the mine there, at Buenke, it wasn't anything like that, it was a proper mine, so . . .'

Jimmy swallows. What?

'So. I don't know,' Conway goes on. 'Apparently he's a very smart guy, from a rich background, educated in Belgium and all of that. What can I say?' He shrugs it off. 'But look, the point is, Bonacci seemed to get more and more puzzled at the idea of a company like BRX wanting to buy a copper mine, and in that particular location. BRX is a private company, he said, and very secretive, so that sort of information doesn't usually get out. Which is when I realised I should have kept my mouth shut. I toyed with the idea of letting Clark Rundle know what I'd done, but I decided against it. I chickened out, basically. I *should* have told him, though.' He pauses. 'Because that might have . . .' He looks away, shaking his head.

Jimmy glances down, and sees the notebook in his hand. He isn't taking any notes. Should he be? Where's his pen? How's he going to remember all of this?

Shut up.

Conway looks back. 'Anyway, at that point Bonacci's attention was very much divided between me and Susie, and of course Susie won out, especially as she started flirting with him, and pretty outrageously. The reason for this was because her ex-fiancé, Gary Lynch, who she was more or less stalking, had appeared in the bar and she was trying to get his attention. She even left with Bonacci, though no one seems to know how far that went. One thing is certain, though, she was doing a lot of coke. What's also undisputed is that Bonacci spent most of the next day trailing along behind her like a lovesick puppy. Now I didn't see any of this. I was off in a conference room with my solicitor poring over the contract. But what also must have happened during the day, at some point, and which *nobody* saw, was that Susie and Bonacci broke into – or somehow inveigled their way into – Clark Rundle's room and went through his papers. Rundle said later on that his stuff had been disturbed, that certain things had been moved. No one can know now, but what seems likely or at least possible is that Bonacci shot his mouth off to Susie about BRX and the mine, maybe trying to impress her, maybe genuinely concerned about it, and that Susie, crazy bitch that she was, suggested they both go and find out more. Sneak into Rundle's room. It'd be a hoot. Come *on*. Carpe *fucking* diem.' He rolls his eyes. 'Now this probably isn't the sort of thing Bonacci would have done in a million years, but there he is, who knows, maybe coked out of it himself, and with this gorgeous woman egging him on, going, have you no *balls*? *I* have. Come *on*.'

Conway stops, stares ahead, seems to be considering what he's just said, trying it out for size. He looks back at Jimmy. 'Maybe that's not how it was, not exactly, but it *fits*. It explains what happened later.'

Jimmy nods. He's reluctant to open his mouth, in case this stops.

He nods again, hoping it will act as a prompt.

'In the meantime,' Conway says after a while, 'I was still locked away with my solicitor, but I had this great idea. I decided to get on the phone to Larry Bolger and persuade him to come down to the conference, swing by for an hour or two, show his face. It was a Saturday, he was due in Cork anyway for a thing that evening, so it wouldn't be a big deal. I'd done a lot of favours for Larry over the years, and this wasn't asking much. I figured if I could be seen hanging out with the prime minister, introducing him around, it'd strengthen my negotiating position with BRX. So after a bit of cajoling Larry agrees. He shows up around six o'clock and before you know it we're all sitting at a table in the main dining room – me, Larry, Clark Rundle, James Vaughan and this other character, Don Ribcoff. There's minimal security, just a couple of guys on the door, and the atmosphere is very relaxed, very congenial. Larry and Vaughan, it transpires, have met before and have plenty to talk about. I'm going over some figures with Rundle, and for those few moments, sitting there at that table, I feel *brilliant*. I mean, think about it, with James Vaughan beside me I'm one degree of separation from *John F. Kennedy*. It's amazing. I feel like I'm a player, like I've arrived or something, and this is just the beginning.' He exhales loudly. 'What a joke.' He looks away again.

Jimmy waits. Then can't wait any longer. 'What happened?'

'What happened? We're all there, in the middle of our various conversations, when Gianni Bonacci arrives into the dining room and walks right up to our table. He says his name, that he's with the UN Corporate Affairs Commission and then he slaps a piece of paper down in front of Clark Rundle and in the space of time it takes for the two guys on the door to get over and grab him he says, *Thanaxite? You've found thanax-*

ite in eastern Congo? And you're going to be extracting it? Does anyone know about this? Then he bangs his fist on the table and says, *We need to talk.* And that's it. They drag him off.' Conway clears his throat. 'Was Susie there in the background, hovering outside? I don't know, maybe she was, I can't remember, I didn't see, but what I *do* remember is the shockwave of panic around that table, Jesus Christ, it was palpable. Rundle was as white as a ghost. He grabbed the piece of paper, looked at it and then flung it at Ribcoff. From what I could see it was a printout of a photo, probably taken on a mobile phone – a photo of a document. I didn't see what was on it, but I didn't need to, we'd all heard what Bonacci said. Anyway, it was the strangest thing, over the next minute or two, no more, Larry and I just sat there, frozen, not even daring to look at each other, as this desperate, whispered conversation took place between Rundle, Vaughan and Ribcoff. I don't know if it was blind panic on their part, or . . . or contempt for *us*, but it was as if we weren't even there. Vaughan asked how Bonacci had gotten a hold of this information, and Rundle said that didn't matter *now*, Jesus, because the situation had to be contained, and immediately. Ribcoff started to say he'd look into it, but Rundle said *no*, looking into it was for later, right now this little fucker, whoever he was, had to be stopped, he had to be prevented from causing any further damage. Ribcoff put his hands up and said, fine, tell me what to do, and Rundle said, whatever you have to . . . clean him out first, bleach him, and then . . . *whatever*, but don't make it obvious, don't make it about *him*, he's UN for Christ's sake, I don't know, cause a diversion, some sort of distraction. There was a silence and then Ribcoff said *right*, and left the table. After another tense pause, Rundle looked at both me and Larry and said, *Gentlemen, listen, I'm really sorry about this* . . . but before he could get any further, more security arrived and there was a bit of a flurry and Larry was whisked away and then Vaughan got up and left as well . . .'

Conway suddenly seems overwhelmed. He turns away and starts massaging his temples. He walks over to the big, grimy window that looks out onto the empty plaza.

Jimmy stands there, watching, waiting. Questions are piling up in his mind now. He tries to filter some of them out and to prioritise others – the obvious first question being, what is thanaxite?

That's the word – the name – Conway used, isn't it?

Jimmy pats his jacket to find a pen. He flips his notebook open and scribbles the word down – a preliminary version of it, at least – and then a few quick notes.

Photo of a document? Taken on a mobile?

Does anyone know about this?

Bleach him?

After a few moments, Jimmy glances up at Conway – at his stooped frame, his hunched shoulders, his head leaning forward against the dirty glass of the window.

Is he losing him?

With no other way to frame the question, Jimmy just blurts it out. 'Mr Conway . . . what is thanaxite?'

*

As the convoy pulls out of the compound, Rundle feels a surge of contradictory emotions – acute relief and intense irritation.

He's relieved that he can go back to Vaughan with the good news, but he's irritated that he had to come all the way down here to hear it in the first place – given that J.J. had apparently heard the very same thing a week earlier.

He's also irritated by Arnold Kimbela himself, this little tin-pot piece-of-shit who insists on being treated like a form of royalty – he won't use phones or e-mail, won't deal with middle-ranking executives, even refuses to work with accountants. If he wasn't sitting on an invaluable deposit of thanaxite, the man would have run out of money, arms, supplies *and* friends a long time ago.

But it doesn't take Rundle more than a minute or two to realise that the relief here far outweighs any irritation. *He* controls the supply chain, which he's just locked down for another couple of years, more or less. Effectively, that now means he's got Jimmy Vaughan by the balls.

He turns to Ribcoff and says, on a whim, 'How far are we from the mine?'

They're on their way back to the airstrip.

'Fifteen miles.' Ribcoff answers. 'About. Why?'

'Can we make a detour?'

Ribcoff calculates. 'Sure. There's time. I guess.' He pauses. 'Is that such a good idea?'

Rundle nods his head firmly. 'I just want to have a quick look.'

Ribcoff leans forward to relay the change of route to Lutz, who radios ahead to the car in front.

About a mile or so farther down the road the convoy takes a left turn and within seconds conditions get considerably rougher – the road twistier, bumpier.

Rundle has never been hands-on when it comes to his business, not really, not the way old Henry C. was, visiting sites, rolling up his sleeves, examining geological charts, talking to foremen, certainly not the way his great-grandfather was, Benjamin Rundle, who apparently used to get down and dirty operating steam shovels, laying railroad tracks and digging irrigation canals. Maybe it's part of the evolutionary process, but Rundle has always been a head-office man, the boardroom and the bank being his natural habitats. BRX has operations worldwide and he has travelled extensively, but how often has he strayed beyond the climate-controlled confines of the airport, the hotel and the conference centre?

He did once visit a BRX mining facility in Brazil, now that he thinks of it. It was to mark the start of a massive drilling project using a new and innovative technology.

Somehow, he suspects, this will be different.

Quite how different he has no idea until they arrive on the outskirts of the mining settlement.

It proves to be something of a shock.

What was he expecting, though? An open pit? Excavators? Dump trucks? Maybe some timber structures and an abandoned copper smelter? He would have seen photos and advanced satellite imagery of the Buenke mine back when they were negotiating the purchase of it from First Continental, but these wouldn't have made any lasting impression on him.

As the convoy stops, Rundle leans forward to get a better view. 'What the *fuck*?' he says.

Just up ahead, on the grassy edge of a steep incline, a group of armed soldiers stand around smoking. Below them, sloping down and stretching out for about a square mile is this rough, brown, hollowed-out patch of earth, with a stream running through it. Surrounding it on all sides is lush greenery and rolling hills. Within it, scores of people move about the pock-marked terrain like ants in a colony. He can't make them out clearly from here, but he understands what's going on, what they're doing.

'This is the mining area, sir', Lutz says from the front, chirpy, like some sort of a tour guide.

Rundle doesn't respond.

He *knows* what it is, Jesus. He'd just forgotten how differently they do things here.

'Look, Clark,' Ribcoff says after a while, 'if you're debating about whether or not to get out of the car, I wouldn't. As you can see, the colonel's men run this place.' He pauses. 'It can sometimes get a bit rough down there, a bit volatile.'

Rundle hesitates, then says, 'Binoculars?'

'Of course.' Ribcoff is clearly relieved.

Lutz rummages up front for a moment, then turns around and holds out a pair. Rundle takes them. They're light and compact. Lutz points out the focus and zoom buttons.

Rundle takes a moment, opens the window and trains the binoculars on the general scene below. The first thing he focuses on is a group of young men squatting at the edge of the stream, one of them sifting something, sand or gravel, in a hand-held sieve. They're all in dirty, raggedy clothes and look lean and scrawny. With his finger, Rundle presses the zoom lever next to the eyepiece and pulls back with a start as the image leaps forward and magnifies. The guy with the sieve appears almost close enough now to touch.

Rundle flicks away from this and lights on another detail, a young man – a teenager, a *kid* really – battering at the hillside rock face with crude-looking tools, a hammer and chisel.

Then, in quick succession, he passes over a series of what look like holes in the ground – what actually *are* holes in the ground – little hand-dug pits, as far as he can make out. One of them is more than that, it's wider, deeper, an improvised shaft, out of which he now sees a small child crawling, like an insect, followed by two others. They are carrying hammers and tin cans. How many others are in there? How deep is it? Rundle swallows and flicks away again. He sees women scrambling in the dirt, and more children. He sees soldiers patrolling along the edges, with Kalashnikovs, and on the far edge he sees a pile of sacks next to a truck. On the side of the truck is a familiar logo – he can just make it out.

Gideon Global.

This is the start of the chain.

Of the arrangement Kimbela spoke about.

His people run the site. They herd in the artisanal miners and supervise the extraction. Then Gideon personnel take over and transport the sacks of rock and dust to the airstrip, from where they're flown to Kigali or Goma, and then on to processing plants in Europe. After that, the processed powder finally makes its way to the various components manufacturers in the US. No *comptoirs*, no *négociants*, no trading posts, no international dealers even. This is a rationalised, streamlined, highly controlled and above all secret supply corridor.

Which took a lot of time and effort to set up.

So many headaches along the way, and right from the get-go.

Rundle moves the binoculars back over the scene, sweeps across it, slides it into a blur. There must be a couple of hundred people here. Then he finds himself doing it again, going back, but this time slowly, scanning, searching for something.

What?

That open mineshaft.

He finds it.

A small, rough hole in the earth.

The three children he saw climbing out of it earlier are around it now, squatting, examining the contents of their tin cans. They are stripped to the waist and covered in a dirty brown dust. He zooms in carefully, and goes from one to the other, studying their faces.

Their big, blank solemn eyes.

He closes his own for a second or two, and then zooms out again, just a fraction.

But when he refocuses, the children have stopped doing what they were doing, all three of them. They've put their tin cans down on the ground and are peering up, looking – he realises – in his direction, *at* him.

He stares back, but only for a moment, before dropping the binoculars. He presses the automatic switch to close the window. Then he turns sideways, towards Ribcoff, and says, 'Get me the fuck out of here.'

*

Conway pulls his forehead back from the grimy window and turns to face Jimmy Gilroy. Now that he's started this, he realises how far there is to go, and he's exhausted.

'Triobium-thanaxite,' he says, with a sigh. 'It's a rare metallic ore. Congo is full of them, niobium, cassiterite, cobalt, uranium. You've heard of coltan, right? It's used to make capacitors for cell phones and games consoles, *every* bloody thing, camera lenses, surgical implants. Well, this one is *extremely* rare. It has a unique chemical composition and until about four years ago had only ever been found in a remote part of Brazil. Then they discovered a deposit of the damn stuff in the mine at Buenke.'

'Who's *they*?'

Conway looks at Gilroy and almost laughs. 'Well, at least you're asking the right questions.'

This Jimmy Gilroy is young and inexperienced and has just admitted he's unemployed, but Conway is fine with that. He doesn't feel he's made a mistake or anything by talking to him. Besides, Phil Sweeney said he was smart, and Phil would know. Phil also said *he'd* worked with Gilroy's father. Conway never met Dec Gilroy, but he's vaguely aware of his reputation – aware that anyone who ever did meet the man really liked him.

So while it might be overstating it to say that Conway likes the son here – they did only meet half an hour ago, and the circumstances are hardly ideal – he *is* comfortable with him. Curiously, as well – and this is crucial – he doesn't seem to resent him.

All in all, he'll do.

He's fit for purpose.

Because this is *it*, isn't it?

Conway's already gone way too far to turn back now, and while he's not quite prepared to admit it to himself yet, he's almost relieved.

'*They*,' he says, 'is an advanced satellite imaging company owned by BRX and the Oberon Capital Group. Obviously, given how rare the stuff is, and how valuable, they decided to try and keep it a secret.'

'What's it used for?'

'To be honest, I don't know. More of the same, I suppose, only bigger and better. Next generation apps.' He shrugs. 'Aerospace, defence turbines, jet engines. Nanotechnology, biotechnology. Who the fuck knows with these people.'

There is silence for a while as this sinks in.

'And Gianni Bonacci discovered your little secret.'

'It wasn't *my* secret, Jimmy. Believe me. I was just trying to flog an old copper mine. But yeah, right after Bonacci dropped his bombshell I won't deny that I put the squeeze on Rundle. He wasn't too happy with that and pointed out to me that unless Bonacci was reined in there wouldn't *be* any sale.' He puffs up his cheeks and then exhales loudly. 'The thing is, because Bonacci had used the words *We need to talk*, Rundle figured that that meant it was a shakedown. Which in turn meant that he probably hadn't told anyone else yet.'

'Right.'

'Which meant there was time. In theory. A window of opportunity. To do something. But when I sat down with Don Ribcoff a while later, at Rundle's request, and fed him every little titbit I knew about Bonacci, everything I'd heard or picked up on in conversation – about him, about Susie, about the two of them, about the coke, about the proposed helicopter trip the next day – I had no idea what I was doing, no idea that there'd be . . .' He pauses, struggling, reluctant to say it straight out. 'Consequences. I mean, it might sound disingenuous now, but at the time I didn't really understand how serious it was, how seriously *they* were taking it. I didn't understand how high the stakes were. Looking back, sure, but –'

'What did you think?'

'That they'd, I don't know, pay him off. I was fully expecting them to pay *me* off, to hike up their offer, which they eventually did, of course.' He then makes a sweeping gesture with his hand to indicate their surroundings. 'It paid for this bloody place. Got it up and running, anyway.' He shakes his head. 'Look, there was a lot of frantic activity that night, a lot of back and forth, so my assumption was that *some* contact was made with Bonacci, and that therefore discussions would be ongoing. Besides, it wasn't really any of my business. Whatever this thanaxite was, I didn't have the knowledge or expertise to even think about getting involved in the extraction process myself. I was just delighted that the mere mention of it was apparently going to lead to a financial bonanza for me.'

There is another silence, during which Conway thinks to himself, *that* was pretty lame. Isn't this meant to be some sort of confession? He looks at Gilroy and actually feels sorry for the poor bastard – having to stand there, having to listen to *this*.

'Jimmy,' he says after a while, a knot tightening in his stomach. 'I don't know what happened exactly, or how, but I can tell you this. Late on the Saturday night, Don Ribcoff came to me with a bag of cocaine the size of a pound of fucking sugar and told me to deliver it to Susie with instructions for her to babysit Gianni Bonacci, that's the phrase he used, *babysit* him. She wasn't to let him out of her sight, she was to go with him on the trip to Donegal. If she did that, there'd be another bag the same size waiting for her when she got back.'

'And did you deliver it?'

A pause. 'Well, what do *you* think?'

'Then what did Susie ask? I mean' – Jesus, the look on his face – 'what did she imagine was going *on*, if she'd been the one who pushed Bonacci into –'

'Remember, *that* was just speculation.' He pauses. 'And no, she didn't ask anything. I'm afraid all Susie could see in front of her was this big fat bag of toot.'

Gilroy stares at him, in silence, no doubt trying to picture the scene. Conway can picture it all too vividly himself. He remembers thinking at the time, *this is fucking insane*.

'So,' he says, 'she did what she was told. Exactly how she went about it, no one knows. Did she go to Bonacci straightaway? Did she go to his room? Did she *fuck* him? Maybe. What she definitely did do, the next morning, was inveigle Niall Feeley and Ted Walker into letting her go along on the helicopter ride. They probably took a bit of convincing, a *lot* of convincing, but no one ever said no to Susie Monaghan.'

'Oh God.'

'Then a few hours later the helicopter crashed along the Donegal coast and they were all killed.'

Conway is aware of what's missing here, of what he's not saying – of the gap, the final piece of the jigsaw, and Gilroy doesn't ask him, doesn't push it.

But he stands there, waiting.

'No one said anything to *me* about it, Jimmy, not Ribcoff, not Rundle, no one, but after what they came out with the previous evening, I just . . . I mean . . . at first there was so much shock over the whole thing, over the crash, the country was convulsed with it, with grief, there was wall-to-wall coverage, and it was *all* about Susie. What had Rundle said? *Don't make it obvious? Cause a distraction?* Well, they certainly did that, because I don't think Gianni Bonacci's name was mentioned more than a couple of times in the reports. And if it was, no one was interested.' He exhales again. 'I mean, sure, it occurred to me that they'd done it, somehow, rigged it, but I didn't for the life of me know *how*, or how they could have done it so fast. It just seemed bizarre. But then as the days went by I discovered more and more about who Don Ribcoff was, *is*. I'd thought he was Rundle's security guy, you know, a glorified bodyguard sort of thing, but then I found out he runs what effectively amounts to a privately owned army. One with unbelievable resources. And reach. So in the light of *this*' – he laughs here, but it's mirthless, more a snort of incredulity – 'the whole thing started to seem horribly plausible.'

He laughs again in the same way, and nods, as though in agreement with what someone else has said.

Gilroy remains silent. He appears to be in shock.

'I had no further contact with Clark Rundle,' Conway quickly goes on. 'It was all through his lawyers after that. They made a new bid for the mine, which was staggering, a multiple of what their original offer had been. It was the price they were prepared to pay for my silence.' He pauses. 'A price I was prepared to accept.'

And there it is, pretty much.

In all its glory.

'But . . .'

'Yes?'

The knot in Conway's stomach tightens a little more.

Gilroy shuffles from one foot to the other, obviously struggling to formulate his question. 'Are you . . . talking on the record here? Am I going to be able to quote you as a source? Because otherwise –'

'How do you prove any of it?'

'Yes.'

He's right, of course. It's all very well to spill this stuff out, but what happens then? Who follows it up? Who takes responsibility?

Conway feels a stinging sensation behind his eyes. 'Now that you mention it,' he says quietly, 'no, I'm *not* talking on the record.'

'Why not?'

'Look . . .' How does he explain this? '*I* can't prove any of it either. Yes, I can tell you what happened, and maybe even why, but I have no real evidence.'

'Then why bother talking to me? Why not tell me to fuck off?'

Conway closes his eyes.

Because, he thinks, *you'll* find evidence. Sooner or later. I know you will. It's there. You'll dig it up. And you *should*. It's your job. But I don't want to be around when you do. Because I'm tired. I've had enough.

He thinks of Ruth and the children.

They won't want him to be around either.

And who'd blame them?

He opens his eyes again. They're still stinging, but he's got them under some sort of control. He takes a step forward. 'Look, Jimmy. You're going to have to come at this from a slightly different angle.'

Gilroy sighs, exasperation showing. 'Angle? What angle?'

Conway clears his throat, hard, bracing himself. 'Listen,' –

he knows this'll have to be quick – 'in the week after the crash I had a couple of conversations with Larry Bolger, but we didn't talk about what happened, not directly, we avoided it, it was a combination of embarrassment, I suppose, and fear, but early the following week he called and told me he'd received some information from a senior garda source, someone in Harcourt Street.' He takes a deep breath here. 'Apparently, a security guard who worked for the helicopter leasing company was making claims that he'd seen something or that something wasn't right at their hangar facility in Kildare. Given the sensitivity of the issue this was passed up the line, and now Larry was in a state about it. I tried to reassure him, but he was frantic, he felt that if there was an investigation, if anything came out, if there was even a hint of involvement, or of collusion, or of cover-up, or whatever, he felt . . . well, that he'd be crucified. At first, I reckoned he was over-reacting, but then I gave it a little thought, and maybe he was right, once something like that got out, there'd be no way of containing it, it'd be guilt by association, and not just him, *I* was there, too. I mean, *fuck*, I had deals in the pipeline, relationships with people, *arrangements*.'

Gilroy looks at him with a mixture of horror and dread.

Where is this going?

'So I made a phone call. I found a number for Don Ribcoff and I called him.'

That's where.

'And?'

'Day or two later the security guard disappeared. Without a trace. Missing person. End of story. Then Ribcoff called me back, said something about the Wicklow hills, local methods, not to give it another thought.'

This proves too much for Gilroy, who deflates right there in front of him. 'Jesus Christ,' he says, 'Jesus *Christ*.'

Conway nods, I know, I know. He feels almost hysterical at this point, unhinged, or drunk, like he could reach out to Gilroy and hug him.

But then he hears a gentle tinkling of bells.

A fucking *ringtone*.

It's not his.

He watches as Gilroy fumbles, reaches into a pocket and extracts his phone.

Then the shift in expression, the apologetic nod.

Yeah, go on, Conway thinks, take it.

'Hello . . . *Maria*?'

Because I'm done here.

Except.

He holds a hand up, waves it.

Gilroy is flustered. 'Sorry . . . just a sec,' he says into his phone, and holds it against his chest.

This'll have to be whispered.

'One quick thing,' Conway says, 'two . . . *two* quick things. That security guard? There was a body found in the Wicklow hills a couple of weeks ago, it was in the papers, check up on that. And . . .' – this is a long shot, his fucking heart thumping now as he realises he hasn't actually mentioned the second call to Don Ribcoff, made only last week – 'has anyone had a look at the CCTV footage?' His mind goes blank for a second. Gilroy is paralysed, staring at him. 'At the hotel in London, at the what's it, the Marlow? Look at the CCTV footage.'

He then nods at the phone and mouths, *Go on, take it*.

Slowly, almost mechanically, Gilroy brings the phone back up to his ear.

Conway steps forward, and around him, pointing, *I'll be over there*.

'Maria . . .' Gilroy says. But it's the only word Conway hears him say, because he's not listening anymore. He's moving too fast. He's already gone.

The stairwell is in almost complete darkness, and when he's halfway up the first flight and looks back he sees nothing, hears nothing.

He moves on, moves upwards, feeling his way with the metal rail.

Counting.

When he bursts through the door and out onto six, he is breathless, but keeps going, muffled voices coming from somewhere, like a chorus deep inside his head. He feels his way along the dark, dusty corridor, tapping the wall until he comes to an open door . . .

Light floods out of the room, early evening light, a bit muted, but that's good. It's enough.

It's all he needs.

He looks around. This is the same room he was in the last time, the bare plastered walls, the damp, acrid smell . . . the sliding glass door to the balcony still open, the way he left it.

As he crosses the room, a current of cool air ripples past him. He swallows, almost gags, that knot in his stomach tighter now than he can bear. It's big, and growing, like a tumour.

He steps out onto the balcony.

He did feel relief, getting all of that stuff off his chest, it was good, but it was fleeting. It's not what he's feeling *now*.

You don't want to know what he's feeling now.

He steps forward, and turns. He leans back against the rail, facing into the empty hotel room. He takes out his phone and looks at it. For a second he considers sending a text to Ruth . . . but that would be too much, too appalling.

He wants to say something, though, to *someone*.

He taps out a message, fumbling over the keys. He presses Send, waits, drops the phone.

He leans back a little further, balancing there for a second. Then loses his balance.

Surrenders it.

Falls.

10

On the return flight to New York, Rundle sits alone in the cabin of his G650, staring out the window.

He's picturing the moment – tomorrow or the next day – when he walks into Vaughan's office, or his library, or the Modern, and nods, *yes, yes, everything's fine*.

A small gesture of triumph.

Then – unable to help himself – he pictures another moment, maybe ten minutes later, in front of a bathroom mirror, or the mirror of an elevator car, but a fucking *mirror* nonetheless.

The inevitable come-down.

Elation, followed by self-loathing.

How do you get them in balance, he wonders.

Then – perhaps not coincidentally – he thinks for a minute or two about Nora, and in cinematic detail, with credit-card production values, but . . . no joy.

No lead.

He reaches for his laptop.

J.J. will have to do.

Since the other day Rundle has been obsessively tracking his brother online. He never used to. Not like this. He was always aware of what was going on, always somehow kept up to date, but not like *this*.

First he checks his web page, then Facebook and Twitter, but he doesn't get very far with those. Then he does what he usually does which is look him up on Google News, where he finds there are two hundred and forty stories speculating that Senator John Rundle is about to file papers to form a presidential exploratory committee.

The fact that it's speculation must mean it's a leak – because J.J. wouldn't do something like this without telling Rundle first, without discussing it with him at least.

Which doubtless means it'll be the first order of business when they next speak.

Rundle closes the laptop.

In his opinion it's too soon. He can see what J.J. is doing, cashing in on the publicity from last week, but it's a risky strategy all the same. The extra attention can only increase the chances that someone will blow a massive hole in the Paris story. It seems incredible to Rundle that the non-appearance so far of the 'motorcyclist' hasn't raised more – or, indeed, any – media suspicion.

And it's not J.J.'s exclusion from the presidential race that Rundle is worried about – although, admittedly, he has been getting comfortable with the idea of his brother in the Oval Office – no, it's the corollary, it's people asking, *well then, what the fuck did happen to his hand?*

And where?

Rundle turns away from the window, in need of distraction. He glances around the cabin.

Empty.

In theory, there could be eighteen people up here, getting served drinks, and . . . what? Cuttlefish, with kimchee, and black radish? Some shit like that.

The mile-high boardroom.

But he actually prefers it this way.

With that thought in his head he drifts off to sleep.

A few hours later, not long after they land in New York, J.J. calls.

Rundle wants to tell him about Kimbela, rub his nose in it, but he doesn't. They talk about the speculation, the exploratory committee.

Though it's clearly more than speculation now.

'So,' J.J. says, 'next Wednesday morning. Are you up for it? The Blackwood Hotel. It's a business thing, an address I'm giving, but I thought I'd take the opportunity to make the announcement official.'

Rundle approaches his waiting car. The driver is holding the door open. Once he gets off the phone with J.J. he's going to call Vaughan. 'Yeah, of course,' he says, rubbing his stomach. 'I wouldn't miss it for the world.'

*

Jimmy sits at the window of his apartment, holding his third cup of coffee since he got up.

Staring out at the bay.

Seagulls squawking and the faint sound of the tide lapping up onto Sandymount strand.

Early morning traffic streaming past.

What you might call a semblance of normality.

Fuck.

But since he got up? Strictly speaking it's not as if he was ever asleep. He's been like *this* the whole time – awake, alert, bug-eyed, like someone on crystal meth – his brain running what happened last night on a continuous loop.

He didn't corner him, did he? Didn't put him in an impossible position? Didn't *push* him?

No.

Conway more or less volunteered all of that information, and it even seemed as if he needed to. But having volunteered it, he clearly then *was* in an impossible position.

At which point Maria Monaghan called.

In a bit of a state.

Apparently after Larry Bolger's sudden death, she felt remorse for the way she'd behaved. What right did she have to expect anything of Jimmy? He'd been offered something better, something more important, and naturally –

But he had to cut her off there, switch frequencies again,

because Conway was walking away, disappearing into the dim shadows.

Was he *leaving*?

Jimmy took a step forward.

Something wasn't right. The rushed tone at the end there, packing everything in.

It was all too –

Jimmy took another step forward, but he couldn't see properly, couldn't see where Conway had gone. It was too dark. So he just stood there, not moving.

It took him a while to realise what he was doing.

He was waiting.

He didn't know what for exactly and when it came – the dense, resonant thud – he was glad to be facing the wrong way.

He immediately turned and went outside. The sight of the body splayed on the concrete was both shocking and horribly compelling – the unnatural configuration of limbs, the blood seeping out from the fractured skull – but already a couple of youths on the far side of the square were on their way over. Some instinct kicked in and he ran.

When he got back to his motorbike on Tara Boulevard he was glad he hadn't locked it and within a matter of seconds was out on the main road again, heading in towards town.

After he got back to the apartment, Jimmy didn't know what else to do except sit around in shock and periodically check for news updates. When the story eventually broke – a few hours ago – he was almost relieved.

On one site it was:

Property developer jumps to his death.

On another:

Embattled tycoon, Dave Conway takes his own life.

Then, a little after seven o'clock, one of the presenters on Newstalk referred to 1929 and the pinstriped bankers queuing up to leap from the window ledges of Wall Street office buildings.

Which meant that a clear narrative was already emerging, and not one with much chance of being influenced or shaped in any way by what Jimmy heard last night.

When another commentator on *Morning Ireland* refers to Conway as an unfortunate 'casualty' and traces everything back to 'the fuse lit by the fall of Lehman Brothers', Jimmy's impulse is to scream. What he does instead is turn the radio off and go over to his desk. He starts making notes, which is something he should have done hours ago – but it's all still fresh in his memory. On the back of what feels like a second wind he sketches out an alternative, more complex narrative than the one taking hold over the airwaves and online.

But when he's finished and he re-reads it . . . it doesn't seem that complex after all.

So before he loses this sense of there being a bigger picture, a comprehensible one, and before his energy levels dip again, he decides to call Maria.

He checks the time and picks up the phone.

As it's ringing, he tries to imagine what he might say to her if she answers.

He can't.

'Jimmy.'

'Maria . . .' He hesitates, his mind blank for a second. Then he rallies. 'Look, I'm sorry I hung up on you last night, but I had no choice, I was in the middle of something really intense,

and not . . . not unconnected to . . .' He sighs. 'I think I've discovered what happened.'

He didn't mean to say that quite so directly – or at all, in fact.

Not without a bit of preparation, a bit of lead time.

'What are you talking about?'

'I think I've discovered what happened to Susie, to all of
them.'

'Jimmy, please.'

'No, listen. I'm not insane. Everything is connected . . . me
stopping the book, taking on the Bolger thing, it's the same
people . . . I was put under a lot of pressure, and . . . even
that guy last night, who jumped off the building, Dave Conway, have you heard about that? *He* was there, at Drumcoolie
Castle, he –'

'Jesus, Jimmy, *stop*.'

He does.

But not for long. 'Maria, please, let's meet. Believe me, you're
going to want to hear what I have to say.'

There is a long silence. Then, 'I'm sorry, Jimmy, but you
sound deranged.'

'Maybe I do. I've been up all night. But *listen* to me.' He
starts whispering. 'The helicopter was sabotaged. The target
was the Italian guy, Gianni Bonacci. He worked for the UN.
The others were collateral damage.' He pauses. 'It's very complicated, Maria' – he hadn't been going to say *this* either, not
yet – 'but you have to understand, it wasn't Susie's fault.'

*

Unpaid leave.

Effective immediately.

If that isn't code for *fuck you, you crazy motherfucker, hit the road and don't come back*, then Tom Szymanski doesn't know what is. That's the downside of working for a PMC, no job security, no guaranteed *de*ployment – and no back-up services either, no Walter Reed.

No tea, no fucking sympathy.

Just a one-way ticket to JFK and make your own way home after that, thank you very much.

Fuck you very much.

He rolls over on the bed and faces the wall.

But come on, six months of having the inside of your head pounded in the Congolese jungle and you're supposed to just ease back into civilian life and switch it *off*?

Szymanski himself, though, never actually had it switched *on* – not over there, that was his thing, his chilled exterior, the quality he was most proud of, like guys who professed to have big dicks or still had hair. But then this bastard Lutz thought he detected . . . what? Early signs of stress, a disproportionate reaction to what had happened? Didn't want his unit contaminated with any hint of darkness? With feelings of remorse or grief or guilt? Didn't want anyone having nightmares?

Good luck with *that*.

Asshole.

The irony, however, is that in the week he's been back all Szymanski has had has been fucking nightmares.

With the neat accompanying trick of never actually seeming to fall asleep.

Chilled exterior, I don't fucking *think* so, not anymore.

He hasn't told anyone he's back yet, and isn't going to either, not for the moment. Instead of taking a connecting flight on to Cleveland he got the AirTrain and then a subway into Manhattan and has been holed up in a hotel here ever since, two hundred bucks a night, and all the junk food, tequila and hookers midtown can throw at him.

He doesn't want to go home. That's why he signed up with Gideon Global in the first place, after his three tours in Iraq – anything to avoid his folks, his ex-wife, his two kids, the ghost of his former life as a solid citizen of C-town.

So maybe he did react, so what? Watching that poor sap get shot in the head at point blank range was pretty fucking intense.

Ashes.

Ray Kroner.

And then those women and kids *he'd* just smoked.

Fuck me.

What is it, you see hundreds of incidents, roadside bombings, IEDs going off, firestorms, shootings, all sorts of trauma and injuries – plus some of that other stuff in Congo, *holy* shit – and you ride it out, you even laugh some of it off, as a survival mechanism. But then *one* thing comes along, a particular incident, and it may not even be such a big deal, if you're looking at it as a scale of one-to-ten sort of thing – intensity-wise, body count-wise – but it *sticks*.

In your brain.

And that's it, you've got it for the rest of your life, like a fucking tattoo, this single image that keeps coming back at you – when you close your eyes, when your mind drifts, when the booze wears off, when your cock goes limp again. It's like what some couples have – our song, listen honey, they're playing our

305

song – well this is *your* song, motherfucker, all yours, and don't you forget it.

In Szymanski's case – with due respect to those two women and the three little kids – it's Ray Kroner's twisted face lying in the mud, twisted because of how the bullet stretched the top of his head off to one side.

He's never going to get that image out of his mind. He didn't know Kroner that well, and didn't even like him, but now he's stuck with him.

And you know who he blames?

Szymanski rolls over, gets off the bed and goes to the window. Some view. The back of another hotel, a much taller one, stacked rows of windows and AC units as far up as he can see. Down to the left there's an alley-way with a thin shard of early morning street action just visible at the end of it – cars passing, MTA buses, yellow cabs, regular New York shit.

He saw him on TV a few days after he got back, on one of the Sunday morning talk shows, *Meet the Press* or *Face the Nation* or *Suck my Dick*, one of those, he doesn't remember, he was flicking around, hungover as shit, waiting for room service, and up he pops on the screen, with a brace on his hand, and they spin this . . . this fucking *fairy* tale about an early morning accident on the streets of Paris. But he doesn't want to talk about it, no, of course not, he wants to talk about the *issues*.

That's who he blames.

The guy on TV.

The guy they were protecting and who Ray Kroner should have blown away when he had the fucking chance.

That's who.

Senator John *fucking* Rundle.

Maria Monaghan can't meet Jimmy until lunchtime.

Which means he has a few hours. He looks at his watch. *Three* hours, give or take.

So maybe he should . . .

Have some breakfast. Establish a little structure.

He eats a bowl of cereal. After that he takes a shower. He gets dressed. He puts on more coffee. Then it's down to work. He has to concentrate. His impulse is to give in here, to let it all overwhelm him – exhaustion, revulsion, confusion – but unless he can clarify certain points, and gather some evidence, he will remain the deranged person he was on the phone a short while ago to Maria.

So.

First. A body found in the Wicklow hills. He locates the story from a few weeks ago. There are reports in four different newspapers on the same day.

Couple out walking their dog.

Remains of a body found in a ditch.

There was some speculation, apparently, about who it might be, but no names were mentioned and no official identification was made. He keeps searching.

These are the only references to the story that he comes across.

He does another search, with a specific date range, and finds the missing person story from three years ago. Thirty-one-year-old Joe Macken, a security guard. He went missing. That's it. No detail about where he worked. No known criminal associations. He had a wife and baby. A further search using his name turns up very little, just two or three other references in more general stories about people who have disappeared.

Is it him? Have they identified him yet? Presumably when they find a body they cross reference it with their database of missing persons.

DNA, dental records, finger prints, stuff like that.

And what if it is him?

Conway said this guy had seen something or had felt that something wasn't right at the place where he worked, the Leinster Helicopters maintenance hangar in Kildare. But *what* specifically? And now that he's dead – which is presumably *why* – how is anyone ever going to find out?

On to phase two.

Jimmy picks up his phone again.

He calls the Missing Persons Bureau. He calls Leinster Helicopters. He calls a guy he used to work with who is now a crime correspondent for a local radio station. He calls a few other people. He leaves messages. He even gets a couple of callbacks.

But what comes from all of this is . . . nothing.

The crime correspondent tells Jimmy in the strictest confidence that although it hasn't officially been confirmed yet the body that was found in the Wicklow hills a few weeks back is probably that of missing Dolanstown drugs kingpin Derek Flood. The woman he talks to at Leinster Helicopters barely remembers Joe Macken and when she checks with a colleague it turns out that Macken worked for an agency in any case. A further inquiry reveals that about a year after he disappeared Macken's wife remarried and emigrated to Australia.

It's as if everything has evaporated.

As for the CCTV footage in the London hotel where Bolger

died, what is *that*, conceivably, going to reveal? And how is Jimmy Gilroy, unemployed journalist, supposed to get his hands on it in the first place?

He looks up from his desk and out across the room.

Let's hear it everybody for the deranged person.

*

'Housekeeping.'

Tom Szymanski turns to face the door, groans.

'Yeah,' he says, half shouting it, 'five minutes.'

He stands up from the bed, flicks the TV off and throws the remote onto the pillow.

There's less work these last few mornings for housekeeping to do. What is it? He looks around the room. He doesn't know. This is Friday. The last time he had a hooker up here was Sunday or Monday. The last time he got properly shitfaced, with all the concomitant fallout, beer bottles, ashtrays, pizza boxes, take-out cartons, was . . . night before last? Or night before that again?

He's not sure.

Last night he did nothing.

Watched TV, smoked a little weed, looked out the window.

It's not that he's getting bored or anything, because if you're a vet, an experienced one, you don't really *get* bored. You don't have the luxury. There's no longer any unoccupied territory in your brain where that can happen.

But you have to keep busy all the same – either working, or overloading your senses – because you *are* fighting something, and if it isn't boredom, maybe it's antiboredom. Like antimatter.

Or whatever that shit is.

Dark matter.

Dark boredom.

Fuck.

Can he stop this, please?

Outside, Szymanski walks around for a while – up and down Fifth Ave, between Thirty-fourth and Forty-second. It's a nice day and there's something easy about New York. It's frenetic and ceaseless, but if you don't bother the place, it won't bother you.

He stops in at a diner for some breakfast.

He takes a booth by the window and sits down. Beside him, there's a newspaper. He picks it up. It's a *New York Post*. Today's. Someone must have left it behind.

He lays it out on the table in front of him.

Waitress comes. He orders coffee and –

It's really all about the coffee.

Coffee and pancakes.

'You want some OJ with that today?'

No, I want it *tomorrow*, you stu—

Easy.

He nods. Goes back to the *Post*. He doesn't buy newspapers. Doesn't believe in them. All the shit you're expected to eat.

Sports coverage maybe, but even that.

He reads a thing about City Councilman Tony Rapello (D-Bronx), who wants to introduce legislation forcing bar and nightclub owners to install a minimum number of security cameras. He reads about a newborn baby that was found abandoned at a subway station in Queens, left in a bag next to a fucking MetroCard machine.

Jesus.

Then, as his pancakes are arriving, he sees it.

Run, Johnny, run.

That *mother*fucker.

John Rundle is rumoured to be setting up an exploratory committee for a possible presidential run next year . . .

Szymanski nearly chokes on his coffee.

Accompanying the article there's a photo of Senator 'Johnny' Rundle, complete with prominent hand brace, standing next to some bearded guy outside an unidentified office building. Although Rundle isn't quoted directly in the article, an aide says that the senator will be attending a reception in the city on Wednesday, at the Blackwood Hotel, and that an announcement may be made then.

The article goes on to explain that the senator sustained a serious injury while on a recent trade delegation to Paris. He was coming to the aid of a motorcyclist, who had collided with a bollard, when his hand was crushed underneath the hapless Parisian's chopper.

Szymanski laughs at this.

Again.

And this time out loud.

Which gets some looks.

He starts his pancakes, and re-reads the article.

What was it Lutz said the day of the incident? That the senator's brother owned the mine at Buenke? That they were a 'big' family? And that consequently Ashes had picked the wrong day to go crazy?

Szymanski leans forward and studies the photo again.

It's well known that politicians lie all the time, but it's not every day you get to catch one out in as blatant and incontrovertible a lie as this.

He pushes his plate aside and drains his coffee.

What day is this? Friday?

He air-signs check to the waitress.

Maybe he'll hang around the city until Wednesday, see what happens.

See what kind of a day *that* is.

*

Walking along Wicklow Street on his way to meet Maria Monaghan, Jimmy's phone rings.

He pulls it out and checks the incoming number.

'Phil?'

'Jimmy.' Phil Sweeney's voice is quiet, muted. 'How are you?'

'I'm in shock. I'm sure you are, too.'

'Yeah, I actually can't believe it. I knew he had financial difficulties, but Jesus, he was always so –'

'That's not why he did it, Phil.'

'*What?*'

'I was there last night. I was with him. Not when he jumped, but up to a few minutes beforehand.'

In the silence that follows, Jimmy slows down and stops. Standing now by the side window of Brown Thomas, he waits. But the silence goes on so long that he eventually has to interrupt it.

'Phil?'

'Yeah. I'm here. Look, this is weird. We have to meet.'

'I'm not so sure about that, Phil. I'm in the –'

'Jimmy –'

'I don't have –'

'*JIMMY.*'

'OK. Fine.' He clears his throat. 'Of course.'

There is silence for a moment, and then in quiet tones, almost whispering, they make an arrangement to meet.

Tomorrow evening. The Long Hall on George's Street.

Jimmy's head is reeling as he puts his phone away.

Ten minutes later he's in Rastelli's sitting down opposite Maria Monaghan.

It takes him a while to adjust. He's also distracted by how Maria looks. There's something different about her, and he's not quite sure what it is.

A girl comes over and they order coffees.

Jimmy is hungry, but this isn't a conversation he wants to have while he's eating.

'Thanks for agreeing to see me,' he says. 'I realise it must seem a bit . . . '

'Yes,' she says, 'it does.' She studies him for a moment. 'You look like shit, Jimmy.'

'Thanks.'

'So what's going on? You made some pretty big claims on the phone there. You'd better explain yourself, because I'm not staying here any longer than I have to.'

Then it hits him what it is. She's not dressed for work. She's in jeans and a zip-up sweater. And she's slightly paler-looking, too, no sign of any make-up.

She seems more relaxed.

'Not at work today?' he says.

'I've taken some time off. I was due a few days.'

He nods, delaying.

'Jimmy?'

'OK.' He launches into it. He may look like shit, and feel like shit, but the one thing he can't afford to be accused of here is talking shit. What he says has to make sense, and not just to her, to *himself* as well. Which it does, largely. But as he proceeds, as he talks, as their coffees arrive, it occurs to him that all he's doing is describing a sequence of conversations he's had – and private, unrecorded conversations. It doesn't help that two of the people he spoke to are now dead. Nor does it help that what he got from the others – from Gary Lynch, from Francesca and Pia Bonacci – was little more than conjecture and speculation.

Jimmy wants Maria to believe what he's saying, partly because *he* believes it, and partly because he hopes the knowledge that Susie wasn't to blame for what happened will bring Maria a certain degree of solace.

But he's not going to convince her with this.

What's to stop her from thinking he's deluded and has made it all up?

Nothing.

It's only when he gets to the end that he sees a flicker in her eye, a response to something he's just said.

He leans forward. 'What?'

Maria doesn't answer.

He glances around, thinking back for a second, going over it in his mind. He'd been telling her about the mine in Congo, about Dave Conway trying to sell it, about the deposit of thanaxite they'd discovered.

About Buenke.

And BRX.

Clark Rundle.

Gideon Global.

'*What?*' he says again, looking directly at her.

She's pale, even paler than before.

'Maria?'

She swallows. 'Did you say *thanaxite*?'

'Yes.'

She holds his gaze, but doesn't speak.

'What's wrong? Have you heard of it?'

She nods her head very slowly. 'Susie mentioned it in that text she sent me from the hotel, before she left. I had no idea what it meant. It seemed like nonsense. I mean, the whole text, it was –'

'What did it say?'

Maria hesitates. This clearly isn't easy for her. Some of the texts that Susie sent to people that morning were leaked to the media and quickly became infamous – evidence that she wasn't in a stable frame of mind. She sent one to her agent screaming, *Get me a decent fucking job before I go completely FUCKING insane!!!!* She also sent a couple to a friend in Dublin in which she said some fairly scurrilous things about a well-known broadcaster who had recently interviewed her.

But the text she sent to Maria that morning has always re-mained private.

She leans back in her chair. 'It said, I can't remember exactly, it was about going on the helicopter ride with some of the guys, along the coast, and then, *Thanaxite baby, that's where it's all at, we're heading for the blood-soaked motherlode*.' She shrugs. 'I never knew what that meant. But it was just *so* Susie, you know, it was typical, she was a messer, she spoke in code, *yo* this and *yo* that, rhyming slang, song lyrics, made-up Dublin rap, whatever. It could have meant anything. Plus she was clearly high as a kite. So it didn't strike me as significant at the time. And after the crash, what did *anything* matter? She was dead.'

Jimmy nods, 'Yeah. Sure.' He lowers his voice a notch. 'But doesn't this corroborate what I'm saying? What Dave Conway told me?'

Maria nods back, reluctantly.

Jimmy can see it in her face. She was sceptical before, impatient even. Now she's putting the pieces together and they seem to fit. 'If what you're telling me is true,' she says eventually, 'then this whole chain of events, from Susie's death right up to what happened last night, it's all the result of a desperate scramble to protect ownership of a *mining* concession?'

'Yes.'

She holds her hands out in disbelief. 'Is that . . . could that *possibly* be true? I mean . . .'

'Well, there seems to be an awful lot of money involved, so on balance I'd say yeah, it could.'

But Maria is barely listening. 'My God. Poor Susie. You know, I think I'm almost glad Mum and Dad didn't live to hear this. It's too awful. It's –'

And then she stops, as something obviously occurs to her. She looks at Jimmy. 'What happens now?'

He isn't sure what to say here. He looks down at his coffee, which he hasn't touched. 'I don't know, Maria. I wanted to tell you this, and I wanted you to believe it. That was important to me. Who else is going to believe it, though? On what conceivable basis could any official investigation of this go forward?'

'On the basis that . . .' She stops, trying to think it through, the ramifications.

But he sees it dawning on her.

'There's no evidence, Maria. Nothing at all. Two of the principal witnesses are gone. If Susie hadn't sent you that text, with that word in it, which in itself hardly qualifies as evidence, would *you* believe it? Would you even still be sitting here?'

Maria considers this, looks at him. 'You've described a conspiracy to murder *six* people, Jimmy. Including my sister. That's *insane*. Can these bastards simply be allowed to get away with it?'

'Well . . .'

'What?'

Jimmy clicks his tongue. 'Leaving aside for a minute the issue of resources, and the fact that I don't have the backing, the *protection*, of an official news organisation, there *is* another avenue of approach here.'

'What do you mean?'

'Two of the people who were at the table that night in Drumcoolie Castle are gone, yeah? Larry Bolger and Dave Conway.'

Maria nods.

'But there were three others. The ones who actually had the incriminating conversation, and who *presumably* carried through on it.'

She nods again.

'Clark Rundle, Don Ribcoff and . . . some old guy.'

11

At around nine o'clock on Saturday morning Rundle and Eve are having coffee in the kitchen of their fifty-seventh-floor apartment in the Celestial Building. They're talking about Daisy, about Oxford, about England, and when Rundle's phone rings he resents the intrusion.

It's Don Ribcoff. He's downstairs in his car and needs ten minutes.

Rundle could ask him to come up, but he's not going to.

'I'll be right down,' he says into the phone, and makes an apologetic face at Eve.

She's used to it. Twenty years of marriage to Clark Rundle and what's she going to do, start getting snippy now?

She reaches for her own phone as he gets up to leave.

Descending in the elevator, Rundle feels relatively relaxed – happy to be back from his trip and looking forward to dinner with Jimmy Vaughan tomorrow night.

Outside, he strolls across the wide plaza towards the kerb, keenly aware of the monolithic slab of bronze-tinted glass shimmering in the sunlight behind him. As he gets near the parked limousine, a door opens, and Ribcoff emerges.

The two men stand on the sidewalk, traffic whipping past.

'Some weird news,' Ribcoff says. 'From Dublin. Dave Conway killed himself on Thursday night. Jumped off a sixth-floor balcony.'

Rundle is surprised, and shows it. 'That *is* weird. Any fallout we need to be concerned about?'

'Maybe. Our asset there is working on it. It turns out someone was with Conway before he did it. The two of them were seen talking, and then this guy was seen leaving. In a hurry. By some local kids.' He pauses, reluctant to go on. 'It might've been that journalist.'

'*Might* have been? I thought you had him under surveillance?'

'We did. But not round the clock. I mean, we checked him out, went to his apartment, trawled through his shit, but there was nothing much there. He wasn't deemed a risk.'

'And now?'

'We're looking into it.'

Rundle glances around. 'What's the take on Conway? What are people saying?'

'Debts, bankruptcy. He was in for a couple of hundred million. Victim of the recession. It seems to be straight up.'

Rundle nods. 'Fine, but this journalist prick talks to Bolger, then he talks to Conway . . . we have to assume he knows something. Or thinks he knows something. We *have* to assume he's a risk.'

'Yeah. But from what our asset could find out the guy is more or less unemployed. Until recently he was working on a book about that actress who was killed in the helicopter crash. That's how he got caught up in this.'

'And *that* doesn't make him a risk? *Jesus*, Don.'

Ribcoff looks around, nodding. 'OK. I'll get our asset to take another look at him.'

'Not just another look, Don. *Sit* on the bastard. We don't want any surprises here.'

'Right.'

Rundle is anxious to get away. 'That it?'

Ribcoff nods.

'Keep me posted.'

'OK.'

As Rundle is turning to go, Ribcoff says, 'By the way, have you seen Mr Vaughan yet? Since we got back?'

'No,' Rundle says, feeling a slight impatience at the question. 'I'm seeing him tomorrow night.'

Back in the elevator, he takes out his phone and calls Regal.

Unfortunately, Nora is not available today. They're about to suggest someone else, another escort, but Rundle hangs up.

*

As he walks along George's Street on his way to the Long Hall, Jimmy keeps turning and looking behind him. He can't shake the uneasy feeling that he's being followed. No one in his line of vision offers themselves up as a likely candidate, but then . . .

He wouldn't expect them to.

Stepping into the pub, Jimmy glances around and spots Phil Sweeney sitting alone at the bar.

He looks tired. There is a glass of whiskey in front of him.

'Jimmy. What'll you have?'

'Pint of Guinness, thanks.'

Jimmy sits on a stool, facing straight ahead, and puts his hands on the bar. 'I'm sorry about Conway,' he says.

'Yeah.' There is a long silence. 'So, what happened?'

Jimmy gets straight into it. Since talking to Maria yesterday he has refined the narrative somewhat. He tells it quickly and leaves no room for interruption.

Sweeney visibly wilts as Jimmy is speaking. At the end he takes a couple of sips from his glass.

Jimmy's pint arrives, but he doesn't touch it. The two men sit for a while without speaking.

Eventually, Sweeney turns to Jimmy. 'I had no idea. I knew *some* stuff, but . . .' He shakes his head. 'I thought he'd had a fling with Susie, that it was all about covering *that* up. Keeping the papers out of it. Saving the marriage. I knew there was a business angle as well, but . . . you know, it was *business*. You learn not to ask awkward questions.'

Jimmy doesn't say anything. He keeps staring at his pint.

'Look, Jimmy, I know you have nothing but contempt for me and for what I do, for the company, and for . . . whatever, I don't want to bring your old man into it, but believe me, what I do, what *we* did, it's not *this*, not what you're telling me.' He reaches for his glass. 'What you're telling me? Way out of my fucking league.'

'OK,' Jimmy says.

'I mean, Conway and Bolger? Whatever bullshit they got involved in that weekend, they kept it a secret all this time. *I* certainly knew nothing about it.' He drains his glass and makes a sign at the barman. 'But I have to tell you, Jimmy, I've heard some ugly shit in my day, but nothing like this. And I don't like it. One fucking bit.'

Jimmy is beginning to wonder how much drink might be in the equation here.

'Look Phil,' he says, fully expecting to be pounced on, 'let me be straight with you. This is a big news story and I intend to pursue it. My only problem is that the two main sources for it are now dead.'

Sweeney looks at him and nods. 'Yeah, I can see that'd be a problem all right.'

'So,' Jimmy goes on, 'I've decided, I'm going to New York. On Monday. See if I can get anything out of BRX.' He pauses. 'See if I can get near Clark Rundle. I've booked the flight. Did it yesterday.'

Sweeney's eyes widen. 'Wow. I don't know if you're insane, Jimmy, or just stupid, but . . .' He stops for a moment. 'You won't get anywhere near Clark Rundle. Guys like him operate in a parallel universe. It's like they live in a bubble.'

'I know. But I have to try. It's a start.'

'He mightn't even *be* in New York.'

'I know.'

Sweeney stops again. He seems to be considering something. 'OK, but you know what . . . you're going to need contacts over there, assistance, *help*.'

'I don't have any contacts.'

'*I* do.'

The barman arrives with the fresh drink. He places it in front of Sweeney, who picks it up and swirls it around gently.

Jimmy isn't sure what's being said here. 'You'll help me?'

'Yeah.' Sweeney puts the drink down. 'There's something I haven't told you yet. I got a text the other night. From Dave. It must have been just before he did it.'

Jimmy turns and looks at him.

'It was fairly cryptic. I didn't know what to make of it. I mean, it's bloody obvious *now*, I suppose, but at the time I thought maybe he was drunk or something. We hadn't been on the best of terms lately, so I didn't reply and I wasn't in the mood to call him.' Sweeney takes a sip from his drink. Then he takes a deep breath. 'He said *Help Jimmy Gilroy any way you can.*'

'I'm sorry, *what*?'

As Sweeney repeats it, Jimmy closes his eyes. He feels a stabbing sensation in his stomach. After a moment he opens his eyes again and says, 'What else was in it?'

Another deep breath. '*No hard feelings. Tell Ruth I'm sorry.* Then the bit about you.'

'*Fuck.*'

'I know, I know.' Sweeney exhales loudly. 'But I was pissed off at him, Jimmy. I barely looked at the damned thing. It made no sense to me. Until the next morning.' He pauses. 'I mean, I never thought he'd do something like that, not in a million years. I can see why now, though.'

Jimmy picks up his pint for the first time and demolishes half of it in one go.

He lets it settle.

There is silence for a while.

'OK,' Sweeney then says, 'I can make a few phone calls, media and PR people over there I know, people I've worked with. It might help. It might be the difference between . . .' He waves a hand in the air. 'I don't know. It might afford you some protection. It'll be a buffer zone. Because you do realise how dangerous this is, Jimmy, potentially? I mean, given what you've told me.'

'Yeah. By definition. It's what the story is about.'

Sweeney half smiles at this. He leans over and pats Jimmy on the arm. 'It's quite a story alright. I'll be putting my credibility on the line with these people, that's for sure.'

'Yeah, Phil, I know.' And then Jimmy can see it, up close like this, what he suspected before. Sweeney is not well. 'Thanks,' he says. 'I appreciate it.'

'Right,' Sweeney says, turning back to his drink. After a moment, he adds, 'And one last thing. I'm not doing this because Dave Conway asked me to. You know that, right? If I'm doing it for anyone at all, Jimmy, I'm doing it for your old man.'

*

'So, how is our friend, the colonel?'

Rundle steps out of the elevator and extends a hand to Jimmy Vaughan. They shake.

'He's good, I guess. He talks a lot.'

'Yeah? What about?'

'Well, it seems he has a thing about the Chinese. Thinks they work too hard.'

'Oh.'

'He prefers our way of doing things.'

'I *see*.' Vaughan holds out an arm and indicates for Rundle to follow him. 'That sounds promising.'

'Indeed.'

They cross the entry foyer. Vaughan is slightly stooped and moves slowly.

'On your own tonight, Jimmy?'

'Yeah. Meredith's away, in LA. Mrs R is here, though. She'll look after us.'

Mrs Richardson is the cook, has been for as long as Rundle can remember.

They enter the dining room. Two places are set at one end of the long mahogany table.

'Please, Clark, sit down.'

Rundle stands at his place and waits for Vaughan to take his.

'If you don't mind,' Vaughan says, looking at his watch, 'we're going to eat straightaway. Otherwise I'll get cranky. This is what old age is like, Clark. And it turns out you don't have a choice in the matter.'

Rundle laughs at this. 'No?'

'No.' Vaughan shakes his head. 'I'm afraid not.' He puts his hands on the table. 'So. Tell me everything.'

Rundle does as instructed. He winds up by expressing the view that Kimbela's hold over the Buenke region appears to be precarious at best. 'We could lose access to the mine from one day to the next. A single swipe of a machete and the balance of power shifts.'

'I know, I know, you've got all these Mobutu wannabes tearing around the place and it's just a mess. We had an amazing run with *him*, though, three decades, at least.'

We?

Rundle leans forward, 'Look, there's a good five- to ten-year offload at Buenke. The latest imaging shows the seam is deeper than we thought. But as far as I can see what we're involved in over there is a smash-and-grab operation, essentially, and it has been from the start.'

'Of necessity, Clark, you know that.'

'Yeah, but' –

Buenke is only the second place on earth where thanaxite

has ever been found and BRX has managed to keep that fact a secret for over three years. Even Kimbela thinks that what they're extracting is coltan. This is because it's extremely difficult to distinguish between the two without sophisticated testing.

– '. . . the mine is so primitive. They practically extract the shit *by hand*. That's not how BRX usually operates. We need to get in there with proper machinery and infrastructure and do this right.'

It's a conversation they've had before.

'We couldn't do it without breaking cover, Clark, and then we'd risk losing everything. We draw attention to ourselves like that and Kinshasa, the Ministry, Gécamines, they'd be down on us like a ton of bricks, then the UN, Global Witness, Amnesty, then Beijing, then every fucking mining company in the world. It'd be a new Klondike.' He pauses. 'Besides, even if we managed to keep a piece for ourselves, it would take too long. It'd slow things down.'

Rundle looks at him for a moment. 'Slow *what* things down, Jimmy?'

He hadn't intended to go along this route, but he's getting frustrated. He's also beginning to accept that he probably has considerably more leverage with Vaughan than he previously imagined. It's a simple equation. Rundle has access to something Vaughan wants, and seems to want badly, so Rundle should be able to call at least *some* of the shots.

Vaughan drums his fingers on the table. Then he looks up. 'Ah, Mrs R.'

Over the next few minutes food arrives and there is a considerable amount of small talk with Mrs Richardson. Vaughan also needs to concentrate when he's eating and tends to go silent for extended periods. Rundle finds the whole business a little trying.

'Slow *what* things down, Jimmy?' he repeats, at the earliest opportunity.

Rundle has worked closely with Vaughan on the Buenke project since the beginning, he's been happy to – flattered even, to have the old man place his trust in him like that – but now he's tired of being shut out, of not knowing the full story. BRX sets the supply chain in motion, but once the thanaxite gets to the processing plants in Europe or the US Rundle has no further involvement with it. What he suspects is that the thanaxite is finding its way to a company, or companies, owned by the Oberon Capital Group, but as to what it's being used for specifically, he has no idea.

And Vaughan has never been inclined to discuss it.

'What do you know about robotics, Clark?'

Until now, maybe.

Rundle leans forward. 'Come again?'

Vaughan puts his fork down and dabs his lips with his napkin. 'You heard me. Robotics.'

'Well, I . . .'

'It's the fastest-growing sector in technology today. Development is exponential. I mean, think Moore's Law, then multiply it by ten.' He puts his napkin down. He reaches for his glass of water and takes a sip. 'But as with most new technologies, where do we look to find the best ideas? To the cradle of war, that's where. Predator drones, Reapers, PackBots, medbots, unmanned this, that and the other. It's a wonderland of possibilities.'

Rundle had been about to say that he actually does know quite a bit about robotics, given that mining is an area where the technology is making a significant impact – in tunnel crawling, for example – but as is often the case with Vaughan, he'll throw a question out there and not really expect or want an answer.

It's annoying but you get used to it.

'In Afghanistan and Iraq,' Vaughan continues, 'back at the start, there were maybe a couple of dozen robotic units in operation, and only on a trial basis. Now there are literally thousands of them being used every single day. It's quite simple, Clark. Automation is the future of modern warfare.'

Rundle nods along, fork suspended over his plate.

'Anyway, a few years ago Jack Drury at Paloma Electronics was contracted by the Pentagon to get something into development – along with almost everyone else in the industry, let it be said. They're all at it now, lining up at the drawing board to strut their stuff.' He pauses. 'But what Jack's guys have come up with?' A smile steals over his face. 'Knocks it out of the park. This thing they have, it's a multipurpose combat UGV, lasers, sensors, antitank rockets, thousand rounds of ammunition, it's amazing. They're calling it the BellumBot. Gives new meaning to the phrase *killer app*.'

Rundle, listening carefully, puts his fork down.

'But that's not all.' Vaughan's smile has become a beam now. 'Because get *this*. They're also designing the damn things to think for themselves.'

Rundle leans forward. 'Think?'

'That's right, Clark. Battlefield management systems that can operate autonomously. They've developed a range of algorithms using game theory and probability models that enable data to be collected in the field, processed and then actually *shared*. We're talking about the holy grail of robotics here. I mean picture it, swarms of units out there collaborating, making decisions, optimising uncertain combat scenarios. And no egos in the mix, no sentiment, no interference. It's beautiful.'

'Holy shit.'

'Yeah, and Paloma have just received a billion-dollar contract to put the first run into production, five, six hundred of them by Christmas.' He lets that sink in. 'And it's just the start, Clark. In terms of where this is going? We're only at the Model T stage.'

Rundle is almost speechless. 'And ... you've been ... helping them? On the supply side?'

'*We've* been helping them, Clark. BRX has. Gideon, too. Thanaxite is essential to the success of this. It allows capacitors to operate at low power levels but extremely high temperatures, which is apparently an unusual combination and criticial for advanced weapons systems. For connectivity and ... speed. I don't know.' He waves a hand dismissively. 'Look, I'm not going to pretend I understand the technical side of this, I'm eighty-two years old, for Christ's sake. Talk to Jack Drury about it. But one thing I do know, that grey powder gives us a serious competitive edge.'

Rundle sits back in his chair and makes a whistling sound. Then he leans forward again, as something occurs to him. 'Why are you telling me this *now*?'

Vaughan sucks his teeth. 'Different reasons. I appreciate your continuing loyalty. Your discretion, as well. And your willingness to take on the Kimbela situation. The timing is also right, with this production deal going through. And now, maybe' – he looks Rundle directly in the eye – 'with J.J. stepping into the ring, I mean, who knows? It might work out. It certainly couldn't hurt.'

Rundle stares at Vaughan. '*J.J.?*'

'Yeah, you can't have too many friends in high places, if you know what I mean, when it comes to . . . certain matters, policy matters, awarding contracts, that kind of thing.' He pauses. 'And by the same token, I'm sure *he* could use some solid backing.'

'Sure, but . . .'

'*What*? I know I've been critical of him in the past, but he's made quite an impression recently. I mean, did you see him this morning, on *Face the Nation*? Man.'

Rundle nods. He saw it all right and J.J. was indeed impressive, with something new about him, a look in his eyes, a touch almost of rapture.

'He's a perfectly credible candidate, Clark.'

Almost as though *he'd* been the one who was bitten.

'I know. He is.'

But not crazy or anything, not hysterical, just the right side of that.

'And if you want to tell him I said so, go ahead. Consider it an endorsement. Tell him I might even show up on Wednesday.'

Rundle is taken aback by this, but he nods vigorously and says *thanks*.

A little later on, in the back of his car, he tries to get everything into perspective. On one level, Jimmy Vaughan's gall, his *ego*, is breathtaking. From his Park Avenue apartment, in his old man diapers, he seems to believe he's personally directing the flow of thanaxite out of Congo and all the way along the supply chain to a privately contracted military robotics programme in Connecticut. He also seems to believe he can personally engineer the process of nominating a presidential candidate for the next election.

And *yet* . . .

He's Jimmy fucking Vaughan.

The man is a legend.

And Oberon does own Paloma Electronics. It doesn't own *him*, BRX, but that hardly matters, Rundle has been in thrall to Vaughan since he was a kid and would do anything for the man. As for political influence, that's hard to quantify, but suffice it to say the chairman of the Oberon Capital Group has been at or near the centre of power in Washington, in one capacity or another, for the best part of fifty years.

And a quick glance at Oberon's current and past board members reveals a dizzying array of luminaries, including former presidents, secretaries of state, secretaries of the treasury, other cabinet members, five-star generals, prime ministers, Nobel laureates and media barons. Manna to conspiracy theorists, the Group was founded in the early 1970s and since then has woven itself into the very fabric of the economic, social and political life of the country. With hundreds of defence, aerospace, telecom and health care companies in its portfolio, Oberon is supposedly responsible for everything from the price of jellybeans to largely shaping US foreign policy over the last thirty-five years.

The car pulls up at the foot of the Celestial.

All of a sudden, Rundle is excited.

He has always craved a closer working relationship with Vaughan and now this is stepping things up several notches. It may well be his last chance, too. Because Jimmy is old and has a slew of medical conditions, all under control, fine, but any one of which, at any time, could flare up and kill him.

Rundle gets out of the car and strolls across the plaza.

The BellumBot.

Fucking incredible.

*

Jimmy gets into JFK a little after two o'clock local time on Monday afternoon. He takes a cab into the city, to the West Village, and checks into his hotel, the Stanley. Even though it's small and a little dingy, the Stanley is pretty expensive, and Jimmy can't really afford it. In fact, this whole trip, along with the one last week to Italy, is being paid for out of the remaining half of the advance he got to write the Susie Monaghan bio – an advance he'll be expected to return in full when his editor finds out he's no longer actually writing the book.

But Jimmy was in a hurry, rooms were available and the West Village is a part of the city he's familiar with, having once shared an apartment there for a couple of months when he was a student.

He arranged the whole thing online in about ten minutes flat. But that was the easy part.

Now that he's here he has no clear idea what to do.

Phil Sweeney gave him some numbers to call, so that should probably be his first task, but for some reason he's reluctant to get started. He's not sure what it is, a lack of confidence maybe, or a fear of being found out? When he expressed doubts like these on Saturday evening, Phil Sweeney told him to feck off, that all he had to do was say he was a freelance journalist working for the *Irish Times* or the *Guardian*.

Or the BBC.

That it was a confidence trick, like most things in life.

That he'd be fine.

Jimmy takes a shower. Then he goes out to walk around for a while and think about getting something to eat. It's hot for April, at least hotter than he expected, and he's overdressed. Life on the streets here has a familiar feel to it, by turns frenetic and chilled out, with lots of smells and colours. He spends some time sitting on a bench in Washington Square Park. A guy comes up and offers him some weed. Jimmy shakes his head and the guy wanders off.

Some skaters roll past.

Jimmy looks around.

What the fuck is he doing in New York?

How does he get from *here*, a park bench, to the fiftieth or sixtieth floor of one of those glass towers up there on the midtown horizon?

And something else he idly finds himself wondering: is he still being followed?

It was a feeling he couldn't shake the other night.

On one level it seems preposterous – deluded, paranoid. But given what he's discovered about these people, what he's been told, isn't it the *least* they would be doing?

Jimmy turns and looks over his shoulder.

Evening has begun to fall and is enveloping the expanse of downtown.

Suddenly, he's hungry.

Behind him here, there are dozens of places he could eat at. He'll find one . . . but in a few minutes.

He reaches for the phone in his pocket.

First he needs to make a couple of calls.

*

'What do you want, a nine mil? I got Sigs, Glocks, Berettas, Mausers, whatever you want.'

Tom Szymanski studies the guy for a moment. This isn't how he'd normally do this. How he'd normally do this would be to stand in a gun store and shoot the breeze with the gentleman behind the counter, a retired serviceman probably, and then proceed to the transaction – only problem *here* is he doesn't have a licence and in New York City getting one takes time.

So it's back channels, it's a bar on Avenue C, it's sitting in a booth opposite this jittery little spic fuck and hoping for the best.

'You got a Beretta M9?'

'Yeah, I got everything, my friend.'

I'm not your fucking –

'How much?'

Haggle, haggle, and then it's back here in half an hour. And half an hour after that again Szymanski's back in his hotel room, loaded M9 on the bed, plus a bag of weed and a gram of coke. The drugs he bought because he could, they were right there in his face.

I got everything.

And it was the minimum he could have bought, really, be-

334

cause this guy had things Szymanski's never even heard of, so-called research chemicals that are guaranteed to . . .

But Szymanski didn't give a shit, he was just being polite.

He's actually not interested in getting high. It's not how he's feeling at the moment, not where his head is at.

Where *that* is exactly, however, he isn't too sure either.

Since he read about Senator Rundle in the paper before the weekend he's had a strange laser-precision focus on everything around him. It's like he's *already* high. It's like he's somehow wired into this, with the story seeming to pop up on his grid every few hours or so – mentions on TV, for example, interview clips, a magazine cover at a newsstand he passes, snatches of a conversation he overhears in a store or in an elevator.

Hey, what do you make of that Senator Rundle?

And each time, in his mind, it jerks him back to Buenke, to this blubbering fuckwad framed in the doorway of the SUV, staring bug-eyed as Tube walks right up and pops one into the side of Ray Kroner's skull. Then Ray's body on the ground, in a heap, his twisted face visible, the top of his head.

Fuck.

Szymanski looks at the gun on the blanket, stares at it, concentrates.

Then Rundle being huddled away, past the other bodies, into a car, on to the airstrip, back to Paris . . . the big lie no doubt already forming, the stench of it everywhere within hours.

Jesus, how long can this go on? How intense can it get? And what if . . . what if Rundle secures the nomination? What if he goes on to win the election, for Christ's sake? Four, possibly eight years of this shit?

Szymanski lowers himself onto the edge of the bed.

And every *day*? Every time he turns on his TV? Or goes on-line? Or walks out on the street? Or wakes *up*? No fucking way, Jack. It'd be intolerable, that's what it would be.

He stretches out his arm.

It would be intolerable, so he's not going to let it happen. It's that simple.

He picks up the gun.

It has to be.

*

Jimmy spends most of Tuesday morning walking around midtown, familiarising himself with various locations – the BRX Building on Fifth, another office building on Lexington (one where he's read that Gideon Global have their headquarters, even though he sees nothing there to indicate that they do), and a restaurant near the Flatiron where he's meeting Bob Lessing, a friend of Phil Sweeney's from what both men referred to, in separate conversations, as the 'old days'.

Jimmy doesn't know how useful any of this is going to be, but it makes him feel like he's doing something.

The restaurant near the Flatiron is French and casual, and Bob Lessing is a guy in his late fifties wearing a grey suit and a bow tie. Apparently, he and Phil Sweeney worked together in the eighties and have been friends ever since. Lessing runs a PR firm here and specialises in strategic communications and risk analysis for large companies working overseas.

Of the three people Jimmy called yesterday evening, from the numbers Sweeney gave him, Lessing was the only one available to meet at such short notice.

'So, Jimmy,' he says, taking a piece of bread from the basket on the table, 'how *is* the big man these days?'

'He's good. I don't see him that often, but he's good.'

Jimmy doesn't know if Lessing is aware that Sweeney is, or might, be sick. Jimmy himself doesn't know, but he's assuming – assuming cancer of some kind.

At the same time, Jimmy is agitated. He's not here to talk about Phil Sweeney.

After a few minutes, Lessing seems to sense this and moves things on. 'Phil told me you might need a little help.'

'Yeah, I'm . . . I'm working on a story.'

Jimmy explains, but couches it in fairly neutral terms, keeps it general. He doesn't make any direct charges against the 'parties' involved or mention the Africa dimension. Phil told him to do this, and that Lessing would read between the lines.

As they eat, Lessing asks a series of questions that demonstrate – to Jimmy's surprise, alarm almost – that he has indeed read between the lines, and very adeptly.

When their coffees arrive, Lessing goes silent for a bit. Then he says, 'OK, here's the thing, I've never worked with BRX, or Gideon, but I can tell you something, you have your work cut out here. BRX is privately owned, so no shareholder meetings, no reports, no *information*, and that's how they like to keep it. Clark Rundle is also notoriously media-shy. As for Gideon Global, what I hear is that they're specialising a lot these days in competitive intelligence and domestic surveillance – NSA contracts mostly – so trying to penetrate *them*? Forget it. One whiff, and they'll penetrate *you*, if you catch my drift.' He stirs sugar into his coffee. 'You see, I work on the opposite side of the fence from you, and a lot of what I do is actually keeping

337

people like you *at bay*. Or subtly veering you in certain directions. Perception management. Therefore even though I don't work for BRX my gut instinct here is to protect them, and to obfuscate. But one thing I will tell you, and this is something I've learned from being in this business more than thirty years, and it's this . . . *that people fuck up*. All the time. They make mistakes, and do stupid things, and in big companies like BRX a huge amount of time and energy goes into covering these mistakes up. And people like *you*, if you dig hard enough, if you make enough of a pain in the ass of yourself, sometimes you get results. *Sometimes*.' He nods at the waiter for the check. 'So what I'm going to do is refer you to one of the biggest pains in the ass on *your* side of the fence. She'll be able to help you with this, whatever this thing is you have. More than I can. Corporate watch, all that stuff, it's her, er . . . her métier.' He takes out his BlackBerry. 'I've dealt with her a good few times, and she's very smart. Ellen Dorsey.' He looks up. 'You ready? Here's her number.'

Fifteen minutes later, sitting on a bench in the park in front of the Flatiron, Jimmy calls Ellen Dorsey. He's heard of her, even read some of her stuff online – from *Rolling Stone*, *The Nation*, *Parallax*, *Wired* – and he's intimidated.

Of course.

'Yep? Ellen Dorsey.'

But that's not going to stop him.

'Hi Ellen, my name's Jimmy Gilroy, I just got your number from Bob Lessing.'

Silence.

That's what Lessing told him to say.

Then, 'Call me back in ten minutes.'

Click.

Ten minutes. He does a quick Google search on his phone. She's thirty-nine. From Philadelphia. There's a roll call of articles she's written, stories she covered, awards won. There's a link to a clip of an appearance she once made on *The Daily Show* with Jon Stewart, but he can't access it.

He checks the time and calls her back.

'Jimmy Gilroy, yeah? So, Bob tells me you've got something. And he assures me that you're not a plant. Bizarrely enough, I trust Bob, so shoot.'

Jimmy pauses. 'Not over the phone.'

'Of course, right. Not over the phone. You know what, let me give you my address. You come here. I'm working, but we can talk.'

This is all happening pretty fast.

She lives near Ninety-third and Amsterdam. He walks a few blocks over and takes the subway. On the train up, he wonders what Bob Lessing said about him on the phone. At no point did Jimmy make it clear to Lessing who he was or wasn't working for. He deliberately left it vague and Lessing didn't ask.

He gets off at Ninety-sixth and Broadway, goes back to Ninety-third and wanders along until he finds her building.

She buzzes him up.

It's still hot and he's still overdressed and as he walks up to the fourth floor he feels like he's going to faint.

He doesn't.

Ellen Dorsey is waiting for him. She's small and lean and spiky, with short dark hair and blue eyes. She's wearing black jeans and a black T-shirt.

'Come on in.'

They shake.

'Thanks for seeing me.'

She holds the door open for him. He walks into the apartment. In a weird way, and though a lot bigger, it's not unlike his own. Books everywhere and a desk covered in shit. Hers backs onto a window, overlooking the street, so when she's working at it, the idea is, presumably, she's facing the room, less distraction.

She goes over and sits behind it now, and indicates for him to take the chair in front of it.

'I'm in the middle of an article,' she says, 'with a looming deadline, so you'll excuse me if I multi-task for a bit here.'

'No, of course, fine, go ahead, I won't keep you long anyway.'

'Tea, you want some, or water, or –'

'No. I'm fine.'

Ellen Dorsey nods and then starts clacking away at her keyboard, looking down at her notes. 'So,' she says, 'talk.'

Jimmy starts, fixing his gaze on a knot in one of the floorboards.

He tells it pretty succinctly, and doesn't hold back as he did with Lessing. He explains about the biography. He describes his conversations with Larry Bolger and Dave Conway. Then he spells it all out – the conference, the mine, the thanaxite, Gianni Bonacci, the helicopter crash.

BRX, Gideon Global.

At one point he realises that the clacking has stopped and he looks up.

Ellen Dorsey is staring at him. 'Holy shit,' she says, holding her mouth open. 'Holy *shit*.' Then she laughs and shakes her head. 'You couldn't make this up, so I'm assuming you haven't.'

'No, I haven't.' He shifts his weight in the chair. He realises he has made quite an impression on her. 'My only problem,' he says, 'as you've probably guessed, is the lack of hard evidence.'

Dorsey nods. 'Sure, sure, but *still.*'

First time he's heard that.

'The other thing I don't have', he goes on, deciding to lay all his cards on the table, 'is a job. This started out as something else, a book about that actress who died in the crash. So I don't have resources, or any kind of support.' He pauses. 'I came here to New York because it seemed like the next logical move.'

Dorsey considers this, swivelling in her chair. 'Have you made contact with any of the principals? Do they know you're looking into this?'

'Not directly, but someone knows.' He tells her about the break-in at his apartment. 'Also, I'm not sure, but I have the impression I'm being followed.'

Dorsey laughs again. 'Well, if you're not, you certainly *will* be when you leave this place. I get a lot of attention from interested parties. You get used to it.' She stops swivelling. 'By the way, what's the connection with Bob Lessing?'

Jimmy explains – the eighties, Phil Sweeney, his old man.

Dorsey seems to get it. 'OK,' she says. 'Look. This is an incredible story, and I'll be honest with you, it doesn't surprise me one bit. The scramble for resources in Africa has thrown up a lot of nasty shit going back for the last, what, hundred, hundred and fifty years? But the problem, as you say, is proving it. With companies like BRX, guys like Rundle, that takes a lot of work, a lot of digging, a lot of *time*. You don't come at them head-on or they'll crush you, in some cases literally. You *gnaw* at them, like a tiny rodent they can't see until it's too late. And that's the thing about this job. It's got a glamorous image, but most of the time it's *mind*-numbingly boring.'

Jimmy wants to say, *I know, believe me*, but he holds back.

'So, what have we got here?' she says, shunting her chair forward and leaning on the desk. 'I'm the one with experience and connections, you're the one with the story, is that it?'

He supposes it is, and nods.

'Well, you're going to have to give me time to think about it, do a little background. How long are you here?'

Jimmy's heart sinks. 'End of the week.'

She clicks her tongue. 'Hhhm. I got to finish this.' She taps the pile of notes on her desk. 'Let me call you tomorrow, OK? Then we can sit down and hammer it out.'

'Yeah, thanks. I appreciate it.'

She smiles. He stands up.

Back out on Ninety-third, Jimmy finds it hard not to be disappointed. Whatever expectations he had coming over to New York were clearly unreasonable. This is a big project, requiring time, and lots of it.

But how much time does he have?

He walks back towards the Ninety-sixth Street subway station – slowly, lost in thought. As he approaches the entrance stairwell, his phone rings. He stops and takes it out.

'Hello.'

'Jimmy? Ellen Dorsey. Listen, I've just been flicking around online and I came across something. Might be an opportunity.'

'Yeah?' He stands there looking out at the passing traffic.

'Clark Rundle's brother – you know, the senator? He's speaking at some thing tomorrow morning at the Blackwood Hotel on East Fifty-eighth Street. Apparently, there's a lot of buzz about it because people are speculating that he might be about to announce his candidacy.'

'Oh.'

'And if that's the case, you should go along, hang around outside, because more than likely Clark Rundle himself will be there, supporting his bro. At least it'd be a chance for you to get a *look* at him. Might be the only chance you ever get.'

*

He can't get a straight answer out of them. They say she's just not available.

But what does that mean?

So when will she be available?

It's not possible to say at the moment.

Jesus *Christ*.

Rundle slams the phone down.

Why can't he just buy Nora, buy her outright, set her up in an apartment and have done with it?

Heading off now to have dinner with J.J. and Sally and Eve, he should be in a good mood, but he isn't. He actually has to remind himself that things are going pretty well at the moment.

Tomorrow morning, for instance.

J.J. announces, then with any luck Jimmy Vaughan shows up, endorses, commits. And that's pretty much it.

It all gets taken to the next level

Clark gets taken to the next level.

Because Vaughan has already brought him in on this Paloma robotics programme, and that's a long game by anyone's definition. On top of which, what, two years campaigning and

343

maybe eight years in the White House? Outstanding. But Jimmy Vaughan won't be around for most of that, which he must know, so Clark can't help seeing this as a process being set in motion.

A sort of . . . *succession* mechanism.

Is it any wonder he's a bit jittery?

Dinner at Quaranta proceeds nicely. J.J. has had a few good days – plenty of media exposure, his celebrity growing at a rate that can only be described as exponential. He seems to have an appeal, something indefinable the camera draws out of him when he's sitting in a studio, an X factor for politicians you couldn't pay for. Tomorrow morning's announcement is set to ramp that up a further few notches.

During the meal, J.J. takes call after call on his cell phone. His staff are setting things up at the Blackwood and J.J. likes to micro-manage. Herb Felder even drops by with the latest draft of his speech, which J.J. asks Rundle to throw his eye over. Sally and Eve tease them about this.

The two brothers.

Echoes.

'Any chance you'll make Clark attorney general?'

The atmosphere at the table is light, even skittish, but everyone understands how this works. They *have* to be excited or it won't play.

It's a confidence trick.

Anything could happen between now and the nomination, let alone afterwards, so they might as well enjoy it while it lasts. At the same time, and up to a certain point, the confidence trick must also apply to themselves. Because if they don't believe, and act as if, they have a reasonable stab at this, who else is going to?

At the end of the meal, as they're finishing their coffees, J.J.'s phone goes off again. Then Rundle's does, too. As they both reach out to answer them, the wives roll their eyes.

Rundle looks at the display and sees that it's Don Ribcoff. 'Don.'

J.J.'s eyes widen and he mouths something at Rundle.

'Clark, I have an update. I need to talk to you.'

Rundle is confused. *What?* This across the table.

J.J. mouths it again. *Jimmy Vaughan.* He points at his phone, then sticks his thumb up.

Rundle's heart skips a beat. Confirmation. This is fantastic. 'Don, what is it, what do you need?'

'Can we meet?'

'No, Don, we can't.' Rundle rolls *his* eyes. 'I'm having dinner. What is it? Tell me.' He's watching J.J. working Vaughan, the way he works a room, but over the phone. Confidence is such a weird thing, he thinks, self-perpetuating, self-regenerating, the more you have . . .

'I don't really –'

'Jesus, Don, just *tell* me.'

'OK. That thing we talked about the other day, the guy?'

What thing? What guy? Rundle is caught now between his excitement and a sudden burst of extreme irritation. 'What the fuck are you talking about, Don?' he whispers into the phone. 'Spell it *out*, would you?'

Ribcoff pauses, then sighs. 'The guy? The journalist? Jimmy Gilroy? He's becoming a problem.' Rundle furrows his brow.

'We took another look at him. He went to Italy last week. He spoke to Gianni Bonacci's widow.'

'What?'

'That was before he met with Dave Conway. And that's not all.' Ribcoff pauses again. Rundle waits, the room around him going slightly out of focus now. 'He's here. In New York.'

'*What?*'

'He arrived yesterday –'

'*Jesus*, Don.'

'I swear to God, Clark, I've only just been given the report this minute.' He sighs. 'Look, there was a delay.'

Rundle can't believe this, any of it. 'He's *here*?'

'Yeah, we tracked his movements online. He booked a room at a hotel in the West Village, five nights. Arrived into JFK yesterday afternoon.'

Rundle gets up from the table, nodding, but not making direct eye contact with anyone. He moves away. 'Are you *on* him? I mean, what's he doing? *Jesus.*'

'Yeah, we're on him, but he doesn't seem –'

'Don, I don't care how he *seems*.' Rundle stops. He's standing between two tables near the side of the room, facing the bar. Quaranta is generous when it comes to table spacing. Acoustics might be a different matter. 'What can you *do* about him?'

There is a pause here, during which Rundle takes a quick look on either side of him. Sitting at the table to his left is Ray Tyner, baby-faced teen star turned serious-contender leading man. At the table to his right, judging from the get-up, is a Roman Catholic bishop, or a cardinal maybe.

'Options are limited,' Ribcoff says, 'because there's something else.'

'Jesus fucking *Christ*.' The cardinal flinches. '*What is it?*'

'He paid a visit this afternoon to Ellen Dorsey, she's an investigative –'

'I know who Ellen Dorsey is. Fuck.'

'So, the point is, she gives him a little cover, some profile. Whatever about him, you don't want *her* on your tail.'

'Meaning?'

Ribcoff hesitates, then whispers, as though he can see the cardinal too. 'We can't just take the motherfucker out. We've got to be careful.'

Rundle swallows. He walks towards the bar and sits on a stool, but turns outward, facing the room. After a while he says, 'You know what, Don? He doesn't know anything. He can't. Maybe he's been told some stuff, but that's as far as it goes. Has to be. It was three years ago. We're covered. There's no proof of anything. He makes a move, says a word, and we'll get legal to shit all over him.'

'OK.'

He catches J.J.'s eye from across the room and nods.

'But don't let him out of your sight, you hear me?'

12

Jimmy gets up early and goes out in search of coffee. It's another really nice day and he just about manages to dress appropriately. He walks along tree-lined, sun-dappled West Fourth Street and tries to imagine living in one of these brownstones.

They're gorgeous, but he could never afford the rents around here.

Besides, he'd miss the sea from his window.

He finds a coffee shop out on Sixth.

Convinced now that he is being followed, he can't help feeling self-conscious, as though every move he makes, every gesture, is being watched and graded. A corollary of this, of course, is that his life might be in danger.

He stays in the coffee shop for an hour, until just after nine, sipping coffee and watching people as they come and go.

When he is out on the street again, he flags down a cab. He does this on impulse. He tells the driver East Fifty-eighth Street and they quickly join the flow of traffic heading uptown.

Jimmy half turns and looks through the rear window.

If he has a tail, could he lose it this easily?

Seems possible.

He turns around again, and looks ahead.

But it isn't as if they'd have much trouble trying to work out where he's going.

They.

Jimmy feels a surge of frustration here. Over three years ago six people died in a helicopter crash. They were murdered. He knows who was responsible, and why. He was told, and he believes it.

But that incident, and what led up to it, is locked away now, in a glass case, perceived by the public at large, and by the authorities, as a tragic accident.

So what does he think, he can come along and change that? He can smash the glass and replace what's behind it?

With what?

The cab turns east at Fifty-seventh Street.

This event at the Blackwood Hotel is supposed to start at ten o'clock. He'll arrive half an hour early and hang around. See what he can see. Without a press pass, he won't get inside the door of the hotel, that's for sure, won't get near it, but he might catch a glimpse of Clark Rundle on his way in.

He gets the driver to pull over between Madison and Park. He pays and gets out. He'll walk the rest of the way, one block north and two over.

From about half a block away he identifies the hotel, sees the marquee, and a small gathering of what look like photographers.

And security.

It's a busy street, lots of midtown bustle, so no need to be overly self-conscious. He comes to One Beacon Court, and peers in at the glimmering, elliptical courtyard as he passes.

A few moments later, two or three buildings before the Blackwood, he stops and leans against some railings. He looks around, up the street, towards the hotel. There are more arrivals, technicians, a camera crew.

People standing around, random individuals like himself, free country.

He takes out his phone, but wishes he smoked, like his old man – standing there in the street, in a three-piece suit, busy with cigarettes and a lighter.

No questions asked.

*

Szymanski is tired. He feels like he was awake all night, but he must have slept periodically, five minutes here and there, enough to keep ticking over – micro doses, but never any of the deep stages, the REM, the restorative shit. That's partly why he steered clear of the coke, which he'll leave for housekeeping maybe. The weed he smoked some of, but most of it's still in the bag.

He'll leave that, too.

He checks out of the hotel at nine thirty.

He carries a canvas holdall with his stuff in it, but not a lot of time passes before he's thinking about discarding it somewhere.

The day's a little warm for the leather jacket he's wearing, but the M9 fits perfectly in the lower inside pocket, so he needs it.

What has he got in the bag anyway? A couple of changes, toiletries, minor personal items. Nothing he couldn't replace in a few minutes at a J. Crew and a Duane Reade's. That was always the Gideon way, travel light, no excess baggage, leave it all behind you – including family, girlfriends, bosses, shitty jobs, whatever.

They didn't have room, and weren't interested.

Passing a construction site he tosses his bag into a dumpster.

There, gone, along with everything else.

But really this particular everything else – *his* everything else – he tossed a long time ago, when he signed up with Gideon in the first place.

Szymanski gets onto Fifth Avenue and starts walking north.

So that's not what this is about, being unable, or unwilling, to go home to C-town – it's about being unable to go back to work.

Unpaid leave.

Effective immediately.

That's all he had left and now it's been taken from him, and even if they'd acted differently, if they'd kept him on, it was all shot to shit anyway, as far as he was concerned, after what happened.

Ray Kroner.

Those people, the women and kids, the man at the wall.

What were their names? At least Ray had a name. *And* he got a body bag.

More than they got.

Szymanski turns right at Fifty-eighth Street. It's a few blocks over.

He wonders about Ray's family, out there in Phoenix, about what kind of an explanation they got, if any, and about the other families, the ones back in the DRC, in Buenke.

He knows *they* didn't get any explanations.

They have to put up with Arnold Kimbela for Christ's sake, day in, day out.

He slows down.

Man, some of the shit he saw over there, slave labour, systematic torture, systematic *rape*.

Explain *that*.

As he gets close to the hotel, Szymanski slows down even more, to a crawl. There's security everywhere.

Naturally.

He's assuming it's all Gideon – their domestic division, the pussy squad, guys in suits, underarm holsters, earpieces. It's unlikely that he'll know any of them, or that they'll know him. Unless Donald Ribcoff himself is around the place, which he probably will be. The CEO of Gideon is notoriously hands-on, especially when it comes to the high-profile jobs. He was in and out of Buenke all the time. But would he recognise Szymanski? Maybe, maybe not.

What does it fucking matter now, though, right?

Szymanski stands across the street from the hotel.

So this is it? He presses a hand against the gun in his jacket pocket. This is what it all comes down to in the end, the life of a spineless, deceitful bastard with a propensity to showboat on TV, who if he hadn't been there that day, and hadn't lied about it afterwards . . .

Szymanski finds the air around where he's standing suddenly heavy with some local cooking smell. He realises his timing may not be the best, but he can imagine lying down now, there on the sidewalk, drifting off to sleep, falling into a pit of dreams.

He looks around.

People everywhere.

Just what exactly does he think he's doing?

*

When Rundle arrives into J.J.'s Manhattan office on Third Avenue he's surprised to see that Jimmy Vaughan is there, sitting on a couch in the corner shooting the breeze with some of the younger staff members. The idea was that Rundle and J.J. would head over to the Blackwood together, from here, wives in tow. Vaughan would show up whenever he chose – but over *there*, at the Blackwood.

Not here.

Rundle didn't expect this.

'Clark,' J.J. calls from across the room. 'Where's Eve?'

Rundle walks towards him. 'She's down in the car, waiting.' He looks at his watch, to reinforce the point. 'Sally?'

'She's over there.' He indicates another office behind him, door closed. 'Some issue with her hair.'

A few feet away, in front of a desk, several of the senior staffers, Herb Felder included, appear to be tinkering – *still* tinkering – with J.J.'s speech.

'We are all of us,' one of them says, 'we are each of us. *Fuck.* We are each of us. We are all of us.'

'Try *we are each of us,*' Herb Felder says.

'OK, OK.' Red pen on paper. 'OK. Because we are each of us shareholders in this great democracy, we are each of us the bearers of a sacred trust –'

Rundle looks at J.J. 'Everything under control?'

J.J. nods. 'Yeah.' He smiles, something he's good at. 'You know what? I think we can nail this thing.'

'So do I.' Rundle smiles as well. But his smile has an in-built smirk to it, always had. He glances over in Vaughan's direction. 'He thinks so too, apparently.'

J.J. widens his eyes in delight. 'I *know.* Let's go over and say hello.'

As they get to the corner, Vaughan looks up. 'Here he is, the *man.*'

'Mr Vaughan.'

This is for the benefit of the junior staffers. Clark and J.J. have known Jimmy Vaughan since they were kids. He's like an uncle to them.

'You ready for this, Senator?'

Vaughan is sitting at one end of the couch, legs crossed, looking small and slightly frail. But his flashing blue eyes mitigate this impression somewhat, and there's no question at all about who's in charge here.

'Absolutely. Bring it on, that's what I say.' J.J. looks around, being inclusive, already working this, the first of the day's, and the season's, many rooms.

Sitting next to Vaughan on the couch is a pretty redhead and standing around in a semicircle are three nerdy-looking guys, all of them in their early twenties.

'So tell me, Senator,' Vaughan says. 'I'm curious. Why are you running?'

J.J. laughs. 'You want to know the truth?'

'Good Lord, no.'

Everyone laughs.

'OK then, because I want to make a difference, because I feel that –'

'Fine, fine, give us the truth.'

More laughter.

'OK, but you know what? It's actually the same answer, maybe framed a little differently. Because the *truth* is, I'm tired of the senate. Doesn't do it for me anymore. Being in the senate these days is all about gridlock and rules and obstructionist bullshit, it's chasing the money and playing to the base, it's exhausting commutes, it's endless press and media and blogging and *tweeting*, Jesus, it's –'

'Whoa, take it easy there, bubba.'

'No, the thing is, I want to be able to *do* stuff. What was it someone once said? It used to be that you spent two years as a senator, two years as a politician and two years as a demagogue. Now you spend the full six as a demagogue. It's crazy.'

Vaughan nods. 'Richard Russell.'

'Right.'

There is a brief silence.

'So, what are you telling me, that's your stump speech? Maybe *I* should run.'

More laughter, but this time it's a little tentative.

Rundle senses J.J. stiffen beside him.

After a moment one of the nerds steps in. 'Can I ask you, Mr Vaughan, what is it that keeps you going? I read about your work rate somewhere recently, projects you're still involved in, companies you've acquired, it's awesome.'

'Fear of death,' Vaughan says immediately, and smiles. Then he points at the senator. 'You think his stump speech sucks? Wait till you hear mine. It's a real downer.' He waves a hand in the air. 'No, but seriously, son, seriously. When you get to my age you just want to grab on to the future, you know, you just want to hold it in your two hands and *look* at it. Now the thing is, most folks don't get the chance to do that, but in my line of work, developing new companies, with new ideas, I sort of can.'

Rundle sneaks a glance at his watch.

'Let me explain,' Vaughan goes on – the nerds and the pretty redhead hanging on his every word now. 'History, right? It's there, undeniably, you can survey it, and mull over it, from the Pyramids to the Renaissance, from the Nazis to 9/11, it's all laid out for us. But the future? You can only ever have access to the tiniest, slimmest portion of it. Beyond what's left of your own life, of whatever few years you've got remaining, everything is a blank, right? It's unreachable. It's unknowable. And *yet*.' He raises a finger in the air and wags it. 'And *yet*. Today, more than at any other time in history, we can guess with some confidence what the future *might* be like. People al-

355

ways used to believe they lived in a time following a golden age, but now it's the other way around. Now we always feel we live in a time just preceding one. You get me?'

Heads nod vigorously.

Some of J.J.'s other staffers, the senior ones, wander over to listen.

'Right, now we're in the infancy stages of various branches of scientific development – biotechnology, nanotechnology, robotics, that sort of thing – and since the rate of change in the next hundred years is probably going to equal or even exceed the rate of change in the last hundred, we can be fairly certain that no matter when we die it will be at a time when great advances are *just* about to take place. Which we won't be around for. Which we'll miss.' He pauses. 'Right? That's the downer part.'

A ripple of nervous laughter.

Vaughan shifts his weight on the couch, shunts forward a bit. 'But what *I* think, and what I try to do with some of these companies – and to answer your question – what *I* think is that if we work harder and faster, and redouble our efforts, and push, I mean *what*ever it takes, if we do that, we can get the jump on next season, next year, the next decade.' He clenches his fist and raises it slightly. 'If we imagine our way into the future with enough vigour and determination, we can somehow actually arrive there. It's a bit like that old slogan from the World's Fair, I remember it as a kid.' He pauses. '*Tomorrow, Now!*'

'Oh my god,' the pretty redhead beside him says, hand on chest, clearly unable to help herself, 'that's *so* inspiring.'

'Thank you, my dear.' Vaughan turns toward her and nods in

acknowledgement. 'Clark there knows what I'm talking about. Right, Clark?'

Rundle is taken by surprise. 'Sure, Mr Vaughan, yeah. Absolutely.'

At that point, Herb Felder intervenes, tapping his watch.

Minutes later, they're all downstairs and piling into various cars.

Rundle sees Don Ribcoff on the sidewalk, but there's no time to talk.

As planned, he and J.J. ride together.

When the car pulls out and joins the flow of traffic, J.J. exhales loudly and says, 'What the fuck was *that*?'

Rundle turns to him, 'Look, he's always been like that. Despite what he says, the old man thinks he's going to live forever.' He turns the other way and looks out the window, Third Avenue flitting past, the corner of Fifty-eighth just up ahead. 'But we know different, right?'

*

Jimmy glances up and sees what looks like a flotilla of black limousines and SUVs turning onto to Fifty-eighth Street from Third Avenue. He leans back against the railings, almost as though he's standing to attention, and watches.

Around the entrance to the hotel there is a flurry of activity – positions are taken, equipment is prepped. On either side of the marquee burly guys in suits line up, enough of them to create an effective blockade, with photographers moving around and behind them, dancing like boxers, already pointing, clicking, whirring.

357

The flotilla moves along the street at a stately pace. It then pulls in and stops, one of the limousines flush with the hotel entrance.

Along the line of vehicles – an SUV, three limos and another SUV, Jimmy can see them clearly now – multiple doors open at once and more burly guys in suits appear, some on the sidewalk, others on the street.

Jimmy steps away from the railings and moves a few paces along to try and see better. But he doesn't get too close. He's assuming he's still under surveillance and doesn't want to draw attention to himself.

Undue attention.

He doesn't want to alarm anyone. Not that there aren't plenty of other people around the place now for them to be worried about.

Passersby, civilians, gawkers.

As the back doors of all three limos are being opened, Jimmy senses a collective, almost gravitational pull, a jolt, like an implosion, *towards* them. This is accompanied by a noticeable increase in the level of clicking and whirring.

From the first car, two ladies appear, in their forties, svelte and elegant. These, Jimmy takes it, are the Rundle wives. From the second car – slightly harder to see now, with the scramble intensifying – the Rundle brothers themselves appear, the senator with the wire brace on his hand and wrist, Clark instantly recognisable from photos in that *Vanity Fair* spread.

They all move from the kerb onto a carpet under the marquee. The pace is leisurely, and Jimmy has the impression that someone from inside the hotel has emerged to greet them. This causes a delay, as there seems to be some handshaking and small talk going on. It's possible they're doing this for the benefit of the photographers and camera crews, but Jimmy doesn't mind, because standing in his direct line of vision at the moment – through an accidental configuration of the crowd, and it surely won't last – is the only person here this morning he's interested in seeing, Clark Rundle.

The chairman and CEO of BRX is tall and distinguished-looking, but in a central casting sort of way. Jimmy would love to be able to read his expression, to decode it, to pick up on something in it, vibes or a signal that would explain, or illuminate, but nothing like that happens.

It's the face of a middle-aged business executive.

What did he expect?

And when a security guy moves and cuts off Jimmy's line of vision, the face goes with it, instantly forgotten, the slate wiped clean.

A second or two later, with a further shift in the crowd formation, Jimmy catches a flash of the senator – telegenic smile in place as he greets someone in the line, pointing at them in recognition.

But then something happens.

From the other side of the street, just up a bit, there's a sudden movement. A man breaks away from a line of people at the kerb and comes rushing across the street in a diagonal line towards the hotel entrance. He's shouting, '*Senator, Senator.*'

Everyone turns and looks. The man is big, in a leather jacket, with a buzz cut and mirror shades.

Reaction is swift.

Two of the security detail double back around the main limousine and head straight into his path, blocking him from getting any further.

'*Senator,*' the man continues shouting, '*tell us the truth, tell us where you were, tell us what you were doing.*'

The security guys push him back, as others arrive to help.

Jimmy and everyone else – including those under the marquee – watch in shock for a couple of seconds. Then, as the senator starts to move, bodyguards bundling him inside, the man lunges forward once more, pushing against the security guys, and shouting, '*Tell us about your trip to Buenke, Senator. Tell us what really happened.*'

Jimmy freezes.

What?

The security guys shove the man back again and this time he breaks loose, taking a few steps away from them. 'Assholes,' he says, standing in the middle of the street now and starting to straighten his jacket. The security guys remain where they are, looking over their shoulders.

Jimmy glances back towards the marquee.

Gone.

Everyone inside, everyone who matters, the rest filtering in slowly, the show over.

Jimmy looks out at the street again. The security guys are shaking their heads at each other as the man in the leather jacket retreats, walking backwards for a bit, but then turning and striding off in the direction of Third Avenue.

A woman in front of Jimmy says to her companion, '*What* did that guy say?'

'I don't know, but what a freak.'

Jimmy stares at the backs of their heads.

Buenke.

He said Buenke.

He said *tell us about your trip to Buenke.*

Before he knows what he's doing, Jimmy has skipped out onto the street and is crossing to the other side.

He walks quickly, glancing back every couple of seconds. When he gets to the corner, he turns right, and scans the sidewalk in front of him.

There he is, half a block away, buzz cut, black leather jacket.

Forward motion.

Keeping his distance, Jimmy follows.

*

'*Fuck, fuck, fuck, FUCK.*'

Standing at the light, waiting to cross at Fifty-seventh Street, Tom Szymanski's insides feel like they're being put through a meat grinder. He can't believe it. That's all he had to offer? That was his A game? Shouting out stuff like some fucking anti-globalisation protester at a G8 summit?

Really?

Jesus.

The light changes and he moves forward, no idea where he's going, that stupid Lipstick Building a few blocks on making him queasy now just having to look at it.

What happened?

He was primed and ready and he could have done it, easily. Granted, there wouldn't have been any fine marksmanship involved, but if he'd positioned himself across the street, up close, clear view.

One shot is all it would have taken.

To the chest, or head.

M9 sliding from his pocket, arm outstretched, element of surprise – it would have been a piece of cake.

So what stopped him?

He doesn't know.

He's too fucking self-aware, maybe, too analytical. Too able to see different points of view at the same time, a potentially lethal trait in this line of business.

He doesn't know.

Too *tired*?

He tried to convince himself he was crazy – and he is, up to a point, sure, given what he's seen – but he doesn't have that extra bit of crazy that Ray Kroner had, the bit that presses too hard on whatever nerve ending it is that causes you to . . . *flip*. And maybe that's it, to stand there in the street and shoot some bastard in cold blood you don't even know, you'd absolutely have to flip. But for him, back there on Fifty-eighth Street, as he gazed across at the entrance to the hotel, fingering the gun in his pocket, he just knew it was never going to happen.

Not today, not ever.

Tom Szymanski, too sane to flip.

But where did that leave him? He still had his sense of out-rage over Buenke, over the 'incident' and the subsequent lies, he still had his raw anger – so he ends up, what, powerless, screaming like a *girl*?

It'd be funny if it wasn't so fucking tragic.

What actually *is* funny is that he's now thinking about going back and retrieving his holdall from that dumpster.

Or looking for the nearest Duane Reade's.

And it's when he stops suddenly, and turns around, to scan this section of Third Avenue for the familiar signage, that something strikes him – it's in his line of sight, a barely perceptible flicker, a reaction maybe to his own action of turning around. That guy at the kerb? The one over there at the camera store window?

Szymanski turns back and moves on.

Someone recognised him. He didn't see Donald Ribcoff at any point, but so what?

Also, he said Buenke.

Which basically means he's fucked. Because Szymanski understands how Gideon works. The company is like some primitive organism – it's lean, it's hungry, and self-preservation is about the sum total of what it knows. Walking on now, crossing Fifty-sixth Street, he can even imagine its physical presence, on his back – and not just eyes, human ones, tracking his every move, but laser pointers as well, from the surveillance equipment they'll be using.

Having to deal with this was never part of the plan.

Because if he'd carried out the plan he wouldn't be here. If he'd shot the senator, they'd have shot him.

No question about it.

Right between the eyes.

So what happens now?

He turns at the next corner, onto Fifty-fifth Street, and speeds up. About halfway along the block he spins around suddenly and comes charging back, straight into the guy who was standing at the window of the camera store on Third, young guy, maybe late twenties, startled-looking, but –

You make a calculation.

He grabs the guy by the lapels of his jacket, steers him to the left and rams him up against the window of a Chinese restaurant.

He ignores anyone passing by and they ignore him.

It's ten thirty in the morning and the Chinese restaurant is closed.

But make this quick.

'You fuckin' following me?'

Stupid question, and when he looks into the guy's eyes one thing he knows straight off. He isn't Gideon.

'Yes,' the guy says, swallowing. 'I am, was, following you.'

And that's not the answer Szymanski expected either. He loosens his grip slightly.

'Who are you?'

'I'm a journalist. I heard what you said back there.'

Szymanski hesitates, screws his eyes up. 'What are you, British?'

'Irish.'

Another moment of hesitation and then Szymanski releases him. He stands back, catches his breath, glances up and down the street.

The guy straightens his jacket and rubs his shoulder.

'OK, Irish,' Szymanski says, staring at him now, 'what the *fuck* do you want?'

*

Inside the ballroom of the Blackwood Hotel, sitting at tables and standing at the back, several hundred people listen attentively as J.J. thumps out what Rundle considers to be a pretty good speech. He knows it's a good speech because he's read it, not because he's listening to it right now.

That's something he can't do.

Listen, focus.

And given what happened outside, he doesn't know how J.J. can do it either – focus on the speech, let alone deliver the damned thing.

From his front-row table, Rundle looks up, cell phone in hand.

'. . . so, friends, in the light of this long, unbroken tradition of public service, it has always been my impulse to get out there and get my hands dirty, to get into the community and get involved, to do the right thing.'

Not only *deliver* it, shit, but do so with such obvious conviction.

It's impressive.

'And for that very same reason, I am now running for president, because I want to get involved, because I want to go on doing the right thing . . .'

The crowd bursts into spontaneous applause.

Rundle glances at his phone. He has texted Ribcoff three times and is still waiting for a reply.

Where the fuck *is* he? And where is Vaughan?

He looks up again, left and right, around the ballroom.

Unable to focus, because . . . *Buenke*.

That man out there said *Buenke*.

'But I know I'm not alone in feeling such an impulse. I know that in your own way you feel it too. And it's not hard to understand why. There's no mystery about it.'

But who was he? Who *is* he? Certainly not the young journalist from Dublin Ribcoff spoke about the other day – not looking like that, he couldn't be.

So *who*?

'It's because, quite simply, we are each of us shareholders in this great democracy, we are each of us the bearers of a sacred trust. And so today, in New York City, I ask you to help me protect that sacred trust. I ask you to support the notions of integrity and accountability.'

Rundle's phone vibrates. He looks at it.

'I ask you to vote for truth, for equality, for justice. I ask you to join me in the greatest journey of our lives. I ask you to be right there by my side as we march on Washington.'

Need to speak, v. urgent, am in reception.

'I ask you to embrace your destiny. I ask you, when the time comes, to vote for John Rundle. Thank you and God bless America.'

Putting his phone away, Rundle rises with the cheering crowd but immediately slips off to the side, head down, and makes for the back of the room, and the exit.

When he gets out to reception, leaving the rapturous applause behind, he spots Ribcoff straightaway. The two men move towards each other at speed, converging by a gigantic potted palm plant in the centre of the lobby.

'The fuck, Don.'

Ribcoff looks furious, barely able to speak.

'He's Gideon. Mother*fucker*.'

'What? What do you mean?'

'He's one of ours, that guy out on the street.' Pointing. 'He was there, in Buenke, when it happened. He helped save your brother's *life* for Christ's sake.'

'I don't –'

'He seemed really stressed by it at the time, by the whole thing, I don't know. They figured he might be unstable. So they put him on leave.'

'Leave.'

'But we're not talking regular army leave, where you come back after a month.'

Rundle can't believe this. 'You *fired* him?'

'More or less.'

'Jesus. And now what? This is some kind of blowback?'

Ribcoff shakes his head, unable even to make eye contact. 'We'd have taken him out already, except . . .'

Rundle waits. '*Except?*'

'Except apparently right now he's down on Fifty-fifth Street talking to Jimmy *fucking* Gilroy.'

13

'So you're what, some kind of a journalist?'

Jimmy nods, seeing himself intermittently reflected in the guy's mirror shades, and finding this disconcerting to say the least. They're both standing at the kerb now, next to a fire hydrant. Every couple of seconds the guy flicks his head left, then right, checking out either end of the street. He's agitated, and seems dangerous. It's not just the buzz cut and the shades, he's brawny and muscular and looks as if he could uproot this fire hydrant with one hand and smash it over someone's head.

Jimmy's, for instance.

But for all that, and the sense they both clearly have that they're being watched, Jimmy feels strangely calm. There's something here, he knows it, and he's not going to let it go.

'That's right,' he says, adopting a tone he hopes he'll be able to maintain. 'Investigative journalist. I'm working on a book about a helicopter crash that happened a few years ago in Ireland and which I *believe*,' looking left and right himself now, 'was perpetrated by some of our friends up the street here.'

The guy looks at him. 'I don't have any fucking friends here.'

Jimmy swallows. 'Figure of speech. I'm talking about BRX, and Gideon Global.'

'Oh really?' the guy says and laughs sourly. 'BRX and Gideon?' He scans the street again, east, west, but when he looks back at Jimmy, he pauses, holding his gaze for a moment, as though weighing something up. 'I could tell you some fucking stories about *them*.'

'Yeah?'

'Yeah.'

'I'd like to hear them.' Beat. 'What's your name?'

The guy hesitates, weighing this up, too. Then, 'Tom.' He shrugs. 'Whatever. That'll do for the moment.'

'Tom. OK.' Jimmy feels a spasm of excitement, giddiness almost, and can't believe what he's about to say next. 'Do me a favour, Tom, will you, and take those fucking shades off?'

This would be the moment for Tom to uproot the fire hydrant, but to Jimmy's surprise and relief he doesn't. He takes off his shades and clips them to his shirt pocket.

His eyes are a deep blue, but a deep something else as well.

They stare at each other for a moment, traffic rumbling past, cars, yellow cabs, vans.

SUVs.

Then the guy extends his hand, 'Tom Szymanski.'

They shake.

'So, Tom,' Jimmy says, 'what do you say we go somewhere and sit down, get a cup of coffee, yeah?'

*

The car pulls into a space across the street from the coffee shop. It has tinted windows, but isn't anything conspicuous, isn't a limo or an SUV – there are enough of those around the place already.

In a booth along the side window of the coffee shop sit Jimmy Gilroy and Tom Szymanski.

Rundle can see them clearly from here.

They're facing each other over cups of coffee, talking.

About fucking *what*, though? Because the thing is, how did *they* hook up?

Rundle has that horrible sensation of being in the middle of a dream you are aware of having but can't direct in any way or put a stop to.

Next to him, Ribcoff sits with an open laptop, a Bluetooth headset and two separate phones on the go. Switching between devices, he taps keys, whispers instructions, waits, listens. There's no point interrupting him. He's doing his job.

Rundle has his own laptop open in front of him and is keeping an eye on developments more generally. J.J.'s speech went really well and is already being blogged about and dissected on various political websites. Only one blogger he's come across so far has mentioned what happened outside the hotel, and that was a throwaway comment about no event in New York ever being complete without its requisite crazy person.

All the live feeds came from inside the hotel.

However, there must have been at least one camera crew outside that caught the incident – even though it only lasted a couple of seconds, even though they'd have been taken by surprise, even though they'd *initially have been facing the wrong way*.

The other straw he's desperately clutching at is the fact that what Tom Szymanski said didn't make much sense.

Because who's ever heard of Buenke? If he'd said *Congo*, now that would have been different. Rundle feels his stomach lurch at the very thought of it. But Szymanski didn't say Congo. And it's unlikely anyone will have picked up on what he did say.

Which means that nothing really bad has happened.

Not yet, at any rate.

'Don,' Rundle says, glancing across the street now, a slight crack in his voice. 'What's next?'

'We're sending an asset in,' Ribcoff replies, without looking up from the laptop. 'He'll be wired every which way to Sunday, so we'll be able to see the subjects at close range and hear what they're saying.'

'But –'

'And out in Jersey they're working on background stuff, see what we can dig up. Just in case.'

Just in case *what*? They have to wage some kind of a PR offensive afterwards? When the dust settles?

That'll be too late.

Jesus.

With the resources they have at their disposal, you'd think they could . . .

Rundle's heart is thumping. 'Look, Don, we *know* what they're saying, or will be saying sooner or later, so . . .'

Ribcoff looks up. 'What?'

'This is an extreme situation. It requires an extreme solution.'

'You think I don't know that, Clark? But it's also a *live* situation . . . it's unpredictable, highly volatile, it's unfolding in real time, and in an exposed, public location.' He pauses. 'I mean, midtown Manhattan? On a busy weekday morning? This isn't fucking Baghdad here. Our options are *very* limited.'

*

The first twenty minutes are awkward, a period of adjustment. A lot of it is linguistic. Tom Szymanski is obviously smart, but he's not familiar with Jimmy's accent or with certain expressions he might use. And while Jimmy himself, like every other person on the planet, is exposed to the lingo here on a daily basis – he finds there's something disconcertingly raw about the way Tom Szymanski speaks.

So, at first, they stumble over each other's words.

'What?'

'Sorry?'

But then it settles down.

They stop at the first coffee shop they come to and take a booth by the window siding onto Fifty-fifth Street. The place isn't that busy, there are only a few people dotted around, sitting at tables or at the counter.

The other four booths along by the window, two ahead of them, two behind, are empty.

The waitress is a grumpy-looking Latina woman in her forties.

Behind the counter two young guys work quietly, chopping and slicing – prepping, Jimmy imagines, for the lunchtime crowd later.

Coffees arrive, both black.

Jimmy takes the lead in offering up information. He's a political journalist who has written for a national newspaper and is currently working on a freelance book project. A significant area of his research concerns the involvement of BRX in a mining concession in the Democratic Republic of Congo.

Tom Szymanski nods along at this, taking occasional sips from his coffee.

'So when we were outside the hotel back there,' Jimmy says, 'and I heard you refer to Buenke, naturally I was curious.'

'Yeah?'

'Well, it's not exactly common knowledge that BRX is in there. They won't talk about it, and certainly not to someone like me. So yeah. Of course.' Jimmy pauses, trying to pace this, but aware, too, that time is short. 'And you seemed to be implying that Senator Rundle himself has been to Buenke? Is that correct?'

'I wasn't implying it. I *said* it.'

'OK.'

'That lying cocksucker was there, let me tell you.'

'How do you know?' This sounds very abrupt. Jimmy braces himself.

'How do I know? Coz *I* was there, too. I saw him.'

'Really?'

Szymanski looks around, nods. 'Yeah, for the last couple of years I've been working as a contractor for Gideon Global. Half of that time I've spent in Congo, shunting people back and forth between the airstrip and the mine. Or guarding the mine. Or escorting shipments of whatever shit it is they're digging up out there from the mine to the airstrip.'

'Wow.'

Wow? Jimmy needs to step it up here, to focus, and get some of this down. He reaches for his pocket. 'Do you mind if I take notes?'

Szymanski shakes his head.

Jimmy pulls out his notebook and pen, flips to an empty page. 'Go on.'

'It's a shithole of a place, believe me.' Then he sighs, impatient at something, or exasperated. 'Actually, that's not true. It's a beautiful fucking country, and I mean *breath*taking, man, like nothing you've ever seen. And I'd hazard a guess that the people are pretty cool, too, but I never really got near any of them. I did see some of the shit they have to put up with, though, and that was enough for me. Basically BRX calls the shots, but the local heavy is a guy called –'

'Arnold Kimbela.'

'Yeah. Fucking dirtbag.' He rolls his eyes. 'Anyway, that's who the senator was down there seeing. The colonel. At his so-called compound.'

Jimmy stares at the page in his notebook. 'When exactly . . . are we talking about?'

Szymanski laughs at this. 'Two weeks ago, more or less.' He holds up his hand. 'This? The injured hand? It didn't happen in fucking Paris. That was all made up. It happened in Congo. We were on our way back to the airstrip.'

As Jimmy continues staring at the page in his notebook, his brain tries to process the information he's just heard, but its significance is almost too huge to take in at once – implications, ramifications, spin off it like pieces of shrapnel.

'Quite a serious claim you're making there,' he says eventually.

Szymanski nods. 'For sure. And that's not all there is.'

No, of course not.

Jimmy is beginning to wonder now if this isn't another of those conversations he's been having recently that subsequently evaporates – unrecorded, uncorroborated, unconfirmed.

'So,' he says, a little wearily, 'tell me more.'

'I will. But first *I* want to know something from you. Tell me about this helicopter crash you were talking about and what it has to do with the mine at Buenke.'

'Fair enough,' Jimmy says, and launches into it. It's like a party piece now, each time modified to suit whoever he's talking to. In this version he holds back on certain specifics, Gianni Bonacci's name, any mention of thanaxite, some other stuff.

As he's talking someone enters the coffee shop, a business-looking guy in a suit, with a newspaper under his arm. He nods at the waitress and takes a seat in a booth by the side window, two down from the one where Jimmy and Szymanski are sitting.

Jimmy can see him over Szymanski's shoulder.

The guy orders coffee and starts reading his paper.

Jimmy and Szymanski exchange looks, each thinking the

same thing, but then Jimmy continues, huddling in a bit, lowering his voice, speeding it up.

He wants to hear what Tom Szymanski has to say.

He wants to get that far, at least.

*

'. . . so this TV actress, the fact that she was there too basically sucked all the oxygen out of the story and meant that the real target, the UN inspector, hardly got a mention. Whether this was intentional or not, I don't know, but from *their* point of view, it couldn't have worked out better.'

Rundle is staring in disbelief at Ribcoff's screen. The image is grainy and a little shaky, but it's fine – the back of one guy's head, and a partial view of the other guy's face. The sound is what counts, though, and that's very good. According to Ribcoff, it travels from inside the coffee shop to Gideon's fusion centre in New Jersey – where it gets a quick 'bath', for interference – and then shoots back here to his laptop, and with only something like a five-second delay.

Otherwise, he says, it might be too hard to make out.

But it's like Ribcoff is showing off, excited about how cool his equipment is – when all Rundle can think about is what they're *hearing*.

'. . . and you're telling me this shit was to cover up their involvement in the *mine*?'

'Apparently.'

There is a pause, then a whistling sound followed by, 'Fuck me.'

'And remember, according to my source, this comes direct

from the top. Sitting at that table was Clark Rundle himself. As well as Don Ribcoff, and some other guy, I can't remember his name.'

'Yeah, but man, *those* two motherfuckers? Jesus Christ.'

Rundle and Ribcoff exchange a quick look, each registering the horror on the other's face.

Then Rundle's phone rings. He fumbles for it.

Shit.

It's Vaughan.

'What's going on, Clark? I expected to hear from you by now. Tell me this situation has been contained.'

Rundle closes his eyes. Vaughan was there, too, outside the hotel, in the third limo, but Rundle wasn't sure if what happened registered with him.

He should have known that nothing escapes James Vaughan.

'We're working on it,' Rundle says, realising how lame that sounds.'

'Oh, I hope so, son, because you know what? Your brother scored big time this morning. A lot of people are talking already. I mean, in respect of fundraising? There's an avalanche of money there, just waiting to be released. So don't fuck it up.' He pauses. 'But Clark?'

'Yeah?'

'If you do?'

'Yeah?'

'You're on your own.'

Click.

Rundle opens his eyes.

Putting his phone away, he sees that his hand is shaking.

He turns to Ribcoff. '*Don . . .*'

'OK, OK.' Hand on ear, clacking keys, another window opening up on his screen. 'This is the plan. We've got . . . we've got to separate them, or wait till they come out and go in different directions, then we can act –'

'Act?'

'Yeah, we can grab Szymanski, that won't be a problem, and we can dispose of him pretty easily. He's more or less off the grid anyway, as far as we can tell. No contact's been made with anyone in Cleveland since he got back, that's where he's from, and he doesn't seem to have any pressing commitments. So we can chalk him up to Congo, put him on our casualty list, MIA, whatever. Gilroy's a little harder, though, with this link to Ellen Dorsey. But if the circumstances are right we could arrange something, an accident maybe. Afterwards we bleach him, phones, laptop, then Dorsey's got nothing.'

Rundle nods along. 'Right, right.' It all sounds so easy.

'But first thing,' Ribcoff says, hitting a key and pointing at the screen, 'we've got to get them out of there, we've got to separate them, and we've got to do it fast.'

Rundle has a stabbing pain in his stomach.

Indigestion? Anxiety? Cancer?

He looks at the screen again. Tom Szymanski is hunched forward. 'So, Irish,' he's saying, 'let me tell you about our next president, yeah, and how he *really* fucked up that hand of his.'

*

'. . . unpaid leave, effective immediately, which in a PMC like Gideon is code for, you know, go fuck yourself and don't come back.'

Jimmy's mind is reeling.

All along he's been focused on the story of the helicopter crash – which is huge in itself, if only he could crack it – but suddenly he's got *this* on his plate? It's essentially the same story, of course, except that it's an upgrade, and one with a much wider application. Instead of a UN inspector and a faked accident, it's got a village massacre and a presidential candidate.

But the people involved are the same, and the motivation is the same.

As a journalist, Jimmy recognises this for what it is – the opportunity of a lifetime. He also knows from experience how easy it would be to let it slip through his fingers.

So he's got to be careful.

But maybe – glancing around now – maybe they've gone beyond careful.

He looks back at Szymanski.

'Then?'

'Then they flew me to JFK.' He shrugs. 'After that I was on my own. If I hadn't seen Rundle on TV peddling this bullshit about an accident in Paris, I don't know, maybe I'd have gone home and forgotten the whole thing.'

Jimmy exhales. 'Yeah, but . . . here we are.'

'Yeah.'

'So what next?'

'What next?'

'Yeah.'

Szymanski lowers his head and shakes it into his chest for a moment. Then he looks up again. 'Jimmy, do you . . . do you have any idea what kind of shit we're in right now, the two of us, sitting here?'

'I've been putting off thinking about it.'

Szymanski laughs. 'Yeah, well, this is your chance, bro, be-cause let me tell you . . . my fucking peripheral vision is clogging up on me. There's a black SUV parked over there on the far side of Third. Don't look. Then there's this car just across the street here with the tinted windows. You see it? *And.*' He throws his head backwards. 'Even money, this prick sitting behind me,' – Jimmy swallows – '*who*, chances are, has got a tiny camera con-cealed on him somewhere and a fucking mic that's probably powerful enough to pick up your heartbeat. Though wait.' He holds up a finger. 'I think I can hear that myself.'

Jimmy makes a face, nervous.

Up to now being under surveillance has been almost aca-demic. They were invisible. It was something he took on faith. But with Tom Szymanski talking like this, all of a sudden it seems very real.

And dangerous.

'We're in a public place,' he says. 'What can they do?'

'They can wait. We're not going to stay here all day, are we?'

'And when we leave?'

'Whatever. Neither of us will get very far.'

'That's insane.'

Szymanski leans forward. 'Have you not been listening to this conversation? Have you not been listening to *yourself*?'

Jimmy looks at him. 'Haven't *you*?' He leans forward as well. 'This is a two-way street.'

'Not as far as they're concerned.' Szymanski yanks up the side of his jacket to the table and partially opens it. With his eyes, he indicates, *down here, look*.

Jimmy looks. What he sees is the barrel of a handgun.

'Jesus Christ.'

'This is the only way I'm getting out of here.'

Jimmy shakes his head. 'Yeah, but not *alive*. If you take that out, you won't stand a chance.' He pauses, then whispers, 'Look, there *is* another way.'

'What other way?' Impatient, unconvinced.

Jimmy hesitates. He nods his head in the direction of the guy two places behind them and makes a face that says, *nah, not if he's listening in*.

It takes a moment for Szymanski to catch on, but when he does – and to Jimmy's shock – he gets out of the booth, stands up and strides back to where the other guy is sitting. With his back to the rest of the coffee shop, careful to conceal what he's doing – not that anyone is paying attention – Szymanski takes out his gun, holding it discreetly, and whispers to the guy, 'Get the fuck out of here. *Right* now.'

The guy doesn't react for a second, then he gives an almost imperceptible nod.

This surely indicates that he isn't what Szymanski might call – or what Jimmy imagines Szymanski might call – a civilian.

After a moment, the guy gets out of the booth, leaves a five-dollar bill on the table, picks up his newspaper and walks out of the coffee shop.

Szymanski returns to his place, sits down, and raises his eyebrows.

OK?

OK.

Jimmy breathes in. 'Er . . . so, first thing, can you prove definitively that you were a Gideon contractor, and that you worked in Congo?'

Szymanski takes a moment to answer. Maybe he's deciding whether or not he's offended by the question, or if he's going to dignify it with a response. Jimmy doesn't know. But eventually, Szymanski says, 'Fuck, yeah. There's a paper trail. Pay cheques from Gideon, the contract I signed, my fucking passport. Plus, I've got a ton of pictures on my phone.' He shrugs, dismissing it. 'Was I there? Yeah, of course I was there.'

'OK,' Jimmy says. 'Good. Now.' He slides over to the edge of the booth. 'You order some refills. I'm going to take a piss and make a quick phone call.'

*

'Where's he going? *Fuck*.'

Rundle punches the back of the driver's seat in front of him.

Beside him, Ribcoff is pressing one hand against his ear and holding the other one out, forefinger raised, looking for quiet.

'He . . . he *what*? Jesus . . .'

He brings his hand down and turns to Rundle. 'Szymanski has a Beretta M9.' He shakes his head. 'This is fucked.'

'It was fucked already, Don. Gun or no gun. One Beretta M9 isn't going to make any difference now.'

'What do you mean?'

'What do you . . . you've got to go in there and take him out, take them both out.'

'But we don't –'

'Or at *least* take Szymanski out, Jesus, while he's on his own, like you said. I mean, look.' He points. 'The guy is just sitting there.'

'Clark, he has a *gun*. There are people in there.'

381

Rundle dismisses this with a flick of his hand. 'People.'

'Oh, so, what, you've got no problem getting into a firefight in a coffee shop on Third Avenue? That's OK with you, yeah?'

Rundle explodes. 'For fuck's sake, Don, you *heard* them in there. I have to *explain* it to you?' He punches the seat in front of him again. 'There's no turning back here. For either of us.'

Rundle knows this is easy to say, and saying it even provides him with some tiny measure of relief, but he does mean it. What route back from this could there possibly be? The weight of responsibility sits on him now like a boulder. In its distinguished, nearly 150-year history, the BRX Mining and Engineering Corporation has never once had to defend its name in court or in the press. For generations the company has been fiercely protective of its privacy and its reputation. And now, what? Clark Rundle comes along and allows it to be dragged through the mud?

The dissolute scion of a once-great family.

Rundle shakes his head. That last part is bullshit and he knows it, but still . . .

If it was just a little bit of corporate malfeasance, they could bring in the lawyers, tie things up for years with depositions and injunctions and all sorts of shit, but this? Allegations of, at best, collusion in *two* multiple homicides? To say nothing of the link to a discredited presidential campaign?

He glances left. 'Oh great, he's back.'

They both watch as Jimmy Gilroy sits into the booth again opposite Tom Szymanski, and then as the waitress arrives and refills their cups.

'That was a chance there, Don, and we blew it. Who knows if we'll get another one.'

'We didn't blow anything, Clark. Jesus Christ, we have to be careful.'

'Careful? Please. Get me a gun and I'll go in there and shoot those two bastards myself. I swear to God, I'm serious. *Careful*.'

Ribcoff exhales wearily, but says nothing.

'Because you know what, Don? They will destroy us. In a fucking heartbeat. And whatever about us? BRX, I mean? Whatever degree of culpability *we're* shown to have? You guys? Gideon? *You* personally? You're going to jail for the rest of your fucking life.'

Ribcoff waits a beat, then snaps his laptop closed. He tosses it beside him and reaches for the door. 'Give me a minute,' he says. 'I'll be back.' He opens the door and gets out.

Rundle turns and watches him scurry back up Fifty-fifth Street. He stops halfway and gets into a parked SUV.

Across the street in the coffee shop Tom Szymanski and Jimmy Gilroy are chatting away. Gilroy seems to be writing stuff down, taking notes. What's he doing, conducting an interview?

Rundle looks away, stares ahead.

Degree of culpability.

Where did he get that one from? Too many billed hours spent in the company of lawyers, he suspects. With many more such hours in prospect, hundreds of them probably, Rundle feels a sudden wave of nausea. What might be beyond those hundreds of hours he can't even contemplate. Because they'll be bad enough in themselves, tedious, contentious, humiliating in the extreme.

And the weird thing is, in anticipating this humiliation the one clear, disapproving face he sees looking back at him is not

Eve's, or Daisy's, or J.J.'s, or James Vaughan's even – it's the old man's.

Not the Henry C. of legend either – the commanding presence, the head of the table, the chairman of the board. No, consistent with the same horrorshow logic unfolding *here*, it's the Henry C. of that Saturday afternoon in the house out in Connecticut, in the study, when his heart failed him and he couldn't reach his medication over there on the desk – couldn't move, while his son Clark just stood in front of him and watched, not raising a hand to help, *waiting*, as he had been for many years . . . the chairmanship now within his grasp, *his* turn, *his* crack of the whip.

That Henry C.

Pale, horrified, desperate, beseeching . . .

Incredulous.

Yeah, degrees of culpability, Rundle thinks to himself, don't get me fucking started.

The car door opens and Ribcoff gets back in.

'OK,' he says, reaching for his laptop, 'here's the new plan.'

*

'And how long had you been working with this guy, this, er . . .?'

'Ray Kroner?'

'Yeah.'

'Few months, I guess. On and off.'

'And what was he like?'

'Ray was OK, you know, but he was always wound pretty fucking tight, I'd have to say, and –'

Jimmy looks up from his notebook. 'Maybe tone the lingo down a bit?'

'Yeah. OK.' Szymanski shuffles, repositions. 'He was always wound pretty tight, but at the same time he was no different from plenty of other guys who get into this business, you know. When they're over there they want to be back here, and once they finally get back here all they can do is dream about packing up and heading over there again. It's the old story. But I mean, that was *me*, too, you get caught up in a cycle of it, and it's just that, you know, you may as well earn good money while you're doing it. Unfortunately, some guys never flush it out of their system, or else they never learn to control it.'

'Right. And on that day?'

'Well, Ray clearly flipped, but what you have to understand is that . . . in Iraq, in Afghanistan, there's at least *some* semblance of a context, *some* sense that a war is being fought. But in Congo, it's just totally insane. It's not *your* war you're fighting, there are no clear sides, and yet you're in the middle of this epic shitstorm, six, seven, maybe eight million people dead in the last, I don't know, fifteen years. You don't have any compass, no flag, just an assault rifle and a fucking *logo*.'

'A logo?'

'Yeah, I mean, whether it's Gideon Global or BRX or any of the others out there, *that's* your point of reference. So it's kind of hard to feel that any of it means anything. And when you witness some of the things we witnessed, well, I sometimes envy Ray Kroner, you know. What he did made no sense, not at all, it was . . . messed up. But in a weird way he escaped, he found release. You know what I'm saying?'

'Yeah.' Jimmy replies. But does he? Not really. He isn't supposed to.

That's what's going to make this such a compelling story.

'Good,' he says, flipping over a page of his notebook, 'let's try another question. Can you tell me when you realised that the man you were escorting in your convoy was, in fact, Senator John Rundle?'

Szymanski glances out the window, then back at Jimmy. 'Sure. It was afterwards. We were standing around waiting for back-up, a few of us, and the company CO, guy called Peter Lutz, more or less told me straight out, he said he had to shoot Ray Kroner because did I know who that was in the back of the car, it was Senator John Rundle, for Christ's sakes, brother of the guy who owns the mine.'

'And you had previously seen this man that your commanding officer identified as the senator having a meeting with Colonel Arnold Kimbela, is that correct?'

'Yes.'

'OK, Tom. That's good.' Jimmy looks down through his scribbled list of questions. 'Right, let's go over the incident again, especially the part where the senator's hand got crushed in the door of the car.'

'Sure.'

'That part needs to be really clear.'

'Yeah, I get that, but believe me, Jimmy, it's clear in my head. It couldn't be any clearer. I can see him now, screaming, leaning back, crying like a fucking baby.'

*

'What's the delay? Send them *in*.'

'They're not ready yet, Clark. They need a little more time. Jesus. This is an improvised operation. They have to be sure of what they're doing.'

Rundle exhales loudly, refraining from further comment, and goes back to his laptop.

Fox and CNN, all they're talking about is John Rundle.

Commentators, panellists, pundits, bloggers.

It's a bit hysterical and hugely premature, Rundle realises that, but it's still a great start.

They'll need to build on this momentum.

He looks up again and across the street.

Assuming they get the chance, of course.

The next few minutes will be crucial.

It seems unreal to him, what's happening – unreal that everything hinges on the suppression of a conversation two guys are having in some coffee shop on Third Avenue.

He closes his eyes.

Ribcoff's plan is audacious. It's based on causing a diversion. Three men definitely *not* looking like Gideon security contractors – and this seems to be what's causing the delay – will show up thirty seconds apart. The first man will enter the coffee shop and go straight to the counter and order something. As the second man is entering, the first man will feign a seizure of some sort and draw as much attention to himself as possible. Using a gun with a silencer, the second man will then shoot and kill Tom Szymanski. At this point the third man will arrive and Taser Jimmy Gilroy, who will then receive a rapid, surreptitious and lethal jab in the back of the neck. The two men will remove Gilroy's notebook and phone and will then carry Szymanski's body out to a waiting vehicle on the street.

Amid the confusion, the first man will recover and leave.

What could possibly go wrong?

Right?

Well, apart from the first hundred most obvious things, Rundle did have one question.

Why leave Gilroy behind?

Logistics, was Ribcoff's response, manpower, timing. Szymanski is off the grid, this keeps it that way. Gilroy's disappearance might drag things out, not to mention dredge things *up*. By doing it this way it's open and shut, he's here, he's dead – questions remain, but they're unlikely ever to be answered to anyone's satisfaction.

The whole thing should only take two minutes, max. Most people in the general area won't notice a thing and those who do will inevitably have conflicting memories of it.

It's high risk, no question about it – but really, do they have any alternative?

Rundle opens his eyes. He looks around, out the window, at his watch. 'Come *on*.'

'Few more minutes, Clark, trust me.' Ribcoff texting with one hand, keying something onto his laptop with the other. 'We didn't come here today equipped for this. And the first guy who walks in there *has to* look like a civilian. Otherwise it won't work.' He pauses, nodding his head in the direction of the coffee shop. 'Besides, look at them over there, yakking like two old ladies.' He shakes his head. 'No one's going anywhere.'

His other phone rings and he picks it up. 'Yeah?'

Rundle closes his laptop. He takes out his own phone. As

388

Ribcoff is talking, Rundle dials the number for Regal. He faces away, gives his membership code in as low a voice as possible and asks if Nora is available.

She isn't.

Nora is no longer with the agency.

'*What?*' Too loud. 'Why not?' Whisper 'Where is she?'

They're not allowed to give out that kind of information. It's confidential. But they have many other beautiful and sophis—

He hangs up.

Shit.

Ribcoff looks at him, phone held to his chest. 'Anything wrong?'

'No.' Rundle waves a hand at the window. 'Except for *this* shit. When do we get moving?'

'Now.' Ribcoff says. 'Zero minus thirty seconds.' He nods at the screen of his laptop.

Rundle doesn't understand. 'What?'

'There.' Ribcoff points. 'Asset number one.'

On the screen is a webcam feed from just around the corner, on Third Avenue. The man Ribcoff is pointing at is approaching the main entrance to the coffee shop. He's of medium height, in jeans and a corduroy jacket, has longish hair, looks a little scruffy. A writer type, or an academic.

Looking to score some joe.

Surrounding him, flowing in both directions, are . . . *people* – woman with a buggy, two businessmen, a flock of Japanese tourists, others, random, nondescript, it's all very quick, and as well, to the left, there is a blur of passing traffic.

Intermittent streaks of yellow.

Rundle's stomach turns. Is this really happening?

The guy disappears in through the door.

Rundle lifts his head and glances across the street.

In the long side window of the coffee shop both men turn their heads for a moment, then turn back and continue talking.

'OK,' Ribcoff says, pointing, 'here comes asset number two.'

Rundle looks back at the screen. From halfway along the block comes a second man. He's of similar height to the first but is dressed all in black.

Baseball cap, shades.

Zero minus . . . what must it be now for this one? Twenty seconds? Fifteen?

Rundle stares intently at the screen.

But suddenly, his focus shifts – from the black-clad asset in the centre to a streak of yellow on the left, a streak that solidifies into a cab pulling up at the kerb.

Zero minus ten seconds.

The cab door opens. A man gets out, then a woman.

Seven.

Rundle lurches forward, almost vomits. 'Stop.'

'What?'

Five.

'Abort.' He elbows Ribcoff. 'Abort. *Stop.*'

'*What?*'

Three.

Moving across the sidewalk, striding with intent, the man and woman cut in front of the asset and get to the door of the coffee shop before him.

'That's Ellen Dorsey.'

'*Jesus.*'

One.

Ribcoff raises a hand to his earpiece, squeezes it. 'Abort,' he says. 'Repeat, *abort*.'

*

Jimmy stands up as Ellen Dorsey approaches. He extends a hand, whispering, 'Shit, am I glad to see you.'

They shake. Dorsey has a laptop under her arm. She places it on the table. She turns to the man directly behind her.

He's rugged and tanned, in his fifties.

Expensive-looking suit.

Something about him says lawyer.

'Jimmy, this is Ned Goldstein. He's with Reynolds, Fleischman & Brock.' She pauses. 'Attorneys.'

OK.

They shake, and then Jimmy introduces Tom Szymanski.

The next thirty minutes or so pass in a blur.

Dorsey sits opposite Jimmy, and Goldstein opposite Szymanski.

Goldstein, it turns out, specialises in whistleblower cases and has worked with Dorsey on several occasions in the past. The first thing he does is quiz Jimmy and Szymanski on what they perceive their current level of danger to be. Calmly and discreetly, Szymanski points out three parked vehicles in the vicinity that he judges to be Gideon surveillance units. He also outlines what he believes Gideon's strategy would most likely be in circumstances such as these. Goldstein proceeds to grill Szymanski on his background, his history in the military and his subsequent employment record with Gideon.

While this is going on, Dorsey checks with Jimmy that he

391

has prepped Szymanski for the interview, exactly as they'd agreed on the phone. Jimmy says he has but adds that Szymanski is adamant he doesn't want to be filmed or photographed. Dorsey makes a face. *OK.* They go over the questions again and Jimmy outlines in general terms what Szymanski's answers will be. When Goldstein has given the all-clear, Dorsey says, the interview should go ahead without delay. She will record it, simultaneously transcribing as much of it as she can, and will then immediately upload a text version onto her website and her Facebook page.

She says that given the incendiary nature of the central claim about Senator Rundle's injury, the interview will be picked up straightaway and will go viral on Twitter in a matter of minutes. That level of public awareness will effectively provide cover for Jimmy and Szymanski, but she warns him that it will also be insane and unlike anything either of them has ever experienced before in their entire lives. Avoiding photographers and camera crews will not be easy.

Is he prepared for this?

Jimmy says yes. Nodding. He is. He also says he understands that the Senator Rundle aspect of the story will dominate at first, and probably for days, but that behind it is the even bigger story of BRX and Gideon Global, which is one he fully intends pursuing – all the way back to the hills of Buenke, and even further back, to the rugged coastline of Donegal.

'Absolutely,' Dorsey says, smiling, 'I'd expect nothing less.'

'And listen, thanks for everything you're doing.'

'Hey, this is *your* story, Jimmy, and I'm happy to help out – by doing this, by putting you in touch with people later if you want, whatever. These bastards deserve all they get.' She pauses.

'But remember one thing. If it all goes pear-shaped for some reason, or turns out to be a crock of shit, it'll still be your story.'

Jimmy says nothing, but acknowledges the point with a nod.

He looks at Tom Szymanski and wonders how he's coping. This can't be easy for him.

He seems to be coping fine.

Ellen Dorsey turns to Ned Goldstein. The lawyer shrugs his shoulders. 'All looks kosher to me. I think we're good to go.'

Dorsey opens her laptop. She takes a small recording device from her pocket, checks it and turns it on. She places it on the table between Jimmy and Szymanski.

She places her hands over the keyboard, poised. She looks up. 'Gentlemen?'

Jimmy swallows.

As he is forming the first question in his mind, he notices the car across the street, the one with the tinted windows, starting up and pulling out of its place.

He closes his eyes. 'Mr Szymanski, can you tell me first of all the exact date on which you started working as a private military contractor for Gideon Global?'

When Jimmy opens his eyes, the car has gone.

I 4

A few hours later – and a few blocks northwest of this Third Avenue coffee shop – James Vaughan opens his eyes and yawns. He takes an afternoon nap most days now. Doctor's orders. It's not the hardest thing in the world to do, an hour or so in bed after lunch, but he does find it interrupts his rhythm. Leaves him a little cranky.

He gets dressed and goes into the study.

There'd been no word from Clark by the time he was hitting the hay, and since his nap is sacrosanct, involving a complete communications blackout, Vaughan is anxious that he might have missed something. If there are any messages for him they'll be here on his phone, but before checking he decides to go online first and see what developments there have been.

It's pretty ugly.

On site after site, one story dominates.

Rise and fall, rise and fall . . .

When he heard that guy outside the hotel shout the word *Buenke*, Vaughan figured, at some level, that the game was up. Then when he heard the uncertainty in Clark's voice a while later, he was left in little doubt.

He watches a couple of news clips, and winces more than once.

It's not going to be easy for the Rundle boys, being hounded and savaged like this by reporters. But in a way they were asking for it.

Vaughan himself has never courted publicity. The very idea of it horrifies him, and always has. In fact – thinking about it – the first time he ever encountered the gentlemen of the press was at his grandfather's funeral in the late 1930s, when he'd still only have been a small boy. He can see it now, the crowds on Fifth Avenue for the service, the carriage strewn with violets, the stiff collar and breeches he was made to wear and how uneasy he felt in the church having to file past the open casket. He clearly remembers the texture of his grandfather's hands and face, too, bloodless and waxy.

That haunted him all the way out to Woodlawn.

But in the end, it was the press photographers he remembers most, the *flashbulbs*, dozens of them, all going off like so many tiny explosions, and then these grubby little men with their pencil stubs and notepads.

Who *are* these people, he remembers thinking at the time.

Who indeed.

He trawls through a few more reports. At this stage, the main focus is on J.J. and his trip to Paris. Was there really a motorcycle accident? Was there really a motor*cyclist*? The search is well and truly on now and that can only end one way.

In tears.

But Vaughan knows that the background stuff will come into focus as well, sooner or later, and that it won't be long before the word Buenke is on everyone's lips.

Thanaxite, too.

It's a damn shame.

He checks his phone – a text from Meredith, who's in LA for a few days, and due back tomorrow. Then three voice messages and four texts, all from Clark.

Oh dear.

He deletes them, and turns to go.

What exactly is it about the phrase *You're on your own*, he wonders, that Clark didn't understand?

*

Tom Szymanski paces back and forth between the window and

the bed. In this hotel room he can do that, there's enough space, unlike where he stayed before, in midtown, which was cramped, but at least *there* he was free to get shitfaced, bring a hooker back, whatever. Here he feels constrained, like he's supposed to be on his best behaviour or something. It's only been twelve hours since the interview in the coffee shop and already, *already*, he's acquired an entourage – legal advisors, media handlers, a fucking bodyguard. He probably hasn't gone about all of this in the best way possible – but in his defence, how was he supposed to know what to do, or say? This isn't exactly the kind of shit he's been trained for. Anyway, twenty minutes after Ellen Dorsey posted the interview on her webpage and did whatever Twitter shit it is that people do these days, a couple of photographers showed up, then a local news crew. Dorsey seemed a bit alarmed herself by how fast it was all happening, but then she tried to make out like it was better this way, that if he had his photo out there, his mug in the public domain, he'd be better protected, it'd be the perfect deflector shield against the very powerful and influential people he had chosen to go up against.

What the fuck?

He hadn't chosen to go up against *anyone*, it had all just happened, and continued happening, inside the door of the coffee shop, then outside on the street, moving along the sidewalk, more and more people arriving, so that pretty quickly it became a circus, and he got separated from Jimmy Gilroy and Ellen Dorsey and her lawyer, and before he knew it . . . shit, before he knew *anything* this other woman was shoving a business card into his hand and asking him how'd he like to go on the *Evening News* with Katie Couric, or do *60 Minutes*, or if the sound of a nice, juicy book contract appealed to him at all? If she hadn't been so gorgeous he might have moved on, but really, this woman was like a fucking movie star, with the eyes, and the lips, and the hips, and the OMG rack, and before he could catch his breath he was sitting next to her in the back of a town car, riding up here to this hotel . . .

For a series of . . . *meetings* . . .

It crossed his mind at one point that she might be a Gideon plant, but no, thinking about it, Ellen Dorsey had been right – with the interview out there on the web, and his name, and his history, and pictures now too, actual footage of him on Third Avenue from that morning, BRX and Gideon wouldn't be so stupid as to go anywhere near him.

This Zambelli woman was on the level, she was a *bona fide* PR princess with a pair of stones on her that would put any man to shame.

She'd nabbed *him*, for Christ's sake.

Look at him.

Holed up in a fucking executive suite, waiting for a deluxe cheeseburger he ordered and watching himself on TV, while out there, in the other room, some grand strategy is being devised, tomorrow's assault on the world's media.

He stops at the window and looks out at the shimmering lights of Manhattan's upper east side.

What's he doing here? What's *his* strategy?

He doesn't know.

It felt weird bailing on Jimmy Gilroy and Ellen Dorsey like that, but then, what does he owe *them*? He did their interview, gave them their scoop.

He turns away from the window.

What does he owe anyone for that matter? What does he owe the various people who've been trying to contact him since early afternoon apparently, looking to hook up with him? So-called friends, family members – and obscure ones, too.

His ex-brother-in-law?

Jesus Christ.

He doesn't owe them anything.

He looks over at the end of the bed.

He still has his gun. It's in the pocket of his leather jacket there.

He could . . .

What?

Flip? Work himself up to it? An improvised frenzy, right here in the bedroom maybe? Or how about downstairs in the lobby? Or live on-air in some TV studio? Take his new movie-star girlfriend with him and go out in a blaze of glory?

Yeah.

He wishes he were that insane. It'd be a lot easier.

On Fox now they're showing clips of Paris, the Eiffel Tower, some big hotel, streets, traffic.

The special correspondents, it would seem, are on the case, arriving into the city in their droves. It won't be long before they start arriving in Congo as well, and chartering small private planes to take them as near to the remote village of Buenke as they can get.

And it won't be long before everything Tom Szymanski said in his interview is checked and verified – Ray Kroner going postal and killing all those people, then Senator Rundle getting his hand crushed in the door of an SUV.

That chiefly.

But it won't stop there, it occurs to him, the coverage, the attention, not by a long shot – and it's going to take all his reserves of sanity to get through it.

All his reserves of energy.

Speaking of which.

He looks over at the door.

Where's that fucking cheeseburger he ordered?

*

Over on the west side, standing at a window of his apartment on the fifty-seventh floor, glass in hand, Clark Rundle gazes down at the jewel-encrusted city spread out below like a vast, magnificent cache of pirate's booty.

After a while, and abruptly, he shifts focus and gazes into his glass.

Single malt Scotch whisky. This is the fourth or fifth one he's had, he *thinks*. He's not a big drinker, but he knows that he's reached a tipping point here, the sensation in his stomach – this little red-hot coal of euphoria, burning steadily now for maybe the last twenty minutes – is due to subside, and fade.

Inevitably.

Leaving him with the dying embers of . . .

Oh *please*.

There. You see?

It's gone.

He drains his glass and turns away from the window.

The room before him is enormous, like a downtown loft space –furnished in a minimalist style, with wide, pine floorboards, a couple of bare leather couches, a tinted glass coffee table and two large, modernist canvases hung on walls at either end.

That's it.

Is it any wonder no-one ever comes in here?

He goes over to the coffee table and puts his glass down beside the bottle of smoky Laphroaig.

Outside, the phone rings.

Again.

Eve is under instructions to screen all calls.

His own cell is turned off.

He looks down at the bottle.

Does he pour himself another one? He's not sure he can re-live – as he will inevitably have to, again and again – those final few moments in the car today beside Don Ribcoff . . . without *some* form of . . . of fortification. Especially that final moment, that very, *very* final moment, when he picked up his laptop and swung it sideways straight into Ribcoff's forehead . . . withdrew it and swung it back, even harder this time, aiming better, the right angle of its corner ramming directly into the centre of Ribcoff's now-turned and very startled face.

The bridge of his nose?

Definitely the bridge of his nose the *next* time, going by the sound, and no question about it the time after that, cartilage, sinew, muscle.

Blood.

Spurting, spraying . . . everywhere.

The few times after that? You're talking fucking . . . *serious* laundry bills.

He picks up the bottle, hesitates, then pours himself another measure, a generous one.

He remembers getting out of the car somewhere down around Twenty-third Street and being met – taken in hand, transferred to another car – by some of *his* people. Luckily, the driver of the original car was one of his, too, and not a Gideon driver – well, he's *assuming* luckily – because you never know.

And then?

And then it was busy.

All day.

He's been busy . . . all day.

Talking.

To this one and that one.

Rationalising, explaining, making calls, responding. Earlier on, there was that very long shower he had to take, and then later – he's a little muddled about the sequence of things at the moment – yeah, *later*, watching TV and checking news websites.

Because, Jesus Christ . . .

J.J.

His big brother.

All day he's had to watch the poor bastard being crucified.

Vilified, ridiculed.

While knowing at the same time, that somehow – and sooner rather than later – *he's* next in line.

For the hammer and nails.

And the cheap cracks.

He lifts the glass to his lips, well beyond that tipping point now. No euphoria anymore, just . . .

Oh Jesus.

He was so *angry* in the car today, about Nora . . . and *with*

Ribcoff – for delaying, for maintaining that stupid pretence of military precision, when it was clear what they had to do.

Despite the enormous risks.

Just go in there and . . .

Because two or three minutes earlier and everything would have been different.

Everything would be different now.

Yeah.

He throws his head back and drains the glass, though this time feeling a little sick as he does so.

Like he's had enough.

He stares at the plain wall in front of him, and then down at the floorboards.

How many messages did he leave today for Jimmy Vaughan? A lot. And *that's* what makes him the sickest, that's what –

Rundle looks up. The door is opening.

It's Eve, looking gaunt and exhausted. She remains standing in the doorway.

'Clark.' She whispers it. 'There are two police detectives downstairs. They want to speak with you.'

Rundle swallows. 'OK.' He shrugs. 'Send them up.'

Shit. This is about Don Ribcoff, isn't it? That driver today, he's sure of it. Or one of the others maybe, one of the Gideon contractors. There were so many of them around the place, it was sometimes hard to tell who was with who, and –

Their loyalties would be with Ribcoff, wouldn't they?

Clearly.

He shakes his head.

All they'd need is the laptop. Which of course he doesn't remember taking with him from the car, and that's because he *didn't* take it with him, he left it there.

Do these detectives have it now? This choice piece of evidence?

Definitive, case-busting?

Rundle turns around and does something he's been threatening to do all day. He steps forward, heaves loudly and throws up – all over one of the leather couches.

Half a pint of whisky.

The sum total of what he's got.

And when he's finished, he wipes his mouth with the sleeve of his jacket.

Standing there, facing the window, he takes a few deep breaths.

A moment later, from outside, he hears the door opening, and voices.

*

A little after eleven o'clock the next morning Ellen Dorsey takes Jimmy to the offices of *Parallax* magazine on Forty-first Street. She introduces him to the editor, Max Daitch, an intense guy in his mid-thirties who sits behind a mahogany desk piled high with papers and books.

Within about twenty seconds he has offered Jimmy two things – coffee and a job.

When Jimmy doesn't respond immediately to either offer, Daitch says, 'OK, I can't tell you much more about the coffee, it's coffee, what do you want, but the job . . .' He leans forward on the desk and clicks his tongue. 'Or maybe, I don't know, does the word *job* make you nervous? Would you prefer if I said *commission*?'

Jimmy smiles and says, 'No, no, coffee's fine, thanks. An espresso. Please.'

Daitch looks at him, waits, then says, 'Oh, what are we, playing hardball here?' He turns to Dorsey. 'Ellen, help me out with this guy, Jesus.'

'Shut up, Max,' she says. 'Do you have any idea what he's been through in the last twenty-four hours?'

Jimmy has barely been able to process this himself.

'That interview he did was broadcast all over the world, it was *the* lead news story everywhere and it totally burned up the blogosphere, but people want more, some kind of a follow-up, so *he* spent most of yesterday fighting off offers from editors and booking agents and people like Liz Zambelli. Who by the way appears to have more or less kidnapped Tom Szymanski, because no one knows where he is. But anyway, there's a lot of interest out there, a lot of competition, network producers are salivating, and yet *this guy*, as you call him, chooses to come here.'

Daitch considers what she's said, then nods. 'OK. Fine. An espresso it is.' He buzzes out to his assistant. Then he looks at Jimmy. 'Great interview, I have to say. Really. It was. Every question, every answer, not an ounce of fat.'

Jimmy nods back. 'Thanks. We were under a certain amount of pressure.'

'No shit. But Ellen here tells me that you've got more, a whole back story to go with this. Is that right?'

'Yes. What I've got, I *think*, is the story of how BRX got involved in this thing in the first place. I want to draw a direct line from that right up to yesterday. Right up to *last night*.' He exhales and bobs his head from side to side, as though weighing it all up. 'So, I don't know, a ten-minute segment on a some news show ...'

'Couldn't possibly do the story justice?'

'Right.'

'OK, but you only *think* you've got it?'

'Well, I know what happened, but I need to work on it. There are a lot of gaps to fill in. I need to go to London to check out some CCTV footage. I need to go back to Italy. Ideally, I should go to Congo.' He pauses. 'Actually, I *have* to go to Congo.'

'Sure.'

'It's murky stuff, and it goes pretty deep.'

'Indeed. But you'll need *time*. For travelling. And lots of money as well, presumably. For expenses.'

'I suppose.' Jimmy pauses again. 'Look, I realise –'

'No, no,' Daitch interrupts, holding a hand up, 'it's fine. I get it. Time and money. That's what you want. The two things we've notoriously run out of in this industry.'

Jimmy exhales. 'So I keep hearing.'

Daitch stands up and moves out from behind his desk. He walks around to the front and then leans back against it. He folds his arms. 'That's the conventional wisdom these days, isn't it? News has to be fast and cheap. It has to ride the clickstream to survive. So anything with the word "investigative" attached to it doesn't have a prayer. Why? Because it's expensive, it ties up resources, and more often than not it invites litigation.' He shrugs. 'It's just the wrong model for the digital age.' He leans forward. 'Well, you know what? Screw that. Screw the conventional wisdom. When's the last time anyone in this room paid attention to the conventional wisdom?' He turns to Ellen Dorsey. 'Am I right?' Then back to Jimmy. 'Look, my point is, *Parallax* is a national magazine, print edition comes out once a month, online edition we do what we can, and ad revenues are a constant struggle, a constant pain in the ass, but in the last couple of years you know what stories have made the most impact, where we've seen actual spikes in circulation? That's right, longer, investigative pieces that we put time and resources into. Ask *her*. It's pretty much what she does full time.'

Dorsey nods in agreement. 'He's right. The technology demands concision, the news reduced to a tweet, but people actually want more, *enough* people want more.'

Daitch stands up straight. 'So, Jimmy, here's the deal, if you have what you say you have, I'm prepared to let you run with it. We can at least talk terms and see where we stand, right?'

'Sure,' Jimmy says, 'absolutely.'

He looks behind him. An assistant is coming through the door with a tray of espressos.

'Besides,' Daitch continues, walking over and taking the tray from the assistant, 'this isn't just some tawdry story about John Rundle getting caught out in a lie that we'll all have forgotten about in a week. With Clark now up on a murder charge, it's a lot more serious than that. It's game on.' He holds the tray out to Jimmy. 'I think we're in for the long haul on this one, don't you?'

*

Later on, after he parts ways with Ellen Dorsey – temporarily, they're meeting for dinner at a place called Quaranta – Jimmy takes a cab downtown.

He hasn't been back to his hotel yet, not since he left it yesterday morning.

He needs to shower and change.

Last night he slept on Ellen's couch.

Slept.

He didn't sleep. He was too wound up.

Too wired.

Having been followed and harassed for most of the day, they had a difficult time at the end giving reporters and photographers the slip. As a reporter himself, Jimmy was, and remains, uncomfortable with this.

But still, as the cab glides along Fifth Avenue now – the Flatiron just ahead – it all hits him again, the sheer scale of what has happened.

And the fact that a little over an hour ago he accepted a job offer.

Or, at any rate, a commission.

For a series of articles.

What he can't help thinking is how pleased the old man would be. Jimmy sees him now, reaching up to a bookshelf, pulling down a paperback, studying the cover for a few seconds, as though re-acquainting himself with something, and then handing it over with the words, 'Here, read this.'

This being a primer, a window on a world, a form of code, an exhortation.

One of many.

The cab shoots across Fourteenth Street and Jimmy starts reaching for his wallet. He gets out at Eighth and makes his way over to Washington Square Park. It's sunny and warm, with high blue skies. Was it only Monday that he sat here on a bench, facing uptown, trying to figure out what to do?

Three days.

It seems longer ago than that.

He sits on another bench now.

He still hasn't figured out what to do, of course – not exactly. But he has a much clearer idea.

Just as he has a much clearer idea what direction his story for *Parallax* should take. It's been forming in his mind for some time, coming into focus.

It's a direct line all right, as he explained to Max Daitch, but one that goes far beyond the tawdry self-destruction of the Rundle brothers.

It's a different route.

It's the supply chain.

The blood-soaked motherlode.

Isn't that what Susie Monaghan called it? In that last text she sent?

Which reminds him.

He takes out his phone, checks for messages – there are quite a few, with Maria at the top of the list.

He looks up, and gazes out over the square.

Where was he?

The supply chain. He needs to follow it. He needs to see where it leads. He needs to find out where the thanaxite ends up, who's using it and what for.

Who has the most to gain.

There are other leads, as well. That third name, for instance

– the old guy Dave Conway mentioned, and more than once. Who's *he*? What was *his* role in what happened?

That's definitely something Jimmy ought to chase up.

He holds out his phone, scrolls down for the number.

But first, before he gets down to work, there's an important call he has to make.

*

Vaughan feels it already, creeping up on him as he opens his eyes, the post-nap crankiness – but today he has to fight it, keep it at an acceptable level, because Meredith is due back this afternoon. She's been in LA attending a premiere, and she'll be all sunny and starstruck, full of stories about celebs she met. The last thing she'll want to encounter in her kitchen is a cranky old man whose idea of a movie star is John Garfield.

Not that he gives a damn, not really.

Vaughan was seventy-eight when they got married and she was twenty-six. He'd never been without a companion in his life, and at the time it had seemed like the right thing to do, affirmative, pro-active.

Or how about stupid?

It's a vanity trap he's seen plenty of other guys his age fall into – having a beautiful young wife on your arm when you've already got one foot in the grave. But then he went ahead and fell into the trap himself.

Trap.

It's not a trap exactly, it's an age thing. She talks a lot, which grates on his nerves, not that he blames *her* for that, and she spends his money – mostly on real estate, décor and clothes.

But at least she isn't a monster, like Jake Leffingwell's twenty-four-year-old, Lisa, who insisted on getting involved in the business from the start and has dragged Leffingwell's staid old company through the mud with all sorts of expensive and high-profile litigation. It's ironic, he thinks, poor old Jake has aged about ten years since he married Lisa.

Vaughan goes into the study. He sits at his desk, and looks at the computer, but decides not to turn it on.

He's had enough. All morning, wall to wall.

He thinks of poor Hank Rundle.

Henry C.

Talk about dragging a staid old company – and a respected family name – through the mud! By the time this is over, Clark and J.J. between them will have undone a century and a half of dedicated brand-building.

Pair of jackasses.

But as far as Vaughan himself is concerned, the damage is significant. There's no question about that. At least it's contained, though, it's private.

No one is tweeting about the Oberon Capital Group.

Nevertheless, he *will* have to make a few calls and set something in motion. Paloma Electronics are on target for the first-phase rollout of the BellumBot, but to maintain any kind of competitive advantage they clearly need a new five-year plan, and a new source of thanaxite, one that doesn't depend so heavily on the good graces of a nonentity like Colonel Arnold Kimbela.

Vaughan looks at the phone.

Time and tide, as it were.

He picks it up and dials the number for Craig Howley at the Pentagon. After the usual song and dance, he gets through.

'Jimmy, how are you?'

'I'm good, Craig, I'm good.'

'My God, have you been *following* this?'

'I *know*, it's horrible, isn't it?' He wanders from his desk over to the window. 'Just horrible.'

'I mean, what the hell makes someone flip like that?'

'I don't know. And I guess we'll never know.' Vaughan is gazing down now at the passing traffic on Park Avenue. 'But in a roundabout way, Craig, that's why I'm calling. We need to talk. I want to have another look at Logar Province.'

Afghanistan.

Southeast of Kabul.

Although the discovery here a few years ago of a substantial thanaxite deposit was omitted from a recently published geological survey of the region, Vaughan has been reliably informed that it's there. The trouble with mining in Afghanistan, however, has always been the country's woefully inadequate transportation infrastructure.

But it seems as if that might be about to change.

The Chinese have embarked on a long-term project to establish a new trans-Eurasian corridor, a sort of modernised version of the old Silk Road. Vaughan's idea is to get in early, establish a foothold in Logar. Fly under the radar for a while and see what happens.

He's learnt that you have to take a long view on these matters.

'Sure, Jimmy, of course. I'm actually going to be in New York at the end of the week.'

'Oh?'

'You want me to swing by?'

'That'd be great.'

They make an appointment for Friday afternoon.

As he's closing his phone at the window, Vaughan sees a car pulling up below.

The driver gets out. The doorman appears.

Showtime.

A few moments later Vaughan is in the entry foyer, and feeling, almost in spite of himself, a flutter of anticipation. But not just for the next thirty seconds and his wife's arrival home.

For something more than that.

For the future itself.

The elevator glides open and Meredith steps out, followed by the doorman, who is carrying her bags.

She is wearing a figure-hugging royal-blue pencil dress and black patent leather stilettos. Radiant and fragrant, she also has a new hairstyle, a bob, short and boyish.

Vaughan likes it, likes it all.

'Darling,' she says, opening her arms to embrace him, 'did you miss me?'

An Interview with Alan Glynn

Given the compexity of the story, can you remember what your starting point was when plotting *Bloodland*?

Yes, I started with the idea of a helicopter crash on the Donegal coast. I wanted a shocking event like this to be the raw material for a conspiracy. The thing is, helicopter and plane crashes have been at the centre of a surprisingly large number of conspiracies over the years, where politically or commercially 'convenient' deaths occur – a classic case being that of Enrico Mattei, whose work in restructuring the Italian oil and gas industries posed a considerable threat to the international cartels. Mattei died in a mysterious plane crash in 1962. Officially, it was an accident, but no one really believed that. More recently, there was the Kaczynski crash in Russia, about which questions have been asked, about which theories abound. Of course, these things are enormously difficult to prove, making it one of the purest forms of conspiracy, and also one of the most horrific. In any case, unravelling the causes of my mysterious air crash, finding a nefarious justification for it, is what set the story in motion.

Did the idea for *Bloodland* come out of the global financial crisis or were you already thinking about these ideas before that?

The global financial crisis is not central to *Bloodland*. It's there in the background alright, and it impacts directly on one character, but a lot of what happens in the story could have happened at any time. The scramble for resources in Africa is nothing new, corporate greed and malfeasance is nothing new and the venality of politicians is certainly nothing new. Where the story is rooted in the present, I suppose, is in the area of America's identity crisis vis-a-vis China. That feels like a huge drama that will be unfolding for quite some time to come. But as with *Winterland*, any confluence between the book's plot and current events is almost incidental as far as I'm concerned. What really interests me is the psychology, the interior life, of these people in positions of incredible power, people who seem to have no moral compass and very little awareness of the consequences of their actions.

Bloodland is set in Paris, New York, Dublin and Congo: how did you go about making the sense of place as authentic as it is?

And don't forget Verona, and London. I've lived in a few of these places and I suppose I drew on memory for much of the detail. With the places I haven't lived in, I simply did research - but this then crucially gets filtered through whichever character is involved in the scene. So it becomes a sort of double act of imagination, this person in that place. It was something I was particularly aware of when writing the scenes set in the Democratic Republic of Congo. For these, I was able to buffer

my lack of direct knowledge with the densely layered perspect-
ives of the characters, Tom Szymanski and Clark Rundle.

**Bloodland has the kind of plot where tiny details at the start
lead to huge revelations by the end. How hard is it when
writing a story like this to keep back secrets from your read-
ers?**

It's not easy. I continually re-read, re-write and revise. At the
same time it's an organic process and the subconscious does
a lot of the heavy lifting for you. A connection that in the
context of the story might seem inevitable, something meticu-
lously and very deliberately placed there by the author, will often in fact have occurred to me at the very last minute. Maybe
it was there all along, waiting to be discovered but the poor
sap at the keyboard isn't necessarily the first one to see it. But
then when it all becomes clear, you have the luxury of being
able to go back and re-arrange stuff, to re-weight and re-calib-
rate scenes in the overall context of the story. As the writer, you
just have to pay attention, which I suppose isn't too much to
ask. Another way of keeping secrets back from the reader, of
course is by not knowing them yourself, as you go along. No
plan, therefore, no outline. It's a good way of keeping things
fresh and unpredictable, but it's also fraught with danger. You
can write yourself into a corner. Or fall of the tightrope.

**Bloodland follows in the footsteps of some great thrillers
that have exposed corruption, from films such as *The Parallax View*, TV series such as *State of Play* and novels like**

The Constant Gardener. Do you have any particular favourites in the genre, and did any in particular influence you?

I like all of them: *Klute*, *The Parallax View*, *All the President's Men*, *The Conversation*, *Three Days of the Condor*, *Marathon Man*. These are the great conspiracy thrillers of the 70s that I grew up watching, and there is no question but that they have influenced me a great deal. I also love the later stuff you mention and would add *Syriana* and *Michael Clayton* to the list, as well as what I have seen so far of *Rubicon*. But there is, I think, a key difference between the two periods. In the 1970s – post-Kennedy, post-Vietnam, post-Watergate – America lost its innocence. Back then it was genuinely shocking for people to realise that their government was lying to them. But you can't lose your innocence twice, and now we're not surprised if our governments and corporations lie to us, we expect it even, and often expect them to do much worse, so the key feature we remember from back then – that creepy frisson, that dawning realisation of the truth – is no longer what animates the conspiracy thriller. That can't be replicated anymore. But these days, perhaps, it's a question of scale – corporate power, for example, has grown exponentially in the last thirty years. Perhaps it's a question of the inescapable and controlling nature of power in the modern world. These stories, consequently, are as relevant now, if not more so, than ever before.

Will we be seeing any more from any of the characters in *Bloodland*?

Yes, definitely James Vaughan, who has appeared in both *Win-*

terland and *Bloodland*. I think he has some explaining to do.
Or someone has to do it for him. And I suppose that'll be me.

Also by Alan Glynn

ff

Winterland
(available in paperback now)

'A dark edgy thriller packed with genuine suspense and a real
sense of danger, diving into a world of crime, corruption and
violence that is all too convincing.' *The Times*

'A page turner in the best sense of the word . . . the three set
pieces of the story are as good as anything I've read in contemporary crime fiction.' John Boyne, *Irish Times*

'An enthralling and addictive read.' *Observer*

'Clever and intense; a dark and powerful slice of Dublin noir.
I loved it!' R. J. Ellory

'A terrific read . . . completely involving.' George Pelecanos

'Timely, topical and thrilling.' John Connolly

'A resonant, memorable and uncomfortable read . . .
Winterland is a book that speaks to absolutely now.'
Val McDermid

ff

Limitless
(available in paperback now)

Now a major motion picture starring Bradley Cooper, Abbie Cornish and Robert De Niro.

Imagine a drug that made your brain function to its full potential.

A drug that allowed you to pick up a foreign language in a single day.

A drug that helped you process information so fast you could see patterns in the stock market.

Just as his life is fading into mediocrity, Eddie Spinola comes across such a pill: MDT-48 – a sort of Viagra for the brain. But while its benefits materialise quickly, so do certain unwelcome side-effects. And when Eddie decides to track down other users, he soon discovers that they're all dying, or dead . . .

'Fast, clever and horrifying.' *Daily Mail*